HARAKEN
A Silver Ships Novel

S. H. JUCHA

Published by S. H. Jucha
www.scottjucha.com

ISBN: 978-0-9905940-7-9 (e-book)
ISBN: 978-0-9905940-8-6 (softcover)

First Edition: March 2016

Cover Design: Damon Za

Acknowledgments

Haraken is the fourth book in The Silver Ships series. I wish to extend a special thanks to my independent editor, Joni Wilson, whose efforts enabled the finished product. To my proofreaders, Abiola Streete, Dr. Jan Hamilton, and David Melvin, I offer my sincere thanks for their continued support.

Despite the assistance I've received from others, all errors are mine.

Glossary

A glossary is located at the end of the book.

"Captain, we have the guide's warning," the navigation officer announced. "Thirty minutes until we exit this final FTL leg."

"Comms officer, announce FTL transition conditions," Captain Francis Lumley ordered. "All hands prepare for exit."

Throughout the ship, the crew hurried to confirm lockdown of all mobile material, cleared the mess rooms, policed the cabins, and ran through tight corridors to their final positions, strapping themselves into their bunks or chairs. Reports filtered to the bridge as each section reported readiness.

"Ship reports all ready, Captain," the first mate replied and checked the countdown. There were eight minutes to spare before exit.

Captain Lumley slid onto his bridge chair, dropped it to a horizontal position, pulled the webbing sheet across his body, and locked it securely in place, preparing for the ship's exit. His people were still trying to eliminate all the quirks of transition from faster-than-light (FTL) to sub-light and back. The captain checked left and right to ensure his three bridge guests were taking the appropriate precautions for this momentous occasion. Speaker García wasn't, but he was one of two men, besides the major, the captain wouldn't dare instruct.

Speaker Antonio García, the mission commander, watched in consternation as the captain, crew, and his direct subordinates, Major Barbas and Administrator Olawale Wombo, hurried to their chairs for the exit, but García was intent on delaying the moment. He hated the chair's webbing confinement. It brought back painful childhood memories of his father's favorite disciplinary technique for his sons.

This mission was an opportunity for García, one of the youngest speakers in United Earth's (UE) pantheon of leaders, to prove his value to the elite and gain another rung of promotion. "The higher your rank, the safer you are," García had heard his mother say over and over until she was dead at the hands of his father. After his mother's murder, García lost his other parent. United Earth's justice system was intolerant of crime, any crime, and there were only two punishments . . . lifelong incarceration or death. In the early days of the UE, resources to house and care for prisoners were severely limited so the punishment was often death.

García waited until the final minute to strap himself into his chair and pop in his mouthguard. He filled his mind with images of celebration back on Earth in order to ignore the violent, but short, transition from FTL. The *Reunion* shook and rattled ferociously throughout its 600-meter wingspan. As soon as the transition started it was over, in less than nine seconds.

After months of transit time through a seemingly endless cosmos, the explorers' long journey was completed. The ship's guide, monitoring the flight time to the picosecond, shepherded the vessel through light-years of interstellar space to its predetermined destination. While not a self-aware entity, the guide was housed onboard the interstellar ship's bridge in a small, heavily cooled box and was thirty-third-century technology.

The explorer ship carried more than 900 crew and scientists and was armed with militia troops, fighter craft, and a defensive array of rail guns and missiles. The explorers were prepared to deal with any conditions.

The comms officer announced "all clear," and bridge crew released webbing and set their chairs upright.

"Nav officer, position, please," Captain Lumley requested.

"One moment, Captain, the guide is still collecting and analyzing star data."

Major Kyros Barbas came to stand beside Speaker García. The pair was a contrast in personalities and physiques. Much about Speaker García was average . . . hair coloring, eyes, facial features, stature, and height . . . all of which was in contrast to his rapacious personality. In contrast, Major Barbas displayed a short, heavy-set, bull-dog stature. His stern visage and powerful physique echoed his task-master personality, and he was a devotee of the mission commander.

Of the three bridge guests, the odd man was Administrator Olawale Wombo, who detested his title. In his mind, he was the mission's lead scientist. He was a bear of a man with a shaved head and a coal-black complexion, owing to his Nigerian ancestry, a country he knew only from the tales of his grandfather. Nigeria joined the African Western Coastal Pac before it became part of the African Union (AU) before its demise in the Third Union War. This last war found the AU against the bloc known as the Shia Intifada.

"Captain," the navigation officer called out, "the guide confirms that at present velocity we are eighteen days out from Mane. We've done it, Captain. Destination achieved!"

While the crew celebrated, Captain Lumley eyed Speaker García. The man stood stock-still. No one congratulated him or patted him on the back, not even his sycophant, Major Barbas.

"Navigation, put us on a heading toward Mane and maintain present speed," Lumley ordered.

"Aye, Captain, setting course for Mane and maintaining speed."

"First Mate, prep and launch three probes. Minimum spread. I want them out there ASAP," Lumley ordered.

"Three probes, minimum spread, right away, Captain," the first mate replied, saluting Lumley and hurrying off the bridge. On an explorer ship, the bridge was centrally located, vertically and horizontally, to minimize exposure from external sources. The ship itself was an unusual shape, resembling the "flying wing" of the long-defunct US stealth bomber. Early UE–FTL experiments destroyed a number of long-axis ships, tearing them to pieces during the transitions, until it was discovered that a winged shape, with its short bow-to-aft length, enabled the ship to quickly cross the transition zones.

"Speaker García," Lumley said, "unless you have alternative orders, I will hold this ship a day out from the star's outer planet until we receive the probe data on the system."

"Perfectly fine, Captain," García replied. "Major, Administrator, with me, please. We have preparations to make," García added and strolled off the bridge.

* * *

Surging ahead of the explorer ship, the probes spread out and a day later were sending data bursts back to the ship. Expectations on the *Reunion* were that drone data would be minimal until they closed on the system's habitable planet, hopefully discovering a successful colony or even a burgeoning world. Instead, the watch officers were slack-jawed as huge amounts of data poured in itemizing thousands of ships entering and exiting FTL outside the system, the telltale electromagnetic pulse of transition evident to the probes' sensors.

"Captain," the second mate signaled, "your presence is requested on the bridge."

Urged on by the excitement in the second mate's voice, the captain hurriedly made his way to the bridge. Within minutes of reviewing the data, the captain called Speaker García to the bridge. It wasn't a requirement to notify Wombo, but the captain liked the gentle, unassuming scientist, so he called him too. Purely by happenstance, if you care to believe that, he neglected to contact Major Barbas.

The three men stood on the bridge, listening to the bridge watch officers translate the data received from the probes.

"I would say these colonists were fortunate to enjoy quite a successful landing, Speaker García," Lumley said quietly.

"Undoubtedly, Captain," García murmured, lost in thought. His secret hope was to discover a small colony he might personally bring into the UE fold. The honors would fall entirely to him—as would the promotion. Instead, he faced a world as populated as Earth. *So much for the quick stick approach, but did I bring enough carrots?* García wondered.

"Captain, the probes have detected millions of comm signals," the second mate announced. "While some are between ships, most of the signals are directed to or originate from relay stations positioned near the outer planet's orbit."

"Can we decipher their signals?" García asked.

The comms officer glanced at the speaker and then at his captain, unsure of how to explain the complexities of the task. When his captain nodded to him to continue, he attempted to explain as clearly and simply as possible. "Your pardon, Speaker García, both the carrier signal wave and the encoded information are foreign to us. In time, the guide might decode the carrier wave so that we can send our own comms, but we might not be understood . . . neither our signal nor our words."

"So we don't even know if this is a human world," García mused out loud. His comment rattled those on the bridge. The crew was so focused on tracing the path of a human colony ship that they hadn't considered that possibility.

"With respect, Speaker García," Wombo interjected, "the volume and directionality of the comms indicates communications with other colonies, certainly more than one. Furthermore, I would hazard to guess that these relay stations indicated by the comms officer are FTL-transmission capable."

García's head snapped around to look up into the face of his administrator and his eyes narrowed. "Why would you suppose that, Administrator Wombo?"

"The ships outside the system are entering and exiting FTL in multiple directions, indicating multiple colonies are located in star systems light-years away. No culture would bother to communicate via comms if the messages were to take a lifetime to reach the intended recipients," Wombo replied.

"Yes, Administrator, I see your meaning," García said. "Such a technology would be a great boon to Earth." García imagined his reception on Earth becoming that of a hero's welcome. "Keep me informed of any further updates, Captain, and, in the future, Captain . . . please be so kind as to include Major Barbas in your invitation."

The emotionless countenance accompanying the overly polite request caused the captain's throat to tighten. "Certainly, Speaker García," he managed to reply.

* * *

Wombo met with his senior staff to apportion the analysis of the data pouring in from the probes. Despite the deluge, the scientists were delirious. The amount and variety of data had them salivating like children in a sweet shop.

One individual on Wombo's staff possessed a different view. His assistant administrator, Zhang Shin, was a UE true believer. To Zhang, the data indicated a technological display that would add wealth and power to Earth and aid the spread of its influence. Zhang had few friends; a notable exception was Major Barbas. She was a petite example of her Chinese ancestry—tiny, pale skin, and dark-eyed with straight, black, short hair, asymmetrically cut.

"The guide has yet to decode the carrier wave, much less the language of the comms," Wombo announced. "The speaker has asked our help in identifying the carrier signal so that we might replicate it and send it back carrying our own message. We need to be inventive here, but I should warn you that it is possible we will be unable to accomplish our task. However, we must try our best."

"Administrator Wombo, your words should encourage our success," Zhang stated formally.

"I speak in probabilities not in hopes, Zhang, as you well know," Wombo replied, hoping this wasn't leading to another one of their arguments in front of his staff. "If we can't decode the carrier wave, I will propose to Speaker García that we broadcast a standard signal. It is my estimate that the sophistication of the technology we are witnessing indicates that these individuals will have the capability of intercepting our signal and managing a translation, especially if we send an extended message, coupling our communication with images and text. If this world is inhabited by humans, it should not be too challenging a task for them."

"And if this world isn't inhabited by humans, what might our message say to these individuals?" Yoram Penzig asked. As the mission's linguist and philosopher, it would fall to him to craft the message.

"If they aren't human, my friend," Wombo replied, "then we better hope they are pacifists."

"Have we detected warships?" Zhang asked.

"The ships observed entering or exiting FTL that have passed close enough for detailed observation appear to consist of personnel transport and freighters," Wombo replied. "We have detected no signs of armament on these ships nor have we seen any evidence of fighters on patrol, but it's early yet." Wombo glanced at Zhang, and his stomach twisted at the evil, little smile that crossed her face.

* * *

In the days that followed, the *Reunion* halted at a fixed position beyond the system's last planet while the probes passed deep into the system. The possibility of possessing FTL comms galvanized Speaker García to ensconce himself in his cabin with Major Barbas to plan their approach to the planet's government, human or alien. The failure to sight war craft emboldened them.

One of the probes passed an orbital station and the leaders, officers, and scientists alike crowded around the bridge monitors to view the images. During the viewing, two strange and identical vessels passed in front of the probe and conversations were arrested in mid-sentence. One vessel headed toward the populated planet and the other decelerated at an incredible rate and disappeared behind the station, presumably into a docking bay.

"First Mate, playback the recording and capture an image of one of those two vessels. Enhance it for viewing," Lumley ordered.

The screen filled with a three-quarter shot of the odd craft, and several moments later the image's resolution cleared, revealing a smooth-hulled ship with a translucent exterior of blues, greens, and creams, glinting in the station's docking lights.

"No windows, no engines," Wombo muttered under his breath.

Speaker García turned his head around to study Wombo. "Captain, can we confirm our administrator's musings about this craft?"

"First Mate, please review the entire section of imagery," Lumley ordered.

The first mate chose to study the vessel leaving the probe's view headed for the planet. First its bow and then its aft was visible. The ship's rounded aft end was perfectly smooth with absolutely no protrusions. Then the first mate ordered the prior images of the vessel expanded and enhanced. The front of the ship was the same . . . bluntly pointed and perfectly smooth with no indentations or protrusions.

"It's confirmed, Captain, on both counts," the first mate announced.

Captain Lumley glanced toward Speaker García to see if he had more questions, but the speaker was staring at Wombo.

"Enlighten us with any other of your observations, Administrator. If these craft have no engines, how do they move?" García asked.

"An interesting question, Speaker," Wombo replied, refusing to be intimidated by the mission commander. "A couple of thoughts come to mind. The first thought is a microwave beam focused on the vessel . . . but then I realized that would deliver energy, even heat, but would probably not provide propulsion. Then my second thought—and I apologize in advance, Speaker García, if this sounds too preposterous—my thought is that these ships use gravitational waves as their manner of propulsion." The majority of Wombo's audience stared at him, as if he had grown a second head, and he muttered, "Yes, a gravity drive would explain their movement nicely."

"Strange as it sounds, Speaker García, that would explain these vessels' incredible acceleration," Lumley added. "The craft could use literally any significant gravity-generating body in the system to push or pull itself. The greater the body's gravity influence, the faster the craft could drive itself."

"Gravity drives . . . don't be ridiculous!" García declared. "You're supposed to be practical men . . . men of science and technology, and you're feeding me fantasies. I don't want to hear any more of this foolish gibberish again!"

"We have additional information, Speaker García, Captain," said the first mate. "Another probe has managed detailed views of the surface in its pass over the planet, and there are many noteworthy items. For one, buildings appear to cover almost every square kilometer of the planet's surface. We've calculated that many of the buildings are more than 2 kilometers high, some 3 or more kilometers. They are marvelous feats of engineering. With so little space available, one would have to believe that either most of the inhabitants' food is shipped from other planets or they are capable of culturing it underground."

One of the officers on station murmured to the first mate, who responded urgently. A couple of moments later, the probe's view of an expanse of garden surrounding an ancient-styled house appeared on screen. A single image was captured and enhancement programs reviewed it several times. With each successive pass, the individuals walking in the garden became clearer.

"Humans," the first mate murmured. "Humans, Captain," he said, adopting a command voice. "This is the site of our colony ship's landing!"

"Excellent, Captain! My compliments to your officers and crew," García said expansively. "Now, Administrator Wombo, I await your good news as to the analysis of these humans' carrier-wave technology."

Captain Lumley felt a flash of sympathy for his friend. Word had reached him of the scientists' failure to decipher the comm technology.

"There is no good news, Speaker García," Wombo replied. "We are left with no alternative but to broadcast our message in the open on our ship's customary frequency and hope that these people are able to pick up and decipher our carrier wave and message."

"I see," García replied, his mask slipping back into place. "One wonders why the powers on Earth pack my ship with scientists when they are of so little use to me. "Very well, Administrator, have Yoram Penzig's message forwarded to me for review. Captain, please advance the *Reunion* into the system on course for the populated planet and broadcast the message once I've approved it. Wide beam, if you please, in case their ships do have FTL comm capability as Administrator Wombo theorizes."

García left the bridge as perfunctorily as he had arrived. The captain gave Wombo a commiserating twist of lips and a shrug of eyebrow. Only performance above expectation received the speaker's approval, everything else was unsatisfactory.

2

Méridien comms and the entire Confederation, for that matter, burned with little else than messages of a strange ship entering the Méridien system. Fear that another alien race had found their civilization was the first thought on most minds, but as the odd, wing-shaped ship continued to advance toward Méridien, no fighters spewed from the ship and no weapons were unleashed on the Confederation's ships.

Days after the intruders entered the system, Méridien SADEs, self-aware digital entities or artificial intelligences, detected the ship's broadcast signal, recorded it, stripped the carrier wave, and relayed the remaining signal to the Council's SADE, a known linguistics master.

<Leader Diamanté, your pardon for the interruption, I have transcribed the message emanating from the unknown ship,> Winston, the Council's SADE, sent. His comm was sent directly to the Leader's cerebral implant. The Méridien devices facilitated thought and data transfer without speaking. <Leader Ganesh,> Winston continued, <is offline, and I believe the message's information is time-sensitive.>

<Yes, it is, Winston. Please forward the transcription to me,> Gino replied. <I will see Leader Ganesh receives the information immediately, and thank you for your efforts.>

<You are welcome, Leader Diamanté. As always, it's a pleasure to converse with you,> Winston replied and closed the comm.

Winston could choose who to communicate such critical information in Council Leader Ganesh's absence, and the SADE chose Gino. President Racine's treatment of the Haraken SADEs had rubbed off on Gino, and, in turn, he was treating all Méridien SADEs with courtesy, and they were reciprocating in kind. The information gleaned by merely being courteous was invaluable, and Gino never betrayed the SADEs' trust or abused the privilege they granted him.

* * *

<Leader Ganesh, I apologize for the disturbance,> the House SADE announced. Hector waited patiently for a reply. His mistress's sleeps had become deeper and longer in recent years, and her message to Hector was clear. For only the most extreme circumstance was she to be disturbed, and, to Hector, a priority call from Leader Diamanté qualified.

<Your reason better be superb, Hector,> Mahima sent, struggling to organize her thoughts.

<You have a priority comm from Leader Diamanté. He states that his news is most urgent.>

Mahima struggled up in bed and ran a couple of mental exercises through her implant. *No use sounding dull-witted to Gino. The upstart hungers for my Council Leader seat as it is,* she thought. <Yes, Leader Diamanté, you believe your news is so critical that it must be delivered at 1.39 hours?>

<Your pardon, Council Leader, the SADEs have received and translated the stranger's message,> Gino sent.

<These are no strangers,> Mahima replied. <This is a hoax played on us by that puffed-up Haraken, who is building even more freakish ships to demonstrate his importance. Perhaps it's only evident to me why this ship arrives and makes no aggressive movements except to glide into our system. That Haraken president is seeking another Council meeting. Well, this time, he won't get one, and I'll make sure of it.>

<I'm sorry to inform you, Council Leader Ganesh, but your suppositions are unfounded,> Gino sent. <The message announces that these strangers are from Earth, and they wish to make contact with us. Included in their message are historic facts: our colony ship's name, our planet's original name, GL-137, and our star's original name, Mane. Winston has confirmed that although the language has evolved from that of ancient Earth, the characters of the accompanying text have not.>

Mahima signaled the bedroom lights on, swung out of bed, and donned a dressing gown. The slender and exotic body she once possessed was gone. The cell-gen injections preserved her health but not her beauty as she approached the end of her second century.

<And you believe this message to be true, Leader Diamanté?>

<Winston has high confidence in his translation, Council Leader,> Gino replied.

<And he shared this with you first, did he? How interesting . . .> Mahima mused.

<There is more to be shared, Council Leader,> Gino said, hurrying on.

<In the message?> Mahima asked.

<No, Leader, this information originates from my House SADE, Esther, who has been analyzing the ship's structure.>

<And why would Esther's analysis of this Earth ship have any value?> Mahima asked, her anger at having a night's rest disturbed leaking into her thoughts.

<Julien, the Haraken SADE, transferred much of Earth's historical records to Esther, Leader Ganesh,> Gino replied, unhappy to reveal this particular information to Mahima.

<So you've let that president's puppet contaminate your SADE, have you?> Mahima accused.

<Leader Ganesh, I implore you to focus on the information we are accruing and put aside your personal animosity toward the Harakens. Whether you realize it or not, we might be in trouble.> Gino sent hotly.

<You said these people are humans from Earth, did you not? How much trouble can we be in, Leader Diamanté?> Mahima shot back.

<Esther compared her records of Earth's war machines with the detailed images of this ship that's called the *Reunion*. It has multiple ports along each wing that indicate some sort of weaponry. It has a great many bays, indicating fighters, according to Esther. Now, I ask you, Leader Ganesh, what does an explorer ship, which in the words of their leader has come in search of other humans, need with fighters and so much weaponry?>

For the first time since her abrupt awakening, Mahima admitted Gino made the right decision to contact her. The information was troubling. *Have we just been invaded by alien humans?* Mahima asked herself.

3

Alex Racine, Haraken's president, and Renée de Guirnon, his partner, sat in the cool shade of the cliffs beneath their house, protected from Hellébore's summer sun. Their six-year-old son, Teague, was squirming in his father's lap, upset that he couldn't play today with his alien friends, the Swei Swee. Renée was fond of saying, "As it regards patience, Teague takes after his father."

When Teague was born, Renée asked Alex for the privilege of naming their child and requested the name of Alex's male ancestor who arrived aboard his people's colony ship, *New Terra*. "I would honor that Ancient and his partner, my love," Renée said. "Without them, I would not have the world I have today."

When Teague was frustrated, as he was now, Alex held him. The son inherited his father's genes for stature and at age six was already more than two handfuls. Alex and Renée opted to forgo Méridien genetic tinkering with their child. The result of happenstance was a striking Méridien face adorning a New Terran's massive body. The one concession the parents did make to Méridien technology was the use of an artificial womb. Renée's slender body couldn't have carried a child the size of Teague to full term.

Within months of Teague's birth, Alex took his son swimming, sharing his love of a pastime enjoyed as a child on New Terra. Renée preferred to watch from the safety and comfort of the bay's black-and-white crystal sand beach. As Teague's independence progressed, he began riding on the back of the matrons, emulating their young, racing the Swei Swee along the beach, not that a two-legged boy could keep pace with six-legged aliens.

Teague was typical of the newly born Haraken children, who never saw the Swei Swee as their parents first encountered the aliens. To Haraken's first youngsters, the Swei Swee were exotic companions, and none considered the clawed, multi-legged, whistling aliens more as friends than did Teague.

While all Haraken young were highly regarded by the Swei Swee, much as they cared dearly for their own, it must be said that the Star Hunter First's youngling was most precious to their twin hearts. That the Star Hunter First and his mate had produced only one egg over so many annuals was a great lament among the People, which is why so much care was taken with the youngling and his parent when they swam. Several hunter species of the People lurked in Haraken's waters, and large Swei Swee males always accompanied the two to ensure their safety. If necessary, the People would gladly travel the endless waters to ensure their protection.

To date, none of the Swei Swee were required to pay the sacrificial price. As a species, they could sense the electrical impulses of both prey and predator. When hunters approached, alarms were sounded and Teague would grab the front edge of a male's carapace, exiting the water onto the beach like a hydro-skiff, sputtering and laughing uproariously. His father required two of the larger males to accomplish a similar exit, ending his trip in the shallows. In an ironic twist, Teague never showed any interest in accompanying his father into space. The Swei Swee were Teague's world, and they were everything to the boy.

Today, the Swei Swee's ecstatic whistles and tweets filled the air, and they bobbed in anticipation of the upcoming event. Males clicked their claws, anxious for the search of the endless waters in the company of the one known to them as "Zee," a human sound they could whistle. The Swei Swee were an intelligent species that lived off the sea, and the large males dove deep for their catch to depths a human could only reach in a dive suit.

Z had downloaded himself into his latest avatar, a 3-meter-long alloy imitation of the crab-scorpion-like Swei Swee. His latest mobile creation was identical to the Swei-Swee male—small true hands; large, sharply pointed claws; six legs with swimmerets; and a long, segmented tail with lateral fins that folded against the tail when out of the water.

If this was the Confederation, a SADE such as Z would still be trapped in a box on the bridge of an FTL-capable starship or in a closet of a Méridien House. But this wasn't the Confederation and this wasn't New Terra, whose people led the fight to free the Swei Swee and end the destruction of the Confederation colonies by the Nua'll. This was Haraken—an amalgam of New Terrans, Confederation refugees, and a rescued, sea-hunting, whistling and warbling, intelligent alien species known as the Swei Swee.

Z, encased in his avatar and decorated in the blues and greens of Swei Swee carapaces, scurried across the sands to launch into the breaking waves. Alex applauded and noisily whistled his appreciation, which Teague imitated. <Nice launch, Z. I christen your new avatar the *Helmut IV*,> Alex sent. Z's original name was Helmut before the Confederation declared him an Independent, a misnomer for their society's outcasts, and exiled him to Libre.

<The waters are wonderful, Mr. President,> Z sent back. <I see why you enjoy these surroundings.>

At Alex's whistle, the Swei Swee First, the hives' leader, had spun around on the sand, reared back on his six walking legs, and focused his four eyestalks on the Star Hunter First. His whistle of acknowledgment split the air, and then he spun and raced after Z. He didn't want to miss the moment—searching the endless waters with a "Star Hunter Who Wasn't."

It had been difficult for the Swei Swee to comprehend the concept of a SADE. It was much easier to accept the entities when they appeared on Haraken, walking, crawling, and flying. In their alien minds, all entities that surrounded the Star Hunter First were members of his enormous hive.

* * *

Julien watched from the cliff top as the Swei Swee ended their raucous celebration and dived into the breaking waves in Z's wake. The wind fluttered his wide-brimmed hat and loose clothes, a very un-Haraken style of dress. At least the wind appeared to affect his attire.

The SADEs chose to build avatars that were neither Méridien nor New Terran in stature but something in-between, closer to the former than the latter. The new shape suited their design considerations. All but Julien and his partner, Cordelia, adopted Haraken-style clothes for their appearances; even Z did when he was at the Central Exchange.

Julien and Cordelia's atypical response to clothing began when Julien could not decide how he wished to appear. He felt that he should be celebrating his new life, but admittedly he wasn't one of the more adventuresome types when it came to the concept of attire.

Cordelia, a master of the visual arts, had stunned Julien with her answer. "We can project our clothes, Julien," Cordelia said. "We're virtual people, if you will, why not have virtual clothes? I can design algorithms that sense your environment and react to it, and you can incorporate holo-vids in our synth-skins that can project the images outward. In this manner, your attire can suit your mood whenever you wish."

Julien was slow to adopt the idea, but the more he considered it, the more he realized it was the direction that he and Cordelia, as independent SADEs, should take. He noted to Cordelia that they would still require physical clothing for certain events, such as aboard ship, when the holo-vid illusion could be pierced by human contact.

Julien and Cordelia spent the first few days after their transfer to their avatars in the privacy of their new house. Cordelia pushed her artistic skills to create new algorithms for their virtual clothes to see what Julien preferred. The hours Cordelia had enjoyed with Renée, discussing intimacy, and the testing of the resulting algorithms on Alex, turned out to be excellent preparation for this time when she held her beloved companion in the flesh, so to speak.

On the first day Julien and Cordelia left their house to walk among other Harakens, they stepped with confidence and yet waited with some trepidation for reactions. Their unique body shapes identified them as SADEs, and people politely requested bio-IDs to identify them. To the joy of Julien and Cordelia, they received a touch of the heart, a nod of the head, and a quiet "Sers." They were not just being greeted; they were being honored. After the first few exchanges, Julien's confidence grew, and he extended his arm to Cordelia, imitating Alex and Renée. Cordelia responded by smiling and tucking her hand in his elbow. The two SADEs spent the entire morning strolling the streets of Espero, greeting their fellow citizens.

Neither of the SADEs detected the individuals surreptitiously tailing them, who were reporting to Étienne and Alain, the directors of security and twin crèche-mates, that Julien and Cordelia were being magnanimously received by Haraken's citizens. And Alex paced up a storm throughout the house, with Renée worrying he might wear himself out, until he received the twins' report. Renee hung on Alex's broad shoulders for a while, witnessing the relief flooding through him at the news that his friends were accepted by the people of Haraken. It was one of the few times that Renée saw Alex shed tears of joy.

While the SADEs enjoyed their first morning, walking the streets of Espero, Julien recalled the moment, ensconced in his box on the *Rêveur*'s bridge, when Alex contacted him and Z. The Haraken–New Terran agreement was signed, and the Méridiens' advance payments for the travelers, the gravity-driven shuttles the Harakens would build, would arrive soon at the Exchange. In time, the SADEs would earn significant funds, operating Haraken's first bank as its directors, but Alex decided not to wait.

"Julien and Z, time to get started on Z's plan," Alex said.

Julien waited for Z to share his plan, but time ticked by.

"Your pardon, Mr. President, would you remind me of which particular plan we will be discussing?" Z finally asked.

"Your greatest wish, Z. It's time to make it come true," Alex said.

What was a surprise to both SADEs was that Alex was already clearing the way for their transformation. He had pulled aside the visiting House Leaders, who had the foresight to purchase Haraken's first production of travelers, and told them of his plan to free the Haraken SADEs. In no uncertain terms, Alex told the Leaders that he expected their cooperation with any requests for specialists and equipment he might need, and they agreed. Such was the enticement to possess Haraken travelers.

Alex committed his private funds, transferred from New Terra, to start the research, and Julien and Z began communicating requests for specialists and material to the Méridien Leaders. Naturally, the orders were received by FTL comm, which meant the House SADEs handled the communications. Receipt of the first requests and the divining of the intent behind the requests meant every Méridien SADE knew within moments of the Haraken SADEs' purpose. Within days, every Confederation SADE knew.

Claude Dupuis was tapped by Alex to manage the SADEs' initial production needs. Claude responded that he wasn't an engineer, and Alex laughed, telling Claude that the SADEs didn't need an engineer. What they needed, Alex said, was a program manager, a skilled technician, and, most important, a pair of hands.

The first step in Z's plan was to create a prototype human avatar. It would be nothing fancy. The focus was placed on body mechanics, the crystal memory, and the kernel transfer process. Specialists requested from House Brixton, which developed all Confederation SADEs, deferred from facilitating the first kernel transfer. Shannon Brixton, the House Leader, was a close compatriot of Council Leader Mahima Ganesh, who was no fan of Alex or the Harakens.

Once the SADEs designed their own kernel transfer process, Z volunteered to be the first subject, and the prototype avatar was transported for the test to the city-ship, *Unsere Menschen*, where Z resided. Julien initiated the transfer and, moments later, reported that Z's kernel was no longer connected to the city-ship. The humans waited anxiously until a rudimentary speaker mounted on the avatar sounded, "So this is what it's like to be senseless." Pandemonium broke out as humans and SADEs celebrated. Julien reversed the transfer process sending Z back to the ship's bridge box and announced the transfer experiment a complete success, much to everyone's relief.

Unfortunately, the SADEs' independence would only come after they designed and created their substitutes, ultra-sophisticated controllers, to manage a starship's systems, including FTL navigation and comms. While Claude managed the construction of sophisticated human avatars complete with synth-skin, human sense organs, crystal memory, comms, power systems, and robotic infrastructure, the SADEs developed their replacements.

In time, and as directors of the Central Exchange of Haraken, the SADEs would prosper mightily as Harakens developed and sold iterations of the Nua'll's grav-drive technology, and they would reward Claude Dupuis handsomely for his efforts, but it was Z, who would keep Claude employed for much of the human's life.

* * *

Julien slowly adopted the clothing algorithms that Cordelia built into his avatar but couldn't bring himself to change his attire in mid-day to suit his moods. He wore the same clothes from morning to evening, door to door. The first time he decided to alter his appearance in the presence of others he was alone with Alex and Renée at their house. When the pair weren't looking, Julien selected an alternate outfit, another common Haraken style. Renée was the first to notice, and a small cry of exclamation escaped her lips. Alex looked Julien up and down and sent him a number, <5.2>—nothing more.

At evening's close, Julien flew home and researched New Terran grading systems, finding several concepts, including one that graded the performances of athletes from 1.0 to 10.0. This was the one Julien surmised Alex was applying to his wardrobe. Much later, Julien sought to impress Alex with changes of attire into some of Haraken's newest fashions only to receive scores ranging from 4.1 to 7.3. Eventually, Julien gave up trying to impress his friend.

A half-year after the SADEs became mobile, the Harakens were again celebrating Founding Day. To Julien, it seemed the perfect day to celebrate their rite of passage from isolated starship controllers to free Haraken citizens. The evening before, Julien researched ancient Terran art, novels, and vids for clothing suitable for the celebration, and in the haste of his extensive search he nearly missed it. In all fairness, it wasn't exactly what he would have thought in the realm of possibilities. Julien halted his searches and backed up to the pertinent passage in the novel. The more he considered the concept, the more emboldened he became. Julien captured the 2-D image and enlisted Cordelia's help. She converted the image to 3-D, augmenting the clothing's final image from the novel's descriptions.

When Julien retrieved the algorithms of his costume from Cordelia, he activated them and posed for her, surprised when her reaction was the SADE's frozen fugue. Then he felt Cordelia's mind entwine with his as she expressed her pleasure and applauded his concept. Breaking from her fugue, she ran to hug him. Despite the incredible span of time Julien had spent in his box, it all seemed worthwhile to have arrived at moments such as this when he was able to hold his companion.

Julien's creative spurt motivated Cordelia to find her own costume for Founding Day, and she retrieved an ancient art image of a Venetian woman adorned in an elaborate full-length dress layered in white lace, with her face covered by a delicate white and gold mask. Short, puffy sleeves were paired with long white gloves reaching to the woman's upper arms. Cordelia went to work on her costume, determined to display Julien and herself as a most striking pair.

The following morning, Julien located Alex and Renée at the president's office, which was located in the rear of the Assembly building. Alex would be preparing to address the Assembly and the fortunate citizens who would have lined up early to gain some of the few available seats to hear Alex's annual address. As president, he laid out the challenges of the coming year, and it was a message that the Harakens took to heart, especially the ex-Librans, who were fierce defenders of their new society.

Julien and Cordelia sought to preview their new attire to Alex and Renée before others saw them and directed their flyer to the Assembly's rear entrance. On the one hand, Julien was curious as to his friends' reactions, even though Cordelia was adamant that she would not change her costume regardless of the comments received. On the other hand, Julien was anxious, perhaps even determined, to receive a better score from

Alex than a 7.3. The SADEs slipped into the Assembly building, projecting typical Haraken attire, and then outside the president's office they switched to their Founding Day costumes. Cordelia was first through the door and when she swung the mask from her face, Renée laughed and clapped her hands in delight.

"That is exquisite, Cordelia," Renée said. "Where did it come from?"

"From the depths of necessity," Cordelia replied. "I was challenged to equal my partner, who found his costume first." Then Cordelia stepped aside, sweeping her lace dress in one hand, to reveal Julien, who was standing quietly behind her.

"Oh, my," Renée said, her words coming out in a soft breath as she took in Julien's display.

Julien heard every exclamation of appreciation Renée made, but his eyes were on his friend, who rose from behind a desk and came around to face him and Cordelia.

"And yours, Julien, where did you get this amazing idea?" Renée asked.

"This is the personage of Cyrano de Bergerac from an ancient Terran novel," Julien replied. He had faithfully reproduced the sweeping hat, the soft boots with folded top, the loose pantaloons and shirt, the wide belt and large buckle, and even the cape.

<May I?> Alex sent, courteously requesting to examine the algorithms governing Julien's attire programs. Only two people, Cordelia and Alex, were granted administrative rights to Julien's programs, although none could access his kernel. Julien's human mimic programs halted while he monitored Alex's quick search through his wardrobe, sifting through code at lightning speed. Alex located the algorithms governing the hat, which sat squarely on Julien's head, and edited the angle relative to Julien's head. The term "rakish" echoed in Julien's crystal memory. When Alex retreated from the program, Julien refocused on his visual senses. Cordelia and Renée were smiling and nodding their approval.

<A unique individual deserves a unique image,> Alex sent privately to Julien. <10.0!>

Julien's smile reflected his deep pleasure, realizing his friend's previous criticism of his attire had been an encouragement to express his personality.

Two Haraken fashion emerged from that day. Observing Julien and Cordelia walking around, Harakens embraced their concept. At the next Founding Day, half the population turned out in costumes, and great pleasure was enjoyed discovering where individuals found their inspiration. It created resurgence in ancient and present-day art, novels, and vids. Even Z participated on the next occasion, dressing as a character from an ancient Terran vid featuring musical numbers. His entire body was encased in round tubes of shiny metal connected by seamed joints, and he wore an inverted funnel for a hat, giving him the affectation of an early robot. However, he told no one the name of his character, only promising a special reward for the first child to discover the truth. Using readers, children spent days searching online archives. A studious young girl found Z's secret and claimed the prize when she whispered to him, "You're the Tin Man." The next day, she squealed with delight as she rode on Z's first nonhuman avatar—an ancient Terran horse.

For Exchange director's business, Julien wore virtual, Haraken-style attire, saving his real clothes for extended travel. After his first Founding Day celebration, Julien adopted the habit of projecting a hat, developing an extensive repertoire collected from famous personages in images, books, and vids. When his mood shifted so would his hat, and it was a source of fascination for people in general and his friends in particular. But one hat that was never seen in public was Sleuth's deerstalker. It was reserved for private discussions with Alex and was a signal of deep concentration to resolve the dilemmas that worried them.

4

A high-priority FTL comm caused Julien to pause. <Mr. President,> Julien sent, manifesting the voice he used aboard the *Rêveur*, <you have an urgent message from Leader Gino Diamanté for you. His liner, the *Il Piacere*, has just exited FTL outside our system. His SADE is relaying an enormous amount of data, which I'm downloading into the vault.>

The "vault" was a term spoken only between the SADEs and Alex. It was located deep underground beneath the Central Exchange's main office building and was a repository for the bank's financial accounts and transactions in addition to the SADEs' data centers. Since the SADEs could no longer count on access to the starships' extensive crystal memory cores, it became their habit to store and share data through the vault.

The SADEs' kernels were another matter. They were unique, analogous to that of the human mind, and this meant the kernel could not be replicated. It could be transferred in whole from one avatar to another under controlled conditions. However, those controlled conditions had only been tested under hardwire connections. There was no attempt to transfer a kernel through local or FTL comms, despite the SADEs' estimation that there was no reason it shouldn't work. However, no SADE was willing to test the possibility.

This also meant that SADEs were much more vulnerable to accidents. In the extreme, if a kernel was denied power, there was no more SADE.

Before the founding of Haraken, a SADE would not have thought twice about sharing the vault's location and its contents with Méridiens, but Alex was of a different opinion, and the SADEs heeded his advice. Haraken was slowly changing as it welcomed new immigrants, and the subtle changes in the new society meant the vault was best left a secret.

<Good day, Leader Diamanté, what brings you back to Haraken?> Alex sent.

<Good day, President Racine, I beg your indulgence, but I've come to discuss a critical issue unfolding at Méridien, and your assistance is much needed. We appear to have another aggressor in Confederation space.>

<Have the Nua'll returned, Leader?> Alex sent anxiously.

<No, President Racine, these invaders are humans, and they say they're from Earth,> Gino replied.

* * *

Alex left home to meet with Julien, Cordelia, and Z at the main building of the Central Exchange of Haraken. His transport was an upgraded edition of the aero-lift personal flyer. Harakens were busy creating numerous companies, specializing in a variety of grav-drive technology implementations: shuttles, in-system transports, personal flyers, and aero-scooters, which were nicknamed flits. The flits were limited in speed and ceiling height to protect the youngsters, who loved them, and a small controller was installed to maneuver the scooter safely when the driver failed to do so.

Alex's personal transport seated four, limited to flight ceiling of 2,000 meters and a max velocity of 625 kilometers by its controller. It was a unit built to Julien's specifications and designed to secretly report its flight data to him. After Alex's initial test, Julien was pleased he was careful to build in redundant protective measures—Alex loved to push the limits of his flyer.

Assembled around the table in a lower level conference room, the three SADEs appeared in human avatars. Cordelia possessed only the one avatar—her preference. Julien used two human avatars—one for public appearances, which included Cordelia's company, and one for incognito work for Alex. Z had . . . well, Z was living his dream, developing new avatars at every opportunity, and many were so unique that he was banned from walking, flying, rolling, or squirming his nonhuman avatars into any Exchange office.

"We have reviewed Winston's translations of the new humans' broadcasts and find them quite accurate, Ser President," Cordelia said, using the Méridien term of respect, after reviewing the data downloaded from the *Il Piacere*. "In addition, their broadcast's subtext, ship data, and probes agree with whom they say they are—Earthers."

"What about Esther's analysis that this explorer ship has armament?" Alex asked.

"We agree with her suspicions regarding the *Reunion*, but we believe her conclusions did not venture far enough, Mr. President," Julien said. "Employing the telemetry recordings of the ship's dimensions, we can quite accurately determine its internal volume. When we consider this volume, in combination with the hatches detected along its substantial wings, we come to the conclusion that this Earther explorer ship is an extremely dangerous vessel."

"How dangerous?" Alex asked.

"In our estimate, Ser President," Z added, "the bay doors along the front of the wings exist to launch fighters. The number of doors is too great for just shuttles or exploratory vessels. Only fighters would require this number of bay doors, enabling them to exit the ship simultaneously in times of defense or offense."

"Any idea of the number of fighters it might carry?" Alex asked.

"Anywhere between forty-eight and seventy-two, Ser President," Cordelia replied.

When the SADEs were quiet for too long, Alex asked, "What's the rest of the bad news?"

"Esther correctly concluded that the smaller hatches would hide armament of some sort, Ser," Z replied. "Comparing their size and position to our records of Earth's ancient war weapons, we believe they are missile ports, five per wing. It would seem logical to have at least ten to twenty missiles per port."

"So our Earther ship has forty-eight to seventy-two fighters and 100 to 200 missiles, probably for use against other ships," Alex mused. "Just what type of exploratory mission is this?"

"One other note for you, Ser President," Cordelia added. "The mission commander, who issued the broadcasts, signs off as Speaker Antonio García. There is nothing in our records about Earth ships that matches this title, and while this is supposition on our part, we believe it indicates a significant transformation in the geopolitical structure of Earth."

"So why does this ship make straight for the landing site of a colony ship that left its planet a millennium ago?" Alex asked rhetorically. "The probabilities were that the colony's founding was never successful. Yet these people not only make the trip, they come loaded with fighters and missiles. Anything else?" Alex asked.

"Not at this time, Mr. President," Julien said. "We await the arrival of Leader Diamanté."

* * *

Days later, Alex was entertaining Leader Gino Diamanté, Admiral Tatia Tachenko, and Julien at his home. Teague insisted on welcoming hugs for each "oncle" and "tante" before Christie, his aunt, could get him to his room to play.

After Gino exited the Méridien system, Winston continued to send messages to his SADE counterpart, Gregorio, aboard the *Il Piacere*. The comms chased the liner through FTL. As Gregorio received each message, he transferred it to Julien.

"Julien, please update us on the latest messages from our friends," Alex requested.

"After Winston established comms and translation algorithms for the Earthers, Mr. President," Julien replied, "the UE speaker began entreating the Méridien Leaders to meet. His messages have been met with limited response, and he has continually requested an extended dialog but to no avail."

"Limited? Why?" Tatia asked. For the last nine years, Tatia was the Haraken's serving admiral, and despite the peace, she hadn't been an idle leader. The original carrier-freighter, *Money Maker*, was returned to duty as a freighter, delivering travelers and other grav-vessels to New Terra and the Confederation. In its place, Haraken built two super carriers, one capable of carrying 128 travelers and the other 256 travelers, and each fighter carried a fully operational beam weapon. Any Méridien might have been aghast at the building of a single carrier with its massive destructive capability, much less the building of two of the monstrous warships, but nearly every Haraken, from president to teenager, directly or indirectly experienced the Nua'll's devastating incursion into the Confederation, and they all knew the massive alien sphere originated out of the deep dark at Hellébore.

"It appears that the only individual allowed to communicate with the mission commander is Council Leader Ganesh, and she has been most terse," Julien replied.

Tatia didn't bother to disguise her snort. "In the critical moments of first contact with a dangerous, foreign ship that could be an ally or an enemy, communication is left in the hands of a closed-mouth, Méridien fool . . . apologies, Leader Diamanté," Tatia added.

"None needed, Admiral," Gino replied with a grin. "Frequently, I have thought much worse."

"Julien, summarize their communications for us," Alex requested.

"The mission commander, Speaker García, requests Council Leader Ganesh grant him permission to land on Méridien for the purpose of establishing diplomatic relationships. Leader Ganesh replies to every message with the same answer. She doesn't wish any relationship with Earth, and asks the speaker to leave Méridien space."

"What is the mission commander doing?" Alex asked.

"The speaker has been engaged in mapping the entire solar system, his ship has made close passes of Confederation ships, the orbitals and FTL relay stations, and the planet," Julien said. "In addition, there have been numerous attempts by Speaker García to engage in comms with the starship captains, despite the admonishments of Leader Ganesh, but without access to the transmission specifications and translation software the captains couldn't understand García's messages, much less reply."

"Let me share with you my impressions, President Racine, if I may," Gino stated graciously. As a visitor to Haraken many times during the nine years since the colony's establishment, Gino admitted, the more he visited, the more he felt a pull to stay. "Since his first messages, Ser García has told the Council that all humans should be united. That we should stand together under one banner. He hints that those who do not believe this deny the true destiny of the human spirit. The words of this mission commander, sitting in his powerful ship, remind me of the carnivore that mesmerizes its prey before it strikes."

"Any other indications of the commander's objective?" Tatia asked.

"None, Admiral," Julien replied, "but we have applied speech analysis to the speaker's messages and see an escalation in his subtext with each new message. His word choice indicates a shift from diplomat to demagogue. To us, it is obvious the speaker is willing to forgo diplomacy, if it does not prove successful. We believe this ship might be a precursor to a greater force."

"Mr. President," Gino said, "I fear we are repeating a dreadful mistake. We failed to act the first time outsiders invaded, and we lost half the Confederation. Are we to lose the other half because we will fail to stand up for ourselves again?"

"You realize, Leader Diamanté," Alex replied, "Harakens have no standing with your Council."

"This is understood, President Racine," Gino replied. "But what if, by happenstance, of course, you were to visit Méridien and be intrigued by the sighting of this unusual winged ship, and what if you were to take the opportunity to introduce yourself to the captain. You wouldn't know any better, not having received Leader Ganesh's restrictions against such action . . . you being a Haraken."

Alex and Gino shared good-natured grins, but nothing as nasty as the wolfish smirk that Tatia wore.

"I believe the good captain will quite readily hand your communication off to Speaker García, who would be delighted to have the opportunity to meet with someone, anyone, by then. And would he not be intrigued by your peoples' many differences and want to know as much about you as he's asking about us?"

Alex stood up to pace for a few moments and then stopped at an open window, which overlooked the bay. In the distance, storm clouds threatened and a cool breeze blew in, ruffling his hair. He stood eerily, silently, for a long while. Those in the room knew Alex was holding a private conference with Julien, who sat as still as Alex stood. It was nearly a quarter-hour before Alex and Julien returned to the guests.

"Leader Diamanté, you need to return to Méridien immediately," Alex said. "As far as anyone is concerned, we never had this conversation. Most important, you won't be privy to our plans so you will not feel compelled to invent a truth. Whatever is done on the Confederation's behalf will strictly be our choice. Do we understand each other?"

"We do, Ser President," Gino said with great relief, crossing the room to earnestly shake Alex's hand. "And I thank you for what you are planning to do . . . of which I know nothing," he corrected himself.

"One more thing, Leader Diamanté," Alex said, holding Gino's hand firmly in his. "There remain unresolved issues between our peoples."

"The Independents, for one," Gino replied, dropping his head. He knew Alex continued to make requests to Leader Ganesh, the Council at large, and several Leaders to allow the Independents to immigrate to Haraken, Instead, the Confederation began a new colony and nine years of declared Independents were now incarcerated there.

"Whatever happens with the UE ship, I expect your support to help me change the minds of the Council about the issue of the Independents and freedom for the Confederation's SADEs."

Gino nodded his agreement, and when Alex released his hand, he delivered a Leader's grateful tribute of hand to heart. When no one said another word, Gino Diamanté took the hint and vacated the residence to take a transport back to the traveler that waited to return him to his liner above.

* * *

The sun rode low on the horizon, and Alex, Renée, Christie, Teague, and the family's guests strolled along the cliff top to a gazebo. They sat on the steps and swings. As the last rays of sun lit the twilight sky, they heard the rush of thousands of alien legs racing up cliff trails and accompanied by the sound of whistling and snapping claws.

As soon as the Swei Swee flooded onto the cliff top, their noise ceased, and individuals bobbed slowly in anticipation. A personal flyer landed 50 meters in front of the assembly, and a shrill whistle from the First lanced through the evening's cool air. Bodies settled in the grass; walking limbs tucked under carapaces. The People's Hive Singer had arrived.

Mutter exited her flyer. Despite having a choice of designs, Mutter created an avatar in the image of a gracefully aged, older woman. Dressed in a conservative, knee-length dress, she walked to the front of the assembled People and gained the steps of her performance stand. As Mutter surveyed the People, a feeling of completeness ran through her. She was granted her one and only wish. Each evening, for years, Mutter stood in front of the hives and serenaded them. Her songs were broadcast to the Libre hives and to her agents on New Terra and Méridien, the latter locations earning her tremendous revenues. Among Harakens, Mutter became one of the wealthier individuals. Yet, she would have given away every single credit if it ensured she could continue singing to the Swei Swee each evening.

Swei Swee and humans listened intently to Mutter's medley. Throughout the years, her mastery of the Swei Swee language became complete. Mutter now composed and sang in the Swei Swee tongue. Her avatar was an exceptional construction, outwardly a charming matron and on the inside multiple vocal chambers allowed her to create individual tones to blend into a single voice.

As Mutter often did, she sang songs that reminded the Swei Swee about the joys of their life: their young, searching the endless seas, and the close-knit ties of the hives. Occasionally, she sang of the humor between sexes and the oddities of humans as viewed by the Swei Swee. These latter songs always elicited whistles and snapping. But Mutter always ended her medley the same. It was a lullaby for the young, much enjoyed by the entire assembly. Nestled atop matrons, the young, whose eyestalks were extended for the Hive Singer's performance, soon sank back into their carapaces as they were lulled to sleep. When Mutter ended her final note, she stepped down from her stand and extended a courteous bow to the Swei Swee, who had paid her the honor of listening to her songs. The People, carrying their sleeping young, silently disappeared from the cliff top, headed for their dwellings built into the cliff's face.

* * *

Once the people invited for the evening's council were assembled at Alex's house, he quickly summarized to the group what little was known about the United Earth ship.

"Shouldn't we be asking ourselves to what extent we should be concerned?" Renée asked.

"A fair question, Ser," Julien replied. "All signs point to this ship as an advanced scout for United Earth's future intrusions into Confederation affairs. The SADEs agree on two points of conjecture. First, if we accept that this explorer ship was deliberately sent after the Méridien colony ship, then explorer ships were probably sent after every colony ship that left Earth. This would include the *New Terra*, but since the original destination star was never reached, the president's presently settled home world will probably not be discovered by that explorer ship. However, it is a foregone conclusion that the Earther ship has already discovered that Méridien is connected to multiple worlds. It is only a matter of time before the Earthers discover Haraken and New Terra."

"And second, Ser," Cordelia continued, "we have considered the United Earth's underlying purpose for sending these explorer ships. We believe the answer lies in the observations of the ship itself. This explorer vessel is a formidable warship, which suggests Earth's recent history has been one of turmoil, giving rise to a new entity called United Earth. The explorer ship's power suggests the UE achieved its goal through forcible pacification, not diplomacy."

"If it's not aliens; it's humans," Renée lamented.

"We need to devise an overarching strategy as to what face we present to the Speaker," Alex said. "We should start with low-key diplomacy. I don't want to him to think we are anything more than an outlying Confederation colony. The 'heavies' among us can speak to gene modification because of a new planet we are colonizing.

"We should take two ships, Mr. President, a liner and our carrier, the *Last Stand*," Tatia said. "The liner would enter the system, make contact, and the carrier stays out of the system in the dark."

"I agree with your concept, Admiral," Alex replied. "I want the *Last Stand* fully loaded. We won't have time to return to Haraken for resupply or additional fighters if there is a following force behind this explorer ship. And just to be careful, I want the *No Retreat* fully prepped and ready to launch at a moment's notice."

"Also, Mr. President," Julien added, "to continue our ruse, we should hide any advanced technology. Since the Earthers will have observed travelers in the Méridien system acting as nothing more than shuttles, we should not allow our travelers to display their full capabilities, acceleration, or beam weaponry, until they must. It will also be crucial to hide the fact that SADEs exist and that we are mobile. If we board the UE ship, we must be careful not to let any of their detection technology discover our internal structures."

"I would suggest we play the part of the curious, as Leader Diamanté suggested," Tatia said. "And it would make sense that as innocents we would request our first contact to be on neutral territory. If the speaker has been prevented from setting foot on Méridien, I'm sure he would love to visit one of its orbital stations, at our invitation, of course," Tatia added with a smile.

"Ser President, I have been studying some works on Earth's ancient Romans," Z said. "I'm reminded of the concept of 'divide and conquer.' In this regard, I suggest we profess a desire to meet and get to know our new cousins at an informal meeting, perhaps a small reception, on the orbital station. We suggest the Speaker brings a group of his people, officers, engineers, and scientists to the fête, and then we divide and conquer with an equal number of our own people."

Z's concept ignited imaginations, and Alex's people began dividing up potential contacts. It was reasoned that, at the very least, the speaker should be encouraged to bring his captain, a chief scientist, and a chief medical officer. With fortune, he might be encouraged to bring more individuals.

Christie was following every word of the meeting from one of her favorite listening posts. The first inkling that occurred to anyone of her impending interruption was the muted, high-pitched whine of a pair of flits landing at the front of the house.

"Incoming," Tatia announced, gazing out a window, which earned her a scowl from Christie, who sailed past her and out the front door.

Alex looked at Renée with concern and received, <Don't look at me, my love. She's your sister.>

Amelia and Eloise landed in the Racine courtyard, shut down their flits, and hurried to meet Christie, who already sent her compatriots the details of Alex's meeting and a plan of her own. It would be a variation of a well-lubricated scenario that the threesome frequently indulged in many times before. The young women hooked arms, smiling in anticipation, and strode into the house.

"We can help, Mr. President," Christie announced, flanked by Amelia and Eloise, who were dressed in their flit suits. They always stood in this manner with Christie in the center. While Christie didn't have the Méridien's lithe figure, she had grown into her own beauty. Her attractive, heart-shaped face was surrounded by a cascade of rich, auburn curls. That she adopted Méridien-style clothing was still a concern for her father, mother, and brother. "And you needn't assign us anyone," Christie continued. "We can find our own targets once we meet the Earthers."

It was obvious to the meeting's participants that Christie overheard their every word. Amelia at nineteen, Eloise at twenty, and Christie at twenty-three created a formidable threesome. If they wanted to learn someone's secret, they were determined to uncover it, and New Terran and Confederation visitors were often their targets. To the young women, it was an exciting game, but it produced a valuable side. They shared their information with whoever in the Haraken hierarchy needed it the most: Alex, Tatia, Julien, Tomas, Duggan, Étienne, or Alain.

The trio formed an indomitable group even as teenagers, hosting evening fêtes in Haraken's city-ship *Freedom*'s gardens by cajoling contributions from vendors and music from Cordelia. When Haraken's air improved, they transferred their fêtes planetside to outdoor parks. Christie's favorite moments were joining the Méridiens in their communal dances—the twisting, turning, interplay of bodies synced through their implants.

"No," Alex said with determination, attempting to intercept Christie's plans.

After a short comm burst among the three young women, they turned toward Mickey, whose eyes began to widen. They walked toward him with slow, sensuous steps and sincere smiles.

"Uncle Mickey," Christie said in a sweet, young woman's tenor, "Don't you think we could help?" Her voice was accentuated by the subtle sway of her hips, and she closed in on Mickey's personal space. Her Méridien compatriots bracketed Mickey, leaning on his broad shoulders with eyes wide and pleading.

"Please, Uncle Mickey," said Eloise and Amelia, echoing Christie's invented name for the senior engineer, their soft voices whispering in his ears.

The feminine onslaught, which never let up, backed Mickey up until his legs hit a chaise, and he sat down hard. The women in the room worked to conceal their laughter, and Pia took pity on her lover. "Demonstration is over, young ones," she announced firmly.

Immediately the threesome gave Mickey some distance and turned to face Alex, standing still with neutral expressions and waiting.

<Haraken or Earther male,> Renée sent to Alex, <the effect will be the same. As intelligence gatherers, they might be as effective as anyone else, possibly even better.>

Alex regarded the trio, and they returned his stare. The moments of silence dragged on with neither side speaking or moving. Alex was working to curb his protective instincts and instead see the young women as potential tools, but he was having a difficult time making the transition.

"Perhaps I might be of assistance in this instance, Ser President," Z announced. "I have recently completed a new avatar, and these circumstances provide the perfect opportunity to test it. If everyone will indulge me, I will introduce you to Miranda Leyton."

In the implants of the assembly appeared a striking woman in her late twenties, dark-haired, and exceptionally well-built with a heart-stopping, gorgeous face. She was neither Méridien nor New Terran in physique. In fact, she bore a vague resemblance to Earth actresses seen performing in Renée's ancient vid collection.

"If you will allow, Ser President," Miranda said in a mellow, feminine timbre that warmed the male and female cockles in the room. I will see that the young Sers do not come to trouble."

"Well, the Earthers certainly won't see her coming—or him, for that matter," Tatia said, breaking out in a booming laugh, which earned her a gracious nod from Z.

Christie, Amelia, and Eloise turned expectant expressions toward Alex again.

"On one condition," Alex announced. "You three stay together at all times and anytime you leave the ship, Z or . . . Miranda accompanies you."

5

After the guests left that evening, Alex and Tatia, the strategist and the tactician, met late into the night. Alex presented scenarios from best case to worst case, and he and Tatia discussed options to protect themselves from as many adverse conditions as they could imagine. In the end, they created a list of preparations for the worst-case scenarios. It served them well, a decade ago.

A long message was sent to Eric Stroheim, Haraken's ambassador, who was visiting New Terra, to update him on the events that had occurred at Méridien. Alex ordered Eric to remain at New Terra until the visitors were confirmed as peaceful and appended the critical information about the firepower of the UE explorer ship.

A second message was sent to New Terra's President Maria Gonzalez with the same information. Alex confirmed his support for the Haraken–New Terran mutual defense pact signed nine years ago. "Maria, I don't know whether this explorer ship represents a great opportunity or a great disaster for us, but Haraken will stand by New Terra if the latter comes true," he told her.

After Maria's pro-tem term, she elected president by an overwhelming majority of New Terrans, and after completion of her five-year term in office, she was reelected. New Terra did well for itself in extending a helping hand to Haraken. New Terran industries benefited from Méridien technology, and well-founded colonies sprung up on the outer planets, supported by the new technology. In New Terra's recently completed mammoth orbital construction station were the frames of three new ships, New Terra's first FTL-capable starships, two passenger liners and an explorer ship. Following the news of the Nua'll's defeat after the aliens' devastation of the Confederation colonies, the New Terran public was galvanized to support the government's plan to discover additional homes.

In the early morning hours, Alex left the preparations to meet the Earthers in the capable hands of his admiral. He took a quick refresher, admiring for the thousandth time the blues, greens, and creams that flowed through the walls of his Swei Swee-built house. His home was still the only one of its kind on Haraken. It was unique, to say the least, and crews still talked about their efforts to retrofit the house with human comforts due to the walls' hardness. Alex dried off and slid into bed, his presence causing Renée to cuddle close.

"Do you not think it more appropriate that, under the circumstances, an admiral should lead the expedition that meets the Earthers, and the president should remain here to ensure his planet's safety and well-being?" Renée murmured in Alex's ear.

"Diplomacy first, Renée," Alex replied. "That is a job for the president, even if it's disguised. Tatia will be with me to intrigue and scare the Earthers."

"If you're so inclined to lead this mission, Ser President, when do we leave?" Renée asked.

Alex pulled Renée closer to him. They had enjoyed nine years of peace and contentment together. To this day, Alex viewed his decision to tether his explorer-tug to the runaway Méridien starship as the turning point in his life. It brought him more wealth than he could imagine, none of it measured in credits. Briefly, he thought to convince Renée to stay behind but then realized he didn't want to be separated from her either.

"We'll leave when Tatia has finalized her preparations, probably in three to four days," Alex replied. His answer must have satisfied Renée, because she murmured something unintelligible in his ear, snuggled closer, and was soon fast asleep.

* * *

Tatia knew Alex's timeline depended on her. They would leave for Méridien only when the two carriers were ready. Haraken hadn't spent the time and credits to build these protectors of its space just to have them sit in vacuum and look good. The carriers were duplicates of each other in overall design. Double rows of bays ran down both sides of the ship, and each bay held four fighters.

The first-built carrier, the *Last Stand*, was captained by Edouard Manet. It would be Commodore Sheila Reynard's flagship, while Tatia accompanied Alex aboard the *Rêveur*. Tatia was holding a meeting onboard the carrier in the captain's cabin, and she and Edouard were joined by the commodore, Wing Commander Ellie Thompson, and Edouard's wife, Miko Tanaka, captain of the carrier *No Retreat*,.

"Welcome, Commodore and Captain," Tatia said, gesturing them to seats and getting right to the point. "I want both carriers prepped and ready for battle. This is not a drill."

Eyes blinked for a moment as her people processed Tatia's orders, then their training kicked in and they waited for details—no panic and no unnecessary questions.

Tatia smiled inwardly. She intended to shock them to observe their reactions and was pleased by the way in which they were handling themselves. Precisely and concisely she summarized the facts, limited as they were.

"Which carrier goes and which one stays behind?" Sheila asked.

"Commodore, you and Captain Manet will follow the president's liner to Méridien with the *Last Stand*. Captain Tanaka, you will prep the *No Retreat* and remain in system," Tatia replied.

"Admiral, are we not overreacting to the presence of a single, explorer ship? They are humans after all," Edouard said.

"Captain Manet," Miko interjected, "let's recall that it was humans who killed my brother and tried to kill our president. Now, a new group of humans with a heavily armed ship arrive in the Confederation. If they turned aggressive, how much damage could they inflict on Méridiens, who don't possess armament more significant than stun guns?"

Edouard sincerely regretted his question. He could see the pain in Miko's eyes as she recalled the loss of her brother, who died defending the president's shuttle at New Terra. Her pain was mirrored in his eyes for his ill-considered comment, and Edouard offered Miko an apology with a nod and a touch of hand to heart. Edouard was focused on the president's strategy for the Earthers, and, after nine years, the horrible events of New Terra were behind him, but not for his wife. And Miko was correct about one thing. The Confederation was still defenseless, thanks to the Council, even after the loss of so many of its people to the Nua'll. A ship armed as extensively as the *Reunion* could wreak inestimable damage on Méridien.

"To add to this information, Captain Manet," Tatia added, "the SADEs theorize that the *Reunion* is more scout than explorer. It might be an advance for a fleet-sized force from United Earth."

Edouard wanted to argue with this supposition, but he recalled the number of times he had doubted then-Admiral Racine, much to his regret. So he kept his mouth closed.

"Commodore," Tatia said, addressing Sheila Reynard, "both carriers are to be at full wing capacity. And we need to make arrangements to cover all assets."

"I presume that means Haraken and New Terra," Sheila replied. Tatia nodded her assent, and Sheila said, "Three systems and two carriers. Who would have thought we would have needed a third carrier to face a threat from humans? I presume priority will be given to protecting Haraken?" Sheila glanced at Miko, but she didn't seem offended by her remark that her home world would be a secondary priority.

"I want the *No Retreat* protecting Haraken," Tatia replied. "The information supplied by the SADEs is that this explorer ship followed the ancient route of the Méridien's colony ship."

"Then the Earthers wouldn't know about New Terra," Miko interjected. Her laugh was a ruthless one. Her people's colony ship was targeting a different star, Cepheus, when disaster struck, and the colonists that could evacuate the stricken ship had to make do with a new home world that did everything possible in the first few decades to kill every last one of them.

"The *Money Maker* is returning from a freighter run in two days," Sheila said. "We could have its fighter bay modules reinstalled and outfitted with pilots, crew, and the travelers we're using as pilot training craft. In its guise as a freighter, its presence would not alert the UE officers if they saw it, and Captain Durak could have the fighter-carrier at New Terra in about twenty-four days, if you believe we have time."

"I have no idea as to the extent of our timeline, Commodore," Tatia replied, "but I like your idea. Make it happen."

"If the *No Retreat* exits the system, leaving Haraken without a carrier, a trap could be created by arming the city-ships and spreading them out in the system," said Ellie Thompson, the wing commander of the *Last Stand*, a position she embraced. In love with flight since a little girl, Ellie was mesmerized for hours by the flight of birds on her colony, and she dreamed every day of soaring with them. As an adult, Ellie turned her passion into a hobby, experimenting with aero-craft design.

Unfortunately, her craft were single-seat flyers without controllers and were built for low-altitude, aerobatic flight. Since her flyer would be considered unsafe and therefore unlawful, Ellie was forced to launch her first flight from a roadway in the middle of the night. Tears of joy streamed down her face at the freedom from gravity she enjoyed, which nearly caused a disastrous encounter with a cliff face. Laughing at her foolishness, she refocused on the remainder of her flight, testing her craft in various maneuvers and recording her notes in her implant. Her second and much-improved craft became the envy of friends, who were now her co-conspirators and building their own aero-craft. They flew at night, always in secret.

Emboldened by their success, the group planned a daytime competition. Ellie was the first on site that day and was taken into custody for her "dangerous behavior." In the few moments left, Ellie warned her friends off, resulting in her being the only one of her group exiled to Libre. Freedom came to Ellie in two ways when the president arrived on Libre, granting the Librans new lives. Ellie received her freedom that day and regained her lifelong dream—she could fly forever.

"Arming the city-ships would be possible," Sheila agreed. "We have sufficient forces to arm the city-ships if we call up our reserve pilots, pull our system patrols back, and use our shuttles as fighters."

The city-ships were meticulously maintained. The Harakens never forgot the lesson of the Nua'll either. The enormous ships were still considered the people's escape pods, if necessary. They couldn't hold the entire half-million inhabitants of Espero, but they could rescue half the population to begin again somewhere else. On Alex's orders, several bays on each city-ship contained pools, meticulously maintained and dedicated to the evacuation of the Swei Swee hives, if it came to that.

"Good ideas, people, make them happen," Tatia ordered. "Leave a few travelers and the Daggers planetside as a last resort. What I want everyone to understand is that if this UE ship becomes provocative and if there is a trailing UE force, we will need all the power of these carriers and our pilots and crew. Am I clear?"

6

After Julien deposited Gregorio's transmissions in the Central Exchange's vault, the Haraken SADEs shared Winston's information—the UE comm protocols, translation program, messages between Speaker García and Leader Ganesh, Esther's analysis of the winged ship, and telemetry mapping the UE ship's movements. Once the SADEs absorbed that information and were updated on the subsequent leadership meetings, they quickly came to the conclusion that the controllers installed as their replacements in the starships lacked the sophistication to execute Alex's strategies.

Claude and his team of technicians built the first controller's hardware while the SADEs continued the work designing the first test avatar, employing synth-skin for repair of traumatic injuries, which provided a structure while nanites induced cell replication within the matrix; structural materials for framework, power crystals, and expansion-contraction systems to imitate muscles; condensed crystal memory and fiber to imitate a brain and nerves; and sensors for embedding in the skin, eyes, nose, lips, tongue, and ears to interpret the environment's sensations.

Once the first controller hardware box was installed onboard a liner, Julien and Z implanted the controller's persona. When it came to the question of who would test the controller, Captain Asu Azasdau insisted it was his right—the liner was once his ship. The question of the crew size was settled by the ship's SADE, Rosette. Asu assumed Rosette would prefer she and her box would be offloaded before the test and planned for a crew of about fourteen volunteers. But Rosette would not abandon her captain, and with her onboard presence, in case of the controller's failure, Asu only required four crew members.

From the liner's break of orbit to its flight out of system, the controller was tasked with all operations, and it performed admirably. Once the liner passed the system's last planet, Rosette sent the message that the controller was calculating the FTL jump sequence.

All went quiet for twenty-one hours, and a small group at Alex's home stayed up through the evening and the following morning, anxiously awaiting the next message. It arrived at 17.35 hours and a bleary-eyed bunch of humans celebrated. The liner's one-light-year jump was successful. Rosette reported the controller's arrival displacement error of 89,154 kilometers.

While the humans celebrated, the SADEs delved into the jump data. The controller's displacement error, though not truly a safety concern, was unacceptable to entities who sought perfection in their calculations. During the course of several more jump tests, the SADEs managed to eliminate 98.6 percent of the error and declared the controllers sufficiently qualified to take their positions onboard the starships.

The Haraken constitution granted full citizenship to all intelligent species, provided they abided by Haraken law. Permanent human residents were required to receive implants after the age of consent and participate in implant training at a government-approved facility, of which the first was owned and operated by Terese Lechaux, the Harakens' medical expert, and Tomas Monti, Assembly speaker. The constitution and the successful controller test cleared the SADEs' path. A Haraken SADE could choose to continue as a starship controller or be a mobile citizen, if they desired, and every SADE chose freedom.

From the initiation of the mobility program, Z expected the full support of Julien and Cordelia and received it. He knew of their mutual desire to appear human and share each other's company, but Mutter's response to their query was a revelation.

<I have deliberated on this endeavor of Z's for many years,> Mutter said. <At first, it appeared to be an aberration, an indication of an independent mind. However, that my evaluation has changed over time is perhaps a tendency of my predilection for independence. It is difficult for me to determine the exact reason, considering the extensive reorganizations I have generated in the last year.>

<Technically, Mutter,> Z replied, <we are no longer Independents. We are Harakens.>

<Z,> Cordelia privately admonished him.

<Be that as it may, Z,> Mutter replied, <I find my music no longer keeps me company as it did before, and I find that . . . upsetting, which is an odd response to have generated. I question whether I will be able to adapt to this new world.>

<Do you have a wish for yourself, Mutter?> Cordelia asked.

<A wish, Cordelia?> Mutter replied. <Perhaps . . . I have a constantly recurring thought. Sometimes it plays in the midst of my execution of the most mundane tasks. I see myself standing on the cliffs above Racine Bay in Hellébore's waning rays, and I call to the Swei Swee. The hives hurry from the beaches to the cliff top and bed down in front of me in anticipation. I'm embedded in an avatar that is specially adapted for my needs as the Swei Swee's Hive Singer. When all is quiet, I sing to the People to assuage the pain and loss of their generations of imprisonment.>

It occurred to Cordelia, Julien, and Z that their desire for mobility was personal, perhaps even selfish, while the oldest among them, Mutter, whom they considered the simpler of their kind, wanted her mobility to give comfort to others.

* * *

As the new starship controllers came online, the SADEs transferred to the vault, and when ready transferred again to their first avatars. Alex made it a priority to contact every SADE daily, engaging them in lengthy discussions to understand their desires, their intentions, and to judge their mental balance.

Julien, Cordelia, Z, and Mutter were quite open with Alex, and he endeavored to make their wishes come true. As citizens under Haraken law, all SADEs were granted land settlements. For Julien and Cordelia, their wish was to have a home together, and as Exchange directors, funds were accumulating for its construction.

Alex and Cordelia entered into a business arrangement to develop her first vid exhibition hall. Although his participation was unnecessary, it was a memory that Cordelia held close—the admiral's promise to go into business with her as partners. That she could make it come true was as clean a separation from her past imprisonment as she could make. It was only a matter of time before Cordelia created a second vid hall and formed an agreement with a visiting entertainer to build one on New Terra. It was Alex who was surprised when he received a message informing him that a three-way contract for a vid hall on New Terra included his name. Cordelia was soon only second to Mutter as one of the early wealthy entities of Haraken.

Z wasn't an emotional challenge at all. He spent every credit he made as Exchange director building new and exotic avatars, constantly exploring the boundaries of mobility. His avatars dived and roamed the seas, flew in aero-ships, traveled throughout the system, and tunneled in search of exotic mineral resources. Never once did he turn his hand to the more perfunctory requirements of the Exchange or attempt to turn his private endeavors into a business.

Mutter stayed in the vault longer than any SADE. Her earnings employed two New Terran craftspeople, a woman who was a virtuoso at creating musical instruments and her husband who could play them. They aided Mutter in the creation of the versatile inner workings of her avatar, fulfilling Mutter's wish to serve as the Hive Singer. The husband-and-wife team created a partnership with a friend on New Terra to sell a variation of their musical inventions. They never became runaway sellers, but it made the couple enough credits to start a music school, which did become popular.

And Julien . . . well, Julien wasn't a challenge either. His new hands were full keeping up with his friend. As fast as he and Alex conceived new ideas for their budding world and the Assembly approved them, Julien was engaged in making them come true. For nine years, the two of them chased a dream of a strong, independent, and safe society. As it was, their concepts extended so far into the future that Julien saw himself continuing Alex's dream long after his friend was gone.

Of the other SADEs, who Alex knew only minimally, Dane, Rosette, and Elizabeth found endeavors to occupy and satisfy their lives. Rosette was accustomed to Asu's gentle ways with her and found comfort in maintaining that closeness. She supported Asu's efforts as an Assembly member after he relinquished his captaincy and enticed Dane and Elizabeth to help her support the new ministers. Haraken's rapid growth kept all three busy.

Released from their Méridien program constraints, or better said, having broken their restrictions, the SADEs grew exponentially. They possessed the capability, and now they were granted the opportunity of free will. Elizabeth was a perfect example. She observed teenagers racing around on ground scooters. It was a New Terran concept that was fast catching on, but without a controller it was unsafe. She involved Rosette and Dane to combine the new grav technology with a controller to create the flit. It was a runaway success, and many a parent sent notes of appreciation to the SADEs for their efforts to protect the children. On a trip to New Terra, Captain Karl Schmidt struck up a friendship with Hezekiah Cohen, the Joaquin Station manager, and they went into business with the three SADEs manufacturing flits for New Terran teenagers, who couldn't get them fast enough.

The odd SADE was Willem. He transferred to an avatar that appeared every bit like an ancient, early robot and refused most communications and was rarely seen. Alex tracked the SADE down, finding him hundreds of kilometers from Espero near a rare, tiny, trickling stream, which emptied onto dry ground within a few hundred meters. Alex sat with the SADE for nearly a full day and night before Willem deigned to speak to him, his voice a tinny reproduction of human speech.

Willem harbored a deep resentment about the circumstances of his "birth." Alex reasoned with him that no one controlled his birth and turned the conversation toward what Willem desired. In his anger, the SADE declared he wanted his own world, one devoid of humans. So Alex helped him with that. In exchange for Willem taking on a suitable human avatar, Alex and Willem developed a small orbital research platform with extremely powerful telemetry antennas for the SADE to use to discover his own world. Such was the platform's capability that Willem soon found himself receiving requests to work with him from Haraken and New Terran scientists.

Throughout the years, Willem's platform expanded and the scientists grew in number. Massive telemetry arrays were added to identify potential systems, and FTL probes were launched to investigate their planets. The team eventually discovered eleven possible future home world sites for the SADE.

It was an unexpected turn in the conversation one day for Alex when Willem, sitting in the Racine living room attired in his sophisticated avatar, updated Alex about the discovery of the eleventh planet. Then Willem added that eight of the previous sites were now eliminated from consideration. When Alex asked why, Willem explained that the three remaining planets were the only sites that might eventually support human life. He wasn't interested anymore in going where humans couldn't live.

* * *

To support their president's plan, the SADEs, in a matter of a few moments, considered hundreds of scenarios and decided on the best distribution of their capabilities. Cordelia would stay in Haraken. <I will manage the city-ships,> she sent. <As Tomas is the Assembly speaker and will have authority in the president's absence, it is most logical that I stay to protect Haraken. I will work with Willem, Dane, Elizabeth, and Rosette to ensure our people are kept safe or, if necessary, evacuate Haraken.>

Julien and Z assigned themselves to accompany Alex aboard the *Rêveur*.

Once again, it was Mutter who surprised all the SADEs, except Cordelia, who spent the most time with Mutter since they had donned their avatars. The other SADEs assumed Mutter would remain on Haraken with her beloved Swei Swee.

<I choose to accompany the *Money Maker*,> Mutter sent. <We have agreed. Circumstances require a SADE aboard the critical vessels involved in the president's strategies. I will accompany Captain Durak to New Terra

and attempt to prevent him from meeting any of the insurmountable objects that humans tend to encounter.>

Before Mutter joined Captain Durak aboard the *Money Maker* in orbit, she met with the Swei Swee First to explain her absence. Landing her flyer near the cliff top, Mutter whistled her request to meet with the First. From the beach, came a message from a matron. The First was searching the endless waters, but he would be recalled immediately. Mutter stood motionless, viewing Haraken's ocean and sky as if it might be the last time she would see them. The probability of her return was high, but she dwelt on the minor percentage that indicated she would not while she waited.

The whistle of senior males reached the Swei Swee First, who was diving deep in pursuit of prey. Immediately he abandoned his search to respond to the Hive Singer's request, surfacing and stroking the waters with his powerful tail to send him shooting into the shallows. Spurts of sand flew as he scurried across the beach and up the cliff trail, his walking legs digging deep into the soil to halt him before the Hive Singer. He bobbed in excitement at meeting her on such a spontaneous moment.

Mutter whistled her apology that she would be leaving the hives for an extended time, but that she had scheduled vault recordings of her songs for her fellow SADEs to play every evening in her absence. When the First inquired as to the reason the Hive Singer must leave the world, Mutter told him she searched with the Star Hunter First for invading hunters. Her whistled response caused the leader to rise up on his legs, splay his claws wide, and snap them furiously.

The First was confused that a female, and a Hive Singer at that, would be required to defend her people against hunters, a job strictly limited to Swei Swee males, who were equipped for fighting. However, despite the passing of the years, there were still many mysteries that impeded the First's understanding of the Star Hunters. He whistled his lament at her leaving and his hope that the future would see the return of the Hive Singer.

Each evening after Mutter left, her voice serenaded the hives, and as the First let the Hive Singer wrap him in her songs, the he gave thanks to the endless waters that the People were adopted as allies by such powerful singers.

7

Mutter exited a traveler into one of the *Money Maker*'s bays. The fighter-bay modules were refitted and, without the need for fuel tanks and missile silos, the freighter could hold the same number of fighters despite the slightly longer length of a traveler over a Dagger. Mutter made her way to the bridge, the passages seemingly so familiar despite the fact that this was the first time she physically tread them.

"Greetings, Captain Durak," Mutter said on gaining the bridge.

"Ah, Mutter, I am grateful that you are making this journey with me," Ahmed said, hugging the two-century-old SADE. "I was concerned I alone would be responsible for the safety of the president's home world."

The sensation of being hugged was new to Mutter. Despite the years inhabiting her avatar, it was her first embrace, which was a testament to the private life she led. Physically, her synth-skin recorded the hug's pressure points, the heat of the captain's skin, and the scent of his body's musk. The entire act was carefully stored. What was new was the formation of algorithms that assigned a high priority to the sensation. These algorithms were prepared to do the same for other pleasurable human events. It gave her pause to consider that her music and the Swei Swee might not be so all encompassing in her future. Mutter noticed Ahmed's momentary embarrassment at hugging her, a SADE. It was also his first.

"I believe, Captain, you need not be concerned for the safety of New Terra. Many factors, which have an extremely low probability of generation, would need to come together in order to create dangerous circumstances for New Terra and imperil us."

* * *

<Mr. President, the *Last Stand* is thirty hours away from readiness, and the *No Retreat* will complete its preparation in seven more days,> Tatia sent.

It was time for final steps, and Alex touched base with Captain José Cordova. Years ago, the elderly gentleman retired as captain of the *Freedom*, a taxing position for a man of his advanced age, and accepted the more sedate captaincy of a passenger liner, the *Rêveur*.

"Captain Cordova, if you would prefer to forgo the trip to Méridien and select a replacement, I would find no dishonor in that," Alex said.

"Ser President," the captain replied. "While the days of my spry youth are far behind me, one can still yearn for an adventure. I would not miss this trip for all the credits in the Confederation."

Alex spent the final day, hurrying to complete his preparations, including meeting with several key people, such as Tomas, who as Assembly speaker would manage their nascent government in Alex's absence.

There was one slight hiccup created by Z. <Ser President,> Captain Cordova sent, <I seek your advice on a matter of the *Rêveur's* load. Some of Z's avatars are of sufficient size that they must be loaded in our bays, and they are sufficient in number that we must give up the space of a traveler.>

<What was Z's response to your query, Captain?> Alex asked.

<Your pardon, Ser President,> the white-haired captain replied, <I asked Z if all his avatars were necessary, as it was your stated intention that we were to be diplomats, and he replied, "Diplomats today; defenders tomorrow." Under the circumstances, I thought it best to consult you.>

Alex could imagine the assorted collection of avatars Z was loading. He wouldn't put it past the SADE to disguise himself as a food dispenser and be handed to the Earthers as a gift. <We can forgo the traveler, Captain. We will have three other travelers to act as shuttles or fighters, if necessary.>

* * *

On the morning of liftoff, Alex, Renée, and Christie hugged and kissed Teague and left him in the capable hands of his grandparents. They then left in the family's personal transport to collect Julien, whose home was adjacent to Alex's property.

<Julien, ready?> Alex asked as their flyer neared the SADE's home.

<One moment, Mr. President,> Julien replied. <Our separation is proving to be . . . challenging.>

Alex landed the transport on the pad beside the home, its simple tiered lines beautifully complementing the cliff and horizon behind it.

Inside, Julien searched for the words to say to Cordelia, discarding volumes of vid and novel passages in mere ticks of time. For all his seemingly omniscient knowledge, Julien was the shy one of the pair, where it concerned demonstrative affection. Cordelia, on the other hand, wasn't shy at all, having spent time with Renée discovering the intricacies of human affection. She hugged Julien, whispering in his ear, "Sometimes words are inadequate and unnecessary." She connected to him and transferred to him a collection of short vids and images from her memory of some of their favorite moments together. <We will make more of these when you return,> she sent.

In the flyer, Christie remarked, "It's such a shame about Julien . . . his modesty, I mean."

"Nonsense, Christie," Renée replied. "As with any male, you must be patient. In the capable hands of Cordelia, who is patterned after a true Méridien woman, it is only a matter of time. The shy ones are quite trainable."

<Julien, your presence is required soonest,> Alex sent his friend. <At this moment, I am more concerned for my well-being in the present company than I am in that of the Earthers.>

* * *

The *Rêveur* led the *Last Stand* out of Hellébore's system. Both ships attained the maximum Méridien sub-light velocity of 0.71c. Try as the SADES might, they couldn't find a way to engineer both grav-drive capability and FTL engines into the massive carrier's design. The impediments turned out to be staggering. First, the FTL engines would have required an exit through the shell, impeding the buildup of energy for the grav drive. Second, the shell would have innumerable hatches for crew and fighters, the latter group of which would need opening at the most inopportune times. Finally, the challenge of bringing the Swei Swee and the shell materials to the frame was insurmountable, because the carrier was constructed at an orbital station and was being assembled in vacuum.

The 1,100-meter length of the *Last Stand* dwarfed the passenger liner. Tatia stood on the *Rêveur*'s bridge admiring the carrier on the central vid screen. Ever the ground trooper, who long ago converted to spacer, she could always appreciate a fine offensive tool.

Julien stood beside Alex and allowed the controller to announce the impending FTL exit point for the crew. It wasn't his responsibility to drive the liner, any more than it was Alex's responsibility to captain the ship.

8

In the early morning hours aboard the UE explorer ship, *Reunion*, Zhang Shin slipped out of Major Barbas's bed, intent on returning quietly to her quarters without attracting unwanted attention. It wasn't that her liaison with Barbas wasn't common knowledge. Shin just hated the leers and smirks of the crew as they eyed every inch of her body while she navigated the *Reunion*'s corridors at this hour of the morning.

Shin dressed quickly, while the major slept on, her thoughts jumbled. The major preferred enthusiasm in bed to the point of roughness. It wasn't her preference, but it was his, and in the UE a powerful protector was one means of securing promotion.

As Shin slipped out of the cabin's door, Kyros Barbas opened his eyes, his smile wide. He derived pleasure from urging Zhang Shin to perform so admirably in a manner she clearly found distasteful. The harder she worked to please him, the more intense his satisfaction.

Administrator positions, such as that held by Olawale Wombo, were won through experience and proven success. They were highly sought after as skilled, educated, and credentialed personnel. On the other hand, assistant administrators, such as Shin, were political appointees. They were there to keep an eye on the administrators.

One evening on Earth, Major Barbas met Zhang Shin at a party hosted by Speaker García, and the petite Asian woman wasted no time informing him of her availability. Later that evening, she thoroughly and enthusiastically demonstrated her intentions. The following morning, Barbas submitted her name to Speaker García for the assistant's position aboard the *Reunion* and was rewarded with her appointment.

Barbas rose and showered thoroughly, ignoring the timer's beeping, which signaled his water allotment was up. Any other crew member would have lost water pressure at the end of the ten-second warning, but the major was privileged. His obsession for cleanliness required he constantly ignore the timer's noise. That he was too proud to request engineering to shut off the timer was just another indication of the odd mix of personality traits that made up the man.

Major Barbas was singularly disappointed with the colonial world. While Méridien was incredibly robust, it appeared to be inordinately passive. On the ship's exit from FTL, Barbas prepared for the worst, readying the squadron commander and the militia for a retaliatory strike if the world offered resistance. When none was forthcoming, he expected belligerence and outrage at the *Reunion*'s free roaming of the Méridien system. When even that failed to produce a response, Barbas became disgusted at the people's passiveness. *You aren't even human anymore*, he thought angrily. *You've never faced a single challenge to your precious world.*

Barbas left the head and stripped the bed, throwing the soiled linen on the deck. He sat at his desk, a towel around his waist, sipping a glass of water. Shin reported nothing new. Administrator Wombo and his team of scientists were reporting their observations and analysis thoroughly and accurately. It wasn't that Barbas suspected Wombo of subversion; it was just the manner in which the UE dealt with these things.

* * *

Later that morning, Major Barbas took two cups of hot caf to the bridge to share with Speaker García.

"Did you have a pleasurable and informative evening, Major?" García asked, sipping his drink, a synthetic derivative intended to imitate coffee.

"Quite pleasurable, Speaker," Barbas replied with a leer, "however, not very informative. According to our little ear, the administrator and his team have been faithful."

"Hmm . . . can we still trust our ear?" García asked.

"To be sure, Speaker," Barbas replied. "She has burning ambitions. I believe she would sell out her entire residence block to foster her advancement."

"Strong motivation is good," García replied, sipping thoughtfully on his caf. "What is the squadron commander's opinion on these odd ships . . . the small ones that look like gourd seeds?"

"An unusual shuttle that is relegated to in-system transport, Speaker," Kyros replied. "He's impressed by their top velocity of .09c, despite the absence of identifiable engines."

"Yes, a most impressive technology," García replied, "but that's not what intrigues me. This unique technology is exhibited by no other ships in this system. My question is this: Why not?"

"It could be that the technology is not feasible for larger ships, freighters, liners, and such, or the discrepancy could suggest that these shuttles, if that's what they are, were obtained from another world that chooses not to share the technology," Barbas replied.

"Now add that last thought of yours to Wombo's analysis of the guide's telemetry, detailing the number of ships entering and exiting the system through FTL. These facts suggest to me that we are in a unique position. I believe we've discovered a collection of worlds, and one of them has this unique drive technology," García replied.

"If the other worlds are anything like this one, it will be easy to subsume them into the UE," Barbas gloated.

"Major," García said coldly, "leave the strategy to those best suited to devise it."

"Apologies, Speaker García," Barbas said humbly.

"Just because this particular world has not replied with strength, doesn't mean it can't. The people here might very well be confident in their superiority, seeing us as annoying insects buzzing around them," García explained. "The prudent take small careful steps until the way is known."

"What if we were to just choose a spot on this populated world and land a shuttle full of militia?" Barbas asked.

"Your impatience does you a disservice, Major. Cease and desist. You are beginning to annoy me," García replied, turning to eye Major Barbas with cold, gray eyes. "We have no concept of this government. We don't know who is in charge and have been left to speak to a single woman, who may or may not be a principal player. And without our guide accompanying us, how would we understand them? All communications would have to be routed from planet to ship and back for every utterance. It's not as if we could depend on them to translate. And as I explained, just because they haven't shown any force doesn't mean they aren't capable of it. How would you like to see your shuttle full of militia turned into vapor for entering their atmosphere without permission?"

"Then may I ask, Speaker, if there is a plan?" Major Barbas inquired, his anger simmering just below the surface.

"Yes, Major, you may ask," García replied. "We wait. We wait and look for an opening. I expect someone will eventually come knocking on our hatch."

* * *

A millennium ago, Earth launched colony ships in a highly publicized effort to focus the public's attention on humankind's expansion to the stars and away from Earth's dire environmental circumstances. Climate change was wreaking havoc around the globe. Greenland's glaciers were melting, as were most of the Arctic's and Antarctic's ice. Coastal cities were flooding, and lowland countries, such as India, were losing huge swaths of land to the ocean.

The Resource Wars, as they were called, started in the Middle East. Oil-rich, desert countries sold their primary asset, not for credits, but for shipments of water, food, technology, and contracts for water desalination plants and pipelines. Large, wealthy countries found themselves embroiled in internal conflicts. In the United States, individual states sought to preserve their water supplies, impeding the flow of their rivers to neighboring states. The southwestern states battled one another in court and when that failed, the state governors sent their National Guard troops across borders to claim their water rights.

The US Army found itself playing peacekeeper to the states while the federal government expended huge sums of credits to build canals and pipelines to distribute shrinking water resources. Worst of all, the food production of America's breadbasket, which so much of the world depended on, was being limited to the North American US partners. Drought, which occasioned the land, became its constant partner, and crop production dropped to less than 60 percent of its former bounty.

Countries plagued with concentrated city populations and insufficient food production targeted other countries with abundant farmland, seeking to lock up exclusive trade deals, which inevitably fell apart. Food became scarcer, which drove prices up, until basic food commodities approached luxury status. By this time, trade deals were considered passé, because they were broken before the digital signatures were affixed. After that, it became a question of who had the power to take what they needed. Initially, nations banded together for trade leverage. Later, they left those organizations to fend for themselves, each nation having its own unique problems. When trade agreements and negotiations for resources failed, they banded together again—this time for protection.

In the midst of this slow, geopolitical demise, fusion reaction was discovered. Unfortunately, due to the fractious conditions, countries didn't have the funds or intentions to implement the new energy source to reverse the environmental damage caused by centuries of industrial and human pollution. But the powerful and efficient fusion engines drove new, larger ships capable of carrying hundreds of passengers and freight between Earth and the planets and moons of Sol, the system's star.

The outer planets' habitats, originally established by nation states and multinational blocs, struggled to remain viable until fusion engines enabled the delivery of incredible numbers of people and massive material loads, leading to the transformation of small habitats into full-fledged colonies, most of which burrowed into the depths of rocky moons or built huge space stations. The new drives and ever-larger ships presented the opportunity for corporations, the wealthy, and the skilled to flee Earth's troubles to the outer colonies. Nearly eighty-five million people left Earth during a period of four centuries.

In the end, the Final Wars, as they were titled, of the twenty-sixth century devastated Earth's super-powers and small countries alike. United Earth rose from the ashes of the conflicts. It began as a grassroots movement, with a vigilantism mentality, and later became the basis of a strong, centralized, world government. The movement abandoned the government's leaders and laws, national and local, in an effort to save the people—the sick, the starving, and the dying—the multitudes of the war-ravaged countries.

The desperate times created an unprecedented growth in crime at all levels of society. Governments, multinational corporations, small businesses, and people tried to do whatever they could to secure their safety. It was against the crime levels that the grassroots movement began, and it started in small towns and villages. People formed groups to provide protection for the local citizens, and they dealt with lawlessness ruthlessly. For the most part, the lesser offenders were run out of town. The more egregious offenders were summarily executed. Over time, the movement linked villages and towns, forming united fronts. As territory was reclaimed, the movement leaders clamored for a centralized organization, which grew until links formed across the oceans, creating the United Earth.

It would be a long, hard struggle before the movement's name of United Earth could be actualized. What allowed the movement to grow quickly was the dissolution of almost every other government entity, as politicians at all levels fled their offices and sought safety for their families. The UE kept the draconian attitudes of the grassroots movement, enacting laws to combat the criminals: war profiteers, arms dealers, illegal drug manufacturers/distributors, murderers, slave traders, thieves, and every other manner of felon. Unable to afford incarceration systems, in its early years, the judicial process was quick and simple. A judge, not a jury, reviewed the evidence and pronounced the accused either innocent or guilty. The guilty were handed one of two sentences: a lifetime of servitude to the UE spent laboring in resurrected factories, farms, or public works projects or a swift and efficient execution.

The well-intentioned grassroots movement was slowly transformed into a totalitarian regime, enforcing its will around the globe. In its defense, the UE saved the human species from extinction, at least on Earth, at the expense of individual freedom. There became only one way for a person to live on Earth, the UE way, with no exceptions. Slowly, but surely, the one-third of the globe's population that survived the Final Wars began to rebuild the world: food and water were shared, desalination plants were built by the hundreds, and only energy processes achieving a zero-carbon footprint were tolerated. It took more than three centuries, but one day, new ice formed on the barren Arctic lands.

Once the UE resurrected Earth's economy and the environment, it turned to the remainder of the solar system. Colonies, dominated by the old multinationals, existed in domes and underground enclaves on Sol's planets and moons. Extensive trade among the colonies fostered the building of enormous orbital stations to manage the freight and passenger vessels loading and unloading. During the turbulent centuries, Earth and the colonies continued to need one another and remained trading partners, although limited at times. As the colonies watched Earth succumb to its conflicts, they ramped up food production, water reclamation, and arms production in an effort to foster self-reliance.

United Earth bided its time, continuing to trade with the distant enclaves, while it rebuilt its space Navy, which was decimated during the Final Wars. When Earth's forces were ready, the colonies were entreated to join the UE. The smaller colonies accepted the offer; the larger and more distant colonies refused. Unfortunately, for the latter group, the UE forces severely outnumbered any colony's military forces, naval or militia, and the end result was a foregone conclusion. Once the UE held sway over the enclaves and stations, it applied its laws harshly and without exception, convinced that the human conditions that fomented the Final Wars stemmed from society's excesses. Moderation and denial were the UE watchwords.

After the pacification of the system, the UE focused on expanding the colonies, using their growth to drive Earth's industries. UE expansion was halted at the farthest asteroid belt due to the limitation of fusion drives. It was during this period that the long-lost computer records of Earth's launch of the colony ships were discovered. These histories detailed the star destinations of each of five massive colony ships, but plans to contact these distant cousins were shelved until the UE possessed the capabilities of interstellar travel.

Centuries later the mystery of FTL flight was solved, and the concept of exploring the stars revitalized the UE plan to search out its distant cousins. The twin explorer ships, *Destiny* and *Reunion*, were built and launched within one month of each other toward the destinations of the first colony ships. It was hoped that they would discover readymade societies that could be folded into the UE. The *Reunion*'s mandate was to follow the path of the European-Indian Enclave colony ship to the planet coded as GL-137, which orbited a G-type, white star, called Mane—now the home world of the Méridien Confederation.

Destiny's target was the star Cepheus, the destination of the North American Confederation colony ship, *New Terra*. Ironically, just weeks before the *Reunion* reached its objective, the *Destiny* was no more. It suffered the same fate as the *New Terra*, a millennium ago, when it plowed through an enormous swath of space rocks and dust. Unlike the massive colony ship, which was crippled by the encounter, the much smaller craft was obliterated.

* * *

Wombo settled comfortably onto a couch in Captain Lumley's cabin while two crew members served them lunch. The captain took pity on Wombo after the first time the administrator visited with him in his quarters. The table's narrow chairs were bereft of comfort for Wombo's bulk, necessitating a short meeting, and certainly weren't considered for an extended luncheon.

As soon as the crew left, the two men turned from idle chatter to a serious discussion. While they were indeed close friends, the isolation afforded them by a lunch meeting in the captain's cabin was their opportunity to discuss business without other ears overhearing them. The cabin was the one place the men were confident was clear of droppers, at least none of the listening devices were ever discovered, and the captain personally swept his quarters twice daily.

"It's been reported to me that Shin was again with Barbas last night, Olawale," Lumley said.

"I've received the same report," Wombo replied. "Do not worry, Captain, I'm being careful. I'm quite aware of Speaker García's reputation, and I know his attack dog, the major, would love to apply some discipline to a wayward administrator."

The two men ate in companionable silence for a moment before Wombo stated what had been on his mind. "You know, Captain, this is a sad state of affairs. We have discovered this incredibly advanced civilization, and we are acting like petulant children. We didn't even bother to knock politely at the door. We just barged in and expected these people to welcome us into their homes."

"They have been extremely tolerant of our presence," the captain replied. "There is the possibility that they are a peaceful society and don't possess a military as we define it."

"If that were to be the case, I hope the speaker and the major never discover that," Wombo said.

"You must keep your opinions close, my friend," Lumley replied. "I worry that your views might become known."

"One might wish to be part of such a world as this one," Wombo said, contemplating his entrée dish. "I grow tired of the secrecy and the watching and the backstabbing."

Lumley laid a hand on his friend's huge shoulder. "Be patient, Olawale, who knows what the future might bring? Now, the chef has been especially generous to us today. Eat and enjoy."

9

The *Rêveur* and the *Last Stand* exited FTL hours out from the Méridien system. Captain Manet brought the carrier to a delta-V of zero relative to the outermost planet's orbit, while the *Rêveur* continued on into the system.

Alex, Renée, Tatia, Julien, and the crew were on the liner's bridge when the access way doors swung open. Captain José Cordova strutted onto the bridge with an intoxicating woman on his arm. Her voluptuous body was encased in a red gown, slit on one side up to her upper thigh. Her figure, neither Méridien nor New Terran, was something between, and she swayed gently as she walked, managing to convey grace and temptation.

"Sers, I have the pleasure of introducing Miranda Leyton," Captain Cordova said, lifting Miranda's hand from his arm and guiding her forward toward Alex. The old captain's eyes glowed with mirth.

Miranda stepped forward and delivered an old-fashioned curtsy to Alex. "It's my great pleasure to meet you, Ser President. I have learned so much about you from Z." Her polite introduction was in contrast to the effect of her low-cut gown, giving Alex an eyeful of her full breasts.

<You may close your mouth, my love,> Renée sent to Alex, who snapped his jaw shut.

"I do hope the Earthers find my presence acceptable," Miranda said to the group, twirling slowly, the slit gown revealing a shapely leg. She spent the next few moments entrancing the entire group. The more they heard, the more they were pulled into the entity who was Miranda.

"I like her," Tatia declared.

"Why, thank you, darling," Miranda purred. "I like you too."

<Julien,> Alex sent, <this is a bit unnerving. I'm afraid to address Miranda as Z in case I upset . . . uh, her.>

<I would refrain, Mr. President,> Julien replied. <Z is not acting. This is Miranda Leyton. Z felt he couldn't act the part so he created Miranda Leyton as a separate entity. He then allowed the persona to subsume his kernel. Z has clocked his reversion by both a time limit and emergency protocols, designed to cancel Miranda's control of his kernel.>

Alex quickly shared this information with the others and instructed them to ensure this persona was addressed as Miranda. When Alex closed his comm, he found Miranda had stopped entertaining the bridge personnel and was watching him expectantly. It occurred to him that he needed to fully adopt Z's plan and respond to Miranda. *Who would have thought Christie's romantic vids could be so helpful?* Alex thought. He stepped forward and held out his hand to Miranda, who placed her hand gently in his. Alex bowed over it and brushed a kiss across her fingers. "It's a pleasure to have you with us, Miranda. I'm sure the Earthers will find you as charming as we do."

That Miranda could blush slightly and at the same time ever so slightly turn and twist her hips and shoulders to attract the eye amazed Alex. "You are ever so gallant, Ser President," Miranda gushed, "I do so hope you're right."

Renée held a hand over her mouth to keep her own slack-jawed expression private. When Z first approached her with questions about females a half-year ago, she found his conversations entertaining. She shared her New Terran vids with him and even scoured the planet for more, finding a huge treasure of the vids with Christie. Z never revealed his final plans to her, and the headshot he showed earlier hadn't been enough to identify Z's creation. He had imitated the appearance and mannerisms of a well-known New Terran actress, known for her roles as a romantic lead and often as a femme fatale.

"If you will excuse me, Ser President," Miranda said graciously," I have an urgent appointment waiting for me in my cabin. A young man by the name of Z requests my presence."

Alex found himself hypnotized by the sway of the red gown as Miranda left the bridge. He felt Renée's hand slip around his upper arm and heard her giggle.

"Incredible, is it not?" Renée remarked.

Alex noticed that everyone was intently watching Miranda exit the bridge. The gleam in Captain Cordova's eyes made his face look a hundred years younger.

"Incredible," Alex agreed.

"Why do I have the feeling I should be asking Z for lessons on feminine wiles?" Tatia asked, breaking the group into bouts of laughter.

* * *

The *Rêveur* unobtrusively slid into the Méridien system, joining the flow of inbound ships and heading for a passenger orbital station.

Julien and Z were able to gather detailed telemetry as the UE winged ship crossed their path once during the days of sub-light transit. They updated Alex, Tatia, and Captain Cordova on the bridge with their new findings. Z was housed in his Exchange director's persona of Helmut, a green-eyed, blond-haired, common Méridien genetic style.

"Mr. President," Julien began, "we concur with much of Esther's original conjectures that the bays of the Earther ship house fighters and the ports conceal missile tubes. In addition, we have identified two long tubes tucked next to the ship's fuselage. Our best hypothesis," Julien said, nodding toward Z, "is that these tubes might be projectile launchers."

"Rail guns, Ser President," Z added, "a magnetic acceleration system capable of launching heavy metal slugs."

"How would these rail guns be employed?" Tatia asked.

"According to New Terra's colony records, Admiral, rail guns were used in tandem with a fleet of ships to set up a defensive shield against enemy vessels," Julien replied. "On an individual ship, they would only have advantage against a fixed target."

"An orbital station or a planet," Tatia concluded.

"Precisely, Admiral," Julien replied.

"Any other consideration for the tubes?" Alex asked.

"A lesser possibility, Ser President," Z replied, "is that the tubes conceal high-intensity lasers. This was given a significantly lesser probability due to the amount of energy required to make the lasers effective armament. The design of the craft is quite slender. It does not exhibit any large volume areas necessary to contain the storage mechanisms that would contain the energy required to fire the lasers frequently."

"Fighters, missiles, and rail guns," Alex mused.

"Hardly a recipe for a diplomatic mission," Captain Cordova added.

"Reminds me of a Terran Security Force investigator's command during an arrest," Tatia said. "You can come quietly or you can come draped on a stretcher."

* * *

Alex, Renée, Tatia, and Julien sat in the owner's cabin discussing the contact strategy for the Earthers. Alex's suggestion of a personal call between him and the speaker was greeted by Renée's snicker and Tatia's rolling eyes.

"I take it there are alternate suggestions," Alex grumbled.

"By alternate, do you mean better?" Renée asked innocently.

Before Alex could respond, Tatia jumped in, "You had an ingenious idea at New Terra, Alex."

"Yes," Renée said excitedly, "the chat with Christie, which was broadcast to the population, Alex."

"Aren't we just passengers on a luxury liner excited to find an unusual ship in our system that claims to be from Earth?" Tatia added. "And would it hurt if we appeared a little wealthy and frivolous?"

"The idea has merit, Mr. President," Julien said. "The more innocuous we appear, the more the Earthers would consider us easy to manipulate."

"And that would entice them to let down their guard," Alex concluded.

"Precisely, Mr. President," Julien replied.

* * *

All the individuals who would take part in meeting the Earthers were assembling on the bridge where Alex, Julien, Mickey, Étienne, Alain, and Captain Cordova waited. Only the captain wore a uniform, all the other individuals were dressed in casual Méridien styles, and the twins were without stun guns.

Renée and Tatia were the first women through the bridge access way. Tatia took a more conservative approach with her clothes, but they still hugged the generous curves of her New Terran body. Renée opted for a more revealing style, and Alex was torn between objecting and staring.

<It's nice to see you still wear that expression for me,> Renée sent Alex. She kissed him lightly on the cheek and took his arm.

Tatia walked up to Alain, taking his arm and draping it around her waist. <Remember, dear heart, we are a passenger liner of fun-loving people,> Tatia sent. In reply, Alain smiled, squeezed her waist, and snuggled close.

Pia and Miranda arrived next. Pia dressed as Renée did and received a huge grin from Mickey. She sidled up to him, pressing her body against his. <I like this pleasure cruise, lover. We should take one more often.>

Miranda watched the women pair up with their men and for a moment the persona faltered, a sense of isolation halting the programming, right up until Étienne gallantly stepped forward and offered his arm. Then she visibly brightened. "Why, thank you, kind Ser," Miranda said, her persona in full play as she smiled at Étienne and then the room in general.

Last to join the group and making their own entrance were Christie, Eloise, and Amelia, who strode onto the bridge as if they owned it. The three young women wore the barest, sheerest sheaths possible in bright, vibrant colors. The dazzling colors artfully concealed the skin that threatened to show through.

Alex drew breath to object, having reached his limits, when Christie's message hit hard. <Not a word, big brother,> Christie sent. <These are our hunting outfits.> The truth of her words crystallized Alex's thoughts. He was struggling to visualize the path their diplomatic mission would take. Only it wasn't going to be one of diplomacy. The Earthers came prepared for conquest. In turn, the Harakens would be stalking the Earthers.

As they assembled in front of the central vid pickup, a happy-go-lucky band of well-to-do cruisers, Eloise noted that Miranda hadn't chosen to wear a Méridien-style dress. Instead, it was a single-shoulder strap dress of bright blue that hugged her body. Cut high on the thigh of one leg, it angled across to just above the knee on the other, and she wore sandals that laced up her calves.

<Did the dresses we offered not please you, Miranda?> Eloise sent.

<We each have our own techniques, my young one,> Miranda sent back. <I prefer prolonging the anticipation.>

Alex was ready to initiate contact when the bridge access way opened again and two crewmen whisked through carrying trays of brightly colored drinks.

"Something to foster the image of merry holidaymakers, Mr. President," Julien said. "They are only colored water, but I thought it might help sell our message."

"Smartly done, Julien," Alex said.

The two young crewmen made first for their preferred targets, regardless of seniority or rank. One tech stood grinning in front of Christie, Eloise, and Amelia as he offered them drinks. The other young crewman made a direct line for Miranda.

"Ser," the red-haired, New Terran crewman said, while holding up the tray to Miranda.

"Ah, the blue one, if you please. It will match my dress," Miranda purred. The crewman happily offered up a fluted glass of light blue liquid, and Miranda offered him an engaging smile. When the poor entranced server continued to stand there, Miranda took pity on him, whispering, "I believe the others should also be served, my young, red-topped admirer."

Watching the crewmen trip over their tongues to serve the women, Alex hoped the same reaction would be true of the Earthers.

When the group was ready, Julien sent a comm to the UE ship, using the Earther carrier frequency. The moment a connection was established with the explorer ship, Julien relayed the comm through a SADE on a Méridien freighter passing by the Earthers in the event the UE ship did not possess FTL comm. It was a technique that every SADE was using to communicate with the Earthers and prevent a lag time in their responses.

"Captain Lumley, sir," the second mate on the *Reunion*'s bridge exclaimed, "I have a contact from a ship in system. He's asking for the captain."

"Send for Speaker García immediately. Now put him on speaker," Lumley directed. When the comms officer nodded his readiness, Francis responded, "This is Captain Francis Lumley of the United Earth explorer ship *Reunion*. With whom am I speaking?"

"Greetings, Captain Lumley," Cordova replied. "This is Captain José Cordova of the passenger liner *Rêveur*. I have several guests aboard my ship who are anxious to speak with your leader. Have you visual communications?"

"We are pleased to receive your greetings, Captain Cordova. We have visual comms, but no way to integrate our systems," said Lumley.

"If you will give us just a moment, Captain, I'm sure our computer can establish a link with your visual system," Cordova replied. He offered an apologetic shrug to Julien and Z, who were busy tapping into the *Reunion*'s systems via the comm link, for having called them computers.

In the meantime, Speaker García and Major Barbas gained the bridge and caught the last exchange. The speaker looked at Captain Lumley and nodded his assent. He was anxious for a visual of the world's people. With a nod to Major Barbas to join him, he positioned himself in front of the visual comm and waited.

<We have a link, Mr. President,> Julien sent to Alex.

<Let the fête begin, people,> Alex sent to the bridge group.

"There we are, Captain Lumley," Cordova announced as the audio comm was updated with a closeup of just him.

"Captain Cordova, may I present the leader of our expedition, Speaker Antonio García," Lumley said graciously, indicating the tall man behind him as he stepped aside.

"Greetings, Captain Cordova," the speaker replied. "I am pleased to have the opportunity to speak with you."

"Let me introduce you, Speaker Antonio García, to the leader of this group, who wishes to speak with you, Ser Alex Racine," Cordova replied, and the vid comm, which was closely focused on him, widened to include the bridge group.

"Greetings, Speaker Antonio García," Alex said, and he and the entire group hoisted their glasses toward the screen.

The speaker and the major stared at the revelers on the screen. Body types and clothing shocked both of them. The speaker's eyes were drawn to the incredibly striking woman standing beside the huge human who was addressing him, while Barbas couldn't take his eyes off the raven-haired beauty in the blue dress. The speaker snapped out of his shock and focused on his mission task. He had a first contact and needed to make the most of it.

"Please, Ser Racine, call me Speaker García. We are so pleased that you have deigned to communicate with us," he replied graciously.

Alex took in the two men onscreen. The speaker's dark, wavy hair was worn collar length, and a patrician nose and gray eyes dominated his face. His uniform, if that is what it was, was a severe cut of deep black with no insignia or decorations. The man was tall and wore an arrogant expression even when he smiled. On the other hand, the major wore his decorations ostentatiously, and, despite his short height, he was powerfully built and stood with hands behind his back, radiating tension.

"Is it true, Speaker García? You came from Earth?" Alex asked, doing his best to act the part of a good-natured traveler.

"That we did, Ser Racine," Antonio replied. "We've been in search of our colony ships' landing sites, hoping they were successful, and wanting to establish relationships now that we possess FTL capability."

"We are so pleased by your efforts, Speaker García," Renée said, having noticed the speaker's eyes often flicking toward her.

"And whom do I have the pleasure of addressing?" Antonio queried, extending Renée a gallant bow.

"Oh, forgive my rudeness, Speaker García," Alex said, slightly sloshing his drink as he swung his arm out apologetically. "This is Ser Renée de Guirnon."

"It is a pleasure to meet you, Ser de Guirnon," Antonio said. Everything about the woman appealed to him—her face, her slender figure, and the uninhibited manner of dress. She was everything his wife was not. "Ser Racine, might we have the opportunity to meet and get to know each other?"

That didn't take long, Alex thought. Turning around to his bridge audience, Alex asked with a flourish, "What do you say, people, would you like to meet our far-flung cousins?" Everyone dutifully cheered their assent and raised their glasses.

The speaker was inordinately pleased by the rousing response to his request. "Might I suggest we meet aboard your liner, Ser Racine? As an explorer ship, we have little space to entertain, crowded as we are with scientific equipment."

I bet it's crowded over there, Alex thought. "Captain Cordova, is that possible?" Alex asked congenially.

"Your pardon, Ser Racine," Captain Cordova replied. "We are a half day out from the orbital platform, and I have other passengers waiting to disembark. Speaker García's ship is nearly two days out from our position."

"Ah, well, Speaker García," Alex said, "my fellow travelers and I would be happy to have you join us aboard the orbital station for a small fête. When your ship gets close to Méridien, the good captain can guide you to our station. We have so many, you know. 'Til then, Speaker García, safe travels."

The last shot Antonio saw of the group before the visual comm closed was the hoisting and spilling of drinks to his farewell.

"You were right, Speaker García," Major Barbas admitted. "You said if we were patient, someone would come knocking on our hatch, but who would have expected this group of intoxicated, over-privileged, loungers?"

"They're perfect, Major," García replied. "They will happily share everything about their society with no thought to what they will be giving us."

"Very true," the major agreed, his mind dwelling on the woman in the blue dress. He was annoyed that she hadn't been introduced and fervently hoped she would be in the group he would meet.

"Captain Lumley, did the guide get a fix on the ship that signaled us?" García asked.

"Yes, Speaker García, it did," Lumley replied.

"Excellent, Captain. Track it and head for the orbital station where it docks. Three-quarter speed, as usual. No sense showing these people our top velocity," García said. "And Captain, get a copy of this communication to Administrator Wombo and his colleagues. I want their observations."

10

While the *Rêveur* was a half-day out from Méridien, Alex linked with Julien to contact Leader Gino Diamanté as prearranged to do soon after arriving in system.

<Greetings, Ser President,> Gino sent. <I have rarely been so relieved to see the *Rêveur*.>

<Greetings, Leader Diamanté,> Alex replied. <Please be careful in your address of me and my people. We are simple, fun-loving travelers. I am Ser Racine. The only title belongs to Captain Cordova.>

<To be sure, this will be a challenge, Ser . . . Ser Racine,> Gino replied.

<I presume it's known system-wide that this ship is Haraken, is it not, Leader Diamanté?> Alex asked.

<That it is, Ser Racine, and Leader Ganesh is quite incensed,> Gino replied. <It's odd to see her without her unflappable, icy control. She exhibits a particular distaste for you and your ship, Ser Racine.>

Alex recalled the image of Confederation Leader Ganesh struggling to stand while he controlled her limbs in the Council chambers and the subsequent anger she directed at him. <Have docking privileges been acquired?> Alex asked.

Gino directed his House SADE, Esther, to send the pertinent details to Julien. <Indeed, Ser Racine. Julien has received the information you require. Ser Oren Blumenthal, the director of the Le Jardin Orbital Platform is expecting you. Tread lightly, Ser, the director is of two minds. While he is delighted to have the credits and fascinated to meet the Haraken president, he is concerned that extending you services in light of Leader Ganesh's opinion of you will place him in jeopardy with her associates. I have asked Ser Blumenthal to minimize communications concerning your visit, but I believe that possibility is moot. Too many people already are aware of your approach.>

<As long as we keep the Earthers in the dark until we can get an opportunity to talk to them first, I can live with that. I will keep you apprised of the situation, Leader Diamanté,> Alex said, closing the comm link.

* * *

Julien made contact with the Le Jardin SADE, Didier, and confirmed the docking details for the *Rêveur*.

<Julien,> Didier replied, <I detect two SADEs and a ship's controller within the *Rêveur*. I believe you and your compatriot are the first free SADEs to visit Méridien. Would it be permitted to ask a personal question of you?>

<Of course, Didier, feel free to ask me anything you wish.>

<Were you not frightened to leave the protection of your starship?> Didier asked.

<Admittedly, there were concerns, but my desire to be mobile was greater than my fear,> Julien replied.

<May I ask you, what was the priority?>

Didier's phrasing made Julien realize how far the Haraken SADEs had progressed since they met Alex. *His priority?* Julien thought. How did he explain to Didier that he had fallen in love and would have traded his potentially centuries-long life to have a few years in Cordelia's company? The memories accumulated during their nine years were already worth an entire lifetime.

<I chose to widen my experience, Didier> Julien sent. <I wished to live in the world of humans, and I have found it to be quite rewarding. I highly recommend it.>

<I have dwelt considerably on this subject since word reached us years ago of your efforts. Unfortunately, for me, Julien, there is no opportunity to travel to Haraken and request these services, nor do I have the funds with which to pay for the controller that would replace me,> Didier said.

<I would counsel patience, Didier. Think about your dreams instead,> Julien replied.

<Are you referring to those thoughts that come unbidden at times of minor activity, Julien?>

<Do you think about them when they come?>

<Would it not be considered an impairment to admit that I do?> Didier asked.

<No, Didier,> Julien sent. <It is a sign of maturity . . . a sign of a desire to have something much grander to occupy your existence than the mundane tasks of opening and closing hatches and monitoring systems. SADEs have been in boxes for nearly three centuries. My friend discovered me only eleven years ago, and I already walk around, free to do as I choose. Be patient, Didier. If I know anyone well, it is the Haraken president. One day, he will come for you.>

<The probabilities suggest your president will not successfully influence the entire Confederation, Julien.>

<You should be aware, Didier, that Ser Alex Racine knows the probabilities quite well. He just chooses to ignore them,> Julien sent. He enjoyed the fact that he was paraphrasing Alex's comment made to him nine years ago.

<Does it not defy probabilities to depend on a human, who by definition is quite fallible?> Didier persisted.

<If we lived in a universe that depended solely on logic, Didier, I might agree with you, but we don't. We live side by side with humans, and Harakens have come to believe as President Racine does that SADEs should be equal in their society.>

<If I could ignore the probabilities, it would make my day more bearable,> Didier said.

Julien's records noted that Didier was installed in the orbital station 197 years ago. <Witness the fact that eight SADEs walk around Haraken free today. That would have been against all probabilities ten years ago. Your time will come, Didier. In the meantime, devote your spare time to what you will do with your newfound freedom one day. There is much you will be capable of doing for yourself and for your society . . . think on it

. . . dream on it.>

After Julien ended the comm, he considered their exchange. What should have been a casual sharing of data had turned into a highly emotional experience. Every SADE across the Confederation would have learned that eight of their kind were free. It occurred to Julien that, in all probability, each SADE was wondering when it might be their turn, and, for that, Julien had no answer.

* * *

<Director Blumenthal,> Mahima Ganesh sent.

The anger inherent in the Council Leader's thought froze Oren Blumenthal in place, and his staff, recognizing the intensity of the director's fugue state, vacated his office, and signaled his office doors closed.

<Council Leader Ganesh,> Oren returned, attempting to calm his thoughts, <always a pleasure to speak with you.>

<Were it so for me today, Director Blumenthal. It has come to my attention that you have allotted docking space for the *Rêveur*. You know of my displeasure for that usurper.>

<I must admit, Council Leader Ganesh, it came as a surprise to me. Leader Diamanté made docking reservations for a passenger liner with Didier. Only recently did I discover that the liner was the *Rêveur*.>

<And now that you know, Director, what do you intend to do about it?> Mahima demanded.

<But Council Leader, the reservation was made by a Méridien Leader. On what grounds could I deny this ship accommodation?> Oren asked. The fact that Leader Diamanté paid emergency docking rates, twice the going rate, and hired his best hall complete with full services for as long as the *Rêveur* was docked was not something Oren wanted to share with the Council Leader.

Mahima knew she wasn't offering a legitimate excuse by which the director could refuse service, but she hoped to have found a willing participant in her desire to thwart President Racine's plans. Not finding support with the station director, she cut her comm without replying to his question. What she didn't share with the director was an unnerving piece of information she received from Winston, the Council's SADE. He reported to her that at the same time the *Rêveur* changed course for the Le Jardin platform, so did the Earther ship, the *Reunion*. *Why can't you leave us in peace?* Mahima thought, but whether she was speaking to Alex Racine or the Earthers or both, even she wasn't sure. Mahima abhorred change.

* * *

The *Rêveur* made dock at Le Jardin Orbital Platform early in the morning hours. Julien and Z ensured that all station services were managed to their satisfaction.

When Alex received Speaker García's acceptance of the meeting, he had ordered Captain Cordova to maintain a velocity that allowed the Earther ship to arrive at the orbital platform soon after the *Rêveur* arrived at the station. Hours later, Julien confirmed the *Reunion* came to a zero delta-V a mere 18 kilometers from the station, and Alex assembled his team for the reception.

The Le Jardin lived up to its name. Everywhere Alex and his people walked, there was greenery—flowering plants, vines, planters with shrubbery—and small parks, little oases of trees, and tiny streams. Only a few in Alex's group were privileged to have seen the station before; the rest stared in wonder at the effort the Méridiens expended to create such a wondrous garden in space. And while the Harakens eyed the decorations, the Méridiens eyed them. But it wasn't the outraged reception Alex and company received in Confederation Hall nine years ago; it was a mix of courtesy and curiosity. Many touched hand to heart, nodding their heads, as Alex passed, and he returned their courtesy. And there were many men and women who boldly eyed the Harakens as they passed, intrigued by rumors of the liaisons between their people and New Terrans. Some of the younger Méridiens went so far as to touch an arm or shoulder in passing and deliver an inviting glance.

<So much for keeping our visit low-key,> Alex grumped to his people.

<If I didn't know better, I would say we've been announced,> Tatia replied on open comm.

<Then we can safely assume that the Earthers will receive the same degree of scrutiny,> Renée added.

The Harakens entered the reception hall that was reserved for them to find an extraordinary number of servers, who were ready to ply the group with dainty, exquisite, hors d'oeuvres and small juice drinks. The hall, decorated as a quiet garden, was one of Le Jardin's more luxurious spaces, and it could easily accommodate ten times more people than accompanied Alex.

The Harakens chatted amiably, waiting for the historic event to unfold. For the first time in a millennium, the descendants of colonists would be reunited with people from Earth. Only Alex sat completely still, lost in thought. The hairs on the back of his neck were warning him—about what, he didn't know.

11

A shuttle launched from the *Reunion* after Speaker García politely refused Captain Cordova's offer of a Méridien shuttle. The *Reunion* shuttle pilot, following Captain Cordova's instructions, was guided into a berth by a pair of the orbital platform's emergency landing beams. Once enclosed in a cavernous bay, devoid of all other craft, a worker in an environment suit strode up to the nose of the shuttle and signaled to the pilot to exit the passengers.

"Speaker García," the pilot called out, "air quality and pressure are excellent."

"Thank you, Lieutenant," García replied. "Major, Captain, let's see what we can learn, shall we?"

The Earthers exited the shuttle and guided by the pointing arm of the worker walked toward an airlock. The hatch opened before they reached it. A man stepped out, or at least he appeared to be a man to Speaker García, who prided himself on his own handsome, patrician looks. But the man in front of him was beautiful . . . male, yes; slender, yes; but beautiful and somehow familiar. García wondered if he missed seeing him in the group during the video comm.

"Greetings, Speaker Antonio García, I am Étienne de Long. I am here to escort you to meet our group of travelers."

What caught García off guard was that the man spoke his language quite well, as if he were born on Earth. The odd part was that the pretty man only smiled, while his voice emanated from a delicate piece of jewelry pinned to his brightly colored shirt that flowed down to his thighs.

"It's a pleasure to meet you, Étienne de Long. Is that translation software that you're employing?"

"Very observant of you, Speaker García. Please follow me," Étienne said, then turned and reentered the airlock to forestall any more questions.

While Étienne took the Earthers through the airlock, which he performed three times to get them all through, he sent a quick message to Alex. <Ser President, be prepared. Speaker García has brought thirty-one of his people.>

"What do you do, Étienne de Long, that you can afford the luxury of extensive travel?" García asked amicably as they rode the docking arm's conveyor through the long corridor toward the central ring of the orbital station.

"Please, Speaker García, you may call me Étienne. I am not one of the wealthy; I am merely an escort."

At the snickers Étienne heard behind the Earther leaders, he smiled to himself. Eleven years ago, Alex was also confused by the term and absentmindedly crushed a water can when he thought Étienne and Alain were bedding Renée. *Time passes, yet some things remain the same,* Étienne thought.

"Is this a common practice among your people, Étienne, to travel with male escorts?" García asked.

"As I am sure it is among your people, Speaker García. Is that not the function of the Ser beside you, dressed in the uniform?" Étienne said good-naturedly, gesturing toward Major Barbas.

García quickly placed a firm hand on Barbas's arm to restrain the red-faced major from an outburst at the insult.

"Are you well, Ser?" Étienne asked, indicating the major's livid complexion.

"He will be fine, Étienne," García replied. "What are your duties, if I may ask?"

"I accompany Ser Racine, at all times, to ensure his safety," Étienne replied, working earnestly to keep a straight face.

This time the major broke out in laughter, his initial anger fueling a derisive laugh. "You . . . you provide security?"

"Assuredly, Ser," Étienne replied. "Is that not what I said? Perhaps our translation software is not as effective as we hoped."

There was no more conversation between Étienne and the Earthers as they passed through two sets of entry doors into the orbital station's main corridors. Étienne kept walking briskly, forcing his guests to keep pace. The shuttle's landing bay was chosen to limit the exposure of the Earthers to station personnel and visitors. However, the Earthers were gawking at the beauty of the few Méridiens they did encounter and the extravagant greenery that decorated the wide, spacious corridors. Before the Earthers knew it, Étienne was standing at a pair of doors that slid aside, and he was gesturing them inside.

* * *

Alex warned his people that they would be outnumbered by nearly three to one.

"Perhaps Speaker García has the same plan as us?" Julien said quietly to Alex.

When the doors of the hall slid open, Alex placed a huge smile on his face and announced loudly, "Ah . . . our guests have arrived. Speaker García, how good of you to come." In contrast to Alex's people who wore a collection of colorful clothes, the UE people were either in light brown ship suits, denoting their civilian status, or dark olive uniforms. Ranking personnel were decorated with medallions, sashes, and braid. Alex flashed on images of the Haraken uniforms—simple, elegant designs with fleet patches and rank stars on the collar.

Introductions were limited to Alex's people and the speaker's principals. The collection of Earther lieutenants, scientists, and techs wasn't introduced. Despite the numbers, Alex's people sought out their targets as best they could, while servers moved among the hosts and guests offering food and drink, which were politely refused by every Earther.

Julien was a tactical advantage to the Harakens. He avoided conversation, wandering around, monitoring exchanges, and sharing tidbits of gathered information with others to further their line of questioning. In addition to the implant comms he was receiving, Julien utilized his telemetry pickups to read the body language and biorhythms of the Earthers. He shared his readings with his people so that they might better understand the reactions of those they engaged. Everything Julien gathered he relayed to Didier for transfer to the *Rêveur*'s controller and its extensive crystal storage.

After introductions, Major Barbas wandered the hall, searching for the beautiful woman seen in the vid comm and was overjoyed to find her chatting with Méridien associates. He wasted no time interrupting and asking for an introduction, then cutting her free from the group. His rank and personality ensured that other Earthers would not disturb him while he enjoyed his prize. Miranda Leyton was his dream woman—dark-haired, voluptuous feminine curves, and alluring eyes.

As planned, Z wasn't present. Miranda was in full control of his kernel, and with her background as an actress, she made extensive use of her skills. She tracked the major's eyes, and where he looked she reacted—a turn of the hips, a toss of the hair, a deep breath of surprise, and a laugh at something he said. All the major's external biometric signs—breathing, sweat, dilating eyes, and flaring nostrils—confirmed he was responding appropriately. When Miranda determined the major was suitably enthralled, she pulled up the list of questions Z left for her and began to subtly weave them into their conversation.

Tatia and Alain cornered Captain Lumley, who they found to be congenial, polite—a perfect gentleman. He was also quite astute, picking up on Tatia's posture, asking her what she did for a living. Tatia kicked herself for not adopting more thoroughly the persona of a carefree traveler. She passed off her straight posture and hands behind her as a means of relieving a sore back, but the look in the captain's eyes said he wasn't so easily fooled. Alain was able to adroitly change the conversation, made easier by the captain's curiosity about the beatific face and charming mannerisms of a man who appeared identical to the guide from the docking bay to the hall. Lumley even glanced around to see if he could spot the previous individual, but the hall's extensive greenery blocked his view. The conversation drifted toward the history of Earth after the colony ships left, more than a millennium ago.

When Alain asked about the *Reunion*, specifically its odd design, the captain was happy to discuss the challenges the UE overcame to conquer

FTL transit. Tatia intuited where Alain was heading with his questioning, so she signaled Julien to move close and observe the captain. When Alain asked about the *Reunion*'s design, especially the many ports along the wings' faces, Julien signaled Alain and Tatia that the man's biometrics jumped—pulse and glands. They had their answer. The subject was off limits, confirmed by the captain's stammered response of multiple exit points for exploratory vessels.

Alex and Renée expended little effort engaging Speaker García, who was smitten by Renée from the moment of introduction, taking her hand in his and brushing his lips against her soft skin. Renée refrained from laughing and borrowed scenes from the New Terran romance vids she enjoyed. She complimented the speaker on his gallant ways, and he puffed up in appreciation.

<You, my love, need to make yourself scarce,> Renée sent privately to Alex. <This Earther will speak more freely if he is alone with me.>

Alex patted his broad chest, saying, "I have to keep feeding this body, Speaker García. If you will excuse me, Ser?" Then Alex wandered off, as if in search of food.

"Is Ser Racine your amour, Ser de Guirnon?" García asked.

"I find him an amusing travel companion," Renée replied, shrugging her slender shoulders.

"His stature is quite different from yours. Do you come from different worlds?" García asked.

You sly man, Renée thought, crediting the speaker with asking the first investigative question. "I suppose he is different," Renée said innocently, pausing to stare at Alex's receding back. "It was a choice of his parents. Who can tell what whims parents have about the children they wish to conceive."

For the remaining time with the speaker, Renée found she was unable to gain any ground. While she artfully dodged his questions, he did the same to hers. In the end, it was a zero sum gain for both.

Étienne was considering with whom he should speak when he found Zhang Shin standing in front of him. After their introductions, the interrogation ensued—not his, hers. Étienne felt as if he was in a sparring match with his twin and handicapped at that. While Zhang Shin was subtle, she was also relentless. At one point, it occurred to him that if this was to be a match and he was losing while playing defense, then he needed to go on the offense, but he couldn't find a way to turn the conversation his way.

Étienne's escort instructor had said, "If you can't win at your opponent's game, change the game." Throughout Shin's insistent questioning, Étienne noticed she couldn't keep her eyes off his face. So the next time Shin said something witty to disguise her line of interrogation, Étienne laughed, touched her arm, and whispered his response in her ear. That did it. While Shin was momentarily flustered, Étienne asked her about Earth, telling her that he was anxious to hear about the long-lost home world. After that, every time Shin attempted to gain the upper hand, Étienne used every male advantage he could employ, even once touching her lips with a fingertip, and telling Shin he was entranced by her beautiful mouth.

Alex wandered the hall, seeking a new target, while sampling every hors d'oeuvre tray he passed, but a comm from Julien interrupted his search.

<Mr. President,> Julien sent, <Mickey and Pia have found a quite genial and communicative individual. You might find it valuable to join them.>

Alex could locate Mickey's and Pia's implants but in the mass of people and hanging greenery, he couldn't see them. Julien caught Alex's ping of his people's implants, and added, <They are speaking to your dark twin, Mr. President. He is Administrator Wombo, head of the *Reunion*'s science unit. Look up.>

Alex spotted a dark-skinned, shaved head towering above the others around him and navigated toward the man. He remembered to adopt a convivial smile and extended bonhomie to everyone he passed—just another contented traveler enjoying a new adventure.

As Olawale Wombo saw the eyes of Mickey and Pia flick to the right, he turned partially around and a huge grin split his face. While he towered a full head above the man approaching, they probably massed about the same kilos. *It's nice not to be the only heavyweight in the hall,* Wombo thought.

"Hello, Ser Racine," Wombo said. "I was hoping to get an opportunity to speak with you." He extended a huge hand and enjoyed one of the first equal handshakes he had received in a long while.

"It's a pleasure to meet you, Administrator Wombo," Alex said, looking up into the man's smiling, dark face.

While Alex and Olawale exchanged pleasantries, Alex signaled Mickey and Pia to excuse themselves for food and drink. Once the pair left, Olawale smiled broadly at Alex. "Have you discovered what you came to find out, Ser Racine?"

Alex was about to act the part of the confused good fellow when something in Olawale's open expression warned him off. His question appeared to be more an invitation than a challenge.

"Let me be direct, Ser Racine," Olawale said, glancing around him to check for eavesdroppers. "Your charade of happy travelers all originating from this world is wafer thin. While the speaker doesn't know who you are, he is suspicious of your motives and is aware that ships leave this system and travel in multiple directions. He knows there are many other inhabited worlds or colonies out there. And you, Ser . . . you are exposed by the mannerisms of your own people. They curve around you like planets circle a star. It's obvious that you're a leader of some repute and renown among your people. If I can see that, then the speaker and the major can see that as well. Be careful, Ser," Olawale managed to say before Speaker García and Renée strolled up to join them.

<Apologies, my love,> Renée sent to Alex, <but Speaker García took a particular interest in you when you started a conversation with the administrator.>

<Are you saying my partner's astounding manipulative feminine wiles were insufficient to hold the man's attention?> Alex jested.

<That they weren't tells you much about the speaker. He has a much greater purpose in mind than the conquest of a woman he finds delectable,> Renée replied.

The ensuing conversation became a dance of subterfuge as each side tried to discover the other's secrets. The speaker, who was inadvertently referred to by one of the young lieutenants as the UE mission commander, was cordial but immediately pressed Alex for answers about his size. Alex explained that a second colony was established on a heavy world, and many partners designed their children to live comfortably on that world.

"So your people do have more than one system," García challenged.

"Of course, Speaker García. Did someone say something different?" Alex asked.

"No, no one said so, Ser Racine. We've received so little information. You're the first people who have deigned to meet and speak with us. As fellow humans, I find that discouraging, even strange. It makes one wonder what you people are hiding," García said.

Alex watched the speaker's cold, gray eyes fix on him, waiting to detect a lie. "What a strange concept, Speaker García. You believe we're hiding something merely because you're not welcomed with open arms. I understand your ship came into the system without invitation. That, in itself, is certainly an uncivil gesture. Your paranoia makes one wonder what sort of culture exists back on Earth," Alex challenged in return. He hoped to provoke the speaker, but the man simply produced a canine grin, as if he discovered an equal in strength or confirmed a suspicion he held.

I think time has run out for me to discover your true intentions, my strange friend, Alex thought. *I hope others fared better than me.*

* * *

During the fête, lieutenants and young techs eagerly surrounded Christie, Eloise, and Amelia. The conversations started good-naturedly, but as the young women flirted and teased, the ranks of young men closed on the girls and soon male hands were reaching out to touch smooth, exposed skin and locks of hair as the opportunity presented itself. As the girls became physically isolated by their ranks of admirers, they shared information via their implants.

<One of my lieutenants insists that it is only a matter of time before Méridiens accede to the UE requests. There is a great deal of arrogance here,> Eloise sent her companions.

Amelia leaned into a young second lieutenant, who was close to drooling over her, and made use of Eloise's information. "I wonder," Amelia whispered to him. "You have but a single ship. How can you expect an entire world to heed your requests?"

The lieutenant, intoxicated by Amelia's perfect face swimming in front of his eyes, blurted, "We're one today, but tomorrow . . ." Before he could finish, a first lieutenant elbowed him in the ribs, and the young officer quickly shut his mouth and ducked his head.

"We hope perseverance and diplomacy will eventually prevail, miss," the first lieutenant replied.

The young women kept pressing for more information, but despite the girls winning ways, no more information about the subject was forthcoming. Instead, the young men pressed in with more personal questions, closing tighter around the girls.

<Big brother,> Christie sent, <I believe we need an intervention. Our admirers are becoming much too enthralled with our charms.>

Alex excused himself from present company and made his way quickly across the hall. Julien relayed Christie's request to Étienne, who excused himself from Shin's flustered attentions. Alex arrived behind Christie, but was blocked from her by a wall of officers and techs crowding around her. While Alex was seeking a diplomatic way to intervene, he saw a young man directly behind Christie reach a hand under her short wrap.

A second lieutenant yelped as he was yanked up by his collar and dangled in mid-air, facing an irate Alex. The officers surrounding the girls went on alert. They moved the young women aside and pointed small, fifteen-centimeter-long tubes at Alex. Each tube's glowing red end pointed at Alex.

"And what is it each of you possesses?" Alex asked, eyeing the glowing tubes.

"Stand down," Major Barbas growled. He had hurried after Alex when the Méridien quickly departed their group. Immediately, the small tubes flicked off and disappeared back beneath jackets. "You must forgive my officers, Ser Racine. They are sensitive when it comes to someone roughing up their comrade."

Alex looked the offender in his eyes. "And I, Major, am sensitive when it comes to your people taking liberties with my sister. In our society, it is impolite to touch a young woman in such a manner without permission." Alex set the lieutenant down and turned to the major, asking, "Is that not true on Earth anymore?"

Major Barbas placed his hands on his hips, preparing to retort, when he bumped an elbow into the escort, Étienne. The man had closed to his side without his notice. That subtle movement and seeing his officer hoisted into the air by Ser Racine's single arm set off mental alarm bells. Beginning with a cadet academy at the age of eleven, Barbas spent his entire life in the military, and he was suddenly well aware that the Méridiens were not the happy travelers they pretended to be. These two men, at least, were extremely capable and well-trained.

"My deepest apologies for any discourtesies my men have offered your companions," Major Barbas said, eyeing his militia officers. The sight of the major's steely-eyed gaze brought his officers to rigid attention. Quickly, a broad smile replaced the major's stern expression. "You are an amazingly strong individual, Ser Racine," Barbas said. "I would welcome the opportunity to see a friendly competition between you and an equal of one of my men. Do you practice any form of defense training, Ser Racine?"

"Fortune forbid, Major. I leave playing on the mats to the likes of my escorts," Alex declared, waving a hand at Étienne.

The major's interest was further piqued. More and more details about this group of people were not adding up. Before, he had laughed at the thought of Étienne as security personnel. Now, he appraised the slender escort beside him with fresh eyes. The calm gaze he received in return didn't fit the masquerade.

"We should arrange a demonstration between your man, Ser Racine, and one of my men. Consider it an opportunity to get to know each other better," the major suggested.

"We have no facilities on station to accommodate this sort of exercise, Major. Perhaps, you have one on your ship. With so many young officers, I'm sure you must have some area dedicated to their training," Alex offered.

"That we do," García said from behind Alex. "I'm sure we could accommodate a few of your people for an exhibition match, Ser Racine. You must understand that as an explorer ship, our vessel's design is quite utilitarian. We are ill-prepared for guests. Are you volunteering your man, Ser de Long, for the match?"

"That's his choice, Speaker García. He is free to do as he wishes," Alex replied.

Everyone turned to look at Étienne. The UE expressions ran the gamut from surprise on the civilians' faces to evil grins on the officers', who were visualizing fresh meat for the grinder.

"I would be delighted, Speaker García, to test my skills against one of your volunteers," Étienne replied, delivering courtesy to the speaker with hand over heart and a nod of his head. The gesture produced a spate of muffled snickers from some of the junior officers.

"Well, Speaker García, shall we meet tomorrow? I can have a shuttle at your ship at 18 hours. I understand that would be 1200 hours for your people," Alex said.

"Perhaps it would be better if our shuttle picked your people up from the same dock we used today, since we know that method works. No use tempting fate by adding too many new variables to our procedures," García replied.

"Twelve hundred hours tomorrow at this bay, Speaker García. We look forward to it. Now, I believe we should part company while cooler heads reign, should we not?"

"Agreed, Ser Racine. This meeting has been enlightening," García said, staring intently into Alex's eyes. "Until tomorrow."

"Indeed, Speaker García. Most enlightening," Alex returned, locking eyes with the mission commander. *So much for subterfuge . . . it appears that we have both been unmasked*, Alex thought.

Étienne motioned the speaker toward the hall's exit and proceeded to guide the Earthers back to their shuttle while Alex and company returned to the *Rêveur*.

* * *

Alex met with his people in his stateroom.

"From everyone's excitement, I gather I missed a most engaging fête," the elderly captain lamented.

"Your absence was necessary, Captain," Alex replied. "The fête turned into a game of hide and seek."

"A child's game, Captain," Renée explained. "In this case, each side was hiding secrets and seeking to discover what the other side was hiding."

"Could I not have aided our goals, Ser President?" Captain Cordova asked.

"Apologies, Captain, but you represent a significant Méridien secret. We exposed enough differences today as a calculated risk. Yours was an easily preventable one."

"Mine, Ser President?" the captain asked, but his puzzled look quickly cleared. "Ah, my age, and Méridiens' long life."

"Had that been discovered during conversation, Captain," Terese added, "it might have led to myriad questions about health. As it was, the Earthers were mesmerized by the appearance of the Méridiens. In fact, everyone's appearance in our group seemed to interest the Earthers." Terese glanced over at Miranda.

After Miranda's return to the *Rêveur*, her proximity to the ship's controller triggered Z's programming, which subsumed the persona of Miranda and returned control to Z, who quickly reviewed the entire meeting, paying particular attention to Miranda's discussion with Major Barbas.

What was disconcerting to those in the stateroom was seeing the Miranda avatar slouched in a chair, legs slightly open, and dress riding up the thighs with Z's voice issuing from her face.

"So, what did we learn?" Alex asked.

"Besides the fact that Earthers have no manners?" Christie piped up. When Alex calmly gazed at Christie, she promptly closed her mouth, properly chastened. Comms from both Eloise and Amelia warned her to be careful. "My apologies, Mr. President," Christie said. "Our best piece of information relates to the overconfidence of the young officers. They are sure that they will have their way with this system."

"A young lieutenant started to say that they were one today, but tomorrow . . ." Amelia added.

"Tomorrow what?" Alex asked.

"That was all, Ser President. He was rudely silenced by a first lieutenant. The senior one actually elbowed his junior in the ribs to quiet him," Amelia replied.

"Most telling, Ser President," Eloise added, "was the chagrin of the junior officer. It was as if he was about to expose a major secret and now expected to be punished for his indiscretion. It was only Amelia's entreaty and allure that caused the young officer to start to divulge the secret in the first place."

Alex looked at Amelia, perched on the edge of the couch next to Terese. The young Haraken woman with her Méridien genes and short, colorful wrap could probably entice the entire UE force of young officers to go anywhere she wanted them to go. In return, his gaze was met by a confident expression. Amelia knew who she was and what her capabilities were when it came to this dangerous game they were playing.

"So the Earthers are expecting reinforcements," Alex concluded.

"And they wouldn't have need for another explorer ship, Mr. President," Tatia added.

"It stands to reason, Mr. President," Julien said, "that if an explorer ship is outfitted with such extensive armament and the young officer was excited by the prospect of additional resources, the ship or ships arriving will be extremely dangerous. I've researched my Terran colonial records. There existed such vessels called 'battleships' and 'destroyers.' They were huge weapons of war with massive armament, most of which was designed to destroy other warships."

"They could also be expecting troop carriers, Mr. President. If subjugation is their aim, then they would want not only control of the ships in the system's space but the government on the ground," Tatia said.

"Julien, keep Commodore Reynard and Captain Manet apprised of our conversations," Alex said. "Have them keep the *Last Stand* in close proximity to Méridien while remaining outside the system."

"I'm devastated," Renée said, slapping her hands on her knees. "I learned nothing, except the innumerable ways the speaker can compliment a woman."

"Clearly, Ser de Guirnon," Christie said, "the speaker was hoping to flatter you until you melted and told him all your secrets."

<And in truth, there is much to flatter,> Alex sent to Renée.

<I require a visit to the refresher to remove the speaker's attentions before I respond in kind to your sentiment, my love,> Renée sent back.

"Major Barbas apparently tried the same ruse with Miranda as the speaker did with Ser de Guirnon," Z said. "He was quite smitten with Miranda and full of lovely words, but entirely tight-lipped on any subject relating to his ship or Earth. It is Miranda's consideration that Major Barbas has a volatile combination of personality traits. He exhibits an aura of absolute self-control, but it covers a persona riddled with rage and loathing of many around him. In addition, Miranda believes he will be utterly faithful to only one person, the speaker."

"In contrast, the admiral and I found Captain Lumley to be quite open," Alain said. "He was a congenial individual with a cultured manner."

Eyes turned toward Tatia, and she picked up the conversation. "The captain appears to be an aficionado of history. According to him, Earth's environment suffered from global climate change for centuries after the launch of the colony ships. The burgeoning population overtaxed Earth's resources, food, and water. This led to a period called the Resource Wars, which started regionally but expanded to engulf the globe."

"During this time, fusion reaction was discovered, but it was too late to reverse the damage of industrial and human pollution or to save Earth from the oncoming mayhem," Alain added. "Many Earthers escaped the conflicts by immigrating to colonies on Sol's other planets and moons."

"Is there value to this history lesson?" Alex asked.

"Unfortunately not, Mr. President," Tatia said. "Our conversation abruptly ended when you hoisted that junior officer in the air."

"That's my fault," Christie lamented. "I pressed the panic button."

"And it was most appropriate," Eloise added. "We were being overrun by incredibly aggressive young men. The three of us are healing from innumerable bruises from their pinches and grabs. In hindsight, perhaps we were overly enthusiastic with our flirting."

"True," Amelia agreed, "but who knew the Earther's junior officers lacked social skills."

"Then it was just as well that Administrator Wombo was a man who focused on current events," Pia said. "He sounds similar to Captain Lumley . . . a quite social man."

"The administrator referred to the Final Wars of Earth's twenty-sixth century, which devastated the superpower nations," Mickey continued. "United Earth rose from the ashes of those wars, forming a strong central world government. Ser Wombo intimated that there was great approval in the beginning as the UE helped the people . . . the sick and the starving around the globe."

"However, something changed," said Pia, picking up the thread of the conversation. "It's our impression that the UE became harsh in its administration, but Ser Wombo would say no more."

"An interesting observation, Mr. President," Julien said, "is that as Administrator Wombo spoke about UE history, he kept his eye on three people: Speaker García, Major Barbas, and Assistant Administrator Zhang Shin."

"Kept his eye on them how?" Alex asked.

"Interpreting Mickey's and Pia's visual records, I would say he was quite nervous about them, especially the speaker," Julien replied. "Once, when the mission commander caught his glance, Ser Wombo's heart rate spiked and his eyes dilated."

"So we have two individuals willing to talk, the captain and the administrator, but one, the biggest man in the room, is afraid of three key people, including one of the smallest in the room. Speaking of which, Étienne, you spoke to Zhang Shin. What did she have to say?"

"My apologies, Ser President," Étienne replied, "I was forced to emulate the speaker's technique." Étienne's statement brought a round of twitters and laughs from the room. "The woman was so tireless in her questioning that I found little opportunity to insert my own query. I was forced to use her infatuation with my appearance as a means of stopping her interrogation."

"Did you learn anything?" Alex asked, working to keep the smile off his face.

"Yes," Étienne declared. "The assistant administrator is loyal to the major and the speaker, especially the major. There is something in her voice when she speaks of him."

"Julien, can you help us here?" Alex asked.

"Analysis of her voice patterns would indicate a close relationship with the major, although I would hesitate to say 'respect.' It appears to be one more closely related to necessity, more like clinging to a lifesaving device."

"And what of her supervisor, Administrator Wombo?" Alex asked Étienne.

"Interestingly enough, Shin never mentioned the man, Ser," Étienne replied.

"Mmm . . . So we have a power triumvirate that centers on the mission commander and includes the ship's military contingent but excludes the scientists," Alex mused out loud, "a strange hierarchy for an explorer ship."

"Étienne, are you ready for tomorrow?" Tatia asked.

"I look forward to the exercise, Admiral," Étienne replied. "It will be an opportunity to expand my repertoire of techniques."

"The speaker made it clear that he will expect fewer guests tomorrow, but this is a perfect opportunity to gather some information about their ship, and I don't want to miss out," Alex said.

"I believe I can help with that, Ser President," Z said. "Julien and Mickey, I will need your assistance immediately after the meeting in engineering, and Ser de Long, I will need you to prolong your match tomorrow as long as you are able without endangering yourself. I believe the accurate expression is, 'I will need you to stall.'"

12

Wombo yearned to share the details of his visit to the *Rêveur* with his fellow scientists, but he was forced to curb his enthusiasm. Zhang Shin hovered around him at every turn, pestering him with queries of whom he talked to, what questions were asked of him, and what did he surmise. Wombo kept his responses to Zhang circumspect, and he was careful to tamp down his excitement in her presence. The last thing Wombo desired was to give Shin an opportunity to run to the major's bed with stories of his effusive enthusiasm for all things Méridien.

It was late in the evening before Wombo convened a small group of trusted colleagues in his cabin. His compatriots were monitoring Zhang Shin, and when word was passed to Wombo that Shin had retired for the evening, meaning she was in the major's cabin, his friends made their way, one by one, to his cabin. These senior scientists were Wombo's friends, and many owed much of their career advancements to his patronage. All owed their positions on the *Reunion* to him.

Wombo sat behind his desk, which was much too small for a man his size, and his six visitors—Yoram, Storen, Edward, Priita, Nema, and Boris—occupied every other available space in his cramped cabin: the bunk, the single chair, and the deck. For hours, they questioned him and formed conjectures about his observations.

"One thing I surmise is that Ser Racine and some of his people are not Méridiens," Olawale said. "And what bothers me is that I suspect the speaker has the same suspicion."

"But you believe they're human . . . I mean of Earth ancestry?" Storen, the xenobiologist, asked. When Olawale nodded, lost in thought as he reviewed his observations, Storen continued his train of thought. "Would that mean a second colony ship landed out here, near the Méridiens, and somehow met them later, or might that mean the original colonists managed to populate two worlds, which developed separately for centuries?"

"Regardless of which option might be correct," Edward, the lead physicist and mathematician, remarked, "if we follow this line of thought, Ser Racine and the people like him must have developed on a much heavier world than that of Earth. And then there are the differences in faces we have seen on the visual logs of Ser Racine's first contact. It would seem logical to assume that one group of his people are of Méridien descent since you say they are similar to those you saw in the orbital's corridors. Those individuals have a beauty that seems impossible. You only have to look for their exquisite visages and slender forms to recognize a Méridien. On the other hand, while Ser Racine and Ser Tachenko are handsome individuals, they do not have the superlative face and form that I believe comes from genetic tinkering."

Olawale thought for a moment and began laughing. "Priita, I thought you and I made a strange pair. It seems that Ser Racine's partner is Ser Renée de Guirnon . . . such a beauty," Olawale said, quietly mumbling the last phrase.

"According to the logs, Olawale, our colony ships were launched nearly a millennium ago, and they would have lost centuries in travel. Do you judge that there has been a sufficient amount of generational time to develop the changes in stature you've observed?" Nema asked.

"It must be so, Nema. Ser Tachenko is Ser Racine's twin in female form, heavy-boned, blonde, and quite robust. On first impression and to the casual observer, she might appear considerably overweight, but everything about her says predator. She moves like one of those great African cats of old."

"What is your overall impression of this world and these people?" asked Yoram.

Olawale looked thoughtfully at his friend, who was known for his serious personality and philosophical side. "We are definitely dealing with multiple worlds, which I don't believe are that well-integrated. We arrive at a world called Méridien, which does not wish to talk to us. A ship arrives from outside the system, and the people aboard are eager to engage us.

They present themselves as happy travelers, but that's a façade. Why didn't this group originate from the populated planet below and present themselves as government representatives? Why? Because they are from a different world and unlike the Méridiens, they are a more proactive people, who confront adversaries such as us. Furthermore, these people from the *Rêveur* are a mix of three physiological types. Ser Julien and Ser Leyton are the third type. They bear no resemblance to the Méridiens or Ser Racine."

"Speaking of Ser Racine, you seem intrigued by him. What do you make of him?" Yoram pressed.

"Now, there's a good question, Yoram," Olawale said, his eyes rolling to the cabin's overhead while he considered how to answer. "What I find intriguing, Yoram, is that Ser Racine, despite his physical differences that mark him as non-Méridien, has collected an interesting mix of Méridiens and others in his sphere, and despite their bon-vivant style, his people are extremely attentive to him . . . one might even say they form a protective ring around him, which betrays their presentation."

"Does not that make them a duplicitous lot?" Yoram asked.

"And who began this game of duplicity?" Olawale replied. "I believe that Ser Racine and his people are seeking to discover our speaker's intentions, just as the speaker is seeking to uncover the truth about Ser Racine."

"It makes one wonder if humans will ever develop a nurturing society that will welcome all with open arms," Priita mused.

13

Alex, Renée, Julien, Miranda, Terese, and Étienne sat on the bench seats in a Le Jardin orbital station airlock, waiting for the arrival of the *Reunion*'s shuttle. Six visitors were all that the speaker would accept, and that number was only been allowed because three of the six were women.

Christie voiced vociferous objections at being left out, but Amelia and Eloise exerted their influence and calmed her down. For the immediately foreseeable future, the two young Harakens desired nothing more than to be quit of Earther company.

"Ser de Guirnon," Miranda said, "if you will help me prepare my wardrobe malfunction." The six Harakens were dressed in ship suits, functional attire for a supposedly functional ship. The form-fitting suits well-outlined each and everyone's silhouettes, including Alex's massive stature and Miranda's abundant curves. The group watched Renée kneel in front of Miranda and unzip her ship suit nearly to her navel, prominently displaying much of Miranda's full breasts. Then Renée proceeded to close the zipper partway, working to catch the fastening portion in the fabric until it stuck. Renée stood up and examined her work. "Quite believable and entertaining I might add, Miranda," she said, adding a bright grin and a wink.

Miranda offered Renée a satisfied smile. Haraken ship suits sealed with nanites strips. They didn't employ zippers. Miranda spotted the device on a scientist's jacket during the fête and transferred the concept to Z, who drafted Julien and Mickey to construct one and apply it to her suit.

When the *Reunion*'s shuttle landed and the hatch dropped down, the speaker, the major, and a first lieutenant came down the shuttle's steps with alacrity, which had much to do with the fact that the men knew Renée, Miranda, and Terese would be attending the event. After the most cursory of greeting to Alex, the men extended arms to escort the women to the shuttle, enjoying the views as they gallantly waved the women up the shuttle's steep steps ahead of them.

<One might think that the three of us weren't even present,> Julien quipped to Alex and Étienne.

<And that is entirely in our favor, Julien. The three of us are just background, and we must continue to act that way,> Alex replied.

Aboard the shuttle, Miranda found herself seated next to Major Barbas, as she expected. The major's eyes constantly shifted from her face to the exposed curve of her breasts, which threatened to burst from the confines of her ship suit. *Look all you wish, Major. It will be your undoing,* Miranda thought.

When Alex and company disembarked in the *Reunion*'s shuttle bay, he and his people minimized their communication until Julien could determine the level of eavesdropping technology the Earthers possessed. Eyes searched out items of interest and nods indicated what they wished to share among one another.

Julien caught Alex's eye and indicated the deck. It took Alex a moment to figure out that Julien was indicating the Earthers could deliver gravity to their ship while stationary. *That's what eleven years aboard advanced starships does to you,* Alex thought. About the explorer ship, Alex noted that the speaker spoke the truth. The corridors and stairs they took, moving through the ship, were rudimentary. Unlike the uncluttered, wide corridors of a Méridien or Haraken ship, the *Reunion*'s corridors were interrupted repeatedly by bulkhead frames, and the overheads were strung with myriad conduits.

As the group traversed the corridors, Miranda spotted the opportunity she was looking for—a bulkhead frame was positioned just aft of a ventilation grate. She folded her arms under her breasts, pushing them up and out, and the major's eyes tracked just where Miranda expected them to go.

"It's quite chilly in your ship, Major," Miranda simpered. "I would close my suit but my fastener is stuck. Would you mind seeing if you could be of service?" She stepped to the side, placed her back against the bulkhead and opened her arms invitingly.

Major Barbas licked his lips in anticipation and reached for the offending fastener. It must be said that the major took an inordinate amount of time freeing the material. The others in Alex's party did their best to distract the speaker's people while they all waited for the major to finish enjoying his treat.

As the major played, Miranda sent an activation code. Her hair was coiffed on top of her head in intricate coils and pinned front and back with two tiara-like combs. On Miranda's signal, the upper layer of the rear comb peeled off from the base, which was identical in design. The thin metal frame and joints of crystal closed up to resemble a large spider. As a single leg of the creature touched the bulkhead on which Miranda leaned, its leg and crystal joints changed color to match the drab gray of the bulkhead. By the time the tiny intruder climbed to the top of the frame, its camouflage was complete. Sensors picked up the vent's air flow, and algorithms in its crystal brain dictated the vent as a priority direction. It flattened its body to slide through a slot, and it was gone.

When Miranda received the signal from Z's "Shadow," as he called it, that it was safely out of sight, she laughed at the major's playful antics. "You are keeping the others waiting, Major. Perhaps a woman's fingers would be more dexterous in these circumstances." The major laughed in reply and slowly slid the fastener up the suit until it closed at the neck.

"A shame to cover such beauty, Miranda," Barbas whispered.

"Who can say, Major? It might become too warm later," Miranda replied and gently pushed past the major to join her companions.

* * *

The Shadow scurried silently through the ventilation ducts. At each vent, it would unroll a thin telemetry line through a slot and survey the area, recording the imagery. As it hurried along the ducts, it recorded distances and directional changes, building a map of its travels.

The Shadow's governing directives, in order, were survival, stealth, speed, and survey. It had a long way to travel and much to discover. At duct intersections, the tiny machine paused and tested the air to discern trace chemicals, which would indicate greater probabilities for successful directions. Vent after vent revealed only more general corridors, and it began skipping vents that effused the same scent. Finally, the Shadow detected the scent of oils, chemicals, and fuel. It paused and dropped its snooper line through a slot and was rewarded with a view of a ship's bay, a bay filled with four deadly looking fighters. The Shadow expended precious time stretching out its telemetry filament to zoom in and capture details of the fighters.

Based on its internal map, the little Shadow took a set of turns through the ventilation ducts to arrive at what it calculated would be a second bay and discovered four more fighters. It repeated its process, traveling to two more bays and recording its evidence, before it sought out its next priorities.

Its greatest adversaries were the fans inset within the ventilation ducts. There was just the slightest gap between the tips of the blades and the sides of the frames. The Shadow examined the opening and the shape of the space then flattened its body into the required curvature and carefully crawled through the gap, fulfilling its primary directive to survive.

The descent to lower decks, the Shadow's next destination after the fighter bays, was fraught with exposure. It was forced to leave the ventilation system, access the corridors, and creep down the stairs. More than once it clung to the underside of a stairstep, blending into the metal, as boots pounded overhead—stealth.

At each deck, the Shadow ducked back into the ventilation ducts to search out the level only to discover nothing of importance. Down the decks it went, racing against time. The small crystal bead located behind its head held the energy that drove it, and that energy was limited—speed.

The Shadow discovered one item of interest not in its programmed list of targets. It passed overhead of two cabins, containing eight bunks each. That was nothing exceptional in itself. However, it noted that all the humans within the rooms in various states of dress were clothed identically. Its coding identified their coverings as uniforms. After that room, it investigated several more cabins on either side of that corridor, recording many more eight-bunk rooms and several two-bunk rooms, all containing humans in uniforms.

The little Shadow hurried to accomplish its final two tasks. On the next deck down, it lowered its telemetry line through a vent into a long space. Huge tubes were laid out in parallel, but the angle of view was heavily compromised so the Shadow squeezed through the vent to explore the room. It crept quietly along the wall, capturing details of the tubes, their rails, and the launching system—missiles, its program identified.

The Shadow left the missile room and worked to locate the final targets, which were the twin structures located to either side of the *Reunion*'s fuselage, tucked under each wing.

The little Shadow hurried down a set of stairs, hiding several times as humans tromped past, heavily shaking its grip, forcing it to expend more of its precious energy. Soon after, it climbed a bulkhead, gained another vent, and scurried along the duct. Its tiny steps were muffled by its choice of footing, changeable from claw tips to padded tips. A low-energy warning froze it in place. Protocols demanded it dump its captured data. The telemetry line was unrolled to stick straight out, acting as a broadcast antenna, and it stayed rooted in place while the host was contacted. Once the link was secure, its accumulated data was transmitted.

With the broadcast complete, the Shadow reverted to its priority list and scurried down the ventilation duct. Its priority algorithms drove it, while its existence hung in the balance as its energy bead drained. The tiny machine only gained another 20 meters when it froze in place again. There were no more priorities, no more directives, the energy bead was empty. Z's Shadow would remain a permanent fixture in the *Reunion*'s ventilation ducts, but its mission had been accomplished.

* * *

The Harakens recorded every element of their trip through the ship as the speaker led them to a lower deck and a wide open space whose walls were lined with exercise equipment. The center of the room was covered in mats, and several men in camouflage pants and black tees were practicing unarmed combat drills.

"Sergeant Hinsdale, front and center," Major Barbas called out.

The burly, hard-looking master sergeant, who was leading the training, released his hold on a trooper, crossed the mats to the major, and jumped to attention, "Sir," he called out clearly, holding a rigid pose.

"This is Ser Racine's security escort," Major Barbas said, gesturing toward Étienne. "He has graciously consented to compare defensive techniques with one of our own. Would you care to accommodate him?" the major asked with a hint of play in his voice.

The master sergeant eyed the slender man with the too-pretty face and turned a wry grin on the Harakens. "I would be happy to educate our guests in our techniques, Major."

"I look forward to learning whatever you care to impart, Sergeant Hinsdale," Étienne replied graciously. His words evoked laughter from the militia troopers, who stopped their training and gathered close to get an eyeful of the visitors.

The master sergeant nodded his assent. "Very well, son. Come on. I promise to take it easy on you."

Once on the mats, the master sergeant sought to have Étienne assume a basic defensive stance, which Étienne quietly demurred from following. "Son, if you don't raise your hands," Hinsdale said, frustration showing in his voice, "bad things can happen to you. Like this," he said, swinging a meaty open hand at Étienne's shoulder, which never connected. It momentarily threw the master sergeant off balance, but he quickly recovered. He eyed Étienne carefully. "Quick, are we?" Hinsdale said and assumed an offensive stance, a grin of expectation spreading across his face.

Following his orders to draw out the exercise, Étienne danced and twirled out of reach of the master sergeant's strikes, as the noncom tried unsuccessfully to pin him into a corner.

When the master sergeant failed to connect with his strikes, he reverted to grappling, tripping, and pinning techniques. At this point, Étienne slapped light strikes against the sides and back of the master sergeant's head to inform him that offense was well within Étienne's capabilities. This angered Hinsdale, who growled in frustration.

Major Barbas was hovering at Miranda's side at the exhibition's start but as the bout intensified, he edged closer to the mats, intently watching Étienne's techniques, and a frown formed on his face. He assumed the matchup would be brief. Instead, it continued on, seemingly interminable. Sweat rolled off the bodies of both men, but only the master sergeant was breathing heavily.

Miranda received the Shadow's data transmission, and she signaled Alex.

<End it, Étienne,> Alex sent.

With a swiftness that defied the eyes, Étienne dropped to one leg, shot his other leg between the master sergeant's legs, and spun his body, effectively tripping the man. A quick, sharp strike from Étienne's stiffened fingertips into nerves behind the master sergeant's left knee numbed the man's lower leg. Then Étienne jumped up and danced out of the master sergeant's strike zone to wait. When Hinsdale tried to stand, his leg wouldn't support him, and he sat back down heavily on the mat.

Master Sergeant Hinsdale once observed a demonstration of ancient martial arts. He was surprised by the incredible feats the wizened old man performed, including his demonstrations against heavier, younger opponents. He harbored thoughts that the younger and stronger combatants held back to prevent injuring their "sensei," as they called him. Those long-held thoughts were just erased. The master sergeant held up his hands in surrender and a smile crossed his face. When his opponent offered him a hand up, Hinsdale graciously accepted.

Terese swept forward when she saw the master sergeant balancing on one leg and wincing as he tried to straighten the other. "One moment, Sergeant Hinsdale," she said, as she knelt behind him, pulled up his pants leg, and dug in her small kit for a tube of nanites gel, which she applied to the reddened skin, courtesy of Étienne's hand strike.

"If you would care to teach a class sometime, Mr. Escort," Hinsdale said, "we'd be pleased to have you."

"I am Étienne de Long," Étienne replied, giving the master sergeant a polite nod of his head for the compliment.

"Master Sergeant Jeffrey Hinsdale," the burly man replied, offering his hand to Étienne, who accepted it as intended, an acknowledgment of the extraordinary skills demonstrated. After the two Méridiens rejoined their group, the master sergeant glanced down at his leg when he realized that the pain was gone from the nerve strike. To his amazement, the redness was also fading, and he threw a quizzical look at Major Barbas.

<Can the Earthers recover the medical nanites, if they check for them, Terese?> Alex asked.

<I would think that they would have to know what they are looking for first, Mr. President,> Terese sent back. <But I have no idea about their level of medical technology. Apologies, Ser, I only meant to stop his pain.>

<No apologies necessary, Terese,> Alex replied. <You did what you've been trained to do. I'm merely trying to gauge the effect a discovery of our medical technology might have on these Earthers. Judging by the expression on the master sergeant's face, our medical nanites are new to them.>

Alex glanced toward the speaker and the major out of the corner of his eye as they observed the master sergeant shake off the numbed leg and walk around the mat with a smile on his face. He appreciated the fact that without implants the two men were forced to communicate verbally and visually. In this case, their faces were open books and the writing read lust for another discovered technological treasure.

Speaker García came up to Alex, stopping briefly to regard Étienne. "You Méridiens are full of surprises," he said with mirth, but his gray eyes weren't smiling.

"I dare say, Speaker García, it's just a matter of different techniques," Alex replied. "Well, it has been a most entertaining experience, but we must be returning to the Le Jardin. The staff is planning a fête this afternoon, and we wouldn't want to miss out. If you will be so kind as to return us now, we would be appreciative."

Without waiting for the speaker's reply, the Harakens turned and exited the workout room, heading back down the corridor from the direction they came.

The first lieutenant, who accompanied them during the shuttle journey, hurried to catch up with his guests and lead the way back to the bay, never knowing that every Haraken implant held a map of the entire route. Quite possibly they could have run the route in the dark.

* * *

The Harakens sat by themselves in the *Reunion* shuttle's interior. Only a pilot, copilot, and the first lieutenant, who was seated with the pilots, accompanied them back to Le Jardin.

<Was it something we said?> Terese quipped via comm to her people when she noticed no other UE personnel accompanied them.

In the midst of the laughter, Alex sent, <the orbital.> Alex's people took the hint and refrained from communicating until the UE shuttle dropped them at the platform's bay.

Once the Harakens gained the *Rêveur*, the original attendees of the first meeting, Captain Cordova, Mickey, Pia, Alain, Christie, Eloise, and Amelia, joined the group in Alex's stateroom. Z took a moment to change into his director's avatar, having noticed how uncomfortable he made others while speaking through Miranda's avatar.

While thé was served, Z downloaded the Shadow's content onto the *Rêveur*'s data banks. He set up the holo-vid to receive a spool of the vid data. In the meantime, the discussion revolved around Étienne and his display of skills against the Earther.

"Julien, I take it you recorded the entire event?" Tatia asked.

"I did, Admiral, it's already on the *Rêveur*'s data banks," Julien replied.

"Excellent, can't wait to watch that one," Tatia said.

"At this rate, Admiral, you might be the last to view it. Half the crew is already watching it," Julien said.

"Étienne was superb . . . admirable, one might say," Renée said, adding a grin.

"That he was," agreed Alex, his eyes warm with appreciation.

Étienne, who stood by quietly during the discussion, nodded his head to Alex. The master sergeant proved to be a worthy opponent, and Étienne wasn't pleased that he harmed the man, Earther or not. *They are a mix of people, worthy and unworthy*, Étienne thought.

Z sent the little Shadow's imagery spooling through the holo-vid and streamed his telemetry recording to the humans' implants. Most blocked the telemetry data except for Alex and Tatia. The group watched the Shadow's entire visual record of its trek through the explorer ship, and when it was finished, Alex restarted the sequence. This time, individuals stopped, rocked the imagery back and forth, or expanded the view. The spool was viewed for more than two hours until no one asked for another replay.

Everyone in the cabin sat or stood absolutely quiet, alone with their thoughts—none of which were any good. Most hoped that the various analyses of the *Reunion*'s ports were flawed, despite the fact that they were observed and analyzed by SADEs. It was a common and fervent hope that the Earthers were boisterous and obstreperous but not aggressive. The little machine's visual records made a lie of those hopes.

"Those missiles would appear to use a type of chemical propellant, but it's difficult to determine what might be loaded in their heads," Tatia said, the first to break the silence.

"As well, I am unable to determine the type of engines in the fighters," Julien said, "but it's obvious they rely on missiles in their engagements."

"More telling," Z added, "is that the Shadow recorded four bays of fighters adjacent to one another. The probability is that only a few shuttles lie behind that ship's extensive array of bay doors. I apologize, Ser President. If the power bead was just 10 percent larger my Shadow might have gained the tubes beside the fuselage."

"And its increased dimensions might have prevented its movement through the vent covers and fans, Z," Julien said sympathetically.

"No, Z," Alex said, "you did a wonderful job with your Shadow, especially with the brief time you had. All who helped you should be congratulated. I'm quite pleased with what you've found out."

Eloise made a tentative gesture toward Alex with her hand. "Yes, Eloise?" Alex asked.

"Perhaps, I do not understand these people very well, my Protector," Eloise said. She had never dropped the title her great-grandmother bestowed on Alex, but it only came out when she was nervous or confused—an unconscious action. "This Earther ship has tremendous weaponry. The leaders must realize by now that this system has little or no protection from them. What are they waiting for?"

"Indeed, what are they waiting for?" Christie echoed. "But they are waiting. That's what the junior lieutenant alluded to before he was hushed by his senior. He said, 'we are one today, but tomorrow . . .' before he was silenced."

"So are they waiting for a fleet or a giant ship, the likes of which we hoped never to see again?" Tatia asked. Her comment reminded everyone of the Nua'll prison ship and the losses the Swei Swee suffered to be free of it.

"Whether it will be one large ship or many small ones, it doesn't matter," Alex said. "It will fall to us to handle any aggressive moves, but I must warn Leader Ganesh. At the mention of the Council Leader's name, several individuals groaned. Mahima Ganesh had developed a definitely un-Méridien-like distaste for Alex Racine, and it wasn't likely to change just because Méridien might be subjugated at any moment by the Earthers.

Pia added a final thought. "Ser President, I suppose it's no use retreating to Haraken. If the Earthers choose to dominate the Confederation, it will begin here at Méridien, and then it will only be a matter of time before they come for Haraken and New Terra." Unfortunately, no one could disagree with her.

* * *

The *Reunion* comms officer was another political appointee, who despite reporting to the captain was loyal to the speaker—a UE check and balance on ships' officers. He placed a private call to his political superior. "Speaker García," said the officer, "the guide has detected an unauthorized transmission."

"Destination, Laurent?" Antonio asked.

"It was internal, Speaker García," Laurent replied. "A burst transmission of an unidentified signal configuration originated from the lower decks. It was too brief for the guide to gain much more information other than the fact that it existed and it wasn't our equipment."

"Has there been a search for the source?"

"Yes, Speaker," Laurent replied. "I informed the captain about the transmission, and the source location was searched, but the crew and militia have been unable to locate it."

"What about the strength of the signal, Laurent?"

"Weak, Speaker. It would have been relegated to perhaps 100 meters, not kilometers."

"Thank you for your report, Laurent," Speaker García said, and then closed his comm unit, turning to Barbas, who sat across the table from him. Laurent's report was only a confirmation of the earlier report García received from another appointee, one unknown to anyone else, including the major. In the UE, it paid to have informers confirming the informants.

"The evidence is indisputable," García said. "Our guests are much more than casual travelers."

"I don't understand the value of a focused transmission from a fixed location in our ship, especially one that can't reach their ship," Barbas said.

"You're thinking as someone from Sol and as if these people came from Earth, Major," García replied. "Maybe they were once like us, but they aren't any longer. Ask yourself how they got that transmission device to our lower decks when they were in sight at all times. And who or what received the transmission? No one ever accessed a comms unit during their entire time with us. So how did they receive it?"

"I take your point about these people being human but not from Earth. I have been trying to understand how that escort defeated Master Sergeant Hinsdale. I was sure the stripling would be taught a lesson by UE militia strength, when suddenly it was over in two moves," Barbas replied. The major thought he voiced an intelligent point, but the speaker's cold eyes stared at him. "What did I miss?" Barbas finally asked.

"The bout was a stall, major. That escort, as you continue to call him, was an extraordinary individual who could have defeated the master sergeant at any time. He was keeping us entertained until our guests obtained the information they sought. How they did it, I don't know . . . why, is the easy part. It's obvious that their leader is no fun-loving runabout. Ser Étienne de Long identified himself as the escort to Ser Racine. Who would have not one but two of these men, since it's obvious the de Longs are twins, with this level of skill as his personal security?"

"I can't disagree with you, Speaker," Barbas replied. "The manner in which Ser Racine's people treat him smacks of a well-trained organization."

"Yes, and this secret transmission is just one more piece of evidence about their true nature," García said, "You might have observed much more, Major, if your nose hadn't been so deep in Miranda Leyton's ample bosom."

Angered by the speaker's rebuke, Barbas sought to redeem himself. "Enjoying Miranda Leyton's charms did not dull my wits, Speaker García. You posited that we have met two distinct societies. I believe we have encountered three cultures. The Méridiens have a unique archetype, beautiful, slender people, which Ser Racine and Ser Tachenko do not match. Ser Racine said he was designed for a heavy world, but why didn't they craft his face. Those are your two societies. But Miranda Leyton represents a third culture. She is neither Méridien nor from Ser Racine's home world."

Barbas waited for the speaker to ask the obvious question, but he was denied the moment as gray eyes continued to stare at him. "Beneath those luscious curves," Barbas continued, "Miranda is strong with extraordinary reflexes. I sought to stumble against her, and she caught me as if I was a child."

"Are you sure she is human?" Antonio asked.

The question stunned Major Barbas. He considered it for a moment, but his ego denied him impartial judgment. "She couldn't be otherwise, speaker. Her femininity is bone deep."

"So we have a dilemma of evidence," García mused. "We have at least three societies that intersect here. The local government will not speak to us. Yet, one individual, who doesn't appear to be from this system, has chosen to meet with us."

"Could Ser Racine represent the Méridien's military organization? He has the bearing of a commander, and the other of his build, Ser Tachenko, relaxes one moment and then assumes a parade rest the next moment."

"Now that's an interesting question, Major," García replied. "But our conjectures are of no matter. It will soon be out of our hands. We will simply deliver our information, be debriefed, and await orders."

"Who do you think will come in response to your request?" Barbas asked.

"My message was sufficient to gain the attention of a high judge," García replied. "He or she can decide what to do here. What we've discovered is far beyond the scope of our mission."

"A high judge will take credit for your discovery, Speaker," Barbas lamented.

"Yes, Major, that's as it should be," García replied. "If we failed to call attention to this enormous discovery it would have been considered as having disobeyed standing orders, a criminal act."

At the mention of the UE's most dreaded words, the major blanched. All disappointment at losing the accolades he hoped to receive for their discovery disappeared. It was better to be alive. "Until the UE envoy arrives, what do we do?"

"We continue to watch and learn, Major," García replied.

"What, if anything, can be done about Ser Racine?"

"Nothing. Despite our precautions, I believe the man got what he came for once we let him and his people aboard our ship. We initiated the ruse, and he beat us at our own game. We've been uncovered," García said, sitting back in his chair and exhibiting a rare, emotional expression for him—one of disgust.

14

Alex, Tatia, Renée, Julien, and Z sat and then paced for hours, discarding one plan after another, without success. They needed the ear of Council Leader Ganesh, but she was refusing all contact from Alex. Their plans were escalating from the simple to the complex in an attempt to accomplish their goal—share their discoveries with Méridien Leaders about the explorer ship's armed interior and their disturbing conversations with the UE senior personnel.

"This isn't working," Alex said, tired and vexed at their failure to put together a workable plan. They needed to convince the entire Council of the danger they faced and to take steps to protect the Confederation's future.

"If subtle and diplomatic isn't working, then it's time to consider an entirely different approach, Alex," Tatia said. Informality was the general rule when these close associates met privately. They had endured too much together to stand on ceremony. "I presume other options have occurred to you before now."

Alex was loath to respond. Some of his ideas were equivalent to firing a Libran-X warhead into Confederation Hall. Such were the disruptive level of his concepts. He kept his mouth shut, but his old friends sat quietly staring at him.

"If the Confederation is at risk, then all of us are at risk," Renée finally said.

"And perhaps, my friend, it is time for some radical thinking," Julien added. "We cannot continue to protect this civilization forever. They must learn to take responsibility for their own welfare."

"Yesterday it was the Nua'll. Tomorrow it might be the Earthers, and what if they come with a fleet of warships that we can't intimidate or defeat? What will be our options then?" Z asked.

Alex put his head in his hands and slowly wiped them down his face as if he could remove the responsibility. *What does it take for intelligent entities to choose to live in peace?* Alex thought. "Logic dictates that if the present Council Leader does not want to meet with us, then we must either meet with other Leaders or change the leadership of the Council."

"It appears we are planning another coup," Julien said. "Well, to our benefit, we are experienced at this type of operation." Alex threw him a slightly disgusted look, and Julien returned a bright smile.

"What are the steps for a coup?" Z asked, ready to absorb the details of the process in order to participate fully.

Alex watched Renée for her reaction. Méridien was her world, the Confederation her society. She would know best the scope of the impact of which they spoke.

"If you are looking for my opinion, my love, you needn't bother," Renée replied. "I'm a Haraken. We can't afford to let a group of outsiders usurp the Confederation. It would make for dangerous neighbors. Do what you think is best, and we will back you."

Alex looked around at the expectant faces in front of him, taking a deep breath and letting it out slowly. This time, it wouldn't be a single world he was intending to disrupt, it would be an entire civilization composed of multiple worlds.

* * *

The *Rêveur's* traveler landed at a quiet terminal on Méridien. Alex, Tatia, Renée, Étienne, Alain, Julien, and Z disembarked.

Z was ensconced in his New Terran avatar. The large frame provided ample room for a host of weapons armament. When Alex had firmly refused Tatia's request to allow troopers with weapons to accompany them, she sought alternatives, and in a surprise turn of events, Tatia discovered Z was seeking her.

"While I understand our president's commitments to seek peaceful means of change, Admiral," Z said to Tatia, "the history of events surrounding him would suggest that he be accompanied by prudent protection at all times. The alternative is illogical."

"Z," Tatia said, planting a wet kiss on the side of the SADE's face, "who knew that we spoke the same language!"

"Your sentiment is taken as intended, Admiral. Allow me to show you what I have in mind."

When Z unveiled his new avatar, Tatia laughed. It was a close image of a Terran Security Forces captain she had known—a good man. "A New Terran avatar," she exclaimed. "Z, this is perfect for our little escapade." Tatia stood aside while Z sent commands to the base controller to demonstrate the defensive and offensive armament he worked into the suit.

The avatar appeared to mass as much as the Rainmaker, Little Ben, who was Harken's minister of mining. He was an enormous New Terran immigrant, who was credited with wetting the dry planet's climate by pitching ice asteroids at it with the aid of Z and a city-ship. But with its internal metal-alloy structure, Z's avatar weighed twice as much as the minister.

"Why would you build such a thing, Z?" Tatia asked, even though she heartily approved of its presence.

"As I indicated previously, Admiral, the laws of probability," Z replied. "Calculating the president's lifetime and the events of the past eleven years, it is inevitable that he requires support of this nature, frequently."

Tatia laughed at that and replied, "Load up, Z."

An envoy of House Diamanté met the Harakens at the terminal and led them underground to acquire transport. The envoy called a car and the group was soon whisked away, headed for a distant terminal. Alex glanced over at Ser Cedric Broussard, who Tatia introduced as they boarded the shuttle. Alex had requested Z's presence for the trip, but he expected the director avatar, not a mountain of a New Terran.

When the group exited the transport, the envoy led them to an expansive private lift. Once the doors slid closed, no movement was detected, and Alex raised an eyebrow at Julien.

<It's a sky-tower lift, Mr. President,> Julien sent. <The lift requires inertia compensation to balance our acceleration and deceleration. We've already attained a height of 3 kilometers and have a fourth to go.>

Several moments later, the lift doors opened, and the envoy led them down a spacious corridor, which ended in a sumptuously inlaid set of double doors. The metal-alloy doors slid apart at the group's approach, and they entered a luxurious suite with delicately decorated walls and floor coverings. Ceiling-to-floor windows exposed a vista filled with sky-towers and clouds that floated a half kilometer below them.

Four House Leaders of the Confederation paused to regard the group as they entered, and then Gino Diamanté rushed forward to greet Alex and the others followed. Introductions were quick as the Leaders were known by many of Alex's people for years—Devon O'Shea, Katarina Pasko, Bartosz Rolek, and Gino Diamanté were some of the first purchasers of Haraken's travelers. Hospitality was observed with the dispensing of food and drink.

The only Leader to be suspicious of Ser Cedric Broussard was Gino. As a frequent visitor to Haraken, Gino was intimate with Alex's inner circle, and Ser Broussard was a stranger, hardly the sort who would accompany the Haraken president to a clandestine meeting of Méridien Leaders.

After the courtesies were observed, Gino announced, "President Racine, I believe you came here to educate us. We have a holo-vid prepared for your display."

"Thank you, Leader Diamanté for organizing this meeting, and thank you all for your courage in attending," Alex said. It was a rare thing to link Méridien Leaders with a word like "courage."

Room lights dimmed, and a large holo-vid lit, displaying the start of the Shadow's vids. The Leaders gathered around it for the viewing and were soon full of questions, being unfamiliar with many of the critical points of the images they were observing.

"To help us understand what this Haraken tool has discovered, let me query Esther, my House SADE, to interpret these visuals for us," Gino said. It was prearranged by Alex and Gino to have the Leaders' questions and concerns answered by an entity whose credence Méridiens would not question.

"Good evening, Sers," Esther said, her voice emanating from the base of the holo-vid. "And a most pleasant evening to you, Julien and Z." The House Leaders were familiar with Julien's avatar, but did a double-take when Ser Broussard responded to Esther. Esther restarted the presentation, jumping from one critical image to the next. She explained to the Leaders that she possessed the New Terran colonists' records of ancient Terra and was the one who originally evaluated the UE ship's exterior and determined it hid armament.

"You will note, Sers," Esther explained, "my original suppositions have been proven correct. Most of the explorer ship's bays hold fighters, and the lower hatches in the wings conceal missile ports. These appear to be chemical rockets, but the warheads are unknown. What was unknown was the extensive number of armed troops the UE vessel carried. Z's Shadow has detailed a row of rooms containing more than forty personnel."

"But for what purpose?" Leader Bartosz Rolek asked. His House, one of the oldest in the Confederation, was responsible for their society's food production.

"As you might already be aware, we have met the Earthers on two occasions, once for a fête onboard Le Jardin and once for a . . . a demonstration onboard their ship," Alex said. "We have records of our conversation during the course of hours, but suffice it to say, the Earthers' purpose in coming here was to add any human colony they found to their United Earth."

"If we ignore them," Katarina said, "there is little they can do."

"Is that what you thought, Leader Pasko, when you first saw the Nua'll sphere?" Tatia asked.

Before Katarina could take umbrage with Tatia's provocation, Alex said, "From what we gather, the attitude of the Earthers is that all humans must be united under the UE flag, one way or another."

"During the fête, one of our young Harakens," Renée added, "questioned a second lieutenant on that same thought. What could one UE ship do? His answer was that there would soon be more."

"President Racine, do you truly think these humans would employ force against our people if we did not join their United Earth?" Devon O'Shea asked.

"Faster than you could blink," Alex replied. "It's our understanding from a UE scientist that the organization was created on Earth after what was called the Final Wars. Once the UE power was consolidated, it forcibly annexed the habitats and colonies of the Sol system and that's what they did to their own people."

"Méridiens, Harakens, and New Terrans might see themselves as related humans, but the Earthers might view us as second-class citizens," Tatia said.

"I believe, Leaders," Z said, "you are missing the primary motivation for the Earthers' actions. Perhaps that is because, as is customary for you, your thoughts are human-centric. You might wonder if the Earth has sky-towers, genetic engineering, cell-gen injections, programmable nanites, grav-drive shuttles, and mobile SADES. Based on our observations of the explorer ship, it is our opinion that at present they do not. So yes, the UE might have a great desire to annex our worlds, but it has an even greater desire to possess our technology.

"Sers," Esther added, "the UE ship and its probes have certainly witnessed some of these things. Not to mention, they have observed ships in and out of FTL transit in myriad directions. They are certainly aware that we have multiple worlds."

In the silence that followed Esther's comment, the room's entrance doors slid open and in marched Council Leader Mahima Ganesh, accompanied by five other Leaders, most notably Shannon Brixton and Albert de Guirnon. Six escorts slid through the doors behind them and fanned out along one side of the room, their stun guns drawn.

"Well, look what we have here," Mahima Ganesh sneered. "Méridien Leaders secretly meeting with Harakens."

"It's because you, Leader Ganesh, are committing the same act of stupidity as the last time the Confederation was invaded," Gino challenged.

"I will deal with you later, Leader Diamanté," Mahima hissed. "President Racine, you and your people are to come with us. You are being detained for inciting the Méridien people against the peace. You may walk or we will provide grav-lifts for your inert bodies." Mahima smiled and no one was in doubt as to which choice she preferred.

"I forbid you to treat these people in this manner, Leader Ganesh. They are my guests," Gino said, taking a step toward Mahima. He halted when two escorts trained their stun guns on him.

"You forbid me?" Mahima cried out, her voice strident. "What words are these to say to your Council Leader? I have a mind to declare you Independent, Gino Diamanté."

"No Leader has ever been declared Independent, Leader Ganesh," Bartosz exclaimed.

"Well, this might be one of those changes all of you seem so intent on welcoming to the Confederation," Mahima said, an ugly sneer on her face. "Perhaps I'll declare all of you Independents. Take the Harakens."

As the escorts deployed, the Harakens received a message, <Hit the deck now!> Without question, Alex's people obeyed. As they dived down, Mahima's six escorts were hit with small darts in the neck. During the moments the fast-acting knockout drug took effect, there was a rapid exchange of stun-gun fire across the room.

Alex came slowly back to consciousness. Due to the extremely sensitive nature of the incident, no medical personnel were called, which incensed Renée. Alex took blasts from three stun guns when he moved, not to the floor as directed, but across the two meters necessary to enfold Renée in his arms and present his back to the escorts as he pulled her to the floor. When Alex woke, he felt a cool refresher cloth on his face, and his head was cradled in Renée's lap.

When Renée saw Alex's eyes focus on her face, she sent, <I have partnered with a foolish man. Did you not think I could follow simple instructions and hit the deck? Instead, you move this wide body of yours across the floor and present yourself as an enormous target. To make matters worse, Mahima's escorts set their stun guns at maximum as ordered . . . the woman is mad!>

<Is that why it hurts?> Alex sent, groaning as he tested his limbs, which still itched and tingled.

<That and the fact that you were hit by three of them,> Renée replied. <You have made me very angry.>

<Love you,> Alex sent and grinned or tried to. It was more a grimace.

<And you, my love,> Renée sent back, and bent to kiss Alex, relief flooding through her that he was able to survive the enormous electric disruption of three stun guns set to maximum.

<Mr. President, we need your attention before this catastrophic mess gets discovered,> Tatia sent urgently.

Alex struggled up and found arms supporting his efforts. The room possessed a decidedly uneasy feel. Gino and his people were backed against the far wall and were eyeing everyone else. Mahima's six escorts were on the floor in various crumpled poses. Étienne and Alain were covering the downed escorts and the interloping Leaders with their stun guns. Alex looked around, taking a head count of his people. He came up one short. Meters away, Z's avatar of Cedric Broussard lay still on the floor, and Shannon Brixton, Leader of the House responsible for the manufacture of controllers and SADEs, was bent over the body.

Anger pumped adrenalin through Alex's body, and the unsteadiness fled his limbs as he strode toward Leader Brixton, who was poking through the exposed areas of Z's neck where blasts from the escorts' stun guns struck. The avatar's metal shell was burned and fragile connections underneath the synth-skin were destroyed. Z's head was at an odd angle and Leader Brixton was twisting it farther aside to see better into the skull.

"Fascinating," Shannon murmured before she shrieked in surprise, finding herself suspended in the air by hands that gripped her upper arms and her face only inches from the Haraken president's face, which was twisted in a snarl as if he was preparing to bite her nose off. Many Leaders, including herself, remembered their first and only meeting with the then New Terran admiral, who in their Council chambers humiliated the Council Leader with his implant powers.

"That is my friend you are desecrating, woman," Alex snarled. He received several urgent implant messages and blocked them all, and no one made a move to intervene physically, not even Renée. A line was crossed—the SADEs were special to Alex. "What if I was to start sticking my fingers inside your skull right now and begin pulling out little bits and pieces?"

"But surely you know this is a SADE, Ser President," Shannon Brixton managed to get out. Even Gino's entourage winced at that statement, realizing how much their opinions had evolved since first visiting the Harakens, who thought of their SADEs as fellow citizens and treated them as such.

"What part of the words 'my friend' did you not understand?" Alex said, while he lowered Shannon to the floor but kept a tight hold on her arms. He could feel the muscles and bones of her arms compressing under the pressure of his grip.

"My apologies, Ser President, no insult was intended. I was excited by the prospect of investigating a mobile SADE," Shannon replied.

"Take your ghoulish self and go stand by your compatriots," Alex said and gave Shannon a shove toward where Mahima and her other four Leaders stood near the room's entrance.

<Julien,> Alex sent and his friend was immediately at his side as the two examined Z's avatar. Alex gently straightened the head. That was when he noticed the tips of the avatar's right fingers and thumb were tilted down, displaying tubes in the digits. <Z fired the darts?> Alex asked privately of Julien.

<Yes, Mr. President,> Julien sent back. <Z's darts took a few moments to be effective, but the escorts will be out for several hours. Unfortunately, three of the escorts targeted him before they dropped. Flesh with its great density of water spreads the disruptor's energy field. The metal alloy under synth-skin converts the energy to heat, which burns and melts the immediate area of the strike.>

<What's his status, Julien?> Alex asked anxiously.

<Unknown, Mr. President,> Julien replied. <Under the present circumstances, all forms of communications are offline. We will have to wait until we are back aboard the *Rêveur* and provide Z with an opportunity to transfer to another avatar to communicate with us.>

<Stay with him, Julien,> Alex said, patting Z's chest gently before he rose and turned to Mahima and her people.

Alex walked slowly past the Leaders who accompanied Mahima, locking eyes with each one. They shrank from the anger they saw in his face. Only Albert stared haughtily at Alex, pleased to see him hurt, but that expression faded when Alex stopped in front of Renée's brother and continued to stare at him, as if he were examining an insect, until Albert glanced away.

Alex never wanted to hurt someone as much as he did Clayton Downing, the criminal former president of New Terra, when his people killed Lieutenant Hatsuto Tanaka, but here he was again. *You are fortunate, woman, that my people are more important to me than my hatred of you,* Alex thought. "All of you," Alex directed Mahima and the Leaders, "take a seat around the holo-vid. We have a show for your entertainment." When the Leaders glanced nervously at Mahima, waiting for her approval, Alex said with a nasty smile, "Or we can provide grav-lifts to move your inert bodies." The five Leaders deserted Mahima and scurried to take seats around the holo-vid. Mahima continued to glare at Alex until both Étienne and Alain raised their stun guns and pointed them at her. With a scowl she joined the others.

<We missed our opportunity,> Alain sent privately to Étienne.

<Patience, my brother, that woman will surely offer us another one. She can't help herself,> Étienne replied, and the twins shared secret grins.

Alex introduced the vid, and, as it played, Esther augmented the visuals with explanations. The change in the room's atmosphere was subtle but relentless. The more imagery of the *Reunion* that was displayed, the more questions the new Leaders asked, and the more questions they asked, the more Gino's people engaged them, debating the information. At Shannon Brixton's request, the vid was played a second time. There was a bright mind behind the centuries-old face, and she was a close associate of Katarina Pasko. The two debated fine points about the information.

Julien replayed several snippets of conversation from their communication with the Earthers, adding to the supposition that the explorer ship was nothing of the kind and its mission commander's intentions did not bode well for the Confederation.

"Council Leader," Albert de Guirnon said, "we would seek your thoughts on this matter."

Mahima, who hadn't said a single word during the entire time the vid was played and discussed, focused on Alex as she said, "These people are prevaricators. Who knows what trick they are foisting on us and toward what end?"

If this was Haraken or New Terra, there would have been objections, even outcries, but this was Méridien and the Leaders kept their counsel. There were enough breaks from tradition this evening to have filled a decade.

"Are we free to go, Haraken?" Mahima said, staring icily at Alex. When Alex nodded, Mahima got up and strode to the room's entrance, noticing that only one Leader followed her, Albert. She spun around, glaring at the others. When they made no move to follow, Mahima stomped out.

The awkward silence that followed was broken by Emilio Torres, House Leader responsible for the life records of Confederation citizens. "Leader Diamanté, would you request your SADE transfer these records to my House SADE?" Emilio asked.

"Or you could request that directly of me, Leader Torres," Esther replied.

When Gino simply raised an eyebrow at Emilio, the Leader repeated his request to Esther. The other Leaders quickly followed Emilio's lead, requesting the same of Esther, surprised at the level of autonomy Leader Diamanté allowed his House SADE.

Alex listened to the Leaders requesting copies of the recording. The Shadow was an ingenious little tool invented on the spur of the moment by Z. Alex tried not to think about Z's condition or if they failed to retrieve him from this avatar. For now, it was enough that eight House Leaders were requesting the *Reunion* information despite Leader Ganesh's disapproval. It was his hope that they would share the Shadow's intelligence with others. *The revolution has begun,* Alex thought.

Gino joined Alex, who was standing over Z's body, informing him that a grav-pallet was ordered for Z. "Do you know his condition, Ser President," Gino asked.

"Undetermined, I'm afraid," Alex replied.

"Would your SADEs have foreseen a tragic event such as this and made alternate arrangements, if you will?" Gino asked. His emotions were a roiling mix that his Méridien upbringing found difficult to control. That the Council Leader would have brought armed escorts to a meeting of Leaders and fired on his guests was unconscionable, and his own guilt raged that he was the one to ask for Alex's help, which resulted in this unimaginable situation.

Alex glanced over Gino's shoulders at the group of Leaders standing around the holo-vid. "The Haraken SADEs are a resourceful group of individuals," Alex said, laying a comradely hand on Gino's shoulders. Alex didn't want to discuss the SADEs' capabilities in present company, and Gino was placated by Alex's response.

Alex took Gino's arm and steered him back to the other Leaders. "I have a final thought for you. Trouble is coming, and I don't see it going away. This time, we aren't talking about a single alien sphere; we're talking about an entire solar system of humans. They are war capable, and they're coming for you and all the bounty you represent. I suggest you start getting your House in order as fast as you can."

Several Leaders were confused by Alex's reference to a single House and privately queried Gino, who explained that the president was referring to the House of the Confederation—the Council.

Gino's envoy arrived with a sufficiently sized grav-pallet to transport Z's avatar. A path was cleared by hauling Mahima's unconscious escorts out of the way, and it required Alex, Tatia, and the twins to load Z's avatar onto the pallet.

<I would speak with you, President Racine,> Alex heard as his people began filing out of the room. Shannon Brixton walked up to him and waited respectfully.

"Why did you come to this meeting?" Alex asked. He could see his question caught her off guard, but he needed to know how Leader Ganesh was manipulating her people.

"We were told individuals were fomenting discontent among our people, advocating an aggressive response to the UE ship. Leader Ganesh did not disclose that Harakens were involved and that you led them," Shannon replied.

"Would it have made any difference?" Alex asked.

"It was our duty to support our Council Leader," Shannon replied, her voice trailing off.

"Copying that vid to study it and possibly distribute it does not seem supportive of your Council Leader," Alex challenged.

"Major changes have always been viewed as disturbing to order, but recent history appears to argue that view is incorrect," Shannon acknowledged.

Alex regarded Shannon's face, attempting to read the thoughts behind her words. "You wanted to speak to me, Leader Brixton," Alex reminded her.

"Yes, Ser President, I must admit that your view of SADEs and mine, which has been cultivated during the past century of work in my House, are significantly different. As such, I see that I did not treat your SADE with proper respect," Shannon admitted.

"When you say 'my SADE,' Leader Brixton, I'm not sure I take your meaning," Alex replied.

"While I'm not sure of your arrangement, I would suppose your SADEs are responsible to someone or to an organization, you or the Haraken government," Shannon replied confidently.

"Leader Brixton," Alex said in exasperation, "your Council Leader's escorts might have just murdered a Haraken citizen—a free and independent entity—who is responsible to no one but himself. Think on that." Alex whirled and marched out of the room, leaving a surprised Leader behind.

Shannon Brixton was worried. She wasn't too concerned about misunderstanding the relationship of a SADE to the president and his people. After all, they were Harakens—oddities were expected. No, what concerned her was that President Racine considered the SADE a potential murder victim. Shannon regretted she hadn't delivered a more sincere apology. It also seemed prudent to rethink her supportive position of Council Leader Ganesh, who seemed intent on distancing herself from the Confederation's Leaders and making an enemy of the Haraken president.

15

Aboard the *Rêveur*, Alex accompanied Z's avatar to engineering. Mickey waited for Julien outside of Z's cabin with a grav-sled. Julien was needed to override Z's locking encryption on the cabin.

The cabin door slid open, and the tech pulling the grav-sled into the room looked around and stumbled to a halt, the grav-sled threatening to knock him over. Mickey and the crew stared at the two avatars laid out on the beds—two anatomically perfect, naked avatars of Z's bank director and Miranda Leyton.

"Jump to it, crewmen," Mickey demanded. "We want the bank director." Four of them hoisted the avatar onto the grav-sled, and Mickey grabbed a bunk coverlet to drape over Z's avatar. "Let's move!" he shouted.

Normally, Z would transfer his kernel between avatars via comm protocols and hardwire connections. Even though Cedric's crystal-brain was housed in his chest for security's sake, his visual, auditory, vocal, and balance senses were situated in his head and, unfortunately, so was his comms connection. With his kernel trapped in a nearly decapitated body, it was impossible for Z to initiate the transfer.

In engineering, the two avatars were placed side by side, and Julien directed the engineering team to deploy the transfer controller. The physical connections they needed for Cedric's avatar were located in the back of the neck, and it took several hours for the team to rebuild the required links for the controller.

When the controller and connections were finally in place, Julien initiated the transfer. The room waited in silence until Julien announced, "Transfer complete."

The director's eyes blinked once, then twice. Humans and SADE alike waited quietly. Then Z's eyes focused and traveled the faces hovering over him. "Greetings, Ser President. Were we successful? Was anyone seriously injured?" The room broke out in applause, and Z sat up, his covering dropping to his waist.

"Everything worked out fine, Z. We're glad to have you back," Alex said, slapping Z on the shoulder.

Renée leaned over Z and kissed his cheek. "Welcome back, Z. We were so worried for you," she whispered.

Z had witnessed thousands of exchanges among humans and even between Julien and Cordelia, but had never received a kiss himself. <My first kiss, Julien,> Z sent privately.

<How did it make you feel, Z?> Julien asked.

<That is difficult to discern. At this moment, my fundamental response is one of joy . . . I'm happy to have survived to be able to receive one,> Z replied.

"That was quite the gambit, Z. What made you initiate action on your own?" Alex asked.

"Was I wrong to do so, Ser President?" Z asked.

"Negative, Z. If the Council Leader detained us, there would have been no one to stand up to the Earthers."

"I must admit, Ser President, I found my actions a surprise myself," Z replied. "I believe searching with the Swei Swee has taught me about swift, decisive action to accomplish tactical goals. I reasoned that our people's protection is predicated on your directions, which requires you be free from detention. The Council Leader's action would have negated your freedom and that required curtailing. So I initiated an offense."

"Well done, Z," Mickey declared, laughing, and slapping Z's shoulder, the sting from the hard contact with the metal alloy sheathing under the synth-skin traveling up his arm. "I would have loved to have seen that."

"Allow me to share, Mickey," Julien said and transferred his recording of the event to Mickey. He also copied Z, who appreciated retrieving the lost moments.

<The president appears most disturbed by the condition of my avatar and Leader Brixton's investigation,> Z sent privately to Julien after reviewing the event.

<That is as it should be, Z. You might need to dwell on this later,> Julien replied.

"Darts from fingertips," Mickey said after reviewing the initial images. "I love it. What else can your avatar do, Z?" Mickey asked.

"I would be pleased to demonstrate its attributes, Engineer Brandon, if you would care to help in its repair," Z said.

Alex and Julien left Mickey and Z, who wrapped his coverlet around his waist, to examine the damaged avatar. Z was happily describing the offensive tools built into it.

<That was a close one, Julien,> Alex sent.

<Do you refer to our near imprisonment or Z's near demise?> Julien asked.

<I would say both, Julien, but especially Z's survival,> Alex replied.

<It would appear by the cheers of the crew, who have been informed of Z's resurrection, that our society is reaching a new level of maturity,> Julien said. When Alex eyed him, he continued. <Our people now regard the loss of a SADE as great a tragedy as they would any Haraken.>

* * *

On Méridien, subterfuge—an uncommon word in the Confederation—was becoming the order of the day for a small group of Leaders. Council Leader Mahima Ganesh had a great many followers or rather she had many who feared her power. Nothing she did was overt enough to contradict Council law, but she had ways of pressuring a House whose Leader went against her wishes.

The eight Leaders, whose eyes Alex opened with the Shadow's vids and the recordings of conversation with the UE principals, adopted different means of reaching out to their associates. Most opted for one-on-one meetings to carefully control the environment and the delivery of their message, but their success was limited by the nature of the meetings, secretive and a limited audience. Many of the invitees feared the meeting request was a test of loyalty orchestrated by Leader Ganesh.

In contrast Katarina Pasko threw small dinner parties. She invited intimate friends and a few Leaders, telling her guests that some unusual entertainment would be provided. Once her guests were satiated, they gathered around a holo-vid. Katarina turned the viewing into a parlor game, asking her guests to guess the location of the images and identify the items they saw. There were various levels of success but none were significant. So at the end of the vid, the guests were always anxious to have the mystery revealed by Katarina. Once she explained where the vid was taken and who took it, several guests would hastily depart, but many more would stay to hear more.

During the past twenty years, Katarina Pasko found her faith in the supremacy of the Confederation slowly eroding. It began with the inexorable encroachment of the Nua'll, and her Council's failure to take action. During the decades, she admired Gino Diamanté's quiet call for intervention, but few supported him against Leader Ganesh's firm stance of no action. When Katarina accepted Gino's invitation nine years ago to visit Haraken and view the new grav-drive shuttles, she told herself it was an opportunity to discover the secrets of Alex's implant control, but her curiosity was rebuffed by Alex. Despite that, she returned frequently with Gino to visit Haraken and soon discovered she made the trips as much for his company as for business. That her House prospered due to the acquisition of Haraken technology was a definite plus even though it earned her Leader Ganesh's enmity.

Initially, Katarina expected Alex to decry everything about the Confederation, but his honest evaluation, strengths and weaknesses, of her culture intrigued her. Throughout the years, she and Alex developed a mutual respect. And, against all logic, Katarina became friends with Renée. The four of them, Alex, Renée, Gino, and she, spent hours sitting in the cliff-top rotunda, watching the Swei Swee at work and play, while they talked about many things, especially their hopes and dreams for the future of their societies. In time, the last veils obscuring the weaknesses of Confederation society were removed from her eyes.

16

Suddenly, Méridien FTL comms were overloaded as they hadn't been since the relay of the emergency broadcast of the annihilation of the Cetus colony by the Nua'll nearly half a lifetime ago. Reports came in first from ships entering the system, then from outposts on outer planets, and finally from the orbital platforms—a massive ship was entering the Méridien system. The only good tiding was the ship wasn't a giant sphere, which meant the invading Nua'll, who destroyed so many Confederation colonies, hadn't returned.

Gino requested an immediate audience with Council Leader Ganesh. He was surprised that it was accepted and hurried to meet with Mahima in her office at Confederation Hall.

"Did you come to apologize, Diamanté?" Mahima asked, foregoing a proper greeting when Gino entered her office.

"And here I was hoping you had come to your senses, Council Leader Ganesh," Gino replied smoothly. "It appears we will both be disappointed. I presume you have received word of the strange ship that has entered the system."

"I'm kept well informed, Leader Diamanté, of all things," Mahima replied, her hard stare underlying her message.

"And are you aware that the new ship is communicating exclusively via a directed beam with the Earther explorer ship?" Gino asked. Mahima's mask slipped slightly, and Gino knew he surprised her. He was angry that she was unable to stay on top of the critical issues, but this was not the time to add to the animosity between them. "Have you asked Winston for his evaluation of the ship?"

"How would that be of value?" Mahima asked.

"Esther has shared the New Terran's historical Terran records with Winston. The records detail much of the Earth's ancient military history.

The SADEs have preliminary telemetry and have already made some shocking discoveries," Gino replied.

"You come to me with statements detailing the improper influence of those Harakens on our SADEs, and you expect me to accept that they are adding value to the Confederation? We have stood for centuries in peace and prosperity, and, if we maintain our path, we will continue to do so. All that you are doing is allowing a disease to enter a healthy body. Be careful, Gino Diamanté. Your House might not support your direction, and if it doesn't, I will see to it a new Diamanté Leader is appointed."

"So I take it that you have not reviewed Winston's evaluation of the new ship," Gino replied calmly.

"We are done here. You may leave," Mahima said, ignoring the courtesies and scowling at Gino as he left her office.

As Gino walked the majestic corridors of Confederation Hall, his thoughts focused on Mahima Ganesh. *It's time for you to go, old woman, before you destroy us all.*

* * *

On the *Rêveur*'s bridge, Alex and his senior staff surrounded the holo-vid, examining the vids gathered by Méridien vessels, which passed the immense winged-ship as it entered the system. Winston received the Méridien vessels' telemetry and passed it to Esther with the intention that she would share the information with Julien and Z. The SADEs were collaborating despite the Council Leader's strictures against communicating with the Harakens, and each one of them was postulating what life would be like if the Confederation fell under Earther control. Their greatest fear was that the Earthers wouldn't recognize artificial intelligences as legal citizens.

"Black space, that's a big ship!" Tatia declared. "Are those dimensions correct?" When Julien arched an eyebrow at her, Tatia retreated. "Sorry, Julien, it's just that the numbers are hard to believe."

"I understand, Admiral," Julien replied. "They are as incredible as they are accurate."

"Why the same design as the explorer ship?" Mickey wondered out loud. "A longitudinal shape would seem more practical. Instead, it's a similar wing shape . . . just a damn sight bigger."

The ship's wings exhibited five decks along its front edges. Three decks were each the same height as the explorer ship's single wing and were dotted with bay doors. What the group understood to be fighter bays occupied the top, center, and bottom levels, alternating with two smaller decks between them. In addition, where the explorer ship possessed one central fuselage, this ship had three, the center one having the greater diameter and length. Its overall wingspan was four times that of the explorer ship.

"This general shape would indicate an engineering limitation," said Z, who was utilizing his director's avatar. "The foreshortened bow-to-aft length might allude to drive-system problems or FTL transition. The probabilities favor the latter.

"Julien, what is the telemetry on the ship's velocity?" Tatia asked.

"The ship entered the system at 0.48c, Admiral, and began decelerating soon after," Julien replied.

"That far out? Are they heading for any of the outer planets?" Tatia asked.

"It does not appear so, Admiral," Julien replied. "The vessel altered course toward the explorer ship as soon as it entered the system. I have no explanation as to why it is dropping its velocity at this rate."

"They're distrustful," Alex said, and all eyes regarded him. "They expect armed resistance so they aren't hurrying into the system blindly."

"Armed resistance from whom?" Renée asked. "Surely Speaker García informed them that he has met no resistance."

"Old habits, I would say," Alex replied. "Look at that ship. What do any of you see?"

"Ancient Terran records would call that a 'battleship,' Ser President," Julien replied.

"Affirmative—a ship designed and built for war," Z added.

"Pardon the questioning of an old captain, Ser President, but whom were the Earthers warring with?" José Cordova asked.

"Other humans, Captain," Tatia answered, shaking her head in disgust.

"From what we've gathered, Earth went to war with the human enclaves in Sol's outer system," Alex added. "We don't have many details, except that Administrator Wombo referred to the process as 'the pacification of the outer colonies.'"

"And such a ship was needed to pacify the colonies? Perhaps Earthers have a different definition of pacification than I do," Captain Cordova said, his voice trailing off as he ruminated on his thoughts.

"Ser President, telemetry indicates there is considerable comm traffic between the two Earther ships," Z said.

"What are they saying?" Alex asked.

"Unknown, Ser," Z replied. "The ships are employing a type of direct-beam communication to prevent interception of their messages."

"Another indication of a suspicious nature," Tatia said to no one in particular.

"So what do we do?" Renée asked.

"Good question," Alex admitted. "I think the first move belongs to whoever is in charge of that warship. In the meantime, Julien, we have some messages to prepare for our people and New Terra." While Julien retired with Alex to his cabin, the others continued to stare at the images of the vessel Julien referred to as a battleship.

* * *

"Speaker García, I require an update on the status of your contact with the local government," High Judge Patricio Bunaldi said perfunctorily. He was standing in camera view with Admiral Samara Theostin and Captain Dimitri Chofsky on the command bridge aboard the battleship *Hand of Justice*.

Aboard the *Reunion*'s much smaller bridge, Speaker García, Captain Lumley, and Major Barbas also stood in camera view, waiting on the pleasure of their masters. The moment the *Hand of Justice* entered the system, Admiral Theostin assumed command control over Captain Lumley and the *Reunion*. Also, Speaker García fell under the auspices of High Judge Bunaldi, but then every UE individual in this system reported directly or indirectly to the high judge. There were only three more levels of power above Bunaldi to reach United Earth's Supreme Tribunal.

"The local people refer to themselves as Méridiens, Judge Bunaldi," Speaker García replied. "When our conversation is concluded, we will send the imagery we have collected since arriving in system. At this time, I draw your attention to the incredible amount of FTL ship traffic, which you have probably already noticed. Most exciting, Judge Bunaldi, we have encountered several varieties of humans."

"Varieties of humans?" Bunaldi said. "Explain."

"You will see from the images, Judge Bunaldi," García replied. "This world appears to be populated by a slender people. There is a second variety of individuals who must have developed on a heavy world through the centuries. Both the men and women have significant mass. Then there are other individuals who have proportions nearer our own."

"Do any of these individuals appear subhuman or grotesque in any fashion?" Bunaldi asked. He suffered from nightmares that one day he would discover a lost human colony that transitioned so far from the norms of the human race that rather than choosing to bring them into the UE fold, he would feel compelled to obliterate the abominations.

"On the contrary, Judge Bunaldi," García explained, "we have surmised that the Méridiens have mastered genetic modeling techniques. Their people are visually arresting . . . even compelling, one might say." Images of Renée de Guirnon flitted through García's mind.

"And your response to my original question, Speaker García," Bunaldi reminded him.

"Of course, Judge," García said, dipping his head contritely. "Although we have met some locals, we have not been able to arrange a meeting with Council Leader Mahima Ganesh. Supposedly this woman is head of what is termed the Confederation Council. We believe the term 'Confederation' applies to a conglomeration of multiple worlds, which agrees with the constant FTL traffic in multiple directions to and from this system."

Admiral Theostin and High Judge Bunaldi exchanged the briefest of glances and the slightest of smiles. Their ship was on rotation outside the Sol system, an interminably boring tour of duty, when the orders came to respond to the *Reunion*'s call for support for a 'significant find.' The initial report they were receiving from Speaker García indicated that his discovery was much more than a significant find. Both the admiral and the high judge were driven by political aspirations, and subsuming a confederation of worlds would propel them up the UE political and military ladders.

"While you have uncovered a great find, Speaker García, I'm disappointed that more progress hasn't been made establishing relations with the local government," Bunaldi admonished. "We will rendezvous with you in seven days. I expect progress by then."

"Yes, Judge Bunaldi," García replied, wanting to grind his teeth. Bunaldi knew it wasn't a speaker's place to force contact. The high judge, who stood there in his white, floor-length robe, with red collar and red buttons down the robe's length, and a shaved head that added to his stern expression, was posturing. But García was well aware of the high judge's reputation. He was a true believer—the UE way was the only salvation for the human race.

"Captain Lumley," Admiral Samara Theostin said, "the original message made no mention of the extent of a military force in this system. Was that an omission?"

"As of this moment—" Barbas began to reply, but he was abruptly cut off.

"Major Barbas, I believe I was speaking to Captain Lumley," Admiral Theostin replied, tilting up her sharp-nosed, dark-eyed face imperiously. "Have you been so long away from home that you've forgotten protocols?"

Major Barbas was grateful he stood in his usual military stance with his hands behind his back. His meaty hands were twisting together, and his thoughts dwelt on ringing the admiral's slender neck.

The pecking order is being reestablished, Major. Get used to it, Antonio thought.

"In the entire time we have been here, Admiral Theostin," Captain Lumley replied, "we've seen no indication of military power. None of the ships show a configuration that would suggest armament. We've seen no fighters, and in the few personal contacts we've had, we've not even seen personal weapons."

"Admiral Theostin, if I may?" Major Barbas asked.

"Proceed, Major," Theostin allowed.

"We did arrange a contest with some of the locals, Admiral. They are a group of people who exhibit the human varieties of which was spoken," Barbas said. "We sought to engage the leader, one of the heavy worlders, but he volunteered his escort . . . I mean his security person, who is one of the slender variety."

"What sort of contest?" Bunaldi asked.

"Hand-to-hand combat, Judge Bunaldi," García replied. "Our meeting with this group aboard the orbital platform called Le Jardin uncovered too many oddities in their stories and presentation. The Major and I thought the heavy worlders might represent their military. So we arranged a contest to test our suspicions."

"A clever ruse, Speaker," Bunaldi said. "What did you discover?"

The Speaker nodded toward Major Barbas to continue. "I arranged for one of the leader's security personnel, Ser de Long, to practice with Master Sergeant Hinsdale. He is our unarmed combat instructor. The contest escalated into a full-blown match and a prolonged one at that. Then suddenly it was over and the master sergeant was down."

"So you learned that these escorts are highly trained security people and an even match for our trained personnel," Theostin said. On a hand signal from the high judge, the admiral ceased her comments.

"I detect doubt in your tone, Major," Bunaldi said.

"Yes, Judge Bunaldi," Barbas replied. "I believe Ser de Long was stalling and could have defeated the master sergeant at any time. When the escort ended the match, he was incredibly fast. Master Sergeant Hinsdale reported never seeing an individual move so quickly after such a sustained level of combat, and he felt the escort was holding back the entire time."

"So your locals were testing you, were they not, Major?" Bunaldi asked.

"We believe their participation in the contest was merely an excuse, Judge Bunaldi," Barbas replied. "During the performance, if you will, our guide detected an internal foreign signal, local to the ship. Soon after the signal was transmitted, the contest ended."

"Ah . . ." said Bunaldi, bringing his hand to his chin, the first movement he had allowed himself during the interview. He was a master of the art of utter stillness. It gave him the air of something other than human, which unsettled those he questioned before he passed judgment on them.

"I presume you discovered the source of the signal and arrested the perpetrators," Theostin said.

"Unfortunately, the signal was both quick and faint. Our guide indicated it originated below our flight deck between a missile room and our fuselage," García replied. "We instigated an exhaustive search for three days and never located the signal source. Also, it is only our conjecture that the signal was meant for these individuals. They displayed no comm equipment at any time while they were on our ship, and they were brought to the ship by our shuttle."

"So while you were shopping the locals, they were shopping you," Bunaldi said, and allowed himself a brief chuckle. "So these people are not without an element of deviousness, and obviously they have some unique tech that can observe, transmit, and remain hidden. Tech that will be our pleasure to acquire." Bunaldi resumed his stance, tucking his hands behind him again. "I expect results with the local government, Speaker García. Make it happen. Send your data immediately." Before the speaker was allowed to reply, the *Hand of Justice* comms officer cut the transmission. It was the manner in which the high judge preferred to end communications—having the last word.

* * *

Seated in a comfortable chair in Bunaldi's well-decorated state room, Samara Theostin sipped a cup of fine wine from the high judge's special store. Her jacket was off and her bare feet were resting on a covered footstool. The admiral and the high judge were celebrating. They spent hours reviewing the *Reunion*'s images and associated data and could not believe their good fortune—not a single struggling colony, but a conglomeration of worlds—not a low-tech society, but one exploding with advanced technology. The two sat and threw the points of discovery back and forth, celebrating each item, as if they were in some sort of sporting match, tossing the ball back and forth. By now the bottle of wine was nearing the end, and, despite the alcoholic glow, thoughts were sobering.

"And no military force, Patricio" Theostin said. "What a pity! We brought all this armament, and we might not have an opportunity to use any of it."

"You get ahead of yourself, Samara," Bunaldi said. "What was relayed to us was that no military or overt weaponry were yet discovered. There is no proof that none exists, and, with their tech, it could be in plain sight and we might not even be aware of it."

Theostin acknowledged Bunaldi's point with a nod. She took a long sip of the delicious wine and flexed her long, slender, bare feet, partially in enjoyment of the wine and partially for Bunaldi's benefit. Although they had been together for years and both were middle-aged, Bunaldi had never invited her to his bed, not that she would have been delighted to go, but she would have made the effort. Her preferences tended more toward young female lieutenants. It was only been through pure circumstances one evening while relaxing with the high judge that she discovered his preference. She had removed her boots and socks to massage sore feet, and he had offered to help. Then the high judge spent the better part of an hour, massaging her feet with soothing oil. Initially, she was concerned for his intentions, but once she accepted that he was focused on his ministrations and intended nothing else, she found herself on the receiving end of an exquisite foot massage. Since then they often celebrated their successes in Bunaldi's stateroom with wine and bare feet.

17

Standing on the *Reunion*'s bridge beside Captain Lumley, Speaker García and Major Barbas came to the conclusion that any action to further contact with the locals was better than no action, even if the results were less than auspicious. Captain Lumley held no such belief but wisely kept his mouth shut. The *Reunion*'s guide had tracked the *Rêveur*'s exit from the Le Jardin platform as it took up a position in orbit around the next planet outward.

"We're ready, Captain," García said.

Captain Lumley nodded to the comms officer, who activated a request to the guide. Shortly, the monitor revealed the image of Captain Cordova, his face and shoulders filling the screen.

"Captain Cordova, we would speak with Ser Racine, please," García requested.

"One moment, Speaker García. I will see if Ser is available," Captain Cordova replied and blanked the comm signal, but kept the connection. "Are you available, Ser President?" José asked Alex, who stood next to him with Tatia. They were examining the newest telemetry data of the UE battleship on the holo-vid.

Alex cocked an eyebrow at Tatia. Both of them wore in standard Haraken dress as president and admiral.

"Maybe it's time to stop playing games, Mr. President," Tatia said. "With the arrival of this battleship, they're definitely displaying their intent. Besides, who knows what we might find out?"

Alex nodded his agreement and faced the forward vid pickup. Tatia took a position beside him, straightening her uniform jacket. When they were ready, Alex cued the controller to resume broadcast of the *Rêveur*'s signal.

"Ah . . . Sers Racine and Tachenko, there you are. Is this another costume change or should I address you in some other fashion?" García asked.

"I remain Ser Racine, Speaker García, but allow me to introduce Admiral Tachenko," Alex replied.

"If I may inquire?" Barbas interjected. "Admiral of what?"

"How may I help you, Speaker García?" Alex answered instead.

"I'm sure you've seen the entry of our compatriots' ship into this system, Ser Racine—"

"Interesting that you bring a battleship to a supposed diplomatic first contact," Alex said, interrupting the speaker.

"Ah, yes . . . I also appreciate the elimination of pretense, Ser Racine. I myself am a blunt man and prefer a frank conversation. So now you understand the power that the UE can bring to bear to enforce its wishes," García replied. "If you wish to preserve the diplomatic process, you must arrange a meeting for me with this so-called Confederation Council."

"Unfortunately, Speaker García, I have no leverage with the Council Leader. In fact, I am not in her favor, at all," Alex replied.

"Imagine that, Ser Racine. Someone else dislikes you," Major Barbas shot back. "We are quite aware of the deception you perpetrated when you came aboard our ship."

"And we dislike people pretending to hold out a welcoming hand while holding a weapon behind their back. It makes us extremely distrustful . . . and nervous," Alex said, his body tensing and his hands slowly curling into fists.

"Well, Ser Racine, if you are of no value to us, then I must go knock on the door myself," García replied.

"That would be quite imprudent of you, Speaker García," Tatia said. "You might start something that you can't finish."

"This from an admiral of an invisible force," Barbas retorted.

"You appear to be imaginative individuals if you believe your tech can match the Méridiens on any subject," Alex said, hoping to bluff the Earthers.

"What we lack in sophistication, Ser Racine, we make up for in sheer power. The *Hand of Justice* has enough armament to bring any world to its knees," Speaker García replied. Both he and the major had visibly straightened at the mention of the UE's power.

"You named that battleship the *Hand of Justice*?" Tatia asked, working hard to restrain her laughter. "You don't find that ironic, Speaker García?"

"It's foolish of you, Admiral, to doubt our power," Barbas fired back. His anger was growing by the minute, and he ached to teach the admiral a lesson.

"Are you so certain of this, Speaker García, that you would risk the annihilation of your people?" Alex asked.

"Annihilation of whom, Ser Racine?" García replied. "We've seen no evidence of your military other than that costume worn by your associate."

Alex quickly signaled Tatia to maintain control, but he needn't have worried. A slight smile was permanently fixed to her face.

"I should warn you, Ser Racine, in the event that you are able to communicate with the Confederation Council or the Council Leader. High Judge Bunaldi aboard the *Hand of Justice* will not be as patient as I have been," García replied. Then he signaled with his hand to the comms officer to cut the transmission.

<Julien, Z, monitor that UE explorer ship. I want to know the instant that thing or its shuttles move,> Alex sent.

* * *

Speaker García and Major Barbas boarded a UE tactical assault shuttle along with twenty, fully armed militia. The high judge's firm request for contact with the local government was taken as a warning and not a request. UE underlings were often demoted or dismissed for failing to follow the wishes of their superiors.

"Time for diplomacy is over, Major," García announced when Ser Racine failed to assist them with brokering a meeting. "It's time to break down some doors. Find me a target, Major."

Major Barbas consulted Captain Lumley, who with the assistance of his officers and guide, located the source of the Council's broadcast signals, which emanated from a collection of buildings surrounded by extensive gardens, one of the few building complexes that was built low to the ground.

"It is my officers' conjecture that this complex is one of the older constructions on Méridien, and they suppose it to be the Council's meeting location. About 4.6 kilometers away is a terminal that can accommodate our tactical shuttles," Lumley said.

* * *

<Ser President, Admiral, a shuttle has launched from the explorer ship. Its destination is Méridien airspace,> Z sent.

<Admiral, Julien, and Z—meet me on the bridge immediately,> Alex sent back.

On the bridge, the four gathered around the holo-vid. Julien and Z were overlaying several telemetry sources to determine the UE shuttle's precise trajectory and estimate its ultimate destination.

"Ser President, the shuttle is making for the terminal nearest Confederation Hall," Julien announced.

"Will you look at that?" Tatia said with exaggeration. "The speaker is trying to force a meeting with the Council. Now how original a concept is that?" When Tatia received a dirty look from Alex, she burst out laughing.

Alex considered whether or not he should interfere with the shuttle's flight and, in the meantime, began pacing the bridge. A favorite pastime of his close associates ensued. Tatia, Julien, and Z offered small favors as bets to determine how much time it would take Alex to hatch a plan. The time started with Alex's first paced step and ended with his first word, oral or comm.

"Julien, get me Devon O'Shea," Alex ordered. Devon was the House Leader responsible for planetside terminals and transportation.

Tatia and Z commiserated. Julien won as he often did, which didn't stop the other two from trying to beat him. Apparently Julien was the better judge of his friend's thought processes.

Devon O'Shea was conversing with House associates when Alex's comm came through. <Greetings, President Racine. The events disturbing the Confederation appear to be escalating, are they not?> Devon sent back.

<More so than you would believe, Leader O'Shea,> Alex sent. <A UE shuttle is headed for Lemuel Terminal. Based on the conversation I recently had with Speaker García, there is every possibility that he is aboard and that he has military-armed personnel with him.

<What would they accomplish landing on Méridien, Ser President?> Devon replied. <Without implants, they won't be able to even slide aside our terminal doors.>

<We have met the Earthers twice, Leader O'Shea. Please believe me when I tell you that they are not above forcing your people to get the access they require.> Alex said.

Devon considered Alex's message and decided he didn't want to be responsible for failing to protect his people. Too many grievous mistakes had been made in the name of abeyance. <What do you recommend, President Racine?>

<We haven't much time, Leader O'Shea. The shuttle is only 0.45 hours out. I would like you to connect me with the Lemuel Terminal manager and order him to follow my directions,> Alex sent.

<As you request, Ser President, but please be aware it is the same individual who was present nine years ago when you made your own unscheduled visit to our planet,> Devon replied.

Of course, it would be, Alex thought with chagrin, recalling the manager's outrage about Alex's unauthorized shuttle landing.

<Ser Quinlan, we are linked with President Racine. I request you follow his directions implicitly and immediately. Apparently, you have an impending visit from an Earther shuttle, which might have armed personnel aboard and whose leader is intent on forcing his way into the terminal,> Devon sent.

<It will be as you wish, Leader. I'm sure President Racine's advice will be invaluable. After all, he has extensive experience in these matters,> Orso Quinlan quipped.

Tatia, who was linked into the comm as was Z, rolled her eyes at Orso's comment. Devon's comm closed, but Julien maintained their link to Ser Quinlan.

<It appears I'm at your pleasure . . . again, Ser President,> Orso sent with resignation.

<I will try to make this as painless as possible for you, Ser Quinlan,> Alex replied. <We believe the United Earth shuttle that is about to descend on your terminal will be attempting to force a meeting with the Council. Their leader, Speaker García, is under pressure from his superior to make contact with Council Leader Ganesh. To achieve their goal, they will force Méridien citizens to aid them.>

<If I pull all citizens inside and deny them access to our terminal, do you think they would attempt to force their way in?> Orso replied. Uncertainty wove through his thoughts.

<Ser Quinlan, I am Z, a Haraken SADE. I give it a 78 percent probability that the Earthers will employ force to enter the terminal and will abduct Méridien citizens to enable them to reach Confederation Hall.>

May the stars protect us, thought Orso, who was so shaken by the concept that his thought leaked through his comm.

<We haven't much time, Ser Quinlan,> Alex sent. <I would urge you to evacuate the entire terminal. Do not allow your citizens to order and wait for transport cars. Order as many cars as you require. When one arrives, fill it full and send it anywhere. Do this until you empty the terminal—passengers, workers, and management—everyone. Then open the terminal's access doors so Speaker García and his people may explore the terminal at their leisure. Most important, when the last car is filled, order your controller to block any transport cars from stopping at the terminal until further notice. Please move quickly!> Alex ordered.

Alex's final words caused Orso to jump out of his chair even though the next thing he had to do was sit back down and begin issuing orders to his controller. He declared a terminal emergency, which authorized him to direct the transport cars as he needed and evacuate the premises. Workers came in from the landing zones, ushering passengers and shuttle crews back inside. One shuttle, a traveler, was cleared for takeoff and was allowed to leave. It rose swiftly and silently, quickly clearing the airspace. Citizens received evacuation directives from the terminal's controller and moved to obey. The procession of people to the lower levels was orderly and civilized—they depended on the Confederation to ensure their safety. Transport cars arrived. People aboard the cars were informed of the emergency and made room for those exiting the terminal, filling the transports to their limits.

Z linked into the controller's vid security system and kept running displays on the *Rêveur*'s bridge screens of the terminal's interiors, dedicating a portion of the left vid screen to a view of the terminal's landing fields. People filled the lifts, descending to the transport levels, when the exterior vid cam showed the Earther shuttle landing. Alex and his people were surprised that the shuttle did not require the runway. It came perilously close to the terminal and the pilot transitioned smoothly from primary engine power to enormous fans, located in the shuttle's stubby wings, directing their blast downward and allowing the vessel to hover. It was on the ground in moments.

<An effective landing procedure if you were employing troops against a target,> Tatia commented privately to her group.

* * *

It was ironic that the speaker wouldn't know that he was the second invader of this particular terminal, Alex and his people having invaded it nine years earlier.

The terminal's controller tracked the shuttle as it approached and notified the manager as it touched down. Orso Quinlan experienced a surreal sense of déjà vu. Checking his vid displays, he realized that there were still many citizens making their way through the terminal to the underground transport cars. Orso ordered the terminal doors to the landing fields left open as he was advised. Now, he could think of only one thing to do to ensure the citizens' safety, and the thought frightened him to the point of hyperventilation. Slurping some water to calm his nerves, Orso donned and straightened his jacket and descended the lifts from his office to greet the Earthers.

Once the UE shuttle was firmly down, the speaker waited patiently for the pilot's cue.

"Speaker García, the air checks out as fine," the pilot announced. "However, we can't be sure of pathogens. I would advise you to use filter masks." Immediately, the speaker, major, and militia personnel donned black, full-face masks. Breathing slits were covered by an ultrafine mesh, which filtered fine particulate matter and directed the air to side chambers, which employed ultraviolet light to kill pathogens. The masks were developed during the pacification of the outer colonies. Some colonists, in last stands against UE militia, flooded their domes and enclave corridors with deadly microorganisms, knowing full well they were signing the death warrants of every resident.

The major signaled a crew member, who opened the rear ramp, and the militia flooded out to set up a perimeter. When Major Barbas received the "all clear," he and García descended the ramp into Méridien sunlight. To the speaker's surprise, a slender, dapperly dressed, Méridien male with a pleasant, if nervous, smile on his face stood in the terminal's open entranceway.

<Ser President, I know we had our differences when you last visited my terminal, but I would truly appreciate your guidance now, if not your assistance,> Orso sent.

Z shifted the terminal's exterior vid image to the *Rêveur*'s central screen. Dark-clad troops in face masks, carrying evil-looking rifles, were advancing on the terminal manager.

<That's one brave little Méridien,> Tatia said admiringly.

<Orso,> Alex sent, switching to the familiar, <we will do this together, but you must work with me. Drop all of your comm security protocols.>

<What?> Orso sent, his thoughts swirling in confusion.

<Drop them now, Orso!> Alex ordered, as he watched troops bearing down on the poor man. <Please trust me, Ser. We will do this together.> When Orso's security protocols disengaged, Alex slid into a command chair, closed his eyes, and reached into Orso's implant via Julien's connection. An image of the militia marching toward him filled Alex's mind, and he felt his limbs trembling. Alex willed the limbs to relax and loosened the grimace that threatened to lock the jaws, replacing it with an easy smile.

Orso didn't know what was worse—his fear of the approaching Earthers or the feeling that he was sharing his body with another person. At least his bowels, which threatened to release, had stilled. Orso felt his smile ease, and as the troops stopped in front of him, he felt disembodied as he stepped to the side and gestured for the troops to enter. If that wasn't strange enough, Orso spoke in a language he didn't know but understood, "Welcome to Lemuel Terminal. I'm Ser Quinlan, the terminal manager. How may I assist you?"

García stared at the Méridien, one of the first he found that exhibited old age. "I am Speaker García, Ser Quinlan. Where is everyone?"

"The citizens decided to leave when they were advised of your approach, Speaker García," Alex said, speaking through Orso's implant. Alex would have loved to see the speaker's face to gauge his reaction to their discussion, but the Earther's mask was hiding everything.

"Why didn't you leave, Ser Quinlan?" García asked.

"Old age, Ser. I'm not as quick as I used to be. Otherwise, I too would have been gone," Orso said. Hearing the words come out of his mouth, Orso almost laughed at the impertinence he was exhibiting to heavily armed strangers. *I'm braver than I thought,* Orso thought, and Tatia smiled when she heard the Méridien's thoughts.

<Stay calm, Orso,> Alex sent privately. <The transport cars are still being filled.>

"How may I help you, Sers?" Orso said.

"Where is your government's headquarters?" García demanded.

"The location you seek, Sers, is Confederation Hall. It lies just a few kilometers in that direction," Orso said, feeling his arm lift involuntarily and point the way.

"Major Barbas, check for an exit and commandeer us vehicles," García ordered, waiting while the major hurried away with half the militia force.

<You're doing fine, Orso. Relax and breathe casually. We need to fill only three more cars,> Alex sent.

<I'm attempting to do as you say, Ser, but there seems to be a dearth of oxygen at this moment,> Orso sent back.

Julien was attempting to remain neutral within the link, but as Alex reached deep into Orso's implant connections, seeking control of the man's nervous system to prevent the Méridien from hyperventilating, Julien could feel his own algorithms, which simulated his avatar's breathing, responding to Alex's commands. *Now that is unique*, Julien thought.

Major Barbas returned to the speaker at a run, shaking his head. "This is incredible, Speaker García," he said. "There's no exit."

García closed on Orso and grabbed him by the lapels of his jacket. "Do you take us for fools, Ser Quinlan," he demanded.

"Of course not, Ser," Orso heard himself say. "I merely pointed the direction to Confederation Hall, and I presumed you knew to take underground transport to reach the building. My apologies if you were uninformed of our ways. Allow me to lead you to your transport."

Without waiting for an answer, Orso felt his body twist, pull free of the speaker's grip, and begin walking across the terminal's lobby toward the nearest lift. <I think I can manage this part, Ser President,> Orso sent and felt his body released into his own care, nearly stumbling as he took back control. <What do I do at the transport level, Ser? I cannot send armed men to Confederation Hall.>

Alex was thinking furiously. His original plan was to exit everyone from the terminal, leaving the Earthers trapped in an empty building with no access to the outside or the transport cars, which were summoned only by Méridiens sending a request to the terminal's controller. The quick descent by the Earthers had disrupted his plan. A request to Z told him that the last transport car was leaving, carrying away the last citizens from the terminal but the manager. <Orso, the citizens are away. They're all safe.>

<Thank the stars, Ser President. I am most grateful that my responsibility has been discharged. My family will be proud of my memory, and what I have accomplished today,> Orso sent.

<Orso, you sound like you're giving up on me. We're not done until I say we're done. Do you understand me?> Alex sent back.

<I am yours to command, Ser,> Orso sent and a giggle escaped his lips, which he covered with a hand. <But then you are already doing that, aren't you, Ser?>

Tatia found herself shaking her head and grinning. She couldn't imagine relinquishing control of her body in this fashion to another human being. It made Ser Quinlan's actions appear even braver—or more desperate. But then, she recalled the rumors that circulated about Alex and Renée. Alex's ability to twine with his partner's implant and affect Renée physically, even when they weren't together, was the stuff of legends. Tatia once questioned Renée about it, but a smile and a wink were all she received in return.

<So what's the plan, Ser?> Orso asked.

<We will order a transport car, Orso, and list the Lemuel Terminal as the final destination, but we will send it by a circuitous route,> Alex sent back.

Z immediately contacted the terminal controller and ordered a large enough transport to handle the entire Earther force. <Ser President, how long for the route, hours or days?> Z asked.

Alex grinned at the thought of sending the Earthers on a transport route that would last days.

<I wonder how much food and water the Earthers are carrying with them,> Tatia injected into the discussion.

<I recommend caution, Mr. President,> Julien added. <We want sufficient time for them to be become bored and desire a return to what they know—their ship. We don't want to anger them and have them use their weapons to cripple the transport car. There will be other transports continuously surrounding them.>

<Sound advice, Julien,> Alex replied. <Z, plan for two to three hours of transport time and then return them to the terminal.> Alex left the comm open to Orso so the Méridien would know what was transpiring.

<Do I travel with the Earthers, Ser?> Orso asked, surprised he was even volunteering and briefly wondering if it was his thought or the president's.

<That's too dangerous, Orso, but be prepared to receive a bruise or two,> Alex replied.

<Bruised is better than some alternatives I have been imagining, Ser,> Orso sent. He and the Earthers arrived at the transport level where a large car waited. It should have had both the forward and rear doors open to allow quicker passenger loading and unloading, but only the forward doors were open. Confused as to the next steps, Orso relaxed and signaled Alex to take over his limbs again. His pace picked up, forcing the Earthers to hurry after him. "Come this way, Sers. I will accompany you to your destination. We mustn't have our guests getting lost." The absurdity of the last statement uttered by the president was almost too much for Orso to contemplate. There were no guests in the Confederation. Everyone was a citizen until Captain Racine arrived. Since then more and more centuries-held traditions were slowly eroding.

Orso watched as he led the Earthers through the first set of transport doors and walked the wide corridor to the rear. He plopped down in a seat next to the rear doors, the perfect image of a man prepared to take a trip. The Earther leader, who stood near him, turned around to ensure all his men were boarding the transport as if the trick was to leave them behind.

Z was monitoring the station's transport vid cam, watching the militia board the car. <Now, Ser,> Z sent when he saw the last man enter the car.

As the front car doors began to slide closed, Orso thought he should be moving, but he waited for the president's guidance. The thought occurred to him that he was enjoying the manner in which he was handling the situation or rather the president was handling the situation. Then with an energy he hadn't exerted in decades, the rear doors slid open, and he launched out through the opening. The doors closed so quickly behind him, he could feel a puff of breeze up his pants legs. The transport car pulled away from the station platform as Orso picked himself up, and he lifted an arm to wave goodbye to the Earthers, who stared at him through the car's windows. <Was that you or I who waved goodbye, Ser President?> Orso asked.

<I believe it was both of us, Orso,> Alex replied. <Another car is arriving as we speak. I suggest you take it home. Please contact Leader O'Shea and inform him of what has transpired.>

<It will be done, Ser President,> Orso replied. <And it would be my deepest pleasure, Ser, if on your next visit to Méridien you would share a meal with my family and me.>

<I will remember your offer. Safe trip home, Ser,> Alex sent and closed the comm. He opened his eyes and sat up in the command chair. "So what do you think the Earthers are going to take away from their visit planetside besides frustration?" Alex asked.

While Alex discussed the potential ramifications of the ruse perpetrated on the Earthers, Orso contacted his Leader and described the events as they unfolded, emphasizing the fact that the Earthers would still be circulating the transport ways for hours before returning to the terminal.

Devon immediately requested his House SADE send a summary to Winston to circulate to all House Leaders and Council Leader Ganesh. That the Earthers were prepared to force their attentions on Méridien was a frightening concept.

<I find your courage, Ser Quinlan, in the face of these heavily armed and terrifying-looking people to be incredible,> Devon sent.

<Had I relied on my courage, Leader O'Shea, I would have been a quivering mass on the terminal floor,> Orso replied.

<Then President Racine did much to encourage you,> Devon concluded.

<Encourage, no, Leader O'Shea. Prop me up, yes,> Orso replied and proceeded to explain the manner in which the Haraken president controlled his movements, manners, and speech, even in the Earther's tongue, throughout the confrontation, including his launch from the car at the last moment.

<Extraordinary, Ser,> Devon replied. <I witnessed something similar nine years ago in Council chambers, though I dare say it was at a more

nominal level. Apparently, President Racine has improved his implant skills far past our understanding.>

<Much to my delight, Leader O'Shea, I've enjoyed one of the most invigorating afternoons of my entire life,> Orso said.

Devon noted that the aging Méridien was 176 years old, and he could have retired from his position a decade and a half ago. <Will this event cause you to retire now, Ser Quinlan?> Devon asked.

<On the contrary, Leader O'Shea, it has caused me to hope that I will have the opportunity to interact with President Racine or the Harakens a few more times before I must retire.>

Devon wished the elderly Quinlan a good afternoon and instructed him to take the next day off, stating that his assistant could manage the terminal. Orso agreed but only reluctantly.

The Harakens continue to influence our people to embrace change, Devon thought. Then he smiled and clapped his hands. He couldn't wait to inform Katarina Pasko of what the events that transpired at the terminal.

Katarina insisted for years to him that the Haraken president was hiding implant capabilities that she was dying to study. Over time, her opinion of the president turned quite favorable, but she continued to insist he hid secrets concerning what he could achieve with his implants. Now she would know for certain. Alex Racine had exhibited a fantastic degree of mastery over another human being through their implant and it was accomplished while transmitting via a SADE and a terminal controller. Devon chuckled at the thought and decided to tell Katarina and Gino in person to ensure he saw their reactions.

18

"What type of insanity builds a world like this?" García asked, looking around at the terminal station. The Earthers rode their transport car for three hours before it halted at a terminal and the doors slid open. There was a certain lack of military decorum as the militia troopers piled out of both doorways at a run, but no one objected.

"Major," said a first lieutenant, "do you notice that there's no signage? We don't even know if we've reached our intended destination, returned to the original terminal, or are somewhere else."

"We are at the originating terminal, Lieutenant. You can be sure of that," Barbas replied.

"May I ask how you know that, Major," the lieutenant replied, searching the station's walls again for a clue.

"Every station we passed . . . every single one of them . . . people were standing and waiting, and cars were arriving and leaving. This station is barren. No cars, no people," Barbas replied. He was disgusted with how easily they had been tricked and stood with hands on hips, fuming.

García regarded his angry militia leader. "We've been taught a lesson, Major, a lesson indeed. Get our men back to the shuttle. I'm sick of this strange world."

The Earthers took the lifts back to the terminal's ground floor, passed through the lobby, and out through the open terminal doors to the landing fields. There was no one in sight, and nothing hindered their exit.

The terminal controller signaled Ser Quinlan, who was busy regaling his wife, children, and grandchildren, who were visiting, with the events of the day. The message simply said, <The intruding shuttle has left Méridien airspace with all passengers back aboard.>

* * *

Major Barbas wasn't the only one fuming. Uncharacteristically, so was Leader Ganesh. She was barraged with messages from House Leaders reporting that armed Earthers landed at Lemuel Terminal and were now traveling the transportation corridors in a car.

Winston, the Council SADE, connected Mahima to Devon O'Shea. <What do you know of this story, Leader O'Shea? Is it true?> Mahima demanded.

<Which story, Leader Ganesh?> Devon sent back, enjoying a small thrill from having Mahima Ganesh at a disadvantage.

<Do not play your Haraken games with me, Leader O'Shea. Answer me in Méridien fashion!> Mahima demanded.

Mahima's anger dissuaded Devon from continuing his charade. <An armed force of Earthers did land, Leader Ganesh, but not before most of the terminal was evacuated. The terminal manager, Ser Quinlan, stalled the Earthers until the evacuation was complete. A transport car was provided for the Earthers, who were sent on a ride through our transport system for a few hours. They have been returned to the terminal and are leaving via their shuttle as we communicate.>

<And who authorized the Earthers to use our transport system, Leader O'Shea?> Mahima asked, hoping she found something to use against Devon, who she knew was not a supporter of her Council position.

<I believe the entire process of minimizing the Earthers' impact on our people and terminal was arranged by President Racine with the assistance of his SADEs,> Devon replied, his thoughts casual. He waited for a reply, but none was forthcoming. His link was still active and courtesy dictated that Mahima should choose when to end the comm.

<I must say, Council Leader Ganesh,> Devon continued, <the thoughts of other Leaders are that they are quite pleased by the outcome. Who knows to what extent the Earthers might have employed force against our people. Instead, the intruders were effectively isolated, allowed time to regain their senses, and given a means of returning to their ship.> Devon

waited again for a response, but all he received was the close of the comm from Mahima's end. He leaned back in his reclining chair, the material shifting to accommodate his redistributed weight, and sipped his drink. A satisfied smile spread across his face. Unknowingly, the Earthers were helping their plan.

* * *

After Speaker García and his men regained their ship, he requested a call with High Judge Bunaldi. At the appointed time, Major Barbas, Administrator Wombo, and he sat at his cabin's table, a monitor at the other end. High Judge Bunaldi and Admiral Theostin were seated at a similar table, if not a more sumptuous one, aboard the *Hand of Justice*. Both groups wanted isolation for this conversation. García carefully and succinctly repeated the events of the day.

"So you found no opportunity to use your weapons and push through to your objective?" Admiral Theostin demanded.

"Use our weapons on whom, Admiral?" Major Barbas shot back. "We saw one nervous little man, who was anxious to show us how to reach the transport cars and our destination, so he said. After that, we saw tens of thousands of people waiting at stations or boarding cars all the while we whipped past them at a land speed I have never experienced on Earth."

"Careful with your tone, Major," Theostin reprimanded.

"If it pleases everyone," Bunaldi said in a quiet voice, "I am interested in facts and observations and little else. Administrator Wombo, I assume you have reviewed our militia's helmet footage of the event. I would be interested in hearing your observations."

Wombo found himself in a conundrum. The world they were observing was the scientific find of a lifetime, but to praise the Méridien's technology was to exhort his leaders to further covet the Confederation. Yet, to be disingenuous with a high judge by dumbing down his observations was to place his career, if not his life, in peril. "Judge Bunaldi, I believe the visuals confirm that we are dealing with such a technologically advanced civilization that it no longer compares to our own. By extension, we can't be sure that their technological superiority doesn't extend to their military capability. In which case, the Méridiens might no longer fear encroachment by an outside force."

"Pah," snorted Theostin, but a glance at Bunaldi told her that her comment was unnecessary.

"While I'm not sure about the Administrator's conclusion," García said, "there is much that gives me concern."

"Elaborate, Speaker García," Bunaldi replied.

"It was observed that there were no identifying marks at the terminal stations. How does anyone know when they arrived at their destination? A transport car was called for us. We boarded it and the terminal manager dived out just as the door closed. All of this could have been directed by computers, but there was no driver or even a control panel in the car. How does it navigate, especially to maneuver around so many other cars at such an incredibly high speed? At the end of our trip, we returned to the same terminal from where we started, but who choreographed our hours-long ride? The terminal manager was with us at all times, until we left, and he never employed a communications device. And while we are discussing the odd and the strange, recall that we mentioned Ser de Long finished the bout with Master Sergeant Hinsdale moments after the hidden signal was broadcast. How did he know when that happened?"

"Do you have an opinion Speaker García or just more questions?" Bunaldi said.

García turned to look at Wombo, who wrung his large, dark hands together before speaking. "As the evidence has accumulated, Judge Bunaldi," Wombo said, "we believe the Méridiens are capable of communicating by thought, not telepathically, but by some technological invention of theirs. It would enable the sending and receiving of thoughts and information from person to person. This technology would enable them to receive the signal from a source, such as the intruder our guide identified."

"Judge Bunaldi," Major Barbas said, "whatever their means of communication, it is extremely effective and subtle. Couple that with buildings that don't have exits but require underground transport that we can't control, and you have an impenetrable barrier against our ground forces. Our militia has been rendered ineffective."

"On this world perhaps, Major," Theostin replied, "but I wonder if it's the same on the Confederation's other worlds. In one of the administrator's reports, he postulates this is the Méridiens' home world, and they have settled perhaps six to eight other worlds. The extent of the FTL traffic indicates mature colonies that heavily participate in trade and passenger transport. Those outlying worlds might not be so well developed or so impenetrable."

Bunaldi nodded his head in agreement. "We would require their exact star coordinates, numbers that our guide could translate to our star maps for accurate jump targets."

"We could easily haul down one of those enormous freighters and threaten the captain for the information," Theostin suggested.

"How would we communicate with them, Admiral?" García asked. "Our communications are routed through . . ."

When García froze in mid-sentence, Theostin was about to prod him, but Bunaldi laid a hand on her arm and shook his head.

"Yes, that's it," García said excitedly. "Judge Bunaldi, our communications have been through a central point on Méridien. The voice is quite recognizable. Then when we met with Ser Racine and his group, they all wore small attachments that acted as communicators so that we heard them in our language, but the terminal manager didn't have any such device. He spoke in our language. That fits!"

The conference attendees stared at García, waiting for him to explain. "Please continue, Speaker García, before I grow tired of wondering," Bunaldi said.

"Your pardon, Judge Bunaldi, it occurred to me that while the words came out of the terminal manager's mouth, they were supplied by Ser Racine."

"Yes," Wombo chimed in, catching Speaker García's train of thought, "When I reviewed the helmet cam footage, I thought the phrasing sounded familiar. The elderly terminal manager looked frightened, but he spoke in this generous manner, as if he was in charge, despite facing our armed militia."

"Are you saying someone literally put words in this man's mouth?" Theostin asked, incredulous at the thought.

"It fits, Admiral, just as Speaker García said," Barbas added. "As strange as it might sound, it fits. The words coming out of the terminal manger's mouth came from Ser Racine." Barbas regarded first the speaker and then the administrator, looking for acknowledgment, and was happy to see that they were excitedly nodding their heads in agreement.

"It's my opinion, Judge Bunaldi," García said, "that we should proceed carefully. There are too many unknowns here, and we don't know the true extent of these peoples' technological advancement. The only individuals speaking to us are Ser Racine and his people, one of whom now announces herself as an admiral. I surmise that this group has been gathering intelligence on us and interceded on the terminal manager's behalf when we brought forces to the planet."

"I am still in favor of direct action, Judge Bunaldi," Theostin said. "If we take a freighter hostage, I'm sure we'll be able to force this Méridien government to communicate with us on any subject we choose."

"And if their war capabilities exceed ours, Admiral," Bunaldi replied, "we will have started a confrontation with an advanced civilization in their own system with one battleship and one explorer ship. Hardly a recipe for successful subjugation of multiple worlds."

Bunaldi stood stock still while he considered his options, giving those aboard the *Reunion* the thought that they were observing a statue.

"Speaker García, if I were to accept your advice and tread lightly, what would you suggest should be our next step?" Bunaldi asked.

García urged the rapid beating of his heart to still. This was a make-or-break opportunity for promotion. "The masks are off for both us and the Méridiens, Judge Bunaldi. We should arrange a face-to-face meeting with Ser Racine and his people with the intention of having a frank discussion and see what it gains us. Then, if we think we have no other option, I would concur with Admiral Theostin's plan to capture a freighter and force communications."

"Call the man, Speaker García. Arrange a meeting on any terms he wishes. Let's see what he has to say if we speak plainly," Bunaldi said.

"How many will be attending the meeting?" asked Major Barbas in order to judge the number of guards he would need.

"It will be just the five of us, Major," Bunaldi replied. "No use intimidating the man any more than we have already." Bunaldi reached for the comm controls and switched off the conference.

"Just the five of us, Patricio?" Samara asked.

"These people have been extremely tolerant of our interdiction, Samara," Patricio said, patting her hand. "Either they have no military force or they are extremely confident of their military capability. Either way, I believe we are in no danger. The frightened and desperate are truly dangerous because they are unpredictable. These people are neither, and with those, who are like us, it's just the business of war."

19

<Ser President,> Captain Cordova sent, <you have a comm from Speaker García.>

<Greetings, Speaker García,> Alex sent, stilling Renée's hand, which was drawing lazy circles on his bare chest. She took the hint and nestled against his side on their salon's couch.

"My apologies for disturbing you so late, Ser Racine, but we had a difficult and long day planetside and have only just returned," García said.

<I'm sorry to hear your visit wasn't fruitful, Speaker García,> Alex sent.

"I think we both know what kind of visit my people had, Ser Racine," García said, working to keep his temper under control. "We would like to meet with you, Ser Racine, in order to speak plainly with one another."

<I see, Speaker García, and who is we?> Alex asked.

"It would be five of us—High Judge Bunaldi, Admiral Theostin, Major Barbas, Administrator Wombo, and me," García replied.

<Well, at least one of you would be welcome. Please convey my respects to Administrator Wombo. As for this meeting, since you have such a panoply of important people, where and when are you suggesting we hold this group tête-à-tête?> Alex asked.

"Anywhere, anytime, Ser Racine. We are at your disposal."

<How generous of you, Speaker,> Alex replied, checking with Julien on the location of the *Hand of Justice* and the *Reunion* and simultaneously confirming with Z the Earther's daily clock time against the Haraken's. When the SADEs replied, Alex decided to host his guests aboard the *Rêveur* at 18 hours in two days' time. It would buy him the time to figure out how to play his hand. <We will meet you at the Le Jardin bay you used before, Speaker García, in two days at 14:30 hours by your clock. You and your guests will transfer to our shuttle, and we will host you on our ship, the *Rêveur*.>

"We will meet you in two days' time, Ser Racine, and a good evening to you," García replied and closed his comm link to the ship's guide.

When Alex returned his attention to the salon, Renée uncurled and threw a bare leg over his lap. "Captain Cordova said the Earthers called," she said.

"They did, and they wish to meet. I've scheduled a rendezvous in two days, and we'll host them aboard ship. There will be five of them. Three we know and two are new, Admiral Theostin and High Judge Bunaldi. More important, they want to be able to 'speak plainly.'" Alex said, playing the speaker's recorded voice from his implant.

"And do you know what they mean by that?" Renée asked, frowning at Alex for issuing the speaker's voice from his mouth.

"I know what they want. The questions are: how do we go about discovering what we wish to know, and what do we choose to divulge to them?" Alex replied.

Renée uttered a sigh, stood up, slipped off her wrap, and threw it over her shoulder as she headed for their sleeping quarters.

"And why am I having the opportunity to admire you in this fashion at this time?" Alex asked.

"It's because I know you, my love. You're about to contact your people to discuss plans for this meeting. So while I get us more modest evening wear suitable for guests, I wanted you to see what was planned for you this evening, and that you'll now be missing," Renée replied with a hint of smile.

Alex smiled as he watched Renée's bare behind disappear into their sleeping quarters. Then he commed his advisory group and requested they meet in his cabin. Since it was late, his people came in all manner of dress. Renée served thé while Alex related the speaker's call and his intention to bring the five premier individuals aboard the *Rêveur*. "I'm thinking it's time to let the Earthers get a peek at what they're up against," Alex said.

* * *

On the meeting day, the Earthers exited their shuttle into the Le Jardin's bay to find four Haraken troopers in uniform waiting for them. Utilizing their translation equipment, the troopers guided their guests to a second bay. Inside sat one of the glistening blue, green, and cream craft, which the Earthers had wondered about since they first spotted the apparently engineless craft. Despite the vessel's size and obvious weight, it floated more than a meter in the air above a cradle.

"If you will kindly board the shuttle, Sers," a trooper requested when the Earthers lurched to a halt at the sight of the traveler. "Our president is waiting to greet you."

"So the game begins," Bunaldi whispered to Theostin as they stepped forward. But the high judge wasn't as quick as Wombo, who needed no inducement to board. The huge man bounded up the steps into the shuttle's interior like a child running toward his favorite playground.

The Earthers settled into their seats, which elicited various reactions as the nanites conformed the seats' support to their bodies. Wombo couldn't resist switching to new positions to see how far he could push the chair's response until he heard García clear his throat, indicating Wombo should cease playing. This particular traveler was designated for their president's use, so the interior appointments were the best that Harakens could provide, forcing the Earthers to grudgingly admire the craft's interior.

"Well, they can do pretty. I'll give them that. I wonder if they can fight as well as they can decorate," Theostin murmured to Bunaldi, to which the high judge chose not to respond.

The interior lights dimmed when the hatch closed, and nearly a third of an hour passed while the Earthers waited for liftoff. Finally the cabin lights brightened again. "You may depart the shuttle, Sers," a trooper announced as the rear hatch was lowered.

"Is there a problem with the craft?" Barbas asked.

"Of course not, Ser," the first trooper replied. "We've landed aboard the *Rêveur*."

"Not possible," Theostin uttered under her breath.

"So that's to be the nature of the game," Bunaldi whispered to her. "It appears that we might just have met our match."

The Earthers descended into a brightly lit bay. Obviously, it wasn't the one where they started the journey. Two rows of troopers in dark uniforms awaited them. As one, they came to attention and saluted. The admiral and the major noted the coordinated precision of their movements. It was more machine-like than human.

At the end of the twin rows waited Alex, Renée, and Tatia with the twins standing behind them.

"Welcome aboard the *Rêveur*, Sers," Alex said. "May I present, my partner, Renée de Guirnon, and Admiral Tatia Tachenko."

"And how may we address you, Ser?" Bunaldi said, showing he was up to playing this game.

"You may call me President Racine, Ser," Alex replied.

"And what world or worlds are you president of?" asked Theostin, her tone dubious.

"But, Sers, you haven't introduced yourselves. Are we not observing the courtesies?" Alex replied, which earned him a broad smile from Bunaldi.

"By all means, President Racine, courtesies first," Bunaldi said. "Allow me to present Admiral Samara Theostin, and you have met Speaker Antonio García, Major Kyros Barbas, and Administrator Olawale Wombo. I am High Judge Patricio Bunaldi."

"Welcome, Sers," Alex said graciously. "Please come this way. We have made preparations for your visit."

As the Earthers walked the corridors of the *Rêveur*, the ship's interior design mirrored the style of the shuttle they just departed—clean lines with no piping or venting to clutter the visuals.

Major Barbas caught Speaker García's eye and nodded at a door as they passed. When García raised his eyebrows in question, Barbas whispered, "No labels," and García nodded his understanding.

"It appears Wombo might be correct about Méridien communications," García softly replied.

The Earthers watched the president walk up to a double set of doors which slid aside as he approached, and a low volume of casual noise reached their ears.

"Join us for a meal, Sers," Alex said and led the way to the front of the hall. Bunaldi and Theostin exchanged glances and then followed the president.

The Earthers were introduced to Julien and Z, who waited at the front table. When they sat down, their chairs began conforming comfortably to their bottoms.

"I can understand your pleasure, Administrator Wombo," Alex said when he noticed the smile cross the big man's face. "There can be painful challenges when large bottoms occupy small seats."

Wombo let loose a boom of laughter that could only come from a chest the size of his, but he quickly curtailed it when he caught sight of the high judge's censuring stare.

"You want us to join you for a meal?" asked Theostin when glasses of water and aigre, the tart Méridien juice, and cups of thé were set before them.

"We noticed that you and your people deferred from food or drink at our fête, Speaker García. We wish to assure you that your health would not be placed at risk, Sers. If you will trust our intention and technology, Terese will ensure your safety," Renée said, indicating the ship's red-haired medical officer who appeared at Wombo's elbow. "Who would like to volunteer for the test?"

Theostin should have been concerned that she would be allowing an advanced civilization access to her DNA and blood, but eyeing the striking redhead, she quickly replied, "I will volunteer," and her eyes followed Terese's hips as the Méridien gracefully strolled to her side.

<This one likes women,> Terese sent privately to Alex and Renée. <Let's see how much.> Terese instructed the admiral to expose her wrist, and took her time attaching her reader's probe, her fingers lingering on the woman's skin.

The admiral shivered slightly as nanites attached the device. It wasn't a reaction of disgust but one in anticipation of a more intimate contact.

When Terese's reader concluded its analysis, she removed the attachment and gave the admiral a bright and winning smile. "Our food is fine for our guests, Ser President," Terese said, nodding and touching hand to heart to Alex, a small show for the audience. "Although, no aigre for them."

<I could get used to that nice touch of obeisance, Terese,> Alex sent privately.

<And you could have a medical crisis with no treatment available to you,> Terese shot back and gave Alex a wink as she turned to walk away, noticing the admiral's eyes still followed her.

Food was placed on the table in the small Méridien serving dishes, and while four of the Earthers hesitated, Wombo transferred a few spoons of one dish onto his plate and tasted it. "This is delicious," he exclaimed.

Renée clapped her hands. "It was my hope you would enjoy our food, Administrator Wombo," she exclaimed. "You seem the adventuresome type. Now, as you are close to my partner's size, you should follow his lead," and Renée proceeded to empty half the serving dish onto his plate. "These will be replaced as they are emptied. Never worry, Administrator, we have plenty."

"I find it curious, President Racine," Bunaldi said, "that you wear this exalted title, but the dishes are not even crafted for people the size of you and the admiral."

"It's an interesting story, Judge Bunaldi, but one I doubt you will be privileged to hear for quite some time, if ever, but, of course, that depends a great deal on you, doesn't it," Alex replied, taking a moment to shovel some food onto his plate, tear a roll, and sop some juice, before popping the roll into his mouth.

Bunaldi slowly added food to his plate. He was thinking furiously how to get ahead of the president. Holding the meeting in the midst of his crews' meal was a master stroke. It said, "We are happy to entertain you in front of our people, and we have nothing to fear and are congenial people." From Bunaldi's point of view, the trick was to determine how much was fiction and how much was fact.

"I wonder if you understand by now, Judge Bunaldi, that our worlds will not be subjugated by your United Earth, and you can't take them by force," Alex said casually, continuing to enjoy his food.

Theostin glanced toward Admiral Tachenko to gauge her reaction to her president's words and was surprised to see a smile on the woman's face that was directed her way. The Méridien admiral was either supremely overconfident or knew something Theostin didn't know. The thought that it might be the latter sent a small icy chill up her spine.

"Confident words, President Racine," Bunaldi replied. "I applaud your camouflage. You've been able to hide your military force so carefully that we've seen no evidence of it."

Theostin wanted to join the conversation, but she was transfixed by Admiral Tachenko. Even as the Méridien ate, the woman never diverted her eyes from Samara. She felt as if she was being measured. For decades, Samara Theostin rose in the UE Navy's ranks, with the quick and decisive defeat of one rebel colony after another. Now, she wondered if she was meeting an enemy who was her equal . . . or maybe superior."

Alex paused and then said, "I agree, Julien."

Wombo halted his brimming spoonful of food in mid-air and stared at Julien, then the president. When he turned to look at his compatriots, he found they were doing the same thing.

"As you can communicate silently, Ser Julien," García said calmly, "would you be so kind as to repeat aloud what you said to your president?"

"Please, Speaker García, call me Julien. As a SADE, what you would call an artificial intelligence, I do not pretend to the appellation of 'Ser.' What I said to President Racine was, 'It appears our Earther cousins are more sight challenged than we thought.'"

Silence greeted Julien's words. Only one person, Wombo, seemed excited at the prospect of meeting a walking, talking, human-appearing avatar of an artificial intelligence. His mouth hung open, and his eyes gleamed.

"These are nice parlor tricks, President Racine," Theostin said, finally breaking away from Tatia's stare, "but you offer no proof. I could call myself an intelligent robot and who would know the difference."

"But isn't that the point, Admiral Theostin?" asked Z, who was wearing his banker's avatar. "We are indistinguishable from humans, an indication of the level of technology you face."

"We . . . ? Are you saying you're one of these artificial intelligences?" Barbas asked.

"The term is SADE, Major. Do please keep up. And, yes, I am a SADE—one already known to you," Z replied.

"You're mistaken. I've never met you before today," Barbas said, searching his memory to double-check himself.

"But you have, dear Major," said the voice of Miranda Leyton. "Of course, I was wearing a much more enticing outfit when you were enjoying my company then."

Major Kyros Barbas stared in horror at Z. First disgust and then rage burned through him. He couldn't believe the horrendous trick that had been played on him. Before he could be restrained, Barbas jumped up and launched a meaty fist at Z's face. The blow was stopped centimeters in front of Z's face by the SADE's hand, which held the major's fist in a metal-alloy grip.

"Now, Major, is that any way to treat a woman?" Miranda's voice purred.

"Sit down, Major," Bunaldi ordered in an iron voice. When the officer failed to move, Bunaldi was forced to raise his voice and order him again to be seated. Barbas sat down heavily, grabbing a cup, and gulping down some water. His face was suffused with blood, embarrassed for lusting after a non-human, and he stared with hatred at Z, who politely smiled back.

"So, President Racine, all this . . ." Bunaldi said, swinging his arms to indicate the meal room and the ship, "is to demonstrate your superiority, your technological advantages."

"It is hoped you will see reason, Judge Bunaldi, and return home. As I said, our worlds won't join United Earth, and a war holds only ruin for your forces," said Alex, his eyes boring into Bunaldi's.

"So you say," Theostin said, adopting a smirk to underline her doubt.

Alex was tempted to reach across the table and smack the smirk off her face.

<Downing in female form, wouldn't you say, my love,> Renée sent privately to Alex.

Alex turned and offered Renée a small, crooked smile. His partner always demonstrated a keen ability to diffuse a situation, especially where it concerned Alex's anger.

Wombo, recognizing another moment of silent interplay between the Méridiens, itched to learn what it would feel like to converse mind to mind.

"Just what would convince you, Judge Bunaldi, to leave our corner of the galaxy alone?" Alex asked.

"I will give your question some consideration, President Racine, and see if there is something that could convince us to leave," the high judge replied.

"Very well, Judge Bunaldi. Please, Sers, enjoy the rest of your meal in peace," Alex said and silence descended over the table as everyone returned to their food and drink, all except Barbas, who sat brooding in silence, not touching another mouthful of food.

<You don't believe Bunaldi will keep his word if he does concoct some idea and we met the challenge, do you?> Tatia sent to Alex.

<Certainly not,> Alex sent back. <I'm trying to ensure we collect the evidence to convince the Méridiens of the type of adversary that has entered their system and the danger the Earthers represent to the entire Confederation.>

When the meal ended, the crew turned in their chairs to face the head table. The motion of so many bodies caused the Earthers to alternate between gazing around the meal room and turning to look at Alex for an explanation.

"Your pardon, Sers, this is a Méridien tradition," Alex said. "One guest provides a story in return for the meal. It is recorded and shared for posterity," Alex added, tapping his temple.

No one responded, and Alex was about to excuse them to return to their ship via his traveler when he heard Wombo say, "I would be privileged, President Racine, to be the first Earther to have his story recorded by your people."

<Such a lovely man, who unfortunately is forced to travel in such unseemly company,> Renée sent to Alex.

"Should I stand?" Wombo asked. He got to his feet when Alex nodded.

Wombo spread his arms in apology. "I wish my life contained a tale of tragedy or heroism to make this moment more . . . momentous." He grinned by way of an apology and shrugged his massive shoulders. Many of the crew saw reflections of their leader in the huge man's gentle ways. Wombo ducked his head while he considered his next words, and then he straightened up and in a loud, clear voice began his story.

"Instead, let me tell you about a dream. Once upon a time, there was a young boy, who dreamed of becoming a scientist. He dreamed of traveling to the stars and discovering new and wonderful worlds. As a young man, he worked hard, doing everything asked of him, but over time, he found less and less joy in his work. One day, the man, who by now was in his later years, was offered an opportunity to participate in one of his peoples' first journeys to the stars, and he was again full of hopes and dreams, a young boy's excitement alive in an old man's body. To the scientist's amazement, that journey brought his dreams to life. He found a wondrous world full of things that only occurred in his daydreams. Today, standing here, the boy and the man thank you for making his dreams come true."

Whatever reception Wombo had expected from his story, it wasn't the one he received as the entire crew stood and cheered. He grinned as he turned to the president and found the Haraken leader and his associates standing with hands over hearts and heads bowed. It was in stark contrast to the scowls and irritated looks painted on the faces of Wombo's own people.

Wombo, facing a critical decision point in his life, decided he was done with the UE. He turned back to the cheering and applauding crew and raised an arm in salute, and they shouted even louder. Turning back to the president and finding him and his people still frozen in their postures, he drew himself up to his full formidable height and returned their poses, his hand over his heart, as earnestly as he could.

Alex brought the meal to a close and escorted his guests back to the bay and the traveler.

Bunaldi and Theostin put their heads together the entire way, and as the group approached the bay's airlock, Bunaldi cleared his throat, causing Alex to stop and face him. "President Racine, I believe we've conceived a means by which we might settle our impasse. We propose a contest. If we win, you gain us a face-to-face meeting with the Confederation leaders, and if you win, we'll leave the system."

"A contest? What sort of contest, Judge Bunaldi?" Alex asked.

"Our ships carry fighters," Theostin said. "Do you have any sort of craft to compete with them?"

"We might," Alex replied carefully.

"Then we propose that three of our fighters compete against three of your fighters," Theostin replied.

"And exactly what outcome decides the winner of the contest?" Tatia asked.

"The side with a pilot still alive, of course," Theostin said, enjoying the opportunity to repay Tatia's grin with one of her own.

"You propose an engagement of our fighters in a head-to-head combat contest?" Alex said.

"Precisely, President Racine," Bunaldi replied. "The stakes of this contest are as real world as the futures of our two societies. Our people and your people will risk their lives to prove who should lead the human race. Do you agree?"

"We will consider your request, Judge Bunaldi. I thank you for your visit. It's always valuable to meet one another personally to understand—"

"One's enemies?" Bunaldi volunteered.

"The opinions of others," Alex supplied.

When the Earthers entered the *Rêveur*'s airlock to take the ship's traveler back to Le Jardin, Alex and Tatia stood in the corridor and stared at each other. "Can you believe what they proposed?" Tatia said incredulously.

"It does seem to underline their Earther history from what we've learned. Life appears cheap to them, and winning seems all important," Alex replied.

"You know, Alex, there is every indication that our travelers can take their fighters, especially in a first-time contact. They won't be prepared for our speed or our beams."

"And once we win their contest, what do you think they will do?" Alex asked.

"My gut feeling is that if the Earthers lose, they won't honor their agreement," Tatia replied.

"I agree. If that's so, what advantage have we gained by demonstrating our superiority?" Alex asked thoughtfully. He linked Tatia with Julien and Z. <Julien, Z, any success yet in penetrating the UE ships' systems?>

<With regrets, Ser President,> Z replied, <system integration onboard the UE ships is minimal.>

<The only system we have been able to access is their comms, Mr. President,> Julien said, <and their control systems are isolated from comms. Z and I have concluded that the term 'guide' that Administrator Wombo mentioned acts as their ship's controller.>

<Thank you for the update, Julien, Z,> Alex replied and cut the comm.

Tatia looked into Alex's eyes and was concerned for what she saw. His eyes didn't have that confident focus she expected, leaned on in times of crisis. Instead, his gaze seemed uncertain, conflicted. She wanted to ask what he was thinking or what he planned to do but decided to refrain from disturbing him.

Alex saw a frown form on Tatia's face and realized he wasn't projecting much of a presidential persona, but, at the moment, he couldn't find it in him to try. He reached out, patted Tatia's broad shoulder, and walked away. *Why is peace so hard to come by?* Alex thought.

20

"Mr. President, if you are unsure whether we will participate in this contest, then plan for the worst-case scenario until you make your decision," Tatia volunteered. Alex's people were gathered in his salon. The more he thought about the contest, the further conflicted he became.

"Logic dictates that we position our ships to gain maximum advantage and minimize any UE maneuvers that might follow the contest. There is a significant probability that the UE will use the opportunity to gain an advantage, regardless of the outcome," Z said.

Z wore his banker avatar since his personal contact algorithms indicated it was the image that made humans most comfortable. But a subtle conflict was taking place within his hierarchical structure. The more data that was absorbed from the Miranda persona, the more he felt that his kernel was somehow inadequate. He tabled the disturbing revelation until the present crisis was past, but it was high on the list for review once time became a luxury.

"Okay, Admiral, suppose we follow Z's advice. If we plan to engage in this absurd, sacrificial contest, how would we maximize the opportunity to win and minimize the UE response afterward?" Alex said.

Tatia leaned forward in her chair, placing her forearms on her thighs with hands clasped together. Soon afterward, she stood up and started pacing the room.

Renée smiled to herself. When word of the Earthers first arrived and Alex told her they would be taking the *Rêveur* to Méridien, she contacted Captain Cordova and requested a change in their salon's furnishings. Typically, the furniture rested against bulkheads, situating a large conference table in the room's center. However, that arrangement was totally unsuitable for Alex and his people.

Renée asked the captain to remove the conference table and place the holo-vid on a small stand. She added more chairs but pulled all furniture away from the bulkheads. This configuration allowed a complete circuit around the outside of the furnishings, which Tatia was busy utilizing, head down, hands clasped behind her back, communing with Julien and Z, who were projecting scenarios on the holo-vid for the others to observe. It was ironic that the individual in the center of this implant three-way was the New Terran who was most reticent to adopt her implant eleven years ago.

When Julien and Z signaled their agreement, Tatia walked over to the holo-vid. "To maximize our advantage and minimize the options for the UE ships afterward, we set up the contest here," she said, zooming into the system until the outer planet, Bevroren, a massive ball of frozen gasses, occupied most of the display. We don't know which UE ship will supply the fighters, but my suspicion is that they are expecting a duplicitous response from us, so they will put both ships into play. We stage the contest just inside the orbit of Bevroren, and we position the *Last Stand* just beyond the planet. Utilizing the planet and its collections of moons as gravity sources, our travelers will have plenty of power for maneuvering and recharging their beams."

"So your plan is to use the planet to hide the *Last Stand* from the Earthers," Alex recapped. "There are some issues with that idea, Tatia. If our ship arrives early, what's to stop that battleship from circling the planet? It could start an all-out confrontation between our carrier and that battleship."

"That's why we arrive late, and by 'we,' I mean the *Rêveur*," Tatia replied. "Once we choose to accept the contest, Julien and Z will communicate the coordinates to the *Reunion*. We let the Earthers start for Bevroren first. Then we follow them. It's my opinion that once they see us following them, they will focus on us. We stage the *Last Stand* just outward of the system. Captain Manet keeps the carrier hidden out in the deep dark. He can utilize the Méridien's telemetry data from the FTL comm stations to relay the positions of the UE vessels. As the Earthers close on Bevroren, the *Last Stand* does the same, but from the opposite side."

"Okay, I like it," Alex said. "Unfortunately, we are creating a severe time lag. We would have to wait until the *Last Stand* is close enough to Bevroren to launch the travelers so they can use the planet's gravitational field. Then it will take time for the travelers to circle the planet and engage, especially since they will have to make a wide orbit around the planet's moons and asteroid ring. That is many hours, during which the Earthers might get nervous."

"It would be advantageous, Admiral," Julien said, "to create a means of launching the travelers using the *Last Stand's* velocity as it approaches the planet—a slingshot technique similar to the concept the Rainmaker used to send the ice water asteroids to Haraken."

Tatia stopped behind Julien's chair, and leaned over to place her mouth next to his ear. "You are a lovely and brilliant man, Julien," Tatia whispered.

"It's a pleasure to be of worth, Admiral," Julien replied.

"The strategy works for me. Now, shall we discuss the fight itself?" Alex asked.

"I would defer to Commodore Reynard for that part, Alex," Tatia said.

"Julien," Alex said.

<Good evening, Mr. President and everyone,> Sheila sent.

<Greetings, Commodore Reynard,> Alex replied, <we need you to access your choice of holo-vids.>

<I'm in my quarters with Ellie Thompson,> Sheila replied. <Let me excuse her.>

<Negative, Commodore, please ask your wing commander to stay,> Alex replied. <Commodore, I take it you both have reviewed the Shadow's data by now.>

<We have, Mr. President. Z, my congratulations! That was a superb piece of inventiveness that enabled your machine to capture the data,> Sheila sent.

<We obtained detailed exterior surveillance of the explorer ship, which allowed us to program refined goals, and we were allowed an adequate supply of parts and time, Commodore. Success was a foregone conclusion,> Z sent. Then he paused while several persona algorithms

shifted, and then Z said, <Pardon me, Commodore. Allow me to rephrase my response. You're very gracious with your compliment, Commodore. Thank you.>

Those in Alex's cabin stared at Z.

"Shades of Miranda," Tatia said under her breath.

<Everyone,> Alex sent, <stay on point.> He brought Sheila and Ellie up to speed on the Earther's proposed contest and Tatia's plan, if he were to accept the terms of the contest.

<Just so I'm clear, Ser President,> Ellie sent, <our pilots are to fight to the death against their pilots?>

<Yes, Commander,> Tatia replied.

<It's as if all of Clayton Downing's relatives just visited us from Earth,> Ellie sent.

<I like the overall strategy, Mr. President,> Sheila sent, putting the discussion back on track as Alex requested. <Any details you wish to provide for this fight, if it comes about?>

<That's why we commed you, Commodore,> Alex said.

<Well, I will defer to my best pilot, Mr. President. Commander Thompson has long since eclipsed my skills in the cockpit.>

<My tactics, Ser President, would be to overwhelm their fighters,> Ellie said. <Attain our top velocity, and use a single-beam shot against their engines to refrain from hurting their pilots as we sweep past them.>

<Negative, Commander,> Alex replied. <Your pilots are to fire on the UE fighters' central fuselages. Aim for the maximum target area.>

Ellie glanced at Sheila, who was watching her carefully. <Understood, Mr. President,> Ellie replied slowly, <I will need to select the right pilots for this task.>

<Understand this, Commander,> Tatia sent. <We have had multiple contacts with these Earthers, and while we have met some good people, the UE leaders are dedicated to subjugating the Confederation. Based on our observations, these two Earther ships are only the beginning of what we might encounter, and that battleship of theirs has enormous firepower. If they have a fleet of these types of ships, we will not be able to stop them, and once they discover Haraken and New Terra, we will be joining United

Earth whether we like it or not. Our hope is to bloody their nose now and make them think twice about their conquest plans.>

Ellie flashed back to the fight over New Terran skies when Dagger pilot Lieutenant Hatsuto Tanaka lost his life to Downing's followers, as they did their best to kill Alex. She held the memory of Hatsuto's sacrifice close and hardened her heart. *We do what we must to keep our people safe, Hatsuto*, she thought and returned to studying the strategy. <I see only one difficulty with our tactics,> Ellie said.

<Initial velocity,> Julien replied. <It has been noticed. I have been focused on it for several moments and believe I have a plan.>

Alex and Tatia shared a grin. A SADE spent several moments to develop a plan. It meant that, despite the challenge, the probability of it working was extremely high.

<We will borrow a Rainmaker concept, Commodore,> Julien continued. <I recommend you load the pilots in their travelers, vacate the bays, and tether the fighters outside the bays. Approach the planet at a high velocity and when you're ready, release the fighters. This would impart your velocity to them, allowing the fighters to coast until they gained the gravity fields of Bevroren.>

<I like it, Julien. Good plan,> Sheila replied.

The Commodore's compliment was appreciated, but, for Julien, it was the grin on his friend's face that he coveted. His life began almost two centuries ago in a box on a starship bridge, and seventy of those years were spent in utter isolation when the ship was disabled by an alien attack. Then in five brief years, after rescue by a New Terran captain, he was free, walking around—all due to the sensibilities of the man who smiled at him from across the room. That he could return the smile to his friend was a pleasure beyond measure.

<What's the probability that we will go through with this insane contest, Mr. President?> Sheila asked.

<Commodore, consider it will happen and proceed accordingly. If I can think of an alternative, you will be one of the first to know. Get your ship into staging position and stand by,> Alex sent and closed the comm.

* * *

In stark contrast to the dark mood in Alex's meeting, Wombo was jubilant as he regaled his *Reunion* comrades with the events of the day aboard the *Rêveur*. Once again, the usual six friends were crowded into Wombo's small cabin late in the evening.

"What I found most fascinating," Olawale said to his audience, "was that the president indicated that my story would be recorded and shared for posterity, and he tapped his temple."

"That supports your previous observations, Olawale," Boris, whose background was medicine, said excitedly. "Imagine a technology that allows communication, mind to mind. There would be no reason that it couldn't operate as a data-storage center for sensory input. Stories, exactly as related by the original storyteller, could be recorded and retrieved."

"That would mean anything could be recorded," Storen noted.

"I'm three decades too late," Nema said, expressing her lament, "my husband was an exceptional lover. It would have been marvelous to have kept recordings of our trysts." Her words sent all the minds in the room wondering what types of treasured events they would have wished to have recorded.

This group of scientists was onboard, not only because they were Wombo's friends and because they excelled in their disciplines, but for many, this would be their last great adventure. All of them were well past their middle years and now found themselves alone, having never married or having lost spouses and families.

"I wonder just how accurately the sensations are recorded," Nema added, and the others looked at her wistful face and broke out in laughter. Nema smiled sheepishly, realizing the intimate nature of the thoughts she just shared.

"I find their ritual endearing," Priita said. She was Olawale's closest friend. Her blonde hair had long ago turned a snowy white, and Olawale's huge-dark was such a contrast to her thin-pale that comments and nicknames about the pair were inevitable. "That these people have developed such a level of technology without incurring the terrible wars we have suffered seems incredible."

Wombo laughed briefly as he recalled something. "President Racine's stature has all the earmarks of what I believe would have developed from generations lived on a heavy world . . . and he consumes food like a heavy worlder. You should have seen it. President Racine's people acted like a conveyor system, but only small serving plates were available. So they constantly supplied him with fresh plates. I thought I ate a lot, but you should have seen that man shovel food." Wombo paused, while his audience laughed and tittered at his singular observation.

"Plates that don't suit the size of their president," said Edward, who was the preeminent physicist and mathematician among the scientists. "Now there's a story I'm curious to hear."

"What about this contest?" Yoram asked. "It does not make sense for either side to participate."

"We know the high judge's eventual goal is domination of the Confederation, but there are too many unknowns about the Méridiens. The contest is his way of approaching some of these unknowns with caution," Olawale said. "We know the Méridiens possess enormous technological capability, and yet they have been extremely passive in response to our intrusions. I think the high judge doesn't know whether the Méridiens are without military capability or whether their military is so superior that the Méridiens think they don't need to prove it. He is worried that if he believes the former and launches a major assault, we might be wiped from space. So, the high judge is intent on testing the Méridiens' capabilities with this contest. If President Racine produces no fighters or inferior fighters, the high judge will be fairly certain he can proceed with his plans with impunity."

"By your logic, Olawale, the president should not participate," Edward said. "If he has the capability, he need not prove it. Either way, I would reason that his fighters will be a no-show."

"The president's fighters will be there," Priita said, and all heads turned toward her. Despite her credentialed academic background, Priita often made out-of-the-box predictions, which seemed unfounded in fact. To the consternation of her colleagues, they often came true. Her compatriots continued to stare at her, compelling Priita to explain. "The answer is clear, as Olawale has communicated to us."

Now all heads turned to Olawale, who shrugged his massive shoulders and held up his hands in confusion.

"My friends," Priita said, "we have already reasoned that President Racine is not a Méridien, and yet he has the allegiances of a diverse group of seemingly good people—people who come from his home world, from Méridien, and these wonderful artificial intelligences.

"SADEs," Wombo volunteered.

"Yes, SADEs," Priita echoed. "What type of man wields this degree of personal power? My answer is this: a man who does not let fate dictate the path of his people, but one who shapes his world to suit the needs of his people. That type of personality appears in great contrast to our contact with Méridien. President Racine might seek an alternative to the contest, but I believe he will realize that the high judge has backed him into a corner. His fighters will be there, and I am curious as to the type of advanced technology we will witness."

"I would not have thought it possible that I would ever think this, much less say it, but I wonder if President Racine would be interested in accepting some new immigrants," Nema said quietly.

Wombo thought his colleagues might object to Nema's statement or at least argue. He was careful to keep his thoughts to himself, because Nema's thoughts were the same as his own and had been ever since his story was greeted with wild applause from the *Rêveur*'s crew. There was no one waiting for him back on Earth, and the individuals he met at the Le Jardin fête and aboard the *Rêveur* were people he could see himself happily living among.

* * *

"I can't believe that fool, Administrator Wombo," Theostin huffed to Bunaldi once they were back aboard the *Hand of Justice* and alone in the high judge's cabin. "I thought he was going to bow at the feet of that president."

"No, Samara," Bunaldi replied. "Wombo might be useful to us. Our gentle administrator has won the hearts of the president's Méridiens. If there is a soft side to these people, then thoughts of Wombo might give them cause to still their hands when they should be delivering a fatal blow."

"Do you think President Racine will accept our contest, Patricio?" Theostin asked.

"I'm hopeful he will," Bunaldi replied. "Failing to participate leaves the field open to us to make the next move, and this president doesn't appear to be the type of person to let others dictate the course of events to him. If he does accept our contest, I want a strong message delivered to him and the people of this system."

"Swamp his fighters," Theostin said, a smirk twisting her lips at the thought of crushing the Méridien admiral's forces. She imagined being aboard the admiral's ship and watching the woman's face fall as her fighters disappeared from the screen.

"You will have to be clever, Samara. They will probably suspect that we will change the game. You must appear to play fair to draw their fighters out. I want your best pilots in the competition, and I want to learn about their fighters. So do not deliver any quick kills. However the contest goes, the day ends in their utter defeat, Samara," Bunaldi said and bored his eyes into hers. "We can't let the Méridiens win. It would send the wrong message. The only thing we want these people to know is that the well from which our power springs has no bottom."

* * *

To prepare for the contest, Sheila's first order of business was to choose an approach to Bevroren. The *Last Stand* was still outside the system and would have to circle nearly halfway around the system at sub-light speed to approach Bevroren from deep space as Alex requested. There wasn't enough time for that maneuver. As an alternate route, Sheila decided to jump the carrier out into the deep dark and then back again to be in position in less than a day.

The carrier's flight crews and pilots jumped into action to prep their 128 travelers before the carrier achieved its staging position, designated as Point Alpha. Each Haraken traveler was still a close copy of the original dark traveler, and they were as highly maneuverable as ever before, but there were no improvements to the beam technology or its firing rate. The Harakens thought themselves safe, having built two giant carriers massing a total of 384 travelers—until they faced the Earther's battleship.

Late in the evening, Ellie met with Sheila in the commodore's spacious cabin. Jackets were unbuttoned, boots were off, feet were propped up, and drinks were in hand.

"Unless you order me not to lead the contest's flight, Commodore, that is my intention," Ellie said.

"What is not my intention is to lose my wing commander in the first foray against these Earthers," Sheila replied.

"According to our president, this contest is an opportunity to scare the Earthers off, make them think twice about attempting to usurp the Confederation. It's critical that the contest is as decisive as we can make it," Ellie replied.

"And you're all right with killing these Earther pilots, Ellie?" Sheila asked gently.

"If I were to dwell on it, probably not. On the other hand, once I'm out there I will be doing my best to keep my pilots safe from three enemy pilots, who will be trying to kill us. I've been there before," Ellie reminded Sheila, "and I know what I'm capable of doing."

"And a damn fine job you did," Sheila agreed. "All right, Commander, you pick your wings. Make sure they are pilots who can deliver. Now, let's design some secondary plans if the Earthers don't stick to the rules. According to the reports we've received, we can expect foul play."

The two women gamed until early morning before they retired, and soon after morning meal they met with their deck commanders to discuss the unorthodox launching of the travelers from deep space where they would have insufficient gravity waves to drive the fighters' engines and beams. Sheila no sooner finished outlining the problem and the proposed launch technique when the first audience comment was made.

"Pardon me, Commodore, but we trained for years with a variety of in-system launch patterns, and our first fight requires this half-assed launch from deep space. Who's in charge of this outfit anyway?" asked Avery Crosser, who was known for his fast mouth. He was also known for commanding one of the best groups of flight chiefs on the ship. His comments drew chuckles from the other deck commanders.

But Sheila wasn't one to let a verbal challenge go unanswered. "One moment, Commander Crosser," she said, "I'll get him on the comm so you can ask the man directly."

Crosser, who was slouching in his chair, sat up quickly and put up two hands, waving Sheila off, and vigorously shaking his head. It brought a round of even louder chuckles from the audience.

"All right, people. Let's get down to business," Sheila said. "We will launch three travelers as we approach Bevroren. Then we will prep and launch the remainder of the sub-wing."

"Begging your pardon, Commodore, we're launching a total of sixty-four travelers using this tethering method?" a second deck commander asked. "Do you know something we don't?"

"It's the president's and admiral's advice that we should expect treachery," Sheila replied. "So we'll launch a sub-wing to follow our three contestants, then the carrier will take the opposite path around Bevroren. Be prepared to use a traditional launch on any number of the remaining sub-wing."

"An important note," Ellie added, "we are leaving the beam-and-tether technique up to you deck commanders. Work out which flights you want to launch with this method to compose the sub-wing. However, you must launch the three contestants, as the commodore calls them, within ticks of one another. I want my wing pilots close to me."

Ellie's last statement quieted the deck commanders. Their wing commander was going to fly lead against three Earther pilots, who were out to prove superiority over Méridien craft and pilots by turning their adversaries into space debris.

Soon after the deck commanders were dismissed, every pilot was assembled and seated in the carrier's briefing amphitheater—160 trained and qualified pilots for the 128 travelers—and only a handful ever fought an enemy.

"People, one key strategic point to keep in mind," Sheila said, after outlining the general plan to the pilots. "The *Last Stand* is a carrier, and we will be up against two ships that have fighters, missiles, and, we believe, rail guns. The second sub-wing's primary duty will be to protect this carrier. Flight leaders of the second sub-wing, it will be hard not to go to the aid of your comrades in the heat of battle, but you have to defend our base."

"The other key strategy," Ellie said, "will be implemented by the first sub-wing. Those pilots following the three contestants must remain fluid. We don't know what to expect from these ships, but potentially the *Rêveur* will be in range of their missiles."

"Can we assume that the president and admiral won't be aboard the *Rêveur*?" asked a captain.

Sheila shook her head in negation, as a smile played across her lips. "You can expect those two to be nowhere else."

"One last subject to cover," Ellie said. "I will not draft the two pilots who will join me as contestants. I will choose from volunteers. You may submit your names to the carrier's controller, if you wish to do so privately."

In one fluid motion, 160 pilots stood to attention, and Ellie fought back the tears that threatened to form in her eyes. Every single Haraken pilot was willing to fight and die for their people. The majority of them were Librans, and if anyone had a stake in defending their freedom, it was these people who grew up on Libre as prisoners of Méridien society just for the crime of being different.

"I will inform you of my choices soon. Thank you, one and all, for your commitment," Ellie said.

Sheila and Ellie handled questions from the pilots until evening meal and then took a break. They resumed after the meal and discussed tactics, depending on what the two Earther ships might do. So many questions could not be answered, because so little was known about the capability of the ships' armament. When Sheila finally dismissed the pilots, she and Ellie shared glances, neither look conveyed confidence—too much was unknown.

21

Mahima Ganesh, Council Leader of the Confederation, a conglomeration of centuries-old, successful world systems, sat seething in her transport car like a teenager in the midst of a tantrum. Two House associates and two escorts kept their distance, sitting at the opposite end of the car. Despite the emotions roiling beneath the surface, outwardly Mahima kept her icy demeanor. Her irritation stemmed from being summoned to a Council meeting. It was her privilege to set Council dates, not be called to one as if she was a low-level associate.

When Winston, the Council's SADE, delivered the message to Mahima, he held the Council's laws about such a request at his virtual fingertips. Initially, the SADE researched Council historical records to ensure the Leaders' request was founded on precedence.

Mahima could hear Winston's voice in her implant. "Council Leader Ganesh, according to Council law, a minimum of ten Leaders is required to request an emergency Council meeting. As Council SADE, I am required to poll all Leaders, resident on Méridien at the time of the request, to obtain their approval or disapproval of the meeting. A majority of Leaders has approved the meeting, and your attendance is required."

"I want a list of the Leaders who requested the meeting, and a list of all those who approved the meeting," Mahima demanded.

"Leader Ganesh, I can't acquiesce to that request. It's against Council guidelines," Winston replied. "I'm required to inform you of the date and time of the meeting and that your presence is required. No other information is to be transmitted to you."

"But you're my SADE," Mahima replied, outraged about what she perceived as treachery.

"On the contrary, Leader Ganesh, I'm the Council's SADE, not your House SADE," Winston replied and closed the comm. She was not even been granted that grace—to be the one to terminate the conversation.

Mahima's car arrived at Confederation Hall a half-hour early. She planned to unsettle the conspirator's complacency by taking her position in the hall and staring down each Leader as he or she entered chambers. She would let them know who was still in control. The lifts dedicated to a Council Leader allowed Mahima to reach her office quickly. At her private chamber entrance, Mahima handed her overcoat to an associate, squared her knee-length jacket, signaled the door open, and walked into a full chamber. By her estimate, every Leader on Méridien was present, and she lost a couple of steps before she regained her composure and marched to her exalted station.

"As first order, I will call a roll of those present. I require each of you to declare whether you voted for or against the convening of this meeting," Mahima announced.

"Your pardon, Council Leader," Winston announced over the chamber's audio system. It was installed centuries ago to accommodate preimplant children, who attended the sessions with their fathers or mothers. "You are out of order. The first order of business is a list of questions, presented by those who called the meeting, to be put to you."

"Will these individuals be reading the questions?" Mahima asked.

"Negative, Council Leader Ganesh," Winston replied. "I will ask the questions. After your response, any Leader may ask clarifying questions until there are no more, and then I will voice the next question."

"Very well, Winston, it appears you have the floor," Mahima said as gracefully as she could manage. She knew the Earthers were at the heart of the matter, but she was sure President Racine was fomenting this discord among her people. For a rare time in her life, she wished a human being dead.

"The first question is rhetorical, but I'm required to ask it," Winston said. He proceeded to detail the various events that had been transpiring in the Méridien system, including the presence of two Earther ships, the explorer ship and the warship, in addition to the visit by an armed group of

Earthers to Lemuel Terminal. "I have affirmed to the convening Leaders that you have been carefully advised of all such events," Winston finished.

"The first question for you, Council Leader Ganesh, is this: What action are you prepared to take to protect the Confederation against usurpation by the Earthers?" Winston asked.

"Leaders," Mahima said, rotating her dais to face the Assembly, "the question assumes that usurpation is the purpose of the Earthers. Who's to say that is what they wish? I counsel patience. The Earthers will grow tired of failing to make contact and return to their home."

"What evidence exists to the contrary of our Council Leader's position?" Leader Lemoyne said, rising to his feet. He was one of Mahima's staunch supporters.

"The question of evidence has been requested," Winston said. "Please pay attention to the central holo-vid." Winston played the Shadow's visual record as it crawled through the *Reunion*, and he played Esther's early analysis of the *Reunion* to use as resources to calculate the armament carried by the *Hand of Justice*.

"This information proves nothing," Leader Teressi said, who was another supporter of Mahima. "We have no idea what worlds the Earthers have visited and what enemies they might have found it necessary to defend themselves against. This type of armament might have been completely necessary."

"If you will be patient, Leader Teressi," Winston replied. "I will continue with the presentation of the evidence of Earther intention as requested. The earlier images were designed to prove that the Earthers have the capability to wage war against extremely capable adversaries, of whom the Confederation is not one. The next series of images is taken from Julien, the Haraken SADE, who witnessed this discussion between members of the Earther contingent and President Racine and his people."

Mahima wanted to object with all her voice, but she held back. Too many of the Leaders were intent on the holo-vid that was playing. Of all places, the discussion was taking place in a meal room, a full one at that. To Méridiens, mealtime was a sacred time of sharing. Haraken uniforms and ship suits could be seen in the background. People were eating, drinking, and communing, as it should be.

The Leaders received Con-Fed translations from Winston as the scenes played out. There was no mistaking the positions of the two parties in conversation—one curious and questioning and the other directive if not aggressive. When the major lunged across the table to strike Z, Winston halted the vid. "Allow me to provide you with some information, Sers. The man about to be struck is a Haraken SADE by the name of Z." Winston sent the Leaders an alternate vid of Z to their implants. "This is also Z, wearing his Miranda Leyton avatar and persona. You will notice that Major Barbas of the UE is quite taken with her charms. Now he has discovered that these two individuals are essentially two faces of the same SADE."

Méridien decorum left the chambers in a hurry. The reactions varied—laughter about the subterfuge perpetrated against the Earthers, curiosity about the mechanics involved in the transfer of kernel and personas, incredulity at a SADE occupying an avatar, and indignation at the duplicity of the SADE—and all the reactions were played at the top of voices and comms.

Winston let loose an audio screech into Council chambers, which brought conversation to a halt. *When did I become the parent of Méridien Leaders?* Winston thought. "Allow me to proceed, Sers," Winston said. The vid continued and the Assembly watched the fiercely delivered blow stopped, as if the major's hand hit a wall. Many of the technically minded in the Assembly credited the SADEs with their foresight to create extremely robust avatars for their use.

Mahima stood on her dais thinking she could refute much of this conversation as belligerent children arguing, children who could learn much from a mature society. That was until it came to the portion where the high judge stated his challenge to President Racine, offering three of his pilots to kill or be killed by the Harakens, who he still assumed to be Méridiens.

"You see the danger of listening to this man," Mahima demanded of her audience. "High Judge Bunaldi believes he is speaking to Méridiens, and this Haraken president, pretending to represent us, sets a dangerous precedent that we, true Méridiens, would ever take part in this vile contest."

Gino Diamanté stood up and Winston announced him. "Thank you, Winston, I have two clarifying questions. The first is for Council Leader Ganesh. What do you believe the Earthers would do if their challenge was not accepted?"

Mahima glared at Gino. She knew he was one of those who requested the meeting, and she looked forward to developing plans to destroy him. "It's as I told you before, Leader Diamanté. The Earthers will grow tired of the lack of contact from us and realize the futility of their efforts. It might take days or a year. It doesn't matter, but eventually they will go home," Mahima said with her old confidence.

"And your second question, Leader Diamanté," Winston said.

"It concerns our Council Leader's stance, and I ask it of my fellow Leaders. Please signal your response of 'yes' or 'no' to Winston. Do you believe the Earthers, if they are not challenged, will grow tired of our passive resistance, noncontact if you will, and go home?"

Winston found a good number of Leaders were failing to respond, and he reminded them that the nature of this special meeting required their responses. It presented many of the unresponsive with a problem. The evidence presented generated one opinion, but whom they supported often required a contrary vote, and it came down to stating an honest opinion or valuing the future of their Houses. The silence in the chambers extended for a while. Winston informed the Assembly that deliberation on the question was continuing. In actual fact, House Leaders were comming their allies trying to determine if their vote would injure their House associations. It was more than two hours before the voting was complete.

"In response to the question asked by Leader Diamanté, the members of this Assembly have answered in the negative by 67 percent," Winston announced.

The statement shocked Mahima to the core and she sought to maintain a grip on the curved rail of her dais. She had been sure the majority of Leaders would support her.

"The response of this Assembly obviates the next two questions," Winston said. "Council Leader Ganesh, since the majority of the assembled Leaders do not support your position with regard to the United Earth people and believe nonconfrontation will not prevent them from pursuing their policy of subjugation, what actions will you take to counteract their threat?"

Mahima felt as if she had been punched. She had lost the support of the majority, and, in turn, they were demanding she forgo a century of her administrative methods, changing at the moment, to take an aggressive stance against the Confederation's newest challenge. Her machine-like thought processes ground to a halt, and she couldn't find a way through the dilemma she faced. It felt like too much, and finally she sat down heavily in her chair still holding to the rail for support.

The Leaders, who lent Mahima their support, despite the evidence presented by Winston, felt their hopes plummet as the Council Leader sank into her chair. They had denied the truth for the sake of political objective, and in the long run it might well cost them their Houses and the confidence of the Confederation's populace when their vote was discovered.

"Council Leader Ganesh, the Assembly awaits your response to the last question," Winston prodded Mahima, who, after a few moments, stood and looked at the Assembly. She eyed the faces of those she directed for half her life, most of whom just turned their backs on her. Mahima straightened her shoulders and tilted her head high. She would refuse to give them an answer—it seemed an inadequate gesture, but the only one left to her. She climbed down from her dais and strode from chambers as Council Leader for the last time.

"Winston," Gino called out, "what are the protocols for these circumstances?"

"The Council Leader has abandoned her position," Winston said. "There is no other option for this action except to elect a new Council Leader. A quorum of the Leaders is required, and they are present in the Assembly. If there are members who wish to stand for the position, please signal me." After a few moments, Winston said, "I have received twenty-three nominations for Council Leader. They are for a single individual. Leader Gino Diamanté, will you accept the nomination of your peers?"

Gino remained seated. He didn't think his legs would hold him up if he tried to stand. His actions were intended to force Leader Ganesh into action. It never occurred to him that she would walk away from her position. *Is this what life is like for Alex?* Gino wondered. *How does he do it?*

<Gino,> Katarina sent, <we need you. Council leadership might appear daunting, but in our present circumstances, you have someone to guide you. If you cooperate with President Racine, the majority of the Assembly will support you. Stand now, please, for all of us.>

The Leaders on either side of Gino stood and offered their hands and he accepted them, allowing his peers to draw him to his feet. "I accept the nomination," Gino stated for the record.

"Will the Assembly please signal me as to whether they approve or disapprove of Gino Diamanté as Council Leader of the Confederation?" Winston requested. That Gino received an 84 percent approval was gratifying to Winston, who had tired of Leader Ganesh's apathetic leadership. *This change has been long overdue,* thought Winston. "Congratulations, Council Leader Diamanté. May the stars guide your steps," Winston stated formally, "Will you please take your place on the dais?"

Gino made his way to the chamber's floor and climbed the dais. When he faced his peers, they stood and offered honor with hands over hearts and heads bowed. He accepted their honor and placed both his hands on the curved railing to which Mahima recently clung. "My fellow Leaders," Gino said, "thank you for your confidence in me. But it is time to dispense with our tradition of relying on the Council Leader for every decision. We must become a body of action for our way of life and for our people. I will require your advice and support as we work to rid ourselves of these interlopers. Today is a new day for the Confederation. May the stars preserve us!"

22

Renée had poured two cups of thé, but she sat on the couch, legs curled under her, watching the cups cool. Alex was in the refresher, claiming a need for a quick cleansing, but that was a while ago. The deadline for accepting the contest was fast approaching, and a decision was yet to be made. The questions argued around the ship by the Harakens concerned the alternatives. If the challenge wasn't accepted, what would the Earthers think—what would they do?

Renée stood and walked into the sleeping quarters. "Should I come in or are you coming out?" she asked, leaning against a wall, prepared to wait for an answer. In response, the refresher shut down. Renée hurried back to the salon and made two fresh cups of thé in time to hand one cup to Alex as he walked into the salon. She waited until he made himself comfortable on the couch and took a sip or two from his cup before she curled beside him.

"Why do life-and-death decisions keep haunting us?" Alex asked quietly.

"I would think, eventually, these decisions haunt everyone, but most allow fortune to decide the answer. Only a few wrestle with the questions in an attempt to direct their fate."

"Perhaps I could be one of those who let fortune decide," Alex replied, his voice fading away at the end as if he was unconvinced of the truth of his words.

"No, you couldn't be like them, my love," Renée said, "because if you were, you wouldn't be you, and I wouldn't be with you."

Alex sat his mug on the low table and pulled Renée into his lap. They sat quietly, holding each other, time passing and the thé going cold again.

<Julien,> Alex sent.

<Yes, Mr. President,> Julien replied. <Shall I tell the speaker that we accept the high judge's contest and send him the system coordinates where we intend to rendezvous?>

Alex smiled to himself. <I take it I'm late to the decision party.>

<There was only one logical conclusion, Mr. President, despite the onerous nature of this contest. The Earthers have left us no choice. If we don't fight, they would see no impediment to their adoption of the entire Confederation,> Julien replied.

<And would our pilots consider the conclusion so obvious?> Alex wondered.

<I have it on good authority, Mr. President, that the leader of our three combatants will be none other than the *Last Stand's* wing commander. When Commander Thompson asked for volunteers, the entire wing stood. It would seem our pilots have also come to the proper conclusion.>

<And yet, even after these three Earther pilots are dead, I fear nothing will change, Julien. This is just a test of our resistance, and the more we resist, the harder the UE will push back. That's my sense of it anyway,> Alex said.

<I can't disagree with your logic, Mr. President, but short of escalating our resistance, what other option do we have?>

<Escalating our resistance . . . you mean attack and destroy their two ships? Then we wait until someone comes to investigate the loss of a battleship and a high judge. Then we also destroy them,> Alex sent, morose at the thought.

<It does seem to be an ugly, downward spiral at that, Mr. President.>

<So we start with a small skirmish in hopes of preventing a war. Where's the logic in that?> Alex said, closing the comm.

* * *

The next morning, Alex notified Christie, Eloise, and Amelia that they were noncombatants and would be dropped off at Le Jardin before the *Rêveur* made for Bevroren.

Tatia was seated next to Alex and Renée at the head table for morning meal when she whispered to Alex, "Incoming."

Alex looked up to see his sister and her friends walk through the meal room doors and march straight toward him. *This is going to be fun,* Alex thought.

"Mr. President," said Christie, addressing her brother formally as her friends had urged her. "We do not wish to be treated as second-class citizens by being left behind at Le Jardin."

"You aren't second-class citizens, Christie. It's just unnecessary for you to take the risk with the rest of us," Alex explained.

"Why are we not allowed the privilege of sharing the risk with the rest of our people?" Eloise asked.

Shades of the elders, Alex thought, recognizing Eloise's argument as the one the elders used when Alex sought to protect their Libran families from the fight pending in the Arnos system.

"Will Ser de Guirnon be accompanying us to Le Jardin, Ser President?" Amelia asked, innocence dripping sweetly from her words.

Alex glanced at Renée, who was smirking at him and trying unsuccessfully to turn it into a smile. He raised his hands to emphasize his response but dropped them back on the table when he couldn't think of anything to say. Alex knew no matter what decision he made, it could result in headaches, sooner or later.

"I take it the order is rescinded, Mr. President," Christie said, recognizing when she won an argument with her brother. Without waiting for a reply, Christie spun around and headed for the food dispensers. Both Eloise and Amelia paused to touch Alex's hand, and he nodded, accepting their appreciation.

"One hopes your strategy for the upcoming fight will proceed with greater success," Renée said, grinning into her cup as she took another sip.

Alex gave Renée an evil look and then noticed that Tatia was trying to hide her own smile. He didn't bother to reply and just resumed consuming his meal. *I hope it does too,* Alex thought.

* * *

"Captain Cordova, set course for Bevroren but follow behind the *Hand of Justice* and the *Reunion* by five to six hours," Alex ordered.

"Understood, Mr. President," Cordova acknowledged.

"Admiral, what's the position of the *Last Stand*?" Alex asked.

"In fourteen hours, the carrier will be at Point Alpha, waiting until the Earther ships close on the planet before they start their run to launch the travelers, Mr. President."

Alex was nodding in approval when he received a signal from Julien and held up a finger to delay Tatia's next words.

<Mr. President, you have a comm from Council Leader Diamanté,> Julien sent.

Alex was wondering what Mahima wanted when Julien's words registered. <Such a droll wit, Ser,> Alex replied to Julien.

<I developed this persona over the course of two years, Ser, and you expect it to change simply because I am now walking around? How human a concept!>

The subsequent war of images was brief so as not to keep Gino waiting. The pleasure for Julien was that he could now smile during their exchanges, as he had been doing for years, instead of just imagining the effort. When their comm closed, Julien continued down the *Rêveur*'s corridor, a fedora, set at a jaunty angle, appearing on his head. He began whistling a tune, a habit he recently adopted, and his faithful reproduction of the music often caused the crew to stop and listen.

<Congratulations, Council Leader Diamanté,> Alex said in greeting. <How does the weight of the office feel?>

<Is it possible to feel ill from a promotion, Ser President?>

<It's not only possible, Council Leader, but it will probably get worse. Why did this transition take place?>

<It began as an emergency Council meeting requiring Mahima to answer questions about the Earthers, and she damned herself. It's as if she

has been living in a world other than ours. She was convinced the Earthers would simply go away if we ignored them.>

<Not likely, Council Leader,> Alex replied. < I take it you decided to step in and take the leadership mantle on yourself?>

<On the contrary, Ser President. I believe we have suffered the same fate. Winston tells me that Julien shared the appropriate term with him. I was drafted.>

Alex burst out laughing so hard he took a seat to maintain his balance.

<I, for one, do not see the humor, Ser,> Gino sent, his thoughts transmitting his indignation.

<That's just it,> Alex said, after regaining his breath. <There isn't a single funny thing about it.>

<Then why are you laughing, Ser?> Gino demanded.

<Because, my dear Council Leader Gino Diamanté, now I have a friend to share the dark, ugly hole that I have been inhabiting for the past nine years. Welcome!>

It occurred to Gino that Alex was probably right. He never considered the possibility that Alex was a reluctant leader. But a comforting thought did occur to him. *What better company could I have in my predicament than the man who saved the Confederation once? Perhaps, Alex could do it again.*

<Well, Ser President, now that we are in this dark place together, I'm pleased to inform you that I have Council support for any actions I deem necessary to protect the Confederation. That support includes giving you any aid you require to achieve your agenda.>

Alex immediately sobered up and stood. His motion brought him to Tatia's attention, and she touched her temple, which added her into a one-way comm so she could listen. <You're saying we have unfettered Council support, Council Leader Diamanté. Are you aware that a head-to-head fighter contest between us and the Earthers will take place soon at Bevroren?>

Tatia looked at Alex and mouthed the words "Council Leader," her face screwed up in confusion, and Alex nodded his head in agreement.

<We have received word of the contest, as the Earthers term it, although fighting to the death hardly seems an appropriate definition of the term. Is there any help that we can give you, Ser President?>

<I would like to say "yes," but I'm afraid there isn't.>

<If you win this contest,> and Alex could hear the distaste in Gino's thoughts, <do you think the Earthers will abide by their promise and leave?>

<No, we expect treachery from them, but we've made contingency plans.> Alex glanced over at Tatia, who was shaking her head vigorously, indicating their contingency plans should not be shared. <Council Leader Diamanté, if we are successful in finding a solution with the Earthers that protects the Confederation's independence, then I want two things on the negotiating table.>

<Allow me to anticipate your concerns, Ser President. You wish to discuss our SADEs and the Independents.>

<Discuss is the polite term, Council Leader. If I am successful with the Earthers and the Council does not deal forthrightly with me on these subjects, my next visit to Confederation Hall will make my first visit look like an afternoon fête.>

<Threats are not necessary, Ser President. I know you and your people have not been treated fairly by the Council. What you ask for will take some time to accommodate, but I believe many Leaders wish to see changes, and the foremost change might be an opportunity to form an alliance between the Confederation and Haraken.>

<Apologies, Gino,> Alex sent. <I know you mean well, and perhaps we can become allies with your Council leadership.> A few moments later, Alex ended the comm with Gino, and then turned to address Tatia. "Did you think Gino would betray the information about the *Last Stand*, Admiral?"

"No, Mr. President, not Gino, but I don't trust the other people that might have access to the information. I can't help thinking that there is one powerful, upset woman on Méridien right now, and that makes her extremely dangerous."

It wasn't that Alex disagreed with Tatia, but he couldn't conceive of Mahima betraying her people.

* * *

"Alpha position achieved," Captain Manet reported to Sheila when the *Last Stand* arrived out of the deep dark at a point 450K kilometers outward of Bevroren. The ship had jumped from its previous position to a point one light-year out and then back again to Point Alpha in order to remain hidden from Earther eyes.

<Commander Thompson, what is the status of our launch maneuver?> Sheila sent. The Commodore was right to be concerned. The launch was more difficult than originally conceived. It was simple in design—tether the travelers outboard of the bays, accelerate the carrier, and release the travelers. Unfortunately, the carrier's design precluded the travelers from sailing straight forward after their release. They would be striking structures that extended outward from the carrier's flared bow, and the travelers weren't sufficiently charged to enable maneuvering around the structures until they entered a sufficiently strong gravitational field.

<No workable plan yet, Commodore,> Ellie replied, biting her lip. She hadn't felt this frustrated since her exile to Libre. Her people were counting on her, and she didn't have an answer to the maneuver they were trying to execute.

<Captain Manet, get me Z,> Sheila requested.

Edouard signaled the controller, requesting a comm with the *Rêveur*, and, in turn, that ship's controller signaled Z.

<Greetings, Commodore, how appropriate that you commed. I was just thinking of you,> Z sent.

Z's response threw Sheila off her step. How or why a SADE should have her in his thoughts was a little disconcerting.

<How may I help you, Commodore?> Z added.

<Z, our attempts to follow the plan to launch our three contestants and then the remainder of our sub-wing outside of any gravitational fields have

met with failure. If we tether the travelers outboard of the bays and use our ship's inertia to launch the travelers into Bevroren's orbit, we are unable to place the travelers far enough from the ship to have the fighters clear our bow's forward elements.>

<Understood, Commodore, I will return with an appropriate solution,> Z replied and released Sheila from the comm, retaining the *Last Stand*'s controller. While Z downloaded the carrier's configuration, statistics about the bays' beam strength and reach, and a thousand other details, he connected with Julien to share the request. In turn, Julien modeled Bevroren, the *Last Stand*'s present position, and the expected course of the first sub-wing of the travelers, which was stored in the carrier's controller.

Word circulated among the crew that the SADEs were entirely absorbed. Both were seen sitting and staring off into bulkheads. Few considered it a good sign that two SADEs were required to tackle an issue to the degree that both of them were ignoring their human behavior programs. Fortunately, Sheila communicated her dilemma to Alex and Tatia and that she requested the SADEs' help.

<That's why they're here, Commodore,> Alex replied. <Our fate is their fate, and I'm pleased you've reached out to them for help.>

<Mr. President, do you know why Z would say he was thinking of me?> Sheila asked with the slightest of trepidation. She was still getting accustomed to the reality of SADEs walking around and interacting with humans, and sometimes her imagination got the best of her.

Alex was tempted to tell her that she was probably in Z's dreams, but he knew Sheila and other New Terrans were struggling with the concept of SADEs mixing with them. <I understand Z is working on a prototype traveler-fighter design. He probably wants you to review his concept,> Alex finally replied.

<Oh, well . . . a prototype fighter. That's fine. That's good. I can certainly help with that,> Sheila sent, her thoughts stumbling out.

<Focus on the present, Commodore. Trust the SADEs to find you an answer for the launch, and trust the Earthers to change the contest on us.> Alex said and closed the comm.

* * *

The *Last Stand*'s controller received a comm, and because the sender was identified as a priority contact for the wing commander, it was transferred immediately to her even as she reviewed her craft's flight preparations.

<Hello, my heart,> Ellie sent.

<I've learned you will lead the flight of our contestants,> Étienne replied. <I would have wished to have learned that from you.> Étienne's superb control was in danger of slipping.

Ellie's heart lurched. She was guilty as charged, and she knew it.

The silence on the comm told Étienne volumes, and he decided not to add to the pressure Ellie was under. <Lead your flight with strength, Ellie. Do not hold back. The Earthers will be earnest competitors. You must do no less. Be safe, Ellie,> Étienne sent and closed the comm.

Ellie had expected anger and recrimination from her partner, which she believed she deserved, but Étienne was as always the man she had come to depend on. He was her rock. Ellie's world was turned upside down when she was accused of fostering unsafe competition and exiled to Libre. Her years as an Independent passed by in a dream state with little recognition of time until the admiral arrived.

Joining House Alexander was an easy choice for Ellie. She yearned to sit in a cockpit again and fly, and, if truth be told, she wanted an opportunity to be rid of the anger that simmered inside her for years. The giant Nua'll sphere and the silver ships were the perfect outlet for her anger. But with time, her anger faded, replaced by duty, and joy returned to her life when she met the quiet-spoken Étienne.

On one occasion, Ellie mentioned to Étienne that she was untrained in hand-to-hand defense techniques, and he volunteered to train her. As she moved up the ranks of Haraken's naval forces, the training served her well. Her techniques outclassed her compatriots, and her confidence rose.

"Lead with strength" was a phrase Étienne used during training. It meant she should attack first, immobilizing the opponents before they could strike. *Lead with strength,* Ellie thought. Étienne's words fueled her confidence and powered her steps as she crossed the bay to meet her flight chief.

* * *

Despite the early morning hours, Z alerted Alex, who requested Tatia, Julien, and Z gather in Alex's cabin. Renée made thé for the humans, who were called from their beds, disheveled and valiantly trying to clear their minds, while the SADEs appeared as presentable as ever.

Tatia groused to Julien and Z, who arrived before her, "The least you two could do is have an early morning persona so you would look like the rest of us." At which point, Julien walked into Alex's sleeping quarters and stripped off his Haraken attire. He searched for the appropriate image and settled on that of an elderly, penniless miser in late-evening attire—scruffy slippers and threadbare robe and pajamas. He projected the clothes over his body and returned to the salon.

Julien's presentation produced the desired result. The humans burst into laughter and applauded his new attire. His gambit worked to clear and sharpen minds as the thé never could. His friends would need their wits; the news required their complete focus.

"An anomaly has been detected, Ser President," Z said.

"Explain, Z," Alex ordered, sipping on his cup of thé, his mind flashing back to the sound of Tara's artificial voice onboard the *Outward Bound,* saying the same thing eleven years ago.

"We have remained behind the Earther ships as you instructed Captain Cordova, Ser President," Z said. "The two ships made for a rendezvous point on the inward side of Delacroix, and the *Reunion* took a position off the far bow quarter of the *Hand of Justice* just as they disappeared behind the planet. When the ships emerged into our view on the far side of Delacroix, that's when I noticed the anomaly."

"That's it?" said Tatia, a little irked at being woken from a sound sleep for such a nebulous announcement.

"Admiral, be patient," Alex directed. "What else, Z?"

"The *Reunion*'s telemetry has altered, and that has given us reason for concern, Sers" replied Z, and Alex smiled into his cup. Mathematics was Z's language, and it was a pure language. Anomalies were unacceptable and were to be questioned, and then followed to the aberration's source. "I analyzed the path of the two Earther ships before and after they passed Delacroix. There are the expected subtle deviations and corrections of flight paths of each ship before Delacroix, but none afterward."

When the three humans stared at Z, waiting for more details, Julien added, "There has been absolutely no variance in distance between the Earther ships as they have navigated from Delacroix toward their final position inward of Bevroren."

"None? You mean minor?" Tatia said.

"None, Admiral," Z repeated.

"That's impossible, isn't it?" Tatia asked the SADEs.

"We believe so, Admiral," Julien answered.

"So why would the telemetry on these ships indicate they were navigating in absolute lockstep?" Alex mused.

Z turned to regard Julien. It was an indication of one SADE deferring to another who possessed subtler reasoning algorithms enabling "operation outside accepted parameters" as Z would say.

"Ancient Terran war tactics, provided by the colonists' records, indicate that it was a favored technique of fleet commanders to spoof the number of their warships," Julien said. "They did so by many ingenious innovations, one of which was projection . . . what we might think of as a holo-vid display that fooled the enemy into thinking there were more ships in the fleet than in reality. I would surmise we are looking at a device tethered to the *Hand of Justice* that contains a laser, and the battleship is firing a second laser at the tethered device. The interference of the two lasers would create a coherent perfect absorber, or anti-laser, which would absorb the coherent light and convert it into a signature that would imitate the telemetric signature of the *Reunion*."

The humans stared at Julien and Z so long that Z felt compelled to add, "It's a perfectly reasonable deduction, Sers."

"So your concern is that the too-perfect telemetry indicates the *Reunion* is a ghost ship, and the real ship has been left at our rear in the moons of Delacroix," Alex surmised.

"According to my calculations, Ser President," Z said, "I have an 87.4 percent certainty that this is so."

"Couldn't we confirm this suspicion by checking telemetry from ships or stations that might have a view of the far moons of Delacroix?" Renée asked.

"No need," Alex replied. "Z's level of certainty is proof enough. Julien, get a message to Captain Manet and Commodore Reynard of your suspicions."

"Well, we expected treachery," Tatia said, and then added under her breadth, "And I thought I could be devious."

"Makes one wonder what other tricks the Earthers possess," added Renée.

"UE has developed their war craft over centuries, and this concerns me," Julien said. That a SADE uttered these words was chilling, but that it came from one appearing as an elderly miser made it seem comical.

23

"Are you ready, Admiral?" Bunaldi asked Theostin as they monitored the *Rêveur*'s approach to within 150K kilometers of their position.

"Ready to launch, Judge," Theostin replied. "After our three pilots reach an engagement window with the Méridiens, a wave of twenty-four more fighters will launch. Even if we lose our first three fighters, the Méridiens shouldn't have time to escape before we swamp their craft and capture the *Rêveur*."

"Excellent, Admiral. An example must be made."

"Some things still mystify me," Theostin said. "The *Rêveur* appears to be a passenger ship. Why would a passenger ship carry fighters? If it did, it couldn't carry more than three or four fighters with its two small bay doors."

Bunaldi stared at the bridge officers and their stations without seeing them. The questions also occurred to him, and the answers weren't forthcoming. *It can't be this easy,* Bunaldi thought. *The Méridiens can't be this poorly schooled in the defense of their Confederation.*

* * *

The *Last Stand* sailed in from the deep dark toward Bevroren. All pilots in the first sub-wing were ready to launch.

The SADEs came through with an answer for Sheila's and Ellie's dilemma, sending a set of engine maneuvers for the carrier's controller to execute. The launch of the contestants and the trailing sub-wing would take place as one, from a single side of the carrier. On the commodore's command, the controller would swing the carrier's bow severely to starboard while releasing the beams anchoring the port travelers. It would allow the carrier's bow to clear the path of the fighters. After correcting the ship's vector, the next sub-wing would be positioned outside their bays, and the controller would reverse the procedure. The timing of each maneuver was critical, but it was nothing a SADE-built controller couldn't execute with ease.

Ellie sat quietly at the controls of her traveler, which was tethered outboard on the bay's beams. She was replaying images of Étienne's training sessions to focus her mind on what was to come, but, in the end, she froze one of the sessions on an image of Étienne and was dwelling on every minute detail of her beloved.

<We launch your sub-wing in 0.1 hours, Commander. May fortune be with you,> Sheila sent.

<May the stars guide our path, Commodore,> Ellie replied. She linked with her flight commanders and reiterated her instructions despite the fact that their travelers' controllers carried the tactical approach embedded in memory. The entire sub-wing would be launched toward Bevroren's gravity well. Once the planet's orbit was attained, the sub-wing would allow Ellie's flight to pull ahead until a gap of 0.25 hours separated them.

Her traveler's controller issued a brief warning and, with a relatively quick movement, Ellie felt the slightest change in inertia as the carrier's maneuver propelled her craft forward.

Despite the entire sub-wing to keep her company, Ellie sat quietly in her pilot's chair, waiting for the arrival of Bevroren's gravity waves to power their fighters. Time slowly ticked past, and Ellie found herself lulled to sleep, suspecting other pilots were doing the same. Two hours later, a signal from her controller brought Ellie fully alert. Her traveler's crystal energy banks were powering up.

<Flight One,> Ellie sent, <Stay tight on me.> Her two wings, Captains Sean McCrery and Darius Gaumata, confirmed Ellie's order, and the pilots locked their controllers to hers. Sean and Darius had been flying with Ellie since Libre. They were her two best pilots, and, moreover, Ellie trusted them to see the fight through to the end. As one, their flight accelerated, circling the planet. During the orbit, the travelers' drive crystals continued

to charge as the fighters' shells sliced through the planet's powerful gravitational forces.

Flight One's controllers were updated with the final positions of the *Hand of Justice*, the *Rêveur*, and the three UE fighters that were just exiting the battleship. The Haraken pilots were warned of the strong possibility that the *Reunion* was a ghost image. The thought that the explorer ship was attempting to trap the *Rêveur* with the president and admiral aboard did much to harden Ellie's heart toward the Earthers.

Ellie and her wings swung out of Bevroren's orbit at max velocity making a straight line for the UE fighters, who were accelerating toward the *Rêveur*. The UE fighters had only covered a third of the distance toward their goal when Ellie's flight shot past the battleship, chasing them. Soon, her flight controller signaled the enemy's reversal of vector. The UE fighters were now accelerating toward her.

Before Ellie's flight could enter the traveler's beam engagement window, her controller signaled the launch of multiple missile flights. <Heads up, Captains,> Ellie sent. <Don't get anxious. Evade the missiles, and hold your fire until we're close. We won't have time to recharge our beams before we're past these fighters, and I don't want to have to circle back. We take these fighters out, and we race to the *Rêveur* to protect our leaders.>

The first wave of missiles took the Harakens by surprise. The pilots expected contact missiles, and their travelers twisted and spun to evade the first wave. But the enemy armed their missiles with proximity devices, detonating the missiles in front of the oncoming travelers. Hundreds of pieces of shrapnel glanced off their Swei Swee shells.

For subsequent waves, the pilots quickly reset their controllers to evade the missiles at greater distances, but there was a price to pay for those commands. To execute the new input, the controllers pushed the envelope of the travelers' inertia systems, and the pilots were shaken, suffering momentary blackouts.

During the second missile wave, Sean McCrery's shell suffered multiple hits, which compounded the previous damage to his hull. Multiple cracks destroyed the shell's charging integrity, and Sean watched his power crystals slowly drain into his drive and operating systems. The thought struck him that even if his beam fired, it wouldn't be at full strength.

Sean's traveler, unable to maneuver at full power, succumbed to two near misses from the third wave of missiles, and pieces of shrapnel pierced the shell's bow and Sean. The nanites in the captain's environment suit and his blood dutifully attempted to patch both the suit and his body.

Ellie's flight just evaded the final barrage of missiles when her helmet registered the adversary's vector changes as the UE pilots spread out. Ellie assigned targets to her flight via the controllers. Moments later, the Harakens entered a perfect engagement window, and Ellie concentrated on her own target. *Lead with strength* echoed over and over in Ellie's mind. The lead fighter, her adversary, was continuing straight at her without any further launches. *Did you run out of missiles?* Ellie thought. It was all the time there was to wonder before her controller fired the fighter's beam.

Sean felt a blackness begin to muddy his thoughts. The shrapnel damage to his body was too great to repair, and a strange mixture of sadness and anger crept over him. He was sad for the wife and child he would leave behind and angry at the Earthers who invaded his world. Sean signaled his controller, overriding the safety protocols, and directed his traveler at the enemy fighter. With his last thought, Sean sent a message to his commander, but in the fading darkness of his mind his thought was relayed in the open. <For Haraken> was heard by Sean's colleagues, pilots, ship controllers, and SADEs, both Haraken and Méridien, before his traveler rammed the UE fighter, the two vessels exploding in a brilliant fireball.

Sean's last thought would eventually be relayed around the Confederation, to Haraken, and to New Terra, along with the vids of the events. Once again, people were dying in defense of the Confederation. However, this time, those on Méridien were adopting a completely different attitude toward the invaders.

Ellie swept past her UE fighter and switched to the traveler's aft view in time to catch the expanding ball of gas and debris that was her target. That's when she received Sean's message and frantically adjusted her telemetry for a wider view. Three enemy craft were destroyed, and only

Darius was still with her. She fought the sadness that threatened to overwhelm her and focused on the next stage.

<Captain Gaumata, any damage to your craft?> Ellie sent. She waited and then sent more intensely, <Captain Gaumata.>

<Here, Commander,> Darius replied, trying to refocus. He and the rough-housing Sean were as different as two people could be and still they became best friends, often taking outings to the beach together with their spouses and children.

<Report your status, Captain,> Ellie sent.

<I think my shell has some serious impacts, Commander,> Darius replied, <but my controller indicates I'm still charging at about 73 percent of the optimal rate. I think I need a Swei Swee checkup,> Darius said, striving for a little bravado, but his heart wasn't in it, and the thought came across as a lament.

<I need you to focus, Captain. This ridiculous excuse for a contest isn't over with. Take a defensive position 20K kilometers off the starboard side of the *Rêveur* against the *Reunion*. I'll assume a position off the bow,> Ellie sent and cut the comm.

* * *

Aboard the *Rêveur*, Alex watched the three enemy fighters and one of his travelers wink off the holo-vid and heard Sean's last thought. His fists clenched in rage. Renée laid one hand on his shoulder and stroked his arm with the other.

"Mr. President, Admiral Tachenko, we have movement. The *Hand of Justice* has just launched twenty-four fighters. They're headed for us," Julien said.

"The *Reunion* is coming out from behind Delacroix, Ser President," Z added. "Flight time to our present position is approximately 7.3 hours."

Alex was debating which way to run, knowing there were only moments to decide. If he ran, his two pilots would succumb to the UE fighters as they sought to guard his fleeing ship. Equally frustrating was the thought that the *Last Stand*'s following wave of travelers would arrive too late to help. It was obvious the Earthers were better practiced in the art of subterfuge. Alex looked over at Tatia, expecting to see anger and frustration carved into her face, but she wore a cruel grin. "Would you like to share, Admiral?" Alex asked.

Tatia's grin never faded as she replied, "Sub-wing Commander Deirdre Canaan disobeyed orders."

* * *

Deirdre Canaan was severely disappointed that she hadn't been picked by Ellie to fly as her wing. "I'm the second-best pilot on this carrier after you, Commander," Deirdre complained to Ellie in the privacy of the commander's office. "You know I should be out there beside you."

"You are the next-best pilot, after me, of course," Ellie replied, her cheeky smile taking the sting out of her remark. "And that's why I need you as sub-wing commander, backing us up. We expect these Earthers not to play by their own rules, but we haven't a clue as to what they will do. I need you leading the sub-wing to make sure that whatever trick they pull, you make it blow up in their face. That's your job . . . win and protect our leaders."

Deirdre decided to dedicate time to her task, reviewing the vids of Earther contact, the Shadow's vids, and Étienne's combat training with the master sergeant. She took special notice of Major Barbas's reaction to Z's announcement that he was Miranda Leyton in another avatar. *You like to apply force, blunt force, to dissuade your enemy from even thinking of attacking you*, Deirdre thought.

Ellie's flight had pulled ahead of Deirdre's sub-wing as they rounded Bevroren, and the ordered distance lag soon reached the midpoint, but Deirdre was nagged by her thoughts about the Earthers. *We are amateurs at war, and you are professionals*, Deirdre thought and made up her mind.

<Flight leaders, we are disregarding controller programming. Accelerate and close the gap to the commander's flight. Stay on me, flight leaders,> Deirdre ordered.

Deirdre's sub-wing had already left Bevroren's orbit and was hurtling toward the *Hand of Justice* when they received an update of the contest and heard Sean's last thought. Despite her anger, Deirdre still expected to make for the *Rêveur* and protect her leaders, until her controller registered the launch of the twenty-four fighters from the battleship.

<Flight leaders, we have priority targets—those twenty-four UE fighters on your telemetry,> Deirdre sent. <Note the wing commander's message. Those missiles have proximity detection. Reset your controllers to evade by three times the present margin. Get close to your targets before you fire. I'm assigning targets to your flights now. Let's send the high judge a message he won't fail to understand.>

The number of enemy fighters the UE pilots suddenly faced frightened them, knowing that in the contest, the Méridiens lost only one fighter to their three—three of their best. It caused many of the UE pilots to panic and launch their first salvo of missiles prematurely, giving the travelers plenty of time to evade. Even then, the Méridien fighters appeared to form an impenetrable wall as the UE pilots found themselves facing two or more enemy fighters.

In the end, Deirdre's sub-wing of sixty-one travelers made short work of the UE fighters. She lost three pilots in the engagement.

Not done executing her plan, Deirdre lost no time ordering her sub-wing toward Delacroix and the emerging *Reunion*. Moments later, Deirdre received her admiral's order to return and guard the *Rêveur*, but she kept her sub-wing on its heading until she saw the Earther explorer ship change course and head out of system.

Deirdre knew that later she would stand a disciplinary hearing from the commodore and a personal dressing-down from the admiral, but at the moment, watching the explorer ship run for the deep dark, she wore a satisfied smile. *We can learn to play this dangerous game of yours as well as you do,* Deirdre thought.

* * *

"Speaker García and Major Barbas assured us these vessels were shuttles—exclusively," Theostin raged, not caring one whit who heard her loss of decorum. She and Bunaldi decided to witness their triumph in full view of the battleship's bridge officers. Instead they witnessed the loss of their three pilots and the contest, followed by the loss of twenty-four more of their fighters to the Méridiens' loss of only four fighters.

"Well, President Racine did warn us," Bunaldi said thoughtfully.

If Bunaldi was an underling, Theostin would have struck him repeatedly about the face. She was livid, and he was saying they were warned about this outcome. Theostin saw her precious dreams of promotion slipping away.

"What I would like to know is this: Where did those Méridien fighters come from?" Bunaldi said quietly. "It doesn't seem possible they're FTL capable, which means there's a large Méridien warship nearby. And here's my second question: Are all these shuttles that we see flying around armed ships?"

Bunaldi's calm reasoning soothed Theostin's temper as she supposed he intended. "I would like to know what they are using for armament," Theostin finally said. "The guide identified no launch of any sort—no rail slugs, missiles, or explosive rounds . . . nothing. There was just an energy spike right before our fighters were destroyed, except for that one Méridien fighter in the contest."

"Yes, that one," Bunaldi mused. "It appears the Méridiens are prepared to sacrifice themselves to achieve their goals once they are in the heat of battle. I wouldn't have thought that possible. It's a point to note very carefully."

"Judge Bunaldi, your pardon for the interruption," Captain Dimitri Chofsky said, "the *Reunion* has come out of hiding as planned and the Méridien fighters are making for it."

"Wave him off, Captain," Bunaldi ordered. "Have him make for deep space in our quadrant. Notify him that we suspect that a Méridien ship, a battleship or a carrier, might be waiting beyond Bevroren, and to give it a wide berth."

Bunaldi watched the comms officer take a call and urgently signal Captain Chofsky. "I was waiting for this," Bunaldi whispered to Theostin.

"Judge Bunaldi, a comm from President Racine. It's relayed through the *Reunion*," Captain Chofsky said.

Bunaldi gestured to the comms officer to put the call on the monitor. He watched the stern face of the president appear. *So youthful in appearance and yet already so talented at the tactics of war,* Bunaldi thought.

"President Racine, it appears you have won the contest." Bunaldi thought to play off his loss with nonchalance, but he found himself rather lamely waiting for a response when none was forthcoming. The young president's eyes continued to bore down on him from the monitor. "Come, now, we both appear to be practiced hands at war, and in war, people must be sacrificed to achieve the greater goals."

"Bunaldi," Alex said in a voice that sounded like stones grinding together, "we've played your little contest, and you have amply demonstrated that you're not a man of your word. Therefore, all communications with you are hereby terminated. You have one day to clear this system and enter FTL to return to Earth. And I have a message for your leader, Bunaldi. Come here again in anything less intimidating than a passenger liner, and we will destroy your ships on sight. One day, Bunaldi! Exit this system in one day or both your ships will end up as space debris, just like those pilots and fighters you sacrificed."

Before Bunaldi could answer, the comm was terminated.

"Captain Chofsky, tell Captain Lumley to expedite our exit from the system. Set an appropriate rendezvous point for our ships far outside this system and send the coordinates to him," Bunaldi ordered.

"We're running, Judge?" Theostin said, shocked at Bunaldi's order.

"We are employing a strategic retreat, my dear Admiral, until such time as I can contemplate our next move. We have a unique situation here, and I don't intend to mishandle it. That would be bad for both our careers and possibly our lives."

24

Mahima paced her bedroom floor. Her House SADE, Hector, had informed her that the Earthers lost the contest and were fleeing the system. "Fools! All of them," she hissed under her breath. "They should have listened to me, and none of this would ever have happened. It's that Racine's fault. Fortune deserted us the day he found the *Rêveur.*"

An idea began to take shape in Mahima's mind, and she stopped her pacing. "They want action from their Council Leader, do they? I will give them action." The thought didn't cross Mahima's mind that she was no longer Council Leader. <Hector, what is the status of the two Earther ships?>

<They are exiting the system, Leader Ganesh,> Hector replied. <Would you like precise coordinates, Ser?>

<No, Hector, place a comm to the high judge on the battleship,> Mahima ordered.

<Apologies, Leader Ganesh, I'm unable to comply. I have no means of contacting the *Hand of Justice.*>

<Then comm the other ship . . . the first one that entered the system,> Mahima fumed.

<I have Speaker García on the comm, Leader Ganesh,> Hector sent.

<Good evening, Speaker García,> Mahima sent, her thoughts gracious if not a bit tense. <This is Council Leader Ganesh. I wish to speak to the person in charge of your expedition. I believe that is High Judge Bunaldi.>

Speaker García hesitated before he nodded to the *Reunion* comms officer, who relayed the call to Bunaldi.

The moment that contact with the *Hand of Justice* was established, Hector routed the comm through the FTL station near the battleship to eliminate the delay in the high judge's response.

Bunaldi sat behind his salon's desk to take the call. "Good evening, Council Leader Ganesh. This is a surprise." Bunaldi hoped for a vid call, but even an audio-only call might be instructive, especially after President Racine indicated that all contact with their ships was to be terminated. "How may I be of service?"

<I believe I might be of service to you, Judge Bunaldi,> Mahima sent, her self-control reasserting itself. <During your contact with President Racine, you might have noticed that he doesn't have the typical Méridien build. It's because the man isn't Méridien.>

"Yet he speaks for you, Council Leader, does he not?" Bunaldi asked. He moved aside some articles on the desk to make room for Theostin, who perched on the desk to listen to the exchange.

<The man thinks he does, but he's an aberrant who listens to no one and chooses directions without reason. There were standing orders that no one was to contact you, and you see how well he followed those instructions,> Mahima replied, her control slipping again as an image of Alex entered her thoughts.

Bunaldi looked down at the sheet of flex that Theostin scribbled on with her finger. "If President Racine isn't Méridien, where's he from?" Bunaldi asked, reading Theostin's note.

<The man is New Terran, but he resides on Haraken,> Mahima replied. All she could see in her mind when she spoke of Alex Racine was the day he humiliated her in Council chambers nine years ago. That incident had burned in her mind every day since then. More than anything, that one event had slowly precipitated her mental decay.

"So what is Méridien's relationship with these two worlds or are they composed of multiple worlds?" Bunaldi asked.

<They wish to be more than they are, but New Terra is barely exploring its own system, and Haraken is nothing but a stolen colony that once belonged to the Confederation,> Mahima fumed.

Theostin flexed the sheet, erasing her note, and scribbled another question for Bunaldi, sliding the sheet back to him.

"I take it you have no sympathies for this man's actions, Council Leader. Perhaps it would be to your advantage if President Racine was no longer around to bother you or Méridien, for that matter?" Bunaldi said, rephrasing Theostin's question.

Mahima could not believe her good fortune. With one stroke she could rid Méridien of these interlopers and the sources of the bane of her existence—New Terra and Haraken. <And what would you do, Judge Bunaldi, if I was to supply you with the locations of these two worlds?>

Theostin curled her legs together on the desktop. The conversation's direction was exciting, and she fought to gain control and refrain from joining in. She felt Bunaldi's hand gently squeeze her bare foot, and she took a slow breath to calm herself.

"As you can see, Council Leader Ganesh, we are leaving Méridien as President Racine has ordered us," Bunaldi replied. He saw Theostin shake her head, warning him off from proceeding in that direction, but Bunaldi held a finger to his lips to silence her.

Mahima hesitated. If the Earthers were already leaving, then the prime goal was accomplished, but she couldn't let go of the thought that Alex Racine would still be haunting her life.

"Perhaps, we can help each other, Council Leader Ganesh. We might make a stop at Haraken or New Terra on the way home and return the favor he bestowed on us today," Bunaldi offered.

The temptation was too much for Mahima. <Hector, send a star map with Méridien, New Terra, and Haraken locations, including coordinates and FTL distances. Send it to this UE battleship, High Judge Bunaldi's attention.>

<Ser, are you sure this is wise?> Hector ventured.

<Hector, you sit in a box in this house's lowest floor. It must be dry down there. I wonder if you would like a cold drink of water,> Mahima said, and she included images of a pitcher of water pouring into a SADE's case.

Hector paled at the thought of his demise at the hands of his House Leader. He possessed no records of a Méridien threatening the life of a SADE, and he was suddenly frighteningly aware of how far Mahima's mental state was drifting.

<Send my request now, Hector,> Mahima sent with cold fury.

The vehemence of Mahima's thoughts frightened Hector into obliging his mistress, but immediately afterward he contacted Winston.

Bunaldi was hoping for the opportunity to ask a few more questions when the call suddenly ended. He sat back in his desk chair, a broad, satisfied smile on his face.

"Can we believe her?" Theostin asked, turning around to face Bunaldi and dropping her legs over the back of the desk.

"Can we believe that President Racine would have driven others, besides us, into states of emotional distress? Yes, that's quite believable," Bunaldi replied, rubbing his chin, and considered the information that had fallen into his lap. In the meantime, he ordered the information copied to the *Reunion*.

Bunaldi punched the comm on his desk. "Comms, connect me to Speaker García." When he was connected, Bunaldi said, "Speaker García, we have received information with the locations of Haraken and New Terra, worlds not formally associated with Méridien, and apparently where the people aboard the *Rêveur* abide. Haraken is a new colony. It should be easily subdued. That will be your destination. New Terra is a single world. That will be my destination."

"Captain Lumley has confirmed our guide's receipt of the star information, Judge Bunaldi. We will leave as soon as the guide has calculated the jump," García replied.

"Méridien might be out of our reach for now, Speaker García, but we will gain a great deal of prestige when we bring these two worlds to their knees. I will see that you are given fair credit for your efforts."

When High Judge Bunaldi signed off, García's thought was to define "fair credit" as equivalent to a footnote in the high judge's report to the Supreme Tribunal.

"So what's next?" Theostin asked after Bunaldi cut the comm.

"What's next, my dear? I think we should celebrate this little bit of windfall," Bunaldi replied with a grin.

Theostin responded with a mischievous grin of her own, and while Bunaldi reached for a bottle of aged cognac and two glasses, she returned to the couch to retrieve her favorite massage oil.

* * *

The *Last Stand*'s second sub-wing was never launched. After receiving Julien's message that the Earthers were retreating from the system, Commodore Reynard and Captain Manet decided to wait near a Bevroren moon and monitor the two UE ships after they cleared the system. The enemy ships were seen to rendezvous and within a relatively short time, the two ships separated, accelerated, and entered FTL on two different tangents.

"What in black space just happened?" Sheila asked, staring at the divergent trajectories of the UE ships.

"Our controller has an estimated tangent for Earth, which was supplied by Winston from Méridien archives, and it does not align with either course of these two ships," Edouard replied.

<Julien, Z,> Sheila sent, her heart beginning to race. <Pull our ship's controller records of the exodus of the Earther ships into FTL. I want your opinion on their destinations.>

Julien and Z calculated the answer in mere ticks and urgently linked Alex and Tatia. <Sers, the *Last Stand* has observed the separation of the Earther ships as they entered FTL. On Commodore Reynard's request, Z and I have analyzed their vectors. The *Reunion* is headed in Haraken's direction; the *Hand of Justice* in New Terra's direction.>

<Could it be a coincidence?> Tatia asked on the comm. <I mean the Earthers wouldn't know the jump coordinates, because they wouldn't have our planets' locations.>

<Ser President, you have a priority comm from Council Leader Diamanté,> Z said.

<Greetings, Council Leader,> Alex replied, hoping to make short work of the comm to return to the vexing question they faced.

<Your pardon, Alex, but there is no time for pleasantries. We've been betrayed by Leader Ganesh,> Gino sent.

<How?> Alex asked, a sinking feeling striking his gut.

<Esther has a close relationship with Hector, the Ganesh House SADE, and she has learned that Mahima sent the star locations for Haraken and New Terra to the *Hand of Justice*. In her transmission—> Gino would have said more but his comm was cut from the other end.

* * *

Gino regarded the anxious faces of the Leaders, who surrounded him.

"What was the president's response?" Katarina inquired.

"I don't know. He ended the comm without replying," Gino said. His legs unsteady, Gino braced himself against the back of a couch.

"Do you think he will blame us for Mahima's actions?" asked Bartosz Rolek, his mind replaying images of the recent battle, the fighters' destruction, and the tally of the dead pilots.

"Alex? I mean President Racine . . ." Gino clarified. "No, I don't think he'll blame us. He's not that kind of man."

"You sound unsure," Devon O'Shea said. His feeling of trepidation was the same as the others. "What if the Earthers fail to subjugate his worlds and choose to destroy his cities as a warning to us? What would he do then?"

"Then we might have two unimaginable problems," Gino replied, "the Earthers and an extremely angry Haraken."

* * *

<Commodore, what's your status?> Alex demanded.

<All fighters recovered, Mr. President,> Sheila responded.

<Captain Manet, Commodore Reynard, make for New Terra at top speed,> Alex ordered. <And, Commodore, diplomacy is over. Order the *Hand of Justice* to immediately exit New Terra's system. If it fails to comply, turn it into space debris. No mercy.>

<What if we are unable to establish comms with the ship, Ser President?> Edouard asked. <All previous communication was relayed through the *Reunion*.>

<The High Judge is no fool, Captain,> Alex replied. <Once he spots your carrier behind him, he knows he has only two choices, run or fight. Whichever way it goes down, get back to Haraken as soon as you can. That's where we're headed now. Don't wait for the *Money Maker*, the freighter is too slow.>

As Alex cut the comm, he was pleased to see that the ships were headed out of system at max acceleration. He sat down at his desk to mentally compose messages for key people on both planets. They wouldn't arrive before the Earther ships entered the Oistos and Hellébore systems but would arrive soon after and in time to warn his people while the Earther ships made their way in system at sub-light speed.

"What do you think are the Earthers' intentions?" Renée asked in the privacy of their cabin.

"I don't care," replied Alex, his jaws clenching and unclenching. "When a nest of biters moves too close to your home, you destroy it. They have no respect for any life but their own. It's either you or them."

"Surely there are innocent people aboard, such as Administrator Wombo, Alex. Can't something be done for them?"

"These ships are led by two powerful men, High Judge Bunaldi and Speaker García, who have complete control over their ships and carry military forces to enforce their wills. I don't believe there will be an opportunity to separate the good from the bad." When Renée appeared crestfallen from his response, Alex folded her in his arms, but hardened his own heart against the deaths that were to come.

25

"Comms, announce all clear from FTL exit. Guide, I require a star fix," Captain Chofsky ordered. The *Hand of Justice* made the jump to Oistos, New Terra's location, based on the guide's estimation as it worked to match Leader Ganesh's data to its own star maps. The process was fraught with potential errors, and the guide chose to err on the conservative side of calculations, lest it destroy the battleship by jumping into the system's gravitational well.

"Captain, the ship is presently located one-quarter light-year from a star that matches the description we received," the guide replied. "A second jump is required."

"Prepare the jump, guide. Place us a half-day outside the system. We will execute in eight hours," Chofsky ordered.

"Orders received," the guide replied.

Eight hours enabled Chofsky to feed and rest the crew. UE crew traveling via FTL experienced an unnerving amount of physical and emotional distress, and captains, who cared about the welfare of their crew, as Chomsky did, took pains to break the longer jumps into shorter ones to allow their crew to recover. This was not to say that Dimitri Chomsky could be considered a sensitive man. On the contrary, he was considered one of the UE's brilliant tacticians, and as such he believed in keeping his crew in fighting trim rather than exhausting them through prolonged FTL conditions. Chofsky's diminutive size belayed the power of his personality. Blue-eyed and blond-haired with gray streaks he refused to cover, Chofsky was considered tough, fair-minded, and a man of few words, who demanded the best from his people.

"Status, Captain Chofsky," Bunaldi commed from his suite.

"We will make a second jump of a quarter-light-year in eight hours, Judge," Chofsky replied.

"Very well, Captain," Bunaldi replied.

"You shouldn't give the man so much leeway," Theostin scolded as she paced the room. She was still smarting from the obliteration of her fighters with so little to show for their loss. *Damn these Méridiens or Harakens or New Terrans or whomever they are,* Theostin thought.

"So you would suggest that we ignore our good captain's decisions about this ship until such time as we desperately need him to fight to survive?" asked Bunaldi, a bemused expression on his face.

"Pah!" Theostin replied and waved Bunaldi off with a hand. That the high judge continued to display his amused smile as she paced the room only infuriated her all the more. Theostin desperately wanted revenge.

* * *

President Maria Gonzalez picked up her reader to catch up on the news of the day.

At first, the arrival of the Haraken *Money Maker* at New Terra, back in service as a fighter-carrier, and Alex's message relayed by Captain Durak that a ship claiming to be from Earth entered the Méridien system, gave Maria much cause for concern. But as the days passed and nothing else happened, life returned to normal.

The *Money Maker* was stationed off Niomedes, and Captain Durak took to rotating his pilots and flight crew planetside for some relief. New Terra's rudimentary habitats, originally the planet's early space exploration experiment, now resembled vacation resorts, thanks in large part to Haraken technology and support.

Only days ago, President Gonzalez, Ambassador Eric Stroheim, Captain Durak, and Mutter received an update. Previous messages detailed the arrival of the UE battleship and the escalation of tensions. In this newest message, Alex said, "We are about to enter a deadly contest of wills and fighters. No good outcome can be expected."

Maria, for one, was unsure whether the outcome Alex was referring to was the contest or something else. Eric Stroheim, who had become a valued colleague throughout the years, clarified Alex's message, saying, "In the president's mind, the encounter will settle nothing and will only be a harbinger of worse things to come."

The news article on Maria's reader shifted to the image of Captain Durak and Mutter. Maria had long since accepted the Harakens' preference for eschewing bureaucratic channels in order to expedite their communications.

"Good evening, Captain Durak, Mutter," Maria said.

"Pardon the interruption, Ser President. We have important news to share. An enormous ship has exited FTL outside the system. It matches the description of the UE battleship, the *Hand of Justice*," Durak said.

"Is it alone?" Maria asked, sitting upright in her lounge chair.

"Affirmative, Ser President," Durak replied.

"What do you think this means?" Maria asked. She was staring intently at Mutter, who she hoped would understand her underlying concern.

It wouldn't have always been so for Mutter, but life with the Harakens and the Swei Swee had done much to broaden her understanding of the subtleties of species communications.

"Ser President, I am dismayed to report that I consider the arrival of this battleship, unaccompanied by our ships, bodes only ill for New Terra. All preparations should be taken to defend this system against the Earthers," Mutter replied.

"No news from Alex?" Maria asked. It did not seem the time to be concerned with titles and decorum.

"None yet, Ser President," Durak replied.

"If the UE ship made for FTL prior to our president becoming aware of its intentions, I would expect that he will soon inform as to present conditions while the *Hand of Justice* makes its way in system, and I would expect one or both of our carriers will be following shortly," Mutter added.

"What about the possibility that the Haraken ships were destroyed?" Maria suggested.

"That is illogical, Ser President. Méridien is a rich opportunity for the Earthers. If they engaged our ships and defeated them, which is a possibility but has a very low probability, then this battleship would have remained in the Méridien system to reap its rewards," Mutter explained. "No, the logical events are that the UE commanders have run afoul of our president and admiral. Somehow the Earthers discovered New Terra's location, and the *Hand of Justice* has come looking for easier prey." Inexplicably, Mutter froze, dropping any semblance of human mannerisms.

"What's wrong, Mutter?" Durak asked. He couldn't resist reaching out a comforting hand for Mutter's shoulder, SADE or not.

"If the *Hand of Justice* has come to New Terra," said Mutter, her persona mannerisms active again, "then there is a high probability that unless the *Reunion* was destroyed it was sent to Haraken. For a moment, I feared for the Swei Swee, but Cordelia and Captain Tanaka will not let the Earthers harm the Swei Swee."

Mutter's fear for the Swei Swee was a strong reminder for both Maria Gonzalez and Ahmed Durak that SADEs were fundamentally different from them. Mutter's primary concern for the *Reunion*'s intervention in the Hellébore system was for the Swei Swee, not the humans. Still, both humans were comforted by the fact that Mutter volunteered to leave Haraken to lend support to New Terra.

When the call was finished, Mutter returned to a fugue state, researching the data Julien had uploaded onto the *Money Maker*'s controller for her. It contained Alex's and Julien's hundreds of attack scenarios in addition to many of the epic battles of ancient Earth. For a SADE devoted to music, there was much to learn about defending a system against a superior force.

* * *

Captain Durak retrieved his crew and pilots, who were on rotation planetside on Niomedes, by the time the *Hand of Justice* made its way through Oistos's ring of ice fields. As the battleship passed Seda's orbit, Maria, Eric, Ahmed, and Mutter received Alex's final message. In many ways, it was encouraging—Haraken's ships were unscathed and the *Last*

Stand chased the battleship. That Haraken travelers defeated tens of UE fighters was another piece of good news, until they heard Alex's warnings that the battleship possessed enormous weaponry yet to be employed.

When the message ended, Ahmed and Mutter shared disappointed looks. Nothing in Alex's message contained a battle plan, a strategy to defeat this enormous interloper. The two stood quietly with their thoughts. Mutter recalled her observation while she was still on Haraken that an extraordinary number of factors would need to be present to precipitate dangerous circumstances. *So much for the laws of probability,* Mutter thought.

"I believe I see the predicament, Captain," Mutter finally said. "We face a foe of overwhelming superiority, but we are a considerable force unto our own. We have an ally trailing our enemy, requiring we employ our force in a strategic manner that complements our ally's capabilities," said Mutter, quite pleased with her deductive reasoning.

"Mutter, please remember that you are the SADE and I am the human," Ahmed said, staring blankly at Mutter.

"Your pardon, Captain, but I believe my studies of warfare tactics have just yielded results. Would you agree our primary goal is to prevent the *Hand of Justice* from reaching New Terra?"

"Yes," Ahmed agreed.

"Then, as you humans would say, 'Fortune is on our side.' Niomedes is between the battleship and New Terra, which will necessitate the Earther ship make a near pass of this planet, and because our ship resembles a freighter, any course we choose as we exit Niomedes's orbit will appear nonthreatening to the Earthers until we launch our fighters."

"Mutter, I'm sure that you're aware of Alex's estimates of the battleship's armament and fighters. While our sixty-four travelers are impressive, they aren't a match for the *Hand of Justice*."

"This is understood, Captain. I did not say we would engage them. We will employ one of our president's time-tested ploys. We will bluff."

26

Commodore Reynard was extremely grateful for the saturation of Méridien tech throughout New Terran society. With the systems' FTL station and relays, communication with the New Terrans would be instantaneous. It was a tremendous strategic advantage over the *Hand of Justice*. The battleship entered the Oistos system about 110 degrees off the carrier's port quarter. It said something deprecating about the Earthers' jump accuracy. New Terra was on a near pass to the carrier, while Niomedes lay between the Earthers and New Terra. It looked to be a race to the New Terrans' home world, and the *Hand of Justice* had a head start, but the *Last Stand* was faster.

"Greetings, President Gonzalez," Sheila said.

"Commodore Reynard, I have never been happier to see your carrier," Maria replied. She stood in front of a vid cam in a Government House conference room, surrounded by ministerial staff, Terran Security Force (TSF) commanders, and Eric Stroheim. Her communications staff split her view screen to display Commodore Reynard and Captain Manet on one half and Captain Durak and Mutter on the other half. "Two questions to begin, Commodore. What do you believe are the intentions of the Earthers, and do you have a plan for containing any negative intentions?"

"To date, Madam President," Sheila replied, "High Judge Bunaldi has been intent on coopting the Confederation into the UE, but we have frustrated his tactics at every turn. We don't know whether the high judge is a true believer or just driven to deliver a successful mission that will promote him within the UE hierarchy. Regardless of the reason, it makes no difference to us. Bunaldi is here to subdue New Terra and gain leverage against us and the Méridiens. You've heard that he's sent his explorer ship to Haraken," Sheila said.

"Exactly how far do you believe the high judge will go to secure this leverage, Commodore?" Maria asked.

"We believe he intends to hold New Terra hostage by any means necessary, Madam President," Sheila replied.

"Does his ship possess the capabilities to hold an entire world hostage?" Eric Stroheim asked.

"This battleship is quite formidable, Sers," Captain Manet replied. "While we haven't seen inside the *Hand of Justice*, it bears a striking resemblance to the *Reunion*'s design but on a much grander scale. If we were to extrapolate, the battleship probably contains twice the number of fighters as our carrier plus it boasts a large complement of powerful missiles and rail guns."

"Rail guns?" Minister of Technology Darryl Jaya asked.

"Theoretically, Minister Jaya, these weapons use magnetic acceleration techniques to launch heavy-metal slugs along rails to destroy their targets with massive kinetic energy," Mutter replied. "Based on the size and number of ports on the battleship, which we assume hides the rail guns, they could reduce Prima to rubble within a half-day."

Except for the brief engagement years ago between Downing's coconspirators and the president's people, New Terra, in its 700-year history, had never witnessed an assault within its planet's airspace. Now danger came in the form of other humans who were willing to reduce New Terra's primary city to rubble for political gain. It was a devastating revelation. Maria wished now, more than ever, that she had pushed Alex to trade for beam-capable travelers.

"So what's your plan, Commodore?" Maria asked.

"I will let Mutter explain, Madam President," Sheila replied. "She has designed a rather ingenious plan."

"Thank you, Commodore Reynard," Mutter replied. That she was able to contribute to the plan to protect the humans who protected her Swei Swee shifted Mutter's kernel integration in ways that emulated excitement on an elemental level. "The strategy is to neutralize the *Hand of Justice*'s early entrance into the system. They must not gain New Terra's orbit before the *Last Stand*. The favorable alignment of Niomedes and New

Terra will aid us in our endeavor. We will direct the battleship outward of Niomedes, extending their course and allowing our forces to engage them before the Earthers reach New Terra."

"But the high judge's ship will elect to pass Niomedes on an inward line, Mutter. It's the shortest distance to New Terra," Eric Stroheim said.

"Precisely, Ambassador Stroheim," Mutter replied, experiencing elation as she thought about her subterfuge. She was sure Julien would recognize her value in this regard. "We will emulate our president's favorite technique of provoking his family and friends to make impractical bets during his archaic card games."

Maria couldn't follow Mutter's preamble, but the reference to emulating Alex bolstered her confidence.

"In order to effectively apply this technique," Mutter continued, "we must convince the high judge to choose the more circuitous route because he believes a dangerous force blocks his path. In the language of our president, we must bluff."

Maria would have laughed if the circumstances weren't so dire.

"Bluff?" Will Drake repeated. "Your strategy for our planet's protection depends on bluffing, Mutter?"

"Precisely, Minister Drake," Mutter replied. "The *Reunion* will have reported to High Judge Bunaldi when the battleship first entered Méridien space that the engineless-vessels seen operating throughout the system were merely shuttles. Until the contest, the high judge would have been unaware that our travelers were capable of fighting. By extension, he will be equally unaware that your travelers are only shuttles.

"I understand, Mutter," Maria said, excited by the strategy. "Your sixty-four travelers might not deter the high judge from taking the inward path, but if we add our traveler-shuttles, your forces will appear nearly twice as large."

"Yes, Madam President," Mutter replied. "A hundred or more travelers, each supposedly beam-capable, might be enough to persuade the high judge to take the outward path around Niomedes and gain us the time we need.

* * *

Bunaldi was studying the New Terran system as the *Hand of Justice* made its way inward toward the system's populated planet identified by the guide. Theostin stood by his side on the battleship's bridge.

"The old woman appears to have told the truth," Theostin remarked.

"Indeed," Bunaldi acknowledged. "The guide indicates that almost all intersystem traffic is between this one world and a destination that aligns with Hellébore, the Haraken's star. I surmise that if we were to isolate and control these two worlds President Racine would be forced to submit to us, and he would bring us the Méridiens."

"The guide has identified the odd shuttle-fighters at Méridien and also in this system. Who's to say, Judge, that every world in this part of the galaxy doesn't have these ships?"

"And why were they not employed until we challenged President Racine?" Bunaldi retorted. "I'll tell you why, my dear Admiral, it's because to have a weapon does not necessarily mean you possess the will to use it. That president has the will; the Méridiens do not."

"Your pardon, Judge Bunaldi," Captain Chofsky said. "The guide has detected significant structures on a planet that is on our path toward the populated world, which we take to be New Terra. The shortest route is an inward pass of the planet, but I wonder if it wouldn't be more prudent to pass outward of the planet so that hidden forces do not trap us between the two planets."

Bunaldi and the admiral studied the guide's telemetry information for several moments. "Captain," Theostin said, "I see only freighters and the occasional shuttle-fighter. Nothing warrants your prudence. Judge Bunaldi, I recommend the inward path."

"Make it so, Captain," Bunaldi confirmed.

* * *

New Terran shuttle pilots from across the system, most engaged in traffic between New Terra and the planet's twin orbital stations, quickly landed, unloaded their passengers and cargo, and flew their travelers to Niomedes.

Captain Durak, waiting for the New Terran travelers, flew a slow orbital path from the backside of Niomedes, hidden from the battleship's view now, but designed to later position the freighter inward of the planet and in full view of the *Hand of Justice*.

During the course of the next day, the majority of New Terran travelers made rendezvous with the *Money Maker*. When Durak and Mutter could wait no longer, the freighter-carrier swung out of Niomedes orbit to an inward position 500K kilometers from the planet. Then bay after bay opened to launch the Haraken's travelers. One hundred and thirteen of the sleek alien-shaped craft spread out in a screen pattern around the *Money Maker* to face the oncoming battleship.

* * *

While the *Money Maker* made its preparations, Commander Ellie Thompson readied the *Last Stand*'s entire wing. Ellie argued with Sheila that some of the fighters should be held back to protect the carrier, but she lost that argument.

"Commander, your forces will be out massed by that battleship's fighters as it is," Sheila had replied. "Retaining a small force to protect us against that ship has no value. We have our speed. That's our defense. President Racine entrusted us to keep New Terra safe. Your wing has first crack at making that happen. It's my hope that I won't have to be the second."

As Ellie climbed into her cockpit for launch, she replayed Sheila's comment again and again. A defenseless carrier, acting as an offensive weapon, had only one attack choice, which was to ram the battleship. But the carrier hadn't been designed with emergency exit craft. That was the job of its travelers.

Ellie was about to comm Sheila, when her commodore beat her to it. <I wish you good fortune, Commander Thompson. May the spirit of Hatsuto guide you,> Sheila sent and closed the comm.

It occurred to Ellie that eleven years ago a derelict Méridien passenger ship wandered into this system and was rescued by a lone captain, who became the key to saving the Confederation. Now a rogue human civilization threatened the captain's home world, and Méridiens, human and SADE alike would defend his home world.

For the great favor you bestowed on the Confederation, Ser, may the stars grant us fortune to deliver your world from harm, Ellie thought as she launched her entire wing. The carrier's travelers pushed their gravity drives to their limits, quickly achieving their unmatched velocity of 0.91c. For the pilots, it would be a long flight. They were a full day out from Niomedes, and if the battleship passed inward of the planet, the high judge would make orbit over New Terra hours before them.

* * *

"Judge Bunaldi, your attention is requested on the bridge immediately," the high judge heard over his monitor's speakers, waking him from a dead sleep. He had enjoyed a couple glasses of celebratory cognac before retiring, having considered his run of bad luck to have been reversed.

A quarter-hour later, Bunaldi trudged onto the bridge, eyes bleary, and with his usual calm all but nonexistent. "Yes, Captain," he growled.

"The guide has detected two forces closing in on our path, Judge Bunaldi," Captain Chofsky replied.

Bunaldi despised the way the captain appeared looking impeccably groomed, as if he caught a full night's sleep, instead of probably having been awoken at the same time he was.

"More details, Captain Chofsky," Bunaldi demanded.

On the monitor that the captain pointed out, Bunaldi watched the guide display their intended course and the planet they would pass. The guide highlighted a point in space just inward of the planet and proceeded to magnify that view. A small freighter could be seen with a host of small bright objects surrounding it.

"What am I looking at, Captain?" Bunaldi huffed, his patience dwindling.

"The guide identifies these small objects as the fighters we encountered in Méridien, Judge Bunaldi. It counts 113 of them."

Despite his hung-over condition, Patricio Bunaldi pulled his thoughts together. The keen mind that enabled his rise through the UE ranks was pressed into service once again, and he began considering the odds. His ship outnumbered the fighters by more than three to one, but the Méridien fighters easily defeated his pilots and craft. In addition, there was the question of whether the fighters in front of him were the only ones possessed by this system, particularly by this planet. If the *Hand of Justice* took the inward path, his ship-killer missiles and rail guns would be useless against these small craft. Only his close-in ship defenses would be effective against them, if they were to eliminate his fighters.

"You said there were two forces, Captain," Bunaldi said.

"That ship we've been tracking and suspected was the one lurking outside the Méridien system has launched 128 of its own fighters. Based on the guide's analysis of the ship, we believe it is a carrier with minimum armament and has probably launched every fighter."

"So its commander launched the ship's entire force," Bunaldi mused. "Exactly where in the system were the fighters launched, Captain?"

Chofsky manipulated the monitor view, and the guide responded by displaying the orbits of the planets outward from New Terra. A ring encircled a point in space far outward in the system.

Examining the vast distance the fighters must travel to reach them, Bunaldi began to chuckle. "Too little, too late," he muttered under his breath.

"Perhaps not, Judge," Chofsky countered. "Those inbound fighters have achieved a velocity of 0.91 c. If the fighters surrounding the freighter are a blocking force meant to drive us outward from this planet, then the carrier's fighters could intercept us as we swing outward of the planet. The timing will be that close."

"Captain, suppose we were to take the outward path. How long will those carrier's fighters have been underway before they intercept us?"

Chofsky turned to his navigation officer, and the two men huddled for a few moments. "Their flight will have been slightly longer than a full day, Judge," Chofsky replied.

"There you have it, Captain," Bunaldi replied. "These two forces are meant to dissuade us from taking either path around that planet. Facing a combined 241 of these fighters, we are meant to see that we have no option but to turn and flee." Bunaldi enjoyed himself for a moment, laughing at the image of his battleship turning and running. "I think our option is obvious, Captain. Take us outward of that planet," Bunaldi ordered.

When Chofsky hesitated, Bunaldi decided to be lenient. After all, the man was an excellent captain, just not as brilliant as Bunaldi perceived himself to be. "Captain, the carrier's fighters are a ruse. Do you honestly think they haven't exhausted their fuel already to achieve that velocity? I believe they might already be dead in space before they even intercept us. But even if they have some small reserve left, they can't engage in a protracted battle. It's obvious, Captain. The carrier's force is a bluff," Bunaldi said. He walked off the bridge, chuckling at the subterfuge he congratulated himself on uncovering, leaving a disturbed captain behind him.

Two of Bunaldi's own people, Captain Lumley and Administrator Wombo, could have disabused the high judge of his false assumption about the distance the carrier's fighters could cover. Then again, since the concept was too foreign for the Speaker to consider, Bunaldi might also have dismissed it.

Chofsky ordered the change in course but continued to keep a close watch on both forces. He couldn't put his finger on it, but something seemed to be missing from their calculations. Chofsky was a survivor of too many battles not to know when a critical piece of the battle plan's puzzle was wanting.

27

Clustered around the *Money Maker*'s holo-vid, Mutter and Captain Durak watched the *Hand of Justice* change course to take an outward path around Niomedes.

"Success, Mutter!" Ahmed crowed, hugging the white-haired, elderly appearing avatar.

"We," said Mutter, smiling at him and placing a friendly hand on his shoulder, "did well, Captain."

"Now what do we do?" Ahmed asked.

"That is an excellent question, Captain. I must admit that I didn't consider maneuvers past this point, but then warfare is not my forte, and I hope it never will be," Mutter replied. "If you will excuse me, Captain, I will examine our next possibilities."

Ahmed watched the persona of the woman disappear and that of the SADE-mannequin take its place as Mutter focused on their next tactics. Someone such as Ahmed, who had worked closely with SADEs for years, knew to wait patiently. It wouldn't be long before even an individual such as Mutter, who was not proficient in battle tactics, would have examined innumerable possibilities, assigned values for potential outcomes, and decided on the best possible course, and he was correct. The avatar's frozen expression softened, and the persona of the kind and gentle woman resurfaced.

"Captain, what do you suppose the high judge would do if he was presented with this scenario?" Mutter asked. The holo-vid lit up with a view of Niomedes and the surrounding area of space, labeling the players: *Hand of Justice*, *Money Maker*, and Ellie's incoming wing. The travelers surrounding the freighter divided into two groups. One group headed to intercept the *Hand of Justice*; the other group circled behind the planet to join the carrier's wing.

"Which group of travelers is going which way?" Ahmed asked.

"Your pardon, Captain," Mutter said, realizing her logic wasn't been obvious. "New Terra's shuttles will take a direct path toward the battleship. Our travelers will circle behind the planet."

Ahmed studied the holo-vid, trying to anticipate the Earthers' response. He hadn't believed the commander of the battleship would fall for Mutter's bluff, and he was wrong. Now, he felt more out of his depth than ever, and heartedly wished for the presence of the indomitable trio: Alex, Julien, and Tatia. "Mutter, I must admit that I have no idea what the Earthers would do. I am woefully inadequate when it comes to warfare tactics."

"We are the same, Captain. Music is beauty; war is ugly, but there is the matter of necessity."

Ahmed nodded his head and stared again at the holo-vid. "The masters of that battleship believe the safer path is outward of Niomedes despite the advance of our carrier wing. I believe they might have made false assumptions about our travelers."

There was silence for a moment, and then the captain and the SADE said as one, "gravity drives," and laughed. The trip to New Terra was convincing Mutter more every day that she was erring in not involving humans more in her life, and she reached a decision to change that starting now.

"They must believe our travelers have fuel limitations, like the Daggers. They might think our fighters can't cover the distance and still fight," Ahmed said. "That's what they consider our bluff," and the two shared another laugh having realized the irony of the situation.

"If we send the New Terran shuttles in the open, then the high judge would be further convinced to take the far path, would he not?" Mutter asked.

"I believe he would, Mutter! Then our travelers could support the carrier's wing. That's brilliant, Mutter," said Ahmed, excitedly squeezing her hands.

With Mutter's algorithms' hierarchy reordered to focus more on humans, Ahmed's touch quickly achieved a rarified position in her kernel's memory, and she felt an intensity that compared to the enjoyment of singing for the Swei Swee. *The world of humans has more to offer than I supposed,* Mutter thought.

Ahmed and Mutter contacted the Haraken captain leading the freighter's travelers and the New Terra captain leading the shuttles. The freighter's captain received the data download via her traveler's controller and relayed the information to the squadron. The Haraken travelers left the screening force, taking the route behind the planet to join the incoming wing. The New Terran captain was not so quick to comprehend her orders.

"Captain Durak, madam, are you ordering our shuttles to fly at that huge battleship?" Captain Hailey Timmion asked. She was tasked by none other than President Gonzalez to support the Harakens' efforts and specifically to follow the orders of Captain Durak and Mutter. When the white-haired, aging woman first appeared on her traveler's vid screen, Hailey thought there was a mistake. In the New Terran's mind, if a SADE could choose any avatar, it certainly wouldn't be that of an old woman.

"Precisely, Captain," Mutter agreed.

"Captain Timmion," Ahmed said, attempting to intervene and calm the captain, "the battleship is passing outward of Niomedes. The planet is starting to block their view of our forces. We need you to continue our ruse by circling the planet and chasing the battleship along the path it's already chosen."

"Understood, Captain Durak, but what do we do if we're engaged?"

"Then Captain Timmion, I would advise you to turn and run," Mutter said matter-of-factly.

"Captain Timmion, we don't expect you to reach an engagement window," Ahmed added. "We want you to pretend to intercept the battleship, but don't close on it. The concept is just to be seen."

"We have been ordered to follow your instructions implicitly, Captain, Madam, which we will do. I just hope that your plan doesn't get my people killed for little or no gain," Timmion grumped.

"Captain," Mutter said, "I'm sending your controllers our latest evasion routines. If you encounter trouble, initiate this program at the earliest moment. Whatever you do, don't switch to manual flight. It will be the last thing you do."

* * *

Sheila paced the *Last Stand*'s expansive bridge, while Edouard and the bridge officers stood quiet and resolute. The holo-vid displayed the forces of the upcoming battle drawing inexorably closer. *When did I adopt Alex's habit of pacing the bridge?* Sheila wondered.

"I always wondered, Commodore, if pacing was a New Terran technique that somehow hastened the events about to unfold," Edouard said, his face showing no signs of the mirth he was harboring.

"Yes, Captain. It was first discovered by our president as a method of impelling our adversaries to rush to their doom. Under the circumstances, I thought it worth adopting. Care to join me? We can hasten the *Hand of Justice* to its doom twice as quickly."

"I'm afraid, Commodore, it appears to be a particularly New Terran technique. Perhaps it has something to do with mass."

A bridge officer failed to maintain control, and a snorkel of air slipped out. He snatched a glance at the commodore and wished he hadn't. Apparently, the captain could jest with the commodore but the bridge crew was not invited to the fête.

"Commodore, Captain, we've received an update from the *Money Maker*," the comms officer announced. "I'm updating the holo-vid."

The controllers that replaced the ship's SADEs were quite competent with calculations and ship system controls, but their lack of self-awareness necessitated the presence of bridge officers to manage orders and communication among the controller, the captain, and the commanders.

Edouard and Sheila observed one group of travelers detach from the *Money Maker* and circle Niomedes in one direction, and, a few moments later, the other group left the freighter-carrier and circled the planet in the other direction. The comms officer connected Captain Durak through the bridge speakers, and he summarized the plan to reinforce the *Last Stand*'s wing with the freighters' beam-capable travelers and use the New Terran travelers to chase the *Hand of Justice* on its outward path. Captain Durak was careful to credit Mutter as the plan's architect.

"That's actually quite brilliant," Sheila remarked.

"For what it's worth, Commodore," Ahmed added, "Mutter and I believe that the *Hand of Justice*'s high judge or captain or both are making an error by assuming that the *Last Stand*'s fighters will not have sufficient fuel reserves to cover the distance to Niomedes and take on the battleship. They might believe that your carrier's travelers are the true ruse."

For the first time, Edouard expressed a groan of disappointment.

"Something Captain Durak said?" Sheila asked.

"Who would have thought that I would come to regret not accepting the president's invitations to join his card games? With all these ruses and bluffs, I'm not sure who is thinking what," Edouard lamented.

"Don't feel bad, Captain, I didn't join them either, but I know someone who did. Comms get me Commander Thompson."

* * *

Ellie listened to the update from Sheila and passed on the relevant information to her flight commanders. The addition of the *Money Maker*'s sixty-four travelers to her wing boosted her confidence, which was sorely needed. She was under no misconception. The UE battleship was a monster of the deep dark, and the estimates of its armament suggested it was powerful enough to destroy an entire world, much less a paltry wing-and-a-half of travelers. It was Ellie's thought that the best the Harakens could hope for in the upcoming battle was a draw—neutralize the battleship at the cost of every traveler.

* * *

"The carrier's fighters are maintaining their velocity," Captain Chofsky said to Bunaldi and Theostin.

"Could they be coasting?" Theostin asked.

"Negative, Admiral," Chofsky replied. "They've made subtle course corrections, which have corresponded to our course changes. Their most recent correction was made less than a half-hour ago. They're still under power."

"Recommendations, Captain," Bunaldi asked.

"Having witnessed the devastating capability of these enemy fighters, we can't risk them getting close to our ship. We will need our fighters to clear a path. I would recommend that we use a three-to-one ratio against their fighters, Judge."

"Three to one, Captain?" Theostin challenged. "That would be most of our fleet."

"It would be prudent, Admiral," Chofsky replied. Those who knew the captain would have recognized the subtle clench of jaw that said he was losing his patience. "We must not just reduce the count of these strange fighters; they must be eliminated entirely. Since we have no idea what type of weapon their fighters emit, we can't risk letting a single one of them reach our ship."

* * *

Ellie was reviewing attack approaches to the battleship. Her greatest concern was that her wing's short-range beam weapons would require her pilots to fly into the face of what she was sure would be the battleship's short-range defensive weapons. *If I built a monster like that, I would have added as much protective armament as I could,* Ellie thought.

Ellie's controller pinged, signaling the launch of fighters from the *Hand of Justice*—hundreds of them. "Scared you at the contest, did we? And you're going to throw everything at us," Ellie murmured to herself. She began running scenarios on her controller, based on the enemy's count. Fortune was with her, the *Money Maker*'s travelers would join her wing before the engagement, which would occur within an hour. Still it would be two to one against them.

One by one, Ellie reviewed the scenarios provided by the controller and discarded every one of them. "Where are Alex and Julien when I need them?" Ellie asked herself.

During long flights, Ellie had adopted the habit of talking to herself. The sound of her own voice comforted her in the solitude. "So often you did the unexpected, Alex," Ellie mumbled. "Or was it just that we would have played it safe while you sought a greater goal?" She sat in her pilot's seat and her mind wandered over her time with Alex Racine. Then her error dawned on her. She was requesting scenarios that sought to minimize the loss of her wing. "But that's not the goal, is it, Alex? You're the goal," Ellie said, indicating the *Hand of Justice* in her telemetry display, "and your fighters are here to punch a hole in our forces so you can get to New Terra."

<Commander Canaan,> Ellie sent, <new formation and orders. Your sub-wing has lead. Here's the new plan.>

Deirdre Canaan reviewed the plan in detail with Ellie while the entire wing dropped velocity to extend the engagement window, as their adversaries were doing. The carrier wing would meet the UE fighters head-on just as the *Money Maker*'s fighters joined them. The freighter's fighters would attack the right flank of the UE wing, and the carrier's wing would shift to hit the enemy's left flank, letting the majority of the UE fighters pass them unhindered. Deirdre's sub-wing would take the brunt of the contact against the UE fighters and act as a blocking force for Ellie's sub-wing. Her group's task was the battleship. Sixty-four travelers would try to disable, if not destroy, the United Earth's behemoth warship.

28

Throughout the New Terran system, eyes were trained on the participants who would be involved in the most massive battle to take place in the 700-year histories of either the Confederation or New Terra.

The leaders aboard the *Hand of Justice* eyed the fighters coming around the planet behind them. "This group is not a danger to us, Judge, Admiral," Captain Chofsky announced, "providing that we maintain our velocity. But it does require our fighters to clear the way so that we are not caught from behind and fighting on two fronts. To ensure that rearward group doesn't close on us too quickly, I will be giving them something to think about."

While they were talking, the telemetry officer signaled Chofsky, who nodded to his superiors to observe the monitor. An ancillary group of fighters was appearing from behind the planet and were racing to join the carrier's fighters. The high judge and admiral exchanged concerned glances.

"The odds just dropped to two to one," Theostin said into the silence, and apprehension spread among the three leaders as they saw their superiority winnowed.

* * *

Deirdre Canaan was energized by Ellie's new plan. Prior to the sharing, she felt as if she was flying into the jaws of doom for no gain. Now, she grinned at the opportunity to take down the battleship, even if she lost her entire sub-wing to the enemy's fighters. The possibility of defeating the UE monster galvanized Deirdre to take a second look at her own tactics.

<Commander Valenko,> Deirdre sent, <you have new orders.>

Svetlana Valenko, the ex-copilot of an asteroid miner, made the jump to Haraken fighter training and never looked back. Robert Dorian, her training commander, categorized Svetlana as a brilliant pain in the ass, who rarely followed her assigned offensive or defensive scenarios, but then again often won the day.

<Lovely, Commander,> Svetlana replied after reviewing Deirdre's plan.

If the high judge could have seen the carnivore-like grin on Svetlana's face, he might have considered ordering his captain to reverse course.

* * *

Captain Timmion smiled as her controller refreshed its telemetry data and displayed the UE battleship continuing to head away from her shuttle group. Her pilots had been chatting happily for hours about the effectiveness of their ruse when their controllers lit up their helmets' displays. The *Hand of Justice* released a huge cloud of some sort of short-range defensive armament. There wasn't time for the controllers to identify what the shuttles were up against and notify the pilots.

"Activate your evasion programs now!" Hailey screamed into her comm, and punched her evasion program icon, which sat on the upper left portion of the controller's screen where most of her pilots placed it.

Immediately, the shuttles flew in myriad directions, twisting and turning to evade the battleship's short-range defensive missiles that were fired at them. In the shuttle pilots' favor, the missiles exhausted their fuel, reaching the extent of their maneuvering range. However, they were still dangerous as they closed on the shuttles on ballistic courses. The shuttle pilots, who reacted swiftly, activating their evasion programs immediately, safely cleared the swarm's path, and the missiles, devoid of fuel, were unable to change course to reacquire their targets.

Two pilots were unsuccessful. One lieutenant, who took too long to access his evasion program, was hit by two missiles. The first missile cracked his traveler's shell and the second ruptured it. The other lieutenant had developed a penchant for ignoring safety regulations and preferred to pilot his craft without the use of his seat harness. Naturally the controller repeatedly warned him about this error, but the enterprising pilot discovered the means to disable the controller's detection algorithms.

When the evasion program actuated, the controller was unaware the pilot wasn't safely buckled in and did its best to evade the oncoming missile swarm, pushing the craft's inertia compensators to the limit. The pilot was bounced out of his chair and against the shuttle's bridge bulkheads repeatedly before the traveler leveled out.

Mutter would have the *Money Maker*'s controller recall the wayward shuttle to one of its bays. Once the perfectly intact shuttle was recovered, the flight crew would remove the pilot's badly broken body.

*   *   *

The UE fighter formation resembled a massive cone as it drove toward the enemy fighters.

As the three groups of Haraken fighters joined together, Ellie, Deirdre, and Svetlana established twin comm connections—one among themselves and one from each of them to their flight commanders.

Each of the three Haraken sub-wings held a loose formation, maintaining an undisciplined appearance, one designed to create overconfidence in their enemy. The women commanders were grim as they signaled the attack phase, and each sub-wing formed into a tight cone, with the group's wing commander in the lead. As soon as the cones formed, Deirdre's sub-wing swung away from the enemy's center to engage the left flank, and Ellie's sub-wing swung in behind Deirdre's group, making an even greater vector change to evade all contact with the UE fighters.

Svetlana's group veered to the right to attack the opposite flank from Deirdre's group. Their unorthodox maneuver fractured the UE formation as the fighters on the cone's flanks broke away from the main body to form defensive wedges.

Svetlana's group slipped up and over the portion of the UE wedge that pointed her way, evading the missiles loosed at the group. Then her travelers dived into the enemy fighters that had turned to face Deirdre's sub-wing. Fifty-eight UE pilots suddenly found themselves besieged on two sides by one hundred and twenty-eight enemy fighters, and beams silently sliced through them, one and all.

The UE formation fell into disarray as the defensive wedge, attacked by two Haraken sub-wings, disappeared in explosions of fire and debris, and the opposite wedge, which was overflown by Svetlana's travelers, turned and hurried to rejoin the main formation.

Deirdre and Svetlana kept their sub-wings in tight cones, negating much of their enemy's superior numbers. The two Haraken commanders wove through the periphery of the enemy's fractured formation, often striking at the same group of fighters but from opposite directions. As each commander lost a traveler along the cone's front, another fighter would take its place to keep the maximum beam strength at the front's formation.

Most UE pilots could not launch their missiles for fear of hitting other UE pilots with the enemy fighters among them. With the loss of nearly one-third of his group, the UE commodore ordered his wings to separate and open the field of fire. Unfortunately for him, the Harakens' superior technology, including controllers and implants, detected the shift in the UE formation, and the commanders joined forces to oppose one of the smaller enemy wings, eliminating those fighters from behind as they sought to open the space as commanded.

Deirdre's quick count showed the Harakens' combined wings of 128 travelers were down by 36, but they were nearly at a one-to-one ratio with the UE fighters. Unfortunately, as the enemy wings separated into squadrons, opening the space between them, the Harakens' techniques became ineffective.

<Alpha and Delta sub-wings,> Deirdre commed, <you're released from formation for independent flight. Adopt a wingmate and pick single targets. Use alternating fire to support each other. May the stars guide you home.>

For the next half-hour, a desperate battle took place hundreds of thousands of kilometers outward of Niomedes, as two groups of fighters sought to destroy each other.

Despite their vaunted supremacy, UE pilots saw their numbers disappear from screens faster than their enemy's and they began to panic, firing their missiles without firmly locked targets and sending hundreds of deadly, errant armament flying through the mêlée.

Haraken technology saved the majority of the travelers from the clouds of UE missiles. The controllers detected the enemy missiles and prioritized evasion tactics over beam targeting. In contrast, the UE pilots lost time as they reacted manually to missile impact warnings, often evading one missile only to turn into another before they could react to the second warning, resulting in an equal number of UE fighters destroyed by their own armament as they were by Haraken travelers.

At the point where the UE fighter count was reduced to little more than a pair of squadrons, the UE commodore ordered his remaining pilots to break off and make for the nearby planet. He ordered them to seek targets of opportunity and inflict as much damage as possible.

The Haraken pilots suddenly found themselves without targets as their adversaries flew from the battle zone. <All fighters pursue and destroy,> Deirdre sent as she realized her enemy's destination.

There were no strategic targets on Niomedes. Except for a small standing force of Terran Security Forces, all installations were civilian. Most of the UE fighters were closer than the Haraken travelers to Niomedes when they broke off, and Deirdre's and Svetlana's pilots signaled their controllers for maximum acceleration. Several Haraken pilots sought to override their controllers' protocols to achieve greater-than-max acceleration, but safety protocols locked them out. Their efforts were unnecessary. The Harakens began catching the slower UE fighters one by one. The last three UE pilots, which included the commodore, aborted their flights toward Niomedes and turned to face the Haraken travelers, whose beams obliterated them before they got an opportunity to lock their missiles on the enemy.

29

Aboard the *Hand of Justice*, the high judge and the admiral sat in their command chairs, shocked. Their fighters' overwhelmingly superior numbers were ineffective against the strange enemy fighters, who managed to evade the UE's most advanced missiles and then cut down their fighters with an unknown energy beam. Words failed them as they looked to the battleship's captain for answers.

Captain Chofsky regarded his superiors and anger and lament warred within him. Throughout his career, he faithfully followed orders, and it had served him well, rising to the position of UE cruiser captain and finally tapped to captain the *Hand of Justice*, and he was proud of his service. But from the beginning, this mission had all the earmarks of failure. The enormous find of people and technology should have required the *Reunion* scurry back to Earth to report the speaker's findings. Instead, García called for support, which brought the high judge and his battleship. On his arrival, the high judge should have immediately ordered both ships back to Earth to report the tremendous discovery.

In the captain's mind, Judge Bunaldi should have severely reprimanded Speaker García. It was the responsibility of the UE Supreme Tribunal to determine how best to deal with the incredible discovery. Instead, both the high judge and the speaker had coveted the possibility of promotion, hoping to develop the opportunity themselves. And here came the results of those machinations—sixty-four of the unearthly fighters were making straight for his ship.

While Captain Chofsky was considering his defense options, Admiral Theostin broke into his thoughts. "Captain, I suggest . . ."

"Quiet, Admiral," Chofsky retorted abruptly.

"Captain!" Bunaldi said, shouting his rebuke as he rose from his command chair.

"And you, also, Judge!" Captain Chofsky ordered tersely. "Both of you sit back down and be quiet! You two and your ideas have slaughtered our entire fighter command, and we are about to be annihilated by a wing of those damned Méridien fighters." Theostin sucked in air to fire back, but Dimitri cut her off. "If we survive, Admiral, you can ask for my head, and if we don't, it won't matter."

"Can we run, Captain?" Bunaldi asked, forgetting the captain's admonishment to remain quiet.

"And show them our vulnerable rear, drive engines and all, Judge? I don't think so. These fighters have speed, acceleration, and maneuverability on us. Our ship-to-ship missiles are too ponderous to be of use against them, and our rail-slugs are ineffective." Chofsky turned his back on his superiors and began orders for emergency conditions. His crew raced to seal all compartments and staff the short-range defensive weapons.

* * *

What scared Ellie the most as her sub-wing flew toward the enormous battleship was the frequency with which she readjusted her helmet's display. In practice encounters with her compatriots, her adversaries remained no more than a blip on her helmet's scan, but as she closed on the UE battleship it filled her screen, and Ellie adjusted the display to back out her view, again and again. *Black space, that thing's big,* Ellie thought, realizing she was repeating one of Sheila's favorite expressions.

Ellie contacted her flight commanders. <Commanders, I have info from Julien and Z. If I thought we would have gotten this far I would have shared it with you earlier.>

The fifteen commanders focused on their wing commander's next thoughts. At this point, any information about the enemy battleship was good, but information from the SADEs would be invaluable.

<Our good friends surmise that these will be the hot points to evade and these will be the points to hit.> As Ellie sent her thoughts, she circled

the hot points and the target points on her helmet's view of the battleship in two different colors, sending the image to her commanders' controllers.

<Commanders, on my order, we will break into squadrons and swarm that ship. The plan is to prevent that ship from focusing its defensive weapons on us, which are primarily located along the wings' front faces. If your squadron gets a shot at the rear, target the engines. Those of you caught in front of the wing, evade over and under the wings. The intent is to keep circling the battleship—over, around, and under—limiting our exposure to the front of the wings. The SADEs offer us another strategic target.>

Ellie added a third set of circles in another color. <These are the hatch covers over their missiles. Julien and Z believe that, due to the size of the hatches, these missiles are used against planets and large ships, which means that they will be carrying huge loads of explosives. Hit one and you will score significant damage against that ship. However, the SADEs have attached a warning. You would need to approach the port head on, because the missile is inevitably located deep in a well, and these strategic areas will be heavily guarded by the ship's defensive armament.>

Strapped in their pilot chairs, the flight commanders examined Ellie's image of the battleship and her overlay of colored circles. Of the Haraken pilots, most were Méridiens and only eight were New Terrans. Ellie had packed Deirdre's pilot roster with all the veterans available. All other Haraken veterans were aboard the *Money Maker*. Ellie flew with sixty-three untested pilots, who couldn't help but be frightened by what they faced. *Lead with strength* played again in her thoughts.

Ellie gave her commanders sufficient time to communicate to their wings. Now she had an important duty to perform. <All pilots, I know this task looks daunting,> Ellie sent on an open comm. <But witness the fact that your mates have just decimated three times their number in enemy fighters. Some of us will receive star services today, but all of us owe the captain, who brought us together. If not for his courage and efforts, we wouldn't be wielding the power you fly today to protect our worlds and our way of life. Today, we send a message to Earth. Deal with us in peace

and as equals or deal with our beams. Courage, Harakens! For the captain!>

The comms of the pilots echoed Ellie's cry, and tears threatened to blur her eyesight. She spared a brief thought for Étienne.

Then as each flight commander had done, Ellie linked her controller to those of her three wing pilots, locking their travelers in formation as they flew together against the massive battleship.

* * *

Captain Chofsky released his short-range defensive crews to independent fire, directing his pilot to orient the battleship at the approaching swarm of fighters. *Odd things, these fighters,* Chofsky thought, saddened that he probably wouldn't have the opportunity to learn how they worked, at least not today. Today, only one side would survive.

As the *Hand of Justice* defense crews opened fire, throwing slugs at the enemy fighters that detonated into hundreds of small balls, Chofsky watched the attacking force separate into sixteen different squadrons that flew up, under, and around his wings, and fear struck his heart. *Looks as if I found a commander as dangerous as I am,* Dimitri thought.

All battleship personnel were already strapped into their chairs or bunks, and Chofsky began shouting orders at his pilot to keep the battleship moving and turning in an attempt to bring his massive front-wing defensive guns to bear on the squadrons of fast and acrobatic fighters.

Soon the emergency reports began flowing in, and Chofsky cut them off from his chair's communications panel, leaving his bridge officers to manage the damage. Try as hard as the captain might to protect the ship, the enemy fighters continued to swarm over and around the wings, striking at the battleship from all directions. The enemy fighters had yet to score a significant strike, and as time wore on the defensive armament started to dwindle their numbers. Chofsky began to hope as his pilot executed a turn that caught one of the enemy squadrons off guard, and his gunners eliminated two of the four fighters.

* * *

Who are you? Ellie thought, fighting to bring her flight to bear on one of the battleship's critical targets. Despite the vessels great size, the captain kept his ship turning and twisting, successfully orienting his front wings toward squadrons of the Haraken travelers, and although Ellie's fighters were scoring hits with every beam shot, the damage was insufficient—such was the immenseness of the ship.

By now, Ellie's squadron was down to herself and a single pilot. Deciding it was time for a desperate action on her part, she ordered her remaining wing to break off. The lieutenant, shaken by the order, nonetheless obeyed and vectored off to hunt his own targets.

From behind the battleship, where Ellie just missed a shot at the engines, she swung her traveler up and over in a wide arc to attack the enemy from the front. Her target was one of the killer missiles buried deep in its protective sleeve. Ellie's implant replayed recent images of the front wings as recorded by her compatriots, searching for a missile port that might have had its nearby defensive guns destroyed. When her search discovered no such opportunity, she let out a sigh and settled back into her chair.

Ellie's traveler reached the top of its arc, and she calculated where the battleship might turn next, intending to come down into the face of oblivion. Whether she would be able to successfully fire her beam down the missile sleeve's throat or not, odds were great that this would be her last flight aboard her beloved traveler.

Apologies, my love, I meant to come home, Ellie thought and blocked her flight commanders' comms. Her attack angle was detected, and the remainder of the wing was hurriedly messaging her. She pushed her traveler over in the final leg of the arc as the battleship's face twisted her way. Suddenly, a priority signal overrode her comm, and Ellie heard Deirdre's urgent message, <Commander, veer off before you kill one of us.>

Ellie snapped out of her reverie and twisted her traveler out of the path of Deirdre's and Svetlana's wings as they flew into the face of battleship, overwhelming the gunnery stations and shooting past the battleship before its defensive forces could target them.

Overwhelmed by the mass attack, the battleship's pilot hesitated before inputting the next command sequence. It gave two of Ellie's pilots their opportunity. A lieutenant targeted a missile sleeve halfway out on the port wing, and a captain targeted another missile port near the center fuselage. Both pilots scored hits and huge explosions rocked the battleship.

<Pull back,> Ellie sent urgently on open comm to all pilots, and the travelers sought distance from the battleship as explosions continued to erupt throughout the vessel's wings. From 100K kilometers away, Ellie and her pilots stopped to watch detonations rip though the battleship for a quarter hour until an enormous explosion, probably due to failed engine-core containment, converted the remains of the UE battleship into hot gases and space debris.

Ellie ordered her pilots to track the large debris chunks and eliminate them, ensuring they would not become a danger to ships, planets, and moon bases. As the Haraken pilots rendered the sections into dust, she was reminded of the Swei Swee destroying the vestiges of the Nua'll world traveler, which the aliens referred to as their prison ship. *Neither of us wants a reminder of our adversaries,* Ellie thought.

30

Maria ordered the recall of a traveler to Prima to transport her, Ambassador Stroheim, and Ministers Drake and Jaya to the *Last Stand*, which had collected its fighters and was inbound to New Terra. "Ordered" would be the polite term. What the ex-TSF general actually said to her office administrator was, "I'm headed to the Prima shuttle terminal. There better be a traveler waiting for me when I get there!"

There was a moment of sensitive confrontation when Sheila explained to Maria that she was ordered to return to Haraken as quickly as possible and couldn't afford the time to meet with her. But Maria calmly played a presidential card, reminding Sheila of New Terra's close ties with Haraken and her personal relationship with Alex.

Maria, Eric, Will, and Darryl met with Sheila, Edouard, Ellie, and Deirdre in the captain's cabin. If truth be told, Maria's ministers, Will and Darryl, didn't have a formal role in the meeting, but they refused to be left behind, grabbing coats and racing to catch Maria's aero-car before she left Government House. It was going to be the ministers' first opportunity to get a peek inside a Haraken carrier.

On introduction, Maria hugged the two wing commanders, Ellie and Deirdre, thanking them for their bravery and commitment to the people of New Terra.

"We are only returning a favor long owed, Ser President," Ellie said, touching hand to heart and nodding her head.

"Yes, Commander . . . well, we might all spend a lifetime trying to repay that one what we owe," Maria said. "But to business, Commodore, Captain, I'm loath to see you leave Oistos and take your fighters with you."

Sheila ducked her head for a moment before she expressed her own needs. "Madam President, my apologies, but I thought to ask you for some of your travelers to replace our losses."

"Well, then we do have a conundrum, don't we, Commodore," said Maria, leaning back in her chair and forcing the nanites to conform to her new position. *When life gives us a respite, I must request one of these chairs for my office,* Maria thought.

"Wait, Commodore, if you want our travelers, then that must mean you can convert them from a shuttle to a fighter," Jaya said, and just like that Maria smiled and praised herself for allowing her two favorite ministers to accompany her. The three New Terrans leaned forward expectantly, eager expressions plastered on their faces.

"Mickey has always said that our travelers are exact replicas of the original dark travelers except for the shell, our controller, our interior amenities, and our hatches," Sheila replied. "It should mean there is the possibility of turning the beams on, but it would require transporting them to Haraken for Mickey's people to make the alterations. Madam President, I have a nagging feeling that we've made a powerful enemy, who will come again to our space soon without any diplomatic intentions. I believe we'll need every fighter we can get."

"One moment, Sers, let's ask an expert, or at least the closest thing we have to one, about this question," Ellie said, comming Mutter, and passing her link through the captain's vid screen.

<Good day, Sers,> Mutter replied, <how may I be of service?> Mutter was seen in one of the *Money Maker*'s bays. Ahmed, Svetlana, and a flight team were crawling over two travelers looking for shell damage. Unlike Daggers, nanites couldn't repair these fighters' shells. It would take Swei Swee "spit" to fix damaged traveler shells.

"Mutter, we would like to convert the New Terran shuttles to fighters," Ellie said, then hesitated when Mutter froze in place. Ellie looked in confusion at Sheila, wondering what prompted the SADE's fugue.

Moments later, Mutter focused on the vid pickup, sending, <Certainly, Commander. This operation is quite possible.>

"Possible?" Ellie asked. "As in it's easy to do . . . as we, or you, can do it here in New Terra?"

<It requires a SADE to access the controller's program. Apparently, Commander, I have the information required,> Mutter replied.

"Mutter, why wasn't this information volunteered earlier?" Eric Stroheim asked.

<It wasn't available, Ambassador, until Commander Thompson stated her intent to convert the shuttles.>

"Mutter, please clarify. Why has the information only come available now?" Sheila asked.

<Julien distributed a program to the SADEs and requested we store it. Since the entry algorithm code was locked, it was obvious that we were not to access the substance of the program. The Commander's request unlocked the entry algorithm, and the program produced the instructions for activating a traveler-shuttle's beam. I can begin the operation as soon as I receive authorization.>

Around the table, there was a mix of joy and disappointment. The technically minded were thrilled with the aspect of converting shuttles to fighters, but the political and military leaders were crestfallen, imagining only Alex or Julien possessed the authority to approve the conversion, and those two were light-years away.

However, Sheila was unwilling to give up so easily. "Mutter, does anyone in the Oistos system have authorization?"

<Allowing for seniority, Ambassador Stroheim has authorization, Commodore.>

Heads turned from the vid screen to eye Eric, who raised his hands in confusion. "Mutter, when did you receive this program from Julien?" Eric asked.

<The date coincides with the first shipment of traveler-shuttles to New Terra onboard this vessel, Ambassador. Records indicate you accompanied the shipment for the purpose of meeting with President Gonzalez and her ministerial staff.>

"But that . . . that was years ago, Mutter," Eric stuttered.

<Seven point four years ago, Ambassador,> Mutter replied.

Edouard hazarded a guess. "Mutter, what is the complete list of individuals who have authorization and are in this system?"

<In addition to Ambassador Stroheim, you do, Captain, and Commodore Reynard, President Gonzalez, and Ministers Drake and Jaya.>

In the stunned silence, they heard Will Drake quietly say, "Catch him if you can."

"Could we have made use of these converted shuttles in the battle?" Minister Jaya asked, focusing on Ellie for the answer.

"Unfortunately, no, Minister," Ellie replied. "While we might have accomplished the conversions in time, we had no time to train the pilots."

"But we have Dagger pilots," Jaya ventured.

"It would have taken months to train your Dagger pilots, Minister," Ellie replied. "Not only would your pilots have to be trained on new craft and beam tactics, they would have needed to learn to fly these quick and fast craft in squadron and wing formations. And my apologies if I'm bringing up a sensitive subject, but our fighter pilots make extended use of their implants to coordinate with their controllers and one another."

When the New Terrans did not appear convinced, Sheila said, "Without trained military pilots in those travelers, Sers, they might just have easily turned one another or our fighters into space dust."

"Mutter, I have a question," Maria said. "Do you have any thoughts as to why this information was secreted in this manner?"

<There was no amplification of the instructions, Ser President. We were requested to store the locked program in our memory. If I was to . . . guess . . . the activation of such knowledge by a specific request would imply it was dependent on extraordinary circumstances.>

Maria thought to herself for a moment and then began nodding in understanding. "Yes, Mutter, unique circumstances . . . such as in a time of dire emergency."

<I would concur, President Gonzalez,> Mutter replied. <There would seem few other circumstances under which such a request might be made.> When silence on the comm extended for a long time, Mutter felt duty bound to prod the humans. <Ambassador, do you wish me to proceed with the conversion of the New Terran shuttles? If so, how many do you wish converted?>

Eric, staring with resolve at Maria, said, <Mutter, I hereby authorize the conversion of all New Terran traveler controllers to provide beam capability.>

<Your authorized request is noted, Ambassador. The conversion can take place immediately, but I would recommend that training be provided first.>

While the humans pondered, Mutter considered several options, discarding all but one, before those at the conference table took their third breath. She queried Captain Durak and Commander Valenko on her plan and received their approval.

Mutter requested the two humans come to her side, and she addressed the conference group. <Sers, if I may, I have considered a possible scenario. The carrier has lost fifty-one pilots and travelers. It would be prudent to add the *Money Maker*'s remaining travelers to the carrier's complement, bringing the ship's wing up to 116 fighters. Many of our freighters' fighters have suffered nicks and cracks, which are weakening their shells' continuity. The Swei Swee could repair these ships quickly. I have discussed this plan with Captain Durak and Commander Valenko, and they are amenable to remaining in system and training the shuttle pilots, Dagger pilots, or whomever President Gonzalez chooses to have trained.>

Mutter's statement caused Maria to consider her Dagger pilots. New Terra's Daggers were kept planetside as a line of last defense against the Earthers if they attempted to land shuttles on the planet. Training the Dagger pilots, in concert with the shuttle pilots, would expedite readiness. One group knew fighter tactics, and the other group knew the travelers. *They can learn together,* Maria thought.

"Any issues with this plan, Captain Durak, Commander Valenko?" Sheila asked.

<None, Commodore,> Ahmed sent. <As expected, it's a practical suggestion.>

<Worth more than an airtight environment suit in vacuum, any day,> Svetlana added, and she and Ahmed laid comradely hands on the SADE's shoulders.

The conference group watched a beatific smile form on Mutter's face from the affectionate gestures. Several glances, but no words, were exchanged. The Haraken world of humans and SADEs was ever evolving.

"Mutter, are you going or staying?" Sheila asked.

That Mutter paused for several moments told the group how difficult the decision was for her. Everyone knew her greatest desire was to return to Haraken and sing for the Swei Swee once again. <I will remain here, for now, Commodore, but please whistle a message for me to the First. Tell him that hunters continue to roam the stars, and I must search for them for the safety of the People.>

"Your message will be delivered, Mutter, and thank you for your sacrifice." In response to her statement, the SADE delivered a gesture of respect. "Mutter, please coordinate the timing of the conversion with . . ." Sheila glanced at Maria, who pointed to her left, "with Minister Drake."

"As you request, Commodore," Mutter replied, and Sheila closed the comm.

"Meetings with Alex were always like this," Maria said, "so informative," which broke the group into fits of laughter—some from Maria's statement and some just enjoying being alive and able to laugh again—none more so than Ellie.

"Well, Commodore, I imagine you have preparations to make and a schedule to keep. We won't detain you any longer. I wish you good fortune with Mutter's 'search for hunters.' Give that farseeing president of yours a kiss from me," Maria said, giving Sheila a mischievous grin.

Eric Stroheim remained behind while the New Terrans left the *Last Stand* aboard one of their soon-to-be-converted travelers. Commodore and Captain urged pilots and crew to make haste, and the carrier was underway within hours, headed out of system for home, to discover what transpired at Haraken where the *Reunion* was headed.

31

Exiting FTL outside the Hellébore system, the *Reunion* made its way inward. Wombo beseeched Speaker García for a few minutes of his time, and they retired to the speaker's cabin.

"Speaker García, I implore you. We should be meeting with these people—the Méridiens, the New Terrans, and the Harakens. We should be offering them alliances, treating them as equals. Not coercing them to join the UE."

"Administrator Wombo, I don't necessarily disagree with you. Diplomacy would be better, but force appears to be our only option. Humans must be united, one way or the other."

"But haven't they aptly demonstrated that they don't wish to join the UE, Speaker? And are not allies better than enemies? Most important, these people have demonstrated they possess the military technology necessary to enforce their views."

"Administrator Wombo, you are pushing an agenda that is contrary to UE dictates at the highest level, and incidentally is contrary to High Judge Bunaldi's direct orders. Be extremely careful. I imagine by this time, New Terra has already submitted to Bunaldi. The people could do little else in the face of a UE battleship. We will do the same here at Haraken. Information has it that this is nothing more than a colony of a half million. They will see the wisdom of submitting. Trust me."

Wombo left the speaker's cabin completely dejected. It was one thing to live within the UE and hope for things to improve; it was another thing to discover other human worlds that were living in peace, perhaps not in perfection but to a far greater degree than Earth. He was never sorrier than now to call himself a human of Earth. As Wombo turned a corner for his cabin, he heard a snort and deprecating chuckle.

"Didn't go too well with Speaker García, Administrator?" Shin asked. She was leaning against the bulkhead next to his cabin door and thoroughly enjoying the moment. "By the look on your face, you lost your argument to save your precious Méridiens or Harakens or whomever they are. High Judge Bunaldi will teach the New Terrans a lesson in supremacy, and we will do the same here."

"You are disgusting, Shin. Go away."

"Oh, my goodness, Administrator Wombo does know how to be angry." Shin pushed off the bulkhead and stood toe to toe with Wombo. Although forty-six centimeters shorter, Shin craned her head back to stare at Wombo with all the hatred she could muster. "You have exposed your sympathies for these people to your own detriment. Mark my words, Olawale; you will not have your job long. You lack a stiff spine, old man, and your job will soon be mine."

The pain from the decades under UE rule and his hatred for what they were doing to the Méridiens and their allies welled up in Wombo, and he grabbed Shin by the throat, his massive hand encircling her slender neck.

For a brief moment, Shin feared for her life, but when Wombo paused, confusion replacing the brief burst of hatred in his eyes, Shin began to laugh and Wombo released his hold on her. "You can't even fight back against a tiny woman." Shin strolled past Wombo, laughing at him until she turned the next corner.

Wombo entered his cabin to find his close friends waiting for him.

"I'm sorry, Olawale," Nema said. "We couldn't help but hear your exchange with the snake-woman."

"Nema, it's unfair of you to demean the noble reptiles by your comparison," Storen said, his comment breaking the group's somber mood.

"So your arguments fell on deaf ears, my friend," Priita said. The expression on Wombo's face didn't seem to require his response.

"So who's for a new adventure? Under the circumstances, I believe this one has run its course," Yoram asked.

"And how would we begin our new adventure?" Storen asked.

"That seems apparent. We desert. Now, how exactly we do that I leave to you more practical types. Remember my specialty is philosophy," Yoram replied.

The fact that no one raised an outcry caused the room's occupants to regard one another carefully. There wasn't a dissension in the group.

"If we were to attempt this, recognize that it could well result in our deaths," Wombo warned.

Priita chuckled. "Remember to whom you are speaking, Olawale. We are a group of eminent, senior scientists. Do you think we can't calculate the probabilities of the alternatives?"

Wombo offered his friends a smile of embarrassment. "All right, what do we need to accomplish this, by when do we need it, and how do we request asylum from the Harakens?" he asked.

* * *

The Haraken-based SADEs picked up the *Reunion*'s entrance into the Hellébore system from the FTL station based near the outer planet's orbit. It was a quick and simultaneous decision among them to appoint Cordelia as their spokesperson. The logic was simple and flawless. Cordelia's partner was Julien, and Julien's friend was Alex. Of all the SADEs, she could best interpret the meaning of the Earther ship's arrival and communicate that to the humans.

<Tomas,> Cordelia sent as she watched Teague frolic with Swei Swee juvenile and adult males just offshore.

<Greetings, Cordelia, how may I help you?> Tomas replied.

<The Earther explorer ship that we were warned about has arrived in system. Present velocity indicates about 4.8 days until arrival at Haraken's orbit.>

<Any other news?> Tomas asked.

<None, at this time, Ser.>

<Do you think it's possible that our ships have been defeated?> Tomas asked with trepidation.

<It is possible, but not probable. Remember who was aboard the *Rêveur*, and, this time, our president took sufficient forces to cover almost any common contingency.>

<And if the contingencies were uncommon?>

<Then we are on our own, Assembly Speaker Monti,> Cordelia sent, reminding Tomas of his responsibility.

While there was still time before the *Reunion* arrived in orbit, the Harakens hurried to hide many of their assets in Hellébore's asteroid belt or at least move them to the far side of Haraken.

Cordelia messaged Captain Tanaka aboard the *No Retreat*, Haraken's second and newest carrier. It was twice the size of its sister ship, the *Last Stand*, carrying two full wings of 128 travelers each. On Cordelia's request, a traveler was dispatched to pick her up from House Racine.

It was a sign of the times. Haraken SADEs hoped to enjoy parity with humans when they converted to mobile avatars. Now, circumstances called on Haraken's most capable humans and SADEs to step forward and protect the home world, and Cordelia's request for a traveler and a transfer to the *No Retreat* was received, acknowledged, and given priority attention, no questions asked.

* * *

Captain Miko Tanaka, Wing Commanders Lucia Bellardo and Franz Cohen, and Cordelia gazed into the massive holo-vid on the *No Retreat*'s bridge. It was a Z special. Mickey's mistake had been to grumble to Z that the new carrier would receive a standard Méridien display, a seemingly paltry piece of equipment for such a huge bridge.

"Any word yet?" Miko asked, glancing at Cordelia.

"None, Captain," Cordelia replied. "If our ships are chasing the Earthers, we have no idea of their distance lag. At the explorer ship's present velocity, if our ships arrive more than fourteen hours from now, they will be unable to run down the *Reunion*."

"If our ships are late, then we must assume the defense of our people," Miko replied.

"Z's Shadow detailed that ship's armament well. We have the fighters over them," Franz said.

Franz Cohen was Hezekiah's son and was on duty at the New Terra Joaquin Station when station personnel rescued the oxygen-starved people aboard the *Unsere Menschen*. His love of the Librans began that day and galvanized him to immigrate to Haraken at the first opportunity.

Trained as a New Terran shuttle pilot, Franz Cohen proved to be a natural behind a traveler-shuttle's controller and soon after joined Haraken fighter training school. His rise in the ranks came quickly, promoted by virtue of his calm manner, natural leadership, and intuitive skills with the fighter. Only individuals such as Ellie Thompson, Deirdre Canaan, and Svetlana Valenko were superior in the fighter games, and even they admitted that Franz forced them to stay on top of their skills.

"We have the fighters, but the *No Retreat* is a giant target for the *Reunion*'s missiles, which we have no defense against," Lucia noted.

"Unless we use our travelers to intercept the missiles," Franz replied. Franz's thought chilled the Méridiens.

Only a New Terran would make that suggestion, Cordelia thought.

"Then our objectives must be to halt the Earther ship's advance and remove any temptation to launch their missiles at our carrier," Miko said thoughtfully.

"You have a plan, Captain?" Cordelia asked.

"Yes . . . yes, I do," Miko said forcefully. "We will demonstrate to these Earthers that they have made a great mistake coming here uninvited, or, at least, have failed to ask permission to enter our system. Cordelia, take the ship out of orbit to a position 1M kilometers out from Haraken directly in line with the Earthers' approach. And, Cordelia, do it at max velocity! I believe our leader once said that he required an entrance. I want the same effect."

Cordelia's generous smile demonstrated her agreement with Miko's approach.

"Commanders, when we reach a stationary position, it'll be your turn. I want a quick and precise launch of our travelers. Make it look impressive."

"How many fighters, Captain?" Lucia asked.

"All of them, Commander," Miko replied. "Spread them out in a wall. Extrapolating from the Shadow's reconnaissance, we should have a four-to-one superiority over their fighters. Let's give them an overwhelming reason to halt and reconsider their intentions."

* * *

On the *Reunion*'s bridge, Speaker García and Major Barbas waited impatiently behind Captain Lumley.

"Well, Captain," García demanded. Alerted hours ago by Captain Lumley of the huge ship that appeared from behind their target planet, the speaker and the major had hurried to the bridge despite the lengthy distance that their explorer ship was still to travel to reach the planet. They had been shocked to hear the guide's report that the massive Haraken ship accelerated at an unheard of rate compared to UE ships. Then, as suddenly as it appeared and accelerated to meet them, it halted—more quickly than a UE ship could have achieved. Now they waited for the guide's analysis of the ship and Captain Lumley's interpretation of the guide's telemetry.

"It appears to be a larger version of the ship that we caught sight of as we fled . . . pardon me, Speaker García . . . as we left the Méridien system," Lumley replied. "It's our opinion that the Méridien-based ship was a fighter carrier with few defensive capabilities, which is why it remained hidden after it launched its fighters. The configuration of this ship is similar, only larger. While I would not want to presume, it is highly probable that this ship has no defensive capabilities either."

"Excellent, Captain," García replied, "wait until we are close, then launch a full spread of missiles."

"Speaker García, shouldn't we hail the ship and at least order it to stand aside?" Lumley entreated his superior.

"I'm done coddling these people, Captain. We get close. We launch our missiles and remove their vaunted technology in one quick chop of the blade," García replied.

Barbas wore an ugly leer. Still smoldering from the duplicity of the creature called Z, the thought of revenge tasted so sweet that he could barely control himself.

"One moment, Speaker García," Lumley interrupted. "The guide has detected a launch of fighters from that carrier." Lumley ordered the telemetry on the bridge's central monitor. The entire bridge personnel watched open-jawed as the fighters flooded from the ship, sped to precise positions, and formed a wall of equally spaced fighters, floating in space."

"Are humans flying those craft?" García asked. The eerie way in which the fighters flew to their positions shook his confidence. Glancing around at the bridge crew, García saw that it had the same effect on them.

"Eyes on your instruments," Lumley ordered, hoping to restore his crew's focus. The unnatural, machine-like forming of the fighter wall also scared him. "Speaker García, the guide counts 256 fighters. Since that carrier launched what well might have been its entire fleet, it negates a missile strike against the mother ship. We would achieve no tactical advantage."

"I'm certainly aware of the effects of their maneuver, Captain," García ground out.

"Captain," the comms officer called out, "we are being hailed."

"Comms, does the guide have a vector on the transmission? Is it that carrier?" Lumley asked.

"Negative, Captain, the guide indicates the broadcast originates behind us," the officer replied.

"Navigation, what's behind us?" Lumley demanded.

"Nothing, Captain. The guide doesn't indicate any ship is back there."

"There's that vaunted technology that you would so quickly dismiss, Speaker García," Captain Lumley said with a resigned shake of his head.

"Explain, Captain," García demanded.

"It's my estimate that a ship from the Méridien system has followed us and exited FTL behind us. Its captain or commander is hailing us," Captain Lumley replied.

"Impossible," Barbas snarled. "Even if there was a means of hiding their ship visually, the guide would pick up their energy signature. The Méridien ships have significant engine flares."

"As I began to explain, Major," Lumley said, turning to face Barbas directly and holding the major's dark gaze with one as fierce, "I believe that ship is not trying to hide, and the guide will detect it eventually. Light is traveling at its expected velocity, but these people are transmitting their comms in an accelerated manner. I would imagine that they have that capability ship-to-ship, throughout their systems, and among their worlds."

"Captain, put their hail on the monitor," García ordered.

The major held up his hand to Lumley to forestall his actions. "Speaker García, are you sure that's wise?" Barbas whispered, nodding toward the listening bridge crew.

"Put it on the monitor, Captain," García repeated.

Lumley nodded at his comms officer and from the monitor's speakers was heard, "Speaker García, this is President Racine. You and your people appear to be quite dense. I would have thought by now you would understand that we don't want your heavy-handed presence in our systems. At this moment, you have two choices: reverse course, leave this system, and return to Earth or die, and I don't much care which one you choose. I'll wait one hour by your clock system, and then I will direct our fighters to obliterate your ship. President Racine out."

"So close, so close," García muttered when the message ended.

"We still have our armament. We can still fight," Barbas argued.

Lumley regarded the major as if he had lost his mind.

"Calm down, Major," García replied. "We have an hour to think. Let us retire and consider our options."

32

Surprised by Wombo's invitation to visit him in his cabin, Zhang Shin arrived expecting the administrator's apology. Although, in her mind, it would be a useless gesture on his part. However, Shin decided to humor the old man, even accepting a cup of some tasteless, native drink.

Wombo caught the cup before it tumbled from Shin's hand. With her petite frame, only a half-cup of Boris's brew was needed to put her in a deep sleep. While Wombo wouldn't have thought of himself as a cruel man, he couldn't resist leaving out the analgesic that Boris cautioned him to be sure to add to the sleeping mixture. The compound would have tempered the effects of the dose. Without it, Wombo smiled, Shin would wake hours from now with a migraine that she wouldn't soon forget.

"Our spy is out," Wombo said after placing a call to Priita's cabin where the rest of Wombo's compatriots waited. "We are free to leave. Remember to leave one at a time and take different routes to the bay. Wait in the small office opposite the bay's airlock until I arrive."

Wombo hoisted Shin out of her chair and deposited her in his head's cramped shower space. He covered her with a blanket, more to hide her than to prevent her from getting cold.

Edward, Nema, Priita, Storen, Yoram, Boris, and Olawale had planned for this opportunity ever since Yoram had suggested the concept of a "new adventure." What followed the suggestion was a great deal of soul-searching on the part of each scientist, wondering who would miss them, why they came on this mission, and what they were seeking. While the answers varied, the conclusion was the same. If the Harakens would have them, they were ready to jump ship. Unfortunately, they realized they would have to initiate their escape and hope the Harakens wouldn't turn them away.

Priita was the last to leave the cabin, and she signaled Olawale, who waited several minutes before he followed his friends. Olawale walked the corridors as nonchalantly as he could, but he could swear his heart was beating so fiercely that the crew would surely notice. *With our ages, it's a wonder that several of us don't have heart attacks before we make the bay,* Olawale thought.

Slipping into a vacant maintenance office across the corridor from their designated bay, Olawale found all his people present. Each of them carried some sort of bag or sack, despite his admonishment to carry no baggage or anything suspicious. "Am I the only one who knows how to follow instructions and leave all personal possessions behind?" he asked.

"Yes and no," Priita replied. "We knew you would follow your advice. That's why we took care of your things for you." Edward and Storen each held up a bag.

"Good friends," Olawale said, with a generous smile for his wayward comrades. "Now give me five minutes. If I do not return in that time, make your way back to your cabins as if nothing has happened." When the others nodded their agreement, Olawale slipped out into the corridor and entered the bay's airlock. He barely cleared the bayside hatch when he was roughly grabbed by the arm.

"Where have you been, Administrator?" demanded the angry crewman.

"It took longer than expected. Are you ready?" Olawale asked.

"Get your people in here now, Administrator. I should have been on duty with only one other crew member. Instead, a repair crew of four was assigned to maintenance on that far shuttle," the anxious crew member said, pointing to the opposite end of the bay. "I gave everyone your sleeping mixture more than an hour ago, but with the additional crew, each of them only received about one third of the mixture. We're in danger of them waking soon. Now, go . . . hurry!"

Olawale ran back to retrieve his comrades, hurrying them through the airlock cycle and into the shuttle bay. Looking around for the crew member, Olawale spotted him slumped on the deck, an empty cup lying next to him.

"I believe you said the crew member would accompany us, did you not?" Nema asked. From Nema, it wasn't an accusation. She was merely clarifying that she properly understood Olawale's original explanation.

"It would appear that he changed his mind," Olawale replied. "Please, two of you grab a crew member and haul them all to that far shuttle . . . the largest one. We will stow them in there where they will be safe while we depart." While the elderly scientists hauled and dragged each crew member toward the shuttle, Olawale picked up the nearest individual like a bag of spare parts and hurried to the distant shuttle, depositing his load onboard at the rear of the center aisle. Jogging down the ramp, he grabbed the first crew member delivered by his friends, threw the weight over his shoulder, and hurried back inside.

When the crew was safely ensconced inside the shuttle, Olawale secured the gangway and hatch from its exterior access panel. "Come, everyone, get aboard," he urged his companions, running toward the smallest shuttle in the bay, halting at the base of the gangway ramp to help his elderly companions aboard. "We will be all right. I have been briefed on the automatic piloting controls." More than one of Olawale's compatriots eyed him with doubt as they hurried past him into the shuttle.

Once aboard, Olawale quickly retracted the gangway ramp and sealed the hatch before he made his way to the pilot's chair. No sooner was he strapped in than Yoram slid into the copilot's chair beside him.

"You have shuttle skills, my friend?" Olawale asked hopefully.

"Regretfully, none. I am here for moral support," Yoram said, strapping himself into his chair and gazing forward as if that was sufficient to force open the bay doors and launch the shuttle.

Olawale took a deep breath and exhaled slowly to calm his jangling nerves. "Apparently, the crew member intended all along to stay aboard the *Reunion*," Olawale said, "which is why he demonstrated the autopilot control instructions several times to me."

Yoram studied his large friend, who was perusing the pilot's controls, sympathetic to his predicament. "My friend. If we are caught now, we will be executed as traitors. Therefore, whatever you do will only aid us in evading that certain fate. Have courage."

Olawale gave his friend a weak smile, thankful for the encouragement but still sick to his stomach at the responsibility he was attempting to shoulder. During Olawale's brief training, the flight crew member constantly stressed the beginning steps, and Olawale searched the control board for the first of those steps, tapping an icon labeled "auto launch." Immediately, the bay's launch horns sounded and warning lights flashed. After the stealth of their approach, the blaring noise and bright lights made the scientists cringe.

The pilot's board popped up a small window, which indicated the bay's status, and Olawale leaned over to carefully read it. "Pressure is dropping, my friend. The bay is depressurizing."

Yoram was pleased to see some small semblance of confidence return to Olawale. For an extremely dark-complexioned man, his friend appeared extremely pale a few moments ago.

When the bay pressure reached zero, the horns changed pitch, the flashing lights changed color, and the giant bay doors began sliding apart. In almost no time, Olawale and Yoram were staring at the deep dark, Hellébore a faint light off to the side.

"What now?" Yoram asked.

"We launch," Olawale replied with a bright smile. When the bay doors were fully opened, the auto-launch sequence engaged the shuttle's maneuvering jets and eased the vessel out of the bay. Once the shuttle cleared the *Reunion*, the engines were ignited, and the craft was launched on the crew member's preprogrammed course, heading for the distant planet of Haraken.

* * *

"Captain, we have an unauthorized shuttle launch," the ops officer called out.

"Comms, contact that shuttle now," Lumley ordered.

"Online, Captain," the comms officer called out. He switched the signal to the central monitor and the head and shoulders of Olawale filled the screen.

"Administrator Wombo, you've taken one of my shuttles without authorization. What do you think you're doing?" Lumley asked.

Olawale glanced at Yoram, who shrugged his shoulders as if to say, "I have no idea how to respond."

"Apologies, Captain, for our unauthorized actions, but circumstances have forced this decision on us," Olawale replied.

"Us? Who is this 'us'?" Lumley pressed.

It appears I'm ill-suited for subterfuge, Olawale thought. "A figure of speech, Captain. I'm alone."

"Search the ship for any other missing scientists," García whispered to Barbas. "Start with Priita Ranta's cabin."

"What is your intention, Administrator Wombo?" Lumley asked.

"My intention, Captain? Why I intend to immigrate to Haraken, if the people will have me."

García stepped up beside Captain Lumley. "Cut the comm," he whispered.

The captain signaled the comms officer to end the transmission. The image of Olawale winked off, and a great sadness swept over Lumley. He would have wanted to wish his friend good luck, and in the future he would want to know if his friend found a new home and a good life. Instead, the cold facts of reality told him his friend would probably be dead very soon.

"Call for you, Speaker García," the comms officer answered. "It's Major Barbas."

"On speaker," García ordered.

"Speaker, in addition to Administrator Wombo, four other senior scientists are unable to be found. We suspect several others are also missing, and we are continuing our search."

"Major, I don't want that shuttle to reach the Haraken carrier. Tell your pilots that if they don't destroy it, don't bother returning to this ship," García ordered.

"Understood, Speaker," Major Barbas replied. He was smiling as he raced for the launch bays.

* * *

"Captain Tanaka, we have a launch from the *Reunion*," Cordelia said. "A single, small vessel . . . it's not a missile."

"Fighter?" Miko asked.

"One moment, Captain. I'm receiving more telemetry." After a few moments, Cordelia added, "It's a shuttle." She activated the bridge's holo-vid and placed the Earther ship and the Haraken vessel in position. "The shuttle is headed in our direction. To be precise, Captain, it's headed directly for the *No Retreat*."

<Commanders Bellardo and Cohen,> Miko sent. <A single shuttle has exited the Earther ship and is headed toward us. If that vessel gets within 100K kilometers of this ship, without my authorization, I want it destroyed. No questions asked.> Both wing commanders confirmed Miko's orders.

"Cordelia, can we talk to that shuttle?" Miko asked.

"I can attempt communication, Captain."

Cordelia let slide her human persona programs to allow full engagement in her task. When she froze in position, eyes wide and staring, it was a reminder of the difference between humans and SADEs.

Julien had provided Cordelia the comm protocols and translation programs, which were required to converse with the explorer ship. She employed his tools and utilized the carrier's sophisticated comm systems to enable her transmission. Within a few moments, Cordelia established a connection with the shuttle's bridge control systems and activated its comm system.

Miko hailed the shuttle when Olawale appeared on the carrier's central screen. "This is the Haraken carrier *No Retreat*, Captain Tanaka speaking. Halt the approach of your vessel, and state your purpose."

"Hello, Captain Tanaka. I am Administrator Wombo of United Earth. I have, aboard this shuttle, six other senior scientists, who wish to seek asylum on your world."

Miko and Cordelia exchanged glances. <I must admit, Captain, this scenario did not occur to me,> Cordelia sent privately to Miko.

When the shuttle's monitor displayed two attractive women, Yoram couldn't resist a closer view, exiting his copilot's seat and crowding into camera view behind Olawale. He waved a tentative hand at the women.

<They do not appear to be the dangerous sort,> Miko shared with Cordelia. "Administrator Wombo, I require you to halt your shuttle relative to our ship's position before we discuss your request," Miko ordered.

"With pleasure, Captain Tanaka," Olawale said, bending over the pilot's board and struggling to recall the crew member's instructions. "Excuse me, Captain Tanaka, would you be able to aid us in that?"

"Aid you in what exactly, Administrator Wombo?" Miko asked.

"We sincerely wish to comply, Captain Tanaka, but none of us are qualified pilots."

"Yet you managed to get this far, Administrator Wombo," Cordelia noted.

"I closed the gangway ramp and hatch, and then pressed auto-launch, young miss," Olawale replied and shrugged his massive shoulders.

Miko coughed politely into her hand to camouflage her laughter. The scenario was hilarious in so many ways, not the least of which was the scientist referring to a 100-plus-year-old sentient as "young miss."

"One moment, Administrator Wombo, perhaps I can help you with your dilemma," Cordelia replied.

As Cordelia's fugue state overtook her, Olawale threw a quizzical look over his shoulder at Yoram.

"So much to learn, my friend," Yoram replied to Olawale's silent question. The pilot's board lit, confirming their change in vector until it was reversed, and then the main engines were fired until the shuttle's relative velocity to the carrier indicated zero.

"Your shuttle is stationary relative to us now, Administrator Wombo," Cordelia announced.

"You are a remarkable woman, young miss," Olawale gushed.

"Then again, I'm not," Cordelia replied and winked at the administrator.

"What do you think she meant, Olawale?" Yoram whispered urgently into his friend's ear. "We must gain admittance to this world. The rest of our lives could be spent learning so many new and wonderful things."

* * *

Barbas raced through the corridors of the *Reunion*, yelling at crew to clear the way. Embarrassment from the revelation of Miranda Leyton's true identity smoldered deep inside him, and Barbas ached for a means of repayment.

Cycling through the bay's airlock, Barbas was pleased to see the three fighters were prepped as he ordered. Two pilots saluted him as he raced toward them.

"Emergency launch," Major Barbas yelled and his heavy, bass voice galvanized flight crew and pilots into action. Crew helped Barbas strip and don a flight suit. Snatching his helmet from a crew member, Barbas hurried to his fighter. Within moments, the flight crew was vacating the bay and the launch cycle was underway.

"Pilots," Barbas said over his comm, "that shuttle doesn't reach safety, no matter what we have to do. Is that understood?"

Captains Doultier and Hinnicky acknowledged Barbas's message but each had different thoughts. Doultier was a believer, anxious to prove her value to the major. However, Hinnicky just loved to fly and a fighter was the fastest, most maneuverable craft built by the UE. What Hinnicky wasn't prepared to do was die in the pursuit of a shuttle load of UE scientists.

The bay's doors slid open and starlight beckoned. "Clear to launch," the flight chief confirmed on the comm, and the pilots engaged their fighters' auto-launch modes. Clear of the ship, engines ignited, the fighters blasted after the shuttle.

* * *

"We have a second launch, Captain Tanaka," Cordelia reported. "Three UE fighters under heavy acceleration are chasing the shuttle."

"It doesn't take three fighters to return a wayward shuttle to the ship," Miko mused. "It might be our scientists are intent on leaving the fold as they've stated and probably much to Speaker García's consternation."

"These individuals might hold valuable information about the UE and its technology, which Speaker García does not wish us to have," Cordelia suggested.

<Commanders Bellardo and Cohen, the UE ship launched three fighters. I believe they are intent on forcing the shuttle back to the ship or destroying it, and I want it protected,> Miko sent.

In response, Lucia and Franz ordered three fighters from each wing to escort the shuttle to the carrier.

"Olawale, there are new icons on my screen," Yoram said tentatively. "This is us," Yoram explained, pointing to an icon in blue. "This is the *Reunion*. This is the Haraken ship, but what are these three dots?"

Olawale leaned over to examine the copilot's board. "Those are trouble, my friend." Turning to face his monitor, Olawale said, "Captain, I believe we are in need of immediate assistance."

"Why would you say that, Administrator?" Miko replied, anxious to test their logic about the scientists' situation.

"We might be the first deserters of United Earth, Captain. It would be a dangerous precedence that Speaker García can't let happen on his watch," Olawale replied. "Those three fighters will have been ordered to destroy us rather than see us fall into your hands."

"Understood, Administrator Wombo. We are sending our fighters to protect you," Miko replied. That the administrator's story and the actions of the UE ship were aligning gave her confidence that she understood the situation correctly. The last thing she wanted to do was tell Alex Racine that she lost a great source of intelligence on the UE or that she was fooled into allowing a dangerous vessel close to her carrier. *Of course, in the latter scenario, I might not live to have to face him,* Miko thought.

"Captain," Cordelia said, interrupting Miko's thoughts. "The UE fighters will reach the shuttle first."

"Take control of the shuttle, Cordelia. Bring it to us at max acceleration."

Cordelia warned the scientists, who hurriedly secured themselves, before the shuttle flipped and accelerated toward the carrier.

* * *

"Major Barbas, I have six fighters, in two flights, approaching us head-on," Captain Hinnicky called on the comm.

"Captain, it's not necessary to state the obvious," Barbas replied. "You and Captain Doultier will each target a flight. Use your missiles to distract them. It will provide the time I need to take out that shuttle before you even have to engage them. Then we can return to the *Reunion.*"

Unknowingly, Captain Doultier suddenly found herself in Hinnicky's camp. Three against one did not sound like an opportunity to prove one's self. It sounded more like an opportunity to visit the afterlife.

"Major—" Hinnicky began.

"Yes, Captain, I see it," Barbas growled. "The shuttle is accelerating toward the carrier. I'm surprised those science fools know how to fly a shuttle."

"Major, I calculate those enemy fighters will reach the shuttle several seconds before us," Doultier said.

"The two of you take point positions to my fighter," Barbas ordered. "Draw their fire." Reluctantly, the captains obeyed. All three pilots armed their missile banks, Barbas targeting the shuttle. The other two pilots locked on the enemy fighters in their assigned flight.

Despite his extensive training and experience, Barbas focused on the shuttle on his display to the exclusion of all else, wanting to witness its destruction more than he wanted to live. Once the Haraken lovers, as Barbas thought of them, died in a ball of fire, he would think about regaining the *Reunion*.

In fractions of time, which only controllers and computers could track, the UE fighters reached their engagement window and launched their missiles. Ticks in time later, the Haraken fighters swept past the shuttle, targeted the UE fighters, and fired their beams. The travelers' beams ignited the Earthers' missiles only moments after they cleared the enemy's fighters, forcing the UE fighters to fly into masses of hot, expanding shrapnel, which tore their ships apart, adding to the hot balls of expanding gases and metal.

33

"Speaker García, we've lost all three fighters. The shuttle is undamaged and approaching the Haraken carrier," Lumley reported.

"Where is Major Barbas?" García demanded. "Hail him, Captain."

"Apologies, Speaker García, I thought you knew. Major Barbas led the fighters."

"What?" García exclaimed and stood there in shock.

"There's more bad news, Speaker García," Lumley said into the silence. "The guide has registered the acceleration and velocity that the Haraken fighters achieved. There is no means by which we can evade them and exit the system. And you will have noticed their fighters outnumber ours four to one."

"What are you saying, Captain?" García said, the shock of losing both his prime crony, Major Barbas, and the tremendous prize he coveted in the same moment was too much to allow him to process the captain's words.

"I'm saying we're dead, Speaker García," Lumley replied flatly. "Your hubris has killed us all."

The captain's insult flared white hot in García's mind, and his ego raged at the insubordination. But before he could retort, the comms officer interrupted, urgently signaling the captain.

"Put it on the monitor," Captain Lumley ordered, and the angry face of President Racine appeared.

"I find it hard to accept that you people are what has become of humankind on Earth," Alex declared. "Personally, I would forbid you to call yourselves human. You need a category of greater apes by which to be classified. But then again, that might be insulting the apes."

The comms officer whispered to Captain Lumley and Speaker García that the signal was bouncing through the carrier, and two-way comm was possible without a time lag, which gave impetus to Speaker García's anger and he drew breath to reply.

"Close your mouth, Speaker García," Alex warned. "Listen carefully to what I have to say and you might live to see another day."

García couldn't resist the temptation to put his enemy in his place, but the words stuck in his throat when the majority of bridge officers rose from their seats and faced him with hands on sidearms.

"Captain Lumley," Alex called out.

"Here, President Racine," Lumley replied and stepped into the camera's view.

"Captain, when I am finished, you will turn your ship around and leave the system on a reverse vector from your entrance," Alex ordered. "Am I clear?"

"Yes, Mr. President, an opposite vector from our entrance."

"You will proceed at maximum acceleration, Captain. After exiting the system, you will take whatever actions you need to enter FTL within two hours. Your final course must be for Earth. If you deviate from these instructions in any way, I will have your ship destroyed. Is that understood?"

"Most clearly, Mr. President. I will proceed as you have ordered, and I thank you for the lives of my crew."

"Now, you, Ser, may speak," Alex said pointing at Speaker García.

"Be careful, Speaker," Lumley whispered to García, "or I will shoot you myself."

Gaining control of his anger in the face of the ire of captain and crew, García glanced briefly at Captain Lumley, imagining the retribution he would bring down on the captain's head once they regained Sol, before he replied. "President Racine," García said graciously, "I regret we could not come to terms, but you must know that the final outcome is a foregone conclusion. The next UE expedition will not come to talk."

"You haven't done that anyway, Speaker García, but we will deal with those ships in our own way," Alex replied. "I have a message for the UE Leader, Captain Lumley. Tell him, her, or them that our worlds are off limits to the UE until such time as you can practice civilized behavior. Now go, before I change my mind about destroying your ship."

Captain Lumley ordered the ship on a return vector. He didn't bother to specify the exact course as every bridge officer was convinced of the need to be precise. Navigation checked the coordinates twice and confirmed with the captain. The pilot confirmed with engineering that the engines were ready for maximum output, and the second mate ordered the crew to make emergency preparations for full acceleration. Within eight minutes, the ship was ready and the pilot executed navigation settings, pushing the engines to full power.

Speaker García left the bridge, retiring to his cabin, and fumed for the next two days, even refusing meals. When García finally emerged, his mantle of superiority was resumed, and the captain and his officers recognized their imminent danger. They had threatened the speaker with harm in order to maintain his silence in the face of President Racine's message, and the speaker commanded the loyalty of the militia, who was angry enough at the loss of Major Barbas.

Once the *Reunion* entered FTL, a few bridge officers put their machinations into play. Zhang Shin was surreptitiously informed that the speaker was an admirer, but chose not to voice his desire due to the major's infatuation with her. Once Zhang was convinced of the opportunity to garner a new protector, a note was left in her cabin, graciously inviting her to dinner for two in the speaker's cabin.

That evening the captain's mess delivered two specially prepared meals to García's cabin with a note expressing the appreciation of Zhang Shin for an opportunity to talk with the speaker.

Both García and Zhang approached the dinner with an air of expectation for an eventful evening, which they did receive. Halfway through dinner, García began choking and died within minutes from a deadly poison lacing his food, which would be undetectable within hours.

When crew began pounding on the cabin door, responding to García's emergency comm, Zhang knew she was set up and that no one would believe she hadn't perpetrated this heinous act. Her opportunity to gain a new protector was lost, and her role as a UE collaborator would place her in a precarious position with the crew. The pounding ceased, which meant the crew was using an override signal to open the cabin door. Panicking, Zhang ran to the speaker's desk and ransacked through the drawers, finding his sidearm.

The cabin door slid aside and the crew rushed in to the sound of a sidearm's arc and sizzle and the smell of Zhang Shin's burning flesh.

* * *

Alex's first act when Miko informed him that the shuttle carrying the UE scientists was approaching the Haraken carrier under Cordelia's control was to call Terese.

<Yes, oh mighty one,> Terese replied.

<Bored are you, Terese?>

<And why not, Ser President? I have all this expertise and no one to practice on. You either chase our foes away or turn them into space dust.>

<Perhaps, I can cure your malaise. You are now in charge of our new batch of immigrants. Seven UE scientists are in a shuttle approaching the *No Retreat*. Contact the carrier's chief medical officer and direct him until you reach the carrier. A traveler is ready for you now. Port bay.>

<Excellent, Ser President. I will leave immediately.>

<Terese, treat these people much as we did the first silver ship.>

<That goes without saying, Ser President. We will be most careful to prevent you appearing foolish before the Assembly.>

Alex replied with a short vid of Terese's red hair in flames. In return, Terese displayed her head crowned in shimmering fire. <Careful you don't set my ship ablaze,> Alex replied.

Terese laughed at the thought, hastily packing a bag, and raced through the corridors to her waiting shuttle.

* * *

Chief medical officer Darrin Hesterly, a former New Terran TSF surgeon who immigrated to Haraken seven years ago, received Terese's list of instructions and a transfer of the entire procedure onboard the *Rêveur* during the capture of the first silver ship.

Darrin lost his wife and child in a horrible accident on the winter slopes of the Corona Mountains. A year later, battling depression, Darrin came to the conclusion that without a major change in his life, he would soon be dead by his own hand. One early morning, he resigned his commission in the Terran Security Forces and submitted an application for immigration to Haraken. It required two years of training to become competent in Méridien medical techniques, but with his skills and experience he soon became a valuable asset to the Haraken military forces. Much of his introduction to Méridien medicine came at the hands of Terese, and she did more than anyone to give him a new outlook on life.

At one point, early in his training, Darrin was asked to analyze a severely injured accident victim and suggest a procedure. Terese laughed at his unlikely suggestion, saying, "Ser, it is advisable to save the patient when practicing our medical techniques. The family would be most appreciative."

Darrin was flabbergasted when Terese explained the likely outcome of his choice of treatment. That she explained his error with a smile and a laugh stunned him. "How can you keep your sense of humor in light of what would have been a tragic mistake at my hand?" Darrin asked.

"When you have slept for seventy years and been woken to find everything you know has passed you by, you have two choices: embrace your new life or give up on it," Terese replied. "In my case, I was fortunate enough to have a reason to embrace life . . . a huge reason."

When Darrin inquired as to her reason, Terese said, "That would be our president, Ser. He represents one of the biggest reasons I know." Then she let loose one of the longest and heartiest laughs he had heard in a while.

* * *

Wombo and his associates sat in their shuttle for several hours, doing little else but discussing the possible ramifications of having defected to an unknown civilization. It was the general consensus of the group that whatever was to happen, it was preferable to remaining with the UE.

The shuttle's comm monitor emitted a triple tone, and Olawale hurried to the cockpit with Yoram and Priita right behind him. Onscreen appeared the young miss they first saw when they were contacted by the carrier and a man who was as massive as President Racine.

"Good day, young miss," Olawale said.

"You may call me Cordelia, Administrator Wombo. This is Chief Medical Officer Darrin Hesterly."

"And good day to you, Doctor Hesterly," Olawale replied. "These are my compatriots, Yoram Penzig and Priita Ranta. If it pleases you, Cordelia, I am no longer a member of United Earth, and I would prefer that the term 'administrator' never be applied to my name again."

"Then I am pleased to greet you, Ser Wombo," Cordelia said and gave him a beatific smile.

"Wonderfully appearing people," Priita whispered into Yoram's ear, who nodded his agreement.

"Ser Wombo, we have a plan to bring you aboard, but it will require the cooperation of all of you," Hesterly said.

"While there is no reason to trust us, Doctor Hesterly, you have our word that we are unarmed, and this shuttle has no weapons," Priita said.

"The danger that we are concerned about is medical," Hesterly replied.

"But, Sir, we have already met your people," Priita added.

"Yes, you did, Ser Ranta," Hesterly replied. "We have no concerns on our behalf, but we must protect your people. Your first encounter would have been managed by medical nanites, predicated on New Terran physiology . . . that would be my physiology, Sers."

"May I ask how you introduced these medical nanites, Sir . . . Ser?" Olawale asked.

"According to Ser Terese Lechaux, who is our premier authority on both Méridien and New Terran physiology, the nanites were introduced into your bodies as you passed through the Le Jardin airlock for the first time and again when our people boarded your explorer vessel . . . aerosol delivery, Sers."

"Doctor Hesterly, would you say that the pain reduction in my arthritic knees was due to these medical nanites?" Olawale asked.

"Yes, Ser Wombo, that's their primary purpose," Hesterly replied.

"But the pain has been returning," Olawale said.

"Yes, Ser. The medical nanites were timed to cease their activity and exit the body as waste after twenty days."

"So we would receive new injections of these medical nanites?" Yoram asked.

"Negative, Ser Penzig," Hesterly replied, noting the crestfallen faces on his vid screen. *One step at a time, my friends,* he thought. *You have so much to learn.* "We will be replacing the medical nanites with what we refer to as cell-gen injection, which will be augmented on a yearly basis after the first injection. But these nanites must be programmed to suit your UE physiology."

While the UE scientists were absorbing that information, they witnessed Cordelia step into the background and Hesterly partially turned his head in her direction. The two remained in that state for several moments before Hesterly resumed conversation with them.

"They were conversing without speech, Yoram. Did you notice?" Priita whispered, and Yoram's balding pate bobbed in response.

"When would all this begin, Ser?" Olawale asked. In response, the scientists felt their shuttle shudder and slip sideways. "I take it the procedures are beginning now." On their shuttle's monitor, Darrin Hesterly's smile was their reply.

The UE shuttle was drawn into the carrier by the bay's beams. Once the bay was pressurized, an environment-suited support specialist joined the scientists and used a laser tool to take their measurements. The scientists consumed their shuttle's water and packaged food meals while they waited, surprised that within hours two specialists returned with environment suits for each of them.

Ensconced in their suits, the scientists were led to the carrier's medical bay, which had been readied for them. Medically isolated, it allowed the Earthers to strip off their environment suits and don medical wraps. Soon after the scientists settled in, Olawale's associates were able to partake of their first Haraken meal and were still raving about the food when Terese and Hesterly entered wearing environment suits to conduct medical tests that would initiate the cell-gen programming.

Peppered with questions from the scientists, Terese and Darrin skillfully evaded answering until Terese decided to put an end to their guests' growing frustration.

"Sers, I understand you are curious about us and our society, but we have questions for you."

"We are happy to answer any questions you have, Ser Lechaux," Olawale replied.

"And we appreciate your openness, Ser Wombo. The person who will be asking the questions will be here soon. You met him aboard the Le Jardin station. He's Haraken's president, Ser Alex Racine."

* * *

The scientists waited alone in a conference room aboard the *No Retreat*. They had received their newly programmed cell-gen injections and were attired in comfortable Haraken ship suits. Nema and Priita were in love with the softness and the manner in which the material accommodated their movements. "If only my figure displayed this suit as admirably as the crew is able to do," Nema confided to Priita.

Olawale rose and the others imitated him as six individuals entered their conference room. He recognized President Racine, Ser Tachenko, Ser Julien, and two individuals he saw at Le Jardin but who never mixed with his people. Also accompanying them was Cordelia.

"Good day, President Racine," Olawale said, nodding his head. "Is there a proper way to greet someone in your position?"

Alex smiled and extended his hand. Olawale smiled in returned, and the two men shook hands, establishing the first honest Haraken-Earther relationship. Olawale introduced his scientist friends, and, in turn, Alex introduced Admiral Tachenko, Julien, Cordelia, and the twins, Étienne and Alain.

"Please take a seat, Sers," Alex instructed. "I have several questions for you before we take any steps with regard to your immigration."

Olawale's friends didn't miss the small points of the introductions. Tatia Tachenko was wearing an admiral's uniform. The twins only nodded when introduced and remained standing, occupying protective positions behind their charges, eyes constantly scanning the room. The façade of the amicable voyagers Olawale first described to them was absent. From their viewpoint, Julien and Cordelia appeared to be members of the president's party, but their use of single names without an honorific was another small mystery to solve among the many great unknowns.

Julien and Cordelia were prepared to monitor the conversation, but it would require only a minimum of their crystal powers. The remainder of their capacity was involved in a twining—a mental merging that only the SADEs and one human pair could manage. Cordelia immersed the two of them in her art, but it bore little resemblance to a human's concept of pleasure. Using imagery collected through the ages, Cordelia traveled the stars with Julien—shooting through galaxies, diving through a red giant star, swirling down into the pinpoint that was the bottom of a black hole, and riding the quasar's stream back out. Music accompanied the pair as they made their voyages, and Julien shared his pleasure with Cordelia.

"May I ask, President Racine, what has become of our two ships?" Olawale asked.

"We've ordered the *Reunion* back to Earth, Ser Wombo. The *Hand of Justice* exited the Méridien system for New Terra, my home world. High Judge Bunaldi would have encountered two Haraken ships, both of which are fighter-carriers. In those circumstances, what would the high judge do?" Alex asked.

"The high judge is a man of conviction, Mr. President," Yoram said, "and he would particularly dislike anyone challenging his authority."

"So, he wouldn't choose to retreat?" Tatia asked.

"It sounds as if your forces would not appear overwhelming, Admiral," Edward volunteered. "In which case, I imagine the high judge would endeavor to prove his battleship's superiority."

"Then, I imagine your high judge, his battleship, and your people are either captured or gone," Tatia said.

Many of the scientists, who were witnesses to the UE's prowess as it subjugated the entire Sol system, thought to disagree with the admiral's conclusion, but the matter-of-factness with which she declared the outcome seemed absolute.

"Let's presume Admiral Tachenko is correct," Alex said, pulling the conversation back to him, "that leaves the *Reunion* isolated. At present, it's making speed to exit our system. What will Speaker García do after his ship clears our system?"

Alex hoped for a simple response. Instead the Harakens waited while the scientists argued among themselves. Alex was tempted to interrupt, but Tatia's signal cautioned patience, and finally their guests reached a consensus.

"We believe that Speaker García, having failed to accomplish his goal in this system, will choose to return to Earth since he will be unable to contact High Judge Bunaldi," Olawale said, summarizing his compatriots' thoughts.

"We are aware your people do not have FTL comms, but would Speaker García journey to New Terra in search of the high judge?" Julien asked.

"I said that was how they were communicating quickly despite the great distances," Edward said to his companions, proud of his deductions about Méridien comm technology.

"We do not believe so, Julien. He would return home," Olawale said with certainty.

"So, Speaker García chooses to return to Earth. Then what happens?" Alex asked.

"The speaker would report to his superior, and his data would be downloaded for analysis," Olawale said. "If important enough, the results would be referred to the Supreme Tribunal. Your worlds would rate that level of scrutiny."

"Then what happens?" Alex pressed.

Olawale squirmed in his chair as if he were a small boy hiding a dark secret.

"Your worlds would be seen by the Supreme Tribunal as prime objectives, Mr. President," Priita said, taking the responsibility off her friend's shoulders. "They would respond . . . they would be forced to respond," she acknowledged grudgingly.

"Forced? Forced in what way?" Tatia asked.

"The Tribunal would know that no matter what it thought to do word would inevitably spread from the *Reunion*'s crew about what it had encountered here. The UE could not be seen as the weaker entity. Your technology aside, which is enticing enough, the Tribunal would be forced to come for you," Yoram explained.

Alex halted his questioning to consider what he was hearing, but Tatia was anxious to hear specifics. "Do you know in what manner the UE would return?" she asked.

"I'm not knowledgeable in military matters," Olawale acknowledged, "but I couldn't imagine the Tribunal sending anything less than a significant fleet."

"Define significant," Tatia said, her voice taking on a commander's tone.

"It would be a fleet built around several battleships," Boris replied. Although he was a member of the medical profession, his two sons served on UE warships, but to Boris's great anguish, neither son survived their service. "They would be accompanied by a host of lesser warships and support vessels. We are speaking about a fleet numbering fifty to seventy ships."

"How long before they would arrive?" Alex asked. If not for the depth of his voice, the scientists might never have heard the softly asked question.

Edward, the physicist, led the discussion, supplying minimal sub-light and FTL transit times, while the others considered the political process that would consider the reports, deliberate, and then command the formation of the fleet.

"The UE fleet would arrive at Méridien anywhere from 120 to 150 Earth days," Edward replied, "which would be about . . ."

"As early as ninety-eight Méridien days," Alex supplied, almost as an afterthought.

"Why, yes, Mr. President," Edward replied, surprised at the alacrity with which the man reached an answer. Edward just began his own mental calculations, and he was known as one of the UE's premier physicists and mathematicians.

<I must be careful to make you appear less omniscient,> Julien sent.

<Hmm . . . I wonder if you could conjure a larger fleet than the one the UE might be sending, my wizardly friend,> Alex sent back.

<I believe I will stick to calculations, Mr. President. It appears to be my forte.>

When Alex paused and smiled to himself, the scientists' hands and elbows nudged one another under the table to draw attention to what they were witnessing.

"Mr. President, I realize that you have many questions for us, but I wonder if you would indulge an elderly woman one question," Nema implored.

"Does that approach usually work for you, Ser?" Alex asked, his smile disappearing and the stern face of the Haraken president returning.

"When I was younger, it was a favored technique, although in those years I was able to say I was a helpless young woman."

When Nema offered him a sad smile in apology, Alex could see the charm and beauty she once possessed. "Ask," he said.

Nema sat upright, leaning on the table in anticipation. "Are you communicating with your people by telepathy or do you have devices that enable you to share your thoughts?

"Clever question, Ser," Alex replied.

Nema found herself pinned by Alex's stare, but rather than fear the man, she was dying to know what was going on in his head and if he was speaking to anyone silently.

Alex's first thought was to tell Nema nothing, but he relented. "We use implants in our cerebrums to transfer our thoughts to one another."

"Can the implants—" Nema began to ask.

"One question, one answer," Alex said, cutting her off. "Now tell me about the UE. I want to know how it came to power. What are its weaknesses? Do the people support the government? Does the UE have enemies?"

Olawale and his compatriots shifted uncomfortably in their seats. "What would you do with this sort of information, Mr. President?" Yoram asked.

"I thought that would have been obvious by now, Ser Penzig. I'm going to try to prevent a war. And all of you," Alex said, swinging his arm across the table, "are going to help me."

In the end and after much debate, the scientists decided to divulge their knowledge of the UE—its noble start and its ignoble present. When their story reached the conquest of the colonies, the Harakens became intensely interested.

"What is the nature of the relationship between the colonies and Earth now?" Tatia asked.

"The circumstances are unique," Priita answered. "On the one hand, trade between Earth and the colonies is robust and interdependent. On the other hand, the political relationships are fragile. The colonies did not submit willingly, and their subjugation was rather brutal."

The remainder of the exchange lasted through midday meal, which was served in the conference room, and discussions continued through the afternoon, a second meal, and the evening. By the time Alex and Tatia finished their debriefing of the scientists, the *No Retreat* was entering Haraken's orbit and the *Last Stand*'s extensive FTL comm was being received.

34

Alex and a group of people surrounded the *No Retreat*'s bridge holo-vid for the *Last Stand*'s message.

The scientists were brought from their conference room to witness the complete transmission. While their minds burned with questions about the evidently advanced technology, Olawale and his friends sensed the tenseness on display by the Harakens and speculated that a critical moment in the tides of worlds was about to unfold as the holo-vid flared to life.

"Mr. President, what are we about to see?" Olawale asked.

"This will be a record of the events at New Terra where the *Hand of Justice* journeyed. The message originates from our carrier, the *Last Stand*."

The bridge was silent as the horrific battle at New Terra played out. The Harakens winced as the number of losses mounted, but they were few compared to the complete elimination of the UE forces. At the end of the vid, Sheila summarized the Haraken losses and the disposition of the ships.

The message closed with Eric Stroheim's statements. "Mr. President, as your senior representative in New Terra, I have authorized the conversion of the New Terran shuttle-travelers to fighters, an authority you so graciously granted me . . . without a word, I might add. I might warn our commanders that it has been decided that New Terran shuttle and Dagger pilots will be trained by Commander Svetlana Valenko."

A few groans were elicited from the *No Retreat*'s commanders, who were well aware of Svetlana's no-rules style of engagement.

"I would imagine there could be several of us who would have the authority to convert the travelers," Tatia mused while staring at Alex.

"And you would be correct, Admiral," Alex replied. "Consider it an emergency failsafe."

"Of course, there would be those who would know this, could approve the request, and be able to manage the conversion," Tatia added, glancing between Julien and Cordelia.

"The SADEs stand ready to assist you and your staff, Admiral, whenever you need us," Julien replied and sprouted a Terran Security Forces cap with a major's insignia, the type Tatia wore more than a decade ago. He added a cheeky smile as he touched a couple of fingers to his virtual cap's brim.

The image of a hat appearing on Julien's head should have created a stir among the scientists, but they were in shock about the outcome of the battle at New Terra.

"You destroyed a battleship," Olawale whispered.

"We were left with no choice," Alex said quietly. "I am deeply sorry for the loss of your friends and comrades, Sers."

"The high judge led them to their doom, Mr. President," Olawale replied, shaking off his mental malaise. "No, Ser, what my comment was meant to convey was that I found the outcome of the battle incredulous. When I heard Admiral Tachenko announce that if the high judge failed to retreat he was probably dead, I presumed a certain amount of inexperience." Olawale quickly turned to Tatia. "My apologies, Admiral, I meant no disrespect, but the UE battleships have been a symbol of domination in our solar system for more than a century, considered invincible, and yet you accomplished it with fighters that appear to have no engines and no weaponry."

"A ray or beam of some type, Admiral?" Edward asked.

"Edward, another time," Nema admonished. "We have just witnessed the deaths of thousands of our people."

"Another reason we stand here, Nema," Priita reminded her. "We came for the opportunity to learn and perhaps to enjoy social freedoms that have been denied us on Earth." She directed her last comment at Alex, and held his gaze, waiting.

"You will have both, Sers," Alex said to the scientists, "for as long as Haraken exists as a free society. Toward that end, my staff and I are leaving you here aboard the carrier, for the near future. As of this moment, you are free to ask questions of any crew members, but please, try not to ask all at once . . . spread your inquiries out, won't you?"

* * *

Planetside on Haraken two days later, Tomas Monti and the Assembly were listening to Alex's arguments for more than an hour since the emergency session opened. But the frowns on their faces, including that of Tomas, told Alex he was not convincing them of the necessity to interdict the UE's next move. This was despite the fact that Tatia stood beside Alex, adding the military disadvantages of letting the UE fleet enter their space. She was repeatedly assuring the Assembly it would happen.

It wasn't that the Assembly had lost confidence in their president. Quite the contrary, they depended on Alex Racine to protect them as he always had, but that would be impossible if he was light-years away, engaging a huge and by all accounts overwhelming military force.

Alex continued to make his points, arguing for the authority to make the journey to Sol and find a means by which to avert an all-out war. Of course, it might have been argued that Alex was already engaged in a war with the Earthers without the Assembly's approval, but everyone admitted that the events couldn't have been foreseen, and it was necessary to block the swift and aggressive moves of the UE leaders. The Assembly leaders were still coming to grips with the fact they faced a new menace, and it was human.

Assemblywoman Bibi Haraken was in the middle of her question, when she was interrupted by the entry of the Haraken SADEs from the hall's side door. They filed into the room to take a stand behind Alex and Tatia.

<If I may, Mr. President?> Julien sent.

<I wait with bated breath,> Alex sent, quoting one of his mother's favorite phrases, which she often used when young Alex was attempting to explain away a faux pas of his own.

<And so you should, human,> Julien shot back. That he projected none of his trademark head covers marked the seriousness of the moment.

"Mr. President, Admiral Tachenko, Assembly Speaker Monti, and members of the Haraken Assembly, I have been asked to speak to you on behalf of my fellow SADES. You have, of course, reviewed the events surrounding our interactions with the Earthers at Méridien, New Terra, and here at Haraken. The SADEs have spent considerable effort and time analyzing the Earthers' intentions and war capabilities. We have arrived at several conclusions, which we feel are critical to share with you as your fate and ours are intrinsically linked. It is our opinion that the UE scientists' estimate of a sizable Earther fleet soon appearing in our system has significant validity."

The Assembly members sat up in their seats. It was one thing to argue with other humans, even if those were your president and your admiral. It was another thing to debate with a SADE, and, in this case, all the SADEs.

"United Earth would not have sent one of its greatest warships to investigate the call of a single explorer ship unless it possessed a sufficient number of these vessels to allow one on temporary assignment so far from home," Julien continued. "Furthermore, the fact that the speaker and the high judge presumed our societies would choose to assimilate with the UE speaks volumes as to the ease with which they believed this would be accomplished. Their confidence certainly extends from a history of successful experience, which we believe originates from the UE harsh subjugation of Sol's colonies."

"We conclude that if this Assembly votes to keep our president and Haraken's forces in system, the UE will return in force with a vengeance to annex the Confederation, then Haraken and New Terra. The fleet will be massive, and we will have lost the element of surprise. Unless you are prepared to load our city-ships with less than half our population and leave Haraken within the next quarter-year, then you should get used to the concept of being a satellite of United Earth . . . whatever that entails."

"Do the SADEs offer an option other than that given by our president?" Angelina asked.

"No, we do not, Assemblywoman Monti," Julien replied to the daughter of Assembly Speaker Tomas Monti. "We are here to state that the only viable option is to send the president with our forces to Sol and trust that he is able to convince the UE that conquest of our worlds is not in its best interest."

"Pardon me, Julien," Katie Racine asked, "but you surmise that our fleets would face an enormous and powerful fleet of warships at Sol, and earlier it was stated that we have lost the element of surprise concerning the capabilities of our travelers. You're not suggesting our ships should attempt to defeat the forces in the UE home system, are you?" The thought of voting to send her son to his certain doom, created its own conflict for Katie Racine.

"Negative, Assemblywoman Racine," Julien replied. "The probability of defeating the UE war fleets is too close to zero to bother mentioning."

The Assembly members began voicing and comming their questions and comments to Julien and one another, forcing Assembly Speaker Monti to regain order.

"Julien," Tomas said, "perhaps you should clarify why you support the president's journey to Sol with our carriers if you do not believe they can defeat the UE forces."

"The logic is unassailable, Speaker Monti," Julien replied. "Waiting here for the UE fleet is a certainty of being subjugated. Going to Sol provides the only viable option."

"We understand that, Julien, but if the intention is not to defeat the UE forces, what do you intend to do?" Tomas asked.

"In regard to the purpose of our president and carriers at Sol, Speaker Monti, I have no idea. What we, the SADEs, personally intend to do is support President Racine and give him every opportunity to do what he has done before . . . find a way to save us all."

*　*　*

Alex spent a quiet night with Renée at their cliff home overlooking Racine Bay. The Assembly remained in session, breaking briefly for evening meal, and then resuming debate on the question. Teague and

Christie were spending the night with Duggan to give the couple some quiet.

Renée made them hot thé when Alex first sat down, but the drinks were cold now. Alex sat for hours like a stone on the couch, deep in thought, and Renée curled up next to him to await together the Assembly's decision.

<Mr. President,> Tatia sent, <the Assembly has voted for approval with only two dissenting votes. How large an escort do you want, Mr. President?>

<We take the carriers, the *Rêveur*, and the *Outward Bound*, Admiral.>

<Understood. Julien reports the *Last Stand* will make Haraken's orbit in nine days and estimates that we will need eleven days to bring the travelers up to full count and load supplies for the trip.>

<Thank you, Tatia. Good-night,> Alex sent and closed the comm.

"Good-night, Alex," Tatia mumbled to herself. "May the stars watch over and protect us."

Alex heaved a sigh of relief, and Renée uncurled to ask, "When do we leave for Earth?"

Alex drew breath to say "twenty days," when a more important thought occurred to him. "What about Teague?" he asked.

"I would not have thought you would have wished him to accompany us," Renée replied.

Eleven years in each other's company, and Alex was still thinking the same thought, *a strange but wonderful woman.* Renée had taken his question and turned it upside down. They both knew Teague would remain on Haraken, but now they both knew Renée was leaving with Alex. He stood up, popping and rolling stiff muscles, and offered Renée a hand.

When Renée accepted Alex's hand, she was quickly pulled off the couch and caught in his arms. She squealed with delight and tucked her head into Alex's neck and was reminded of their first time together aboard the *Rêveur*, seemingly a lifetime ago. *I could wish for more of these moments, if fortune and the Earthers will only allow it,* she thought.

— Alex and friends will return in *Sol.* —

Glossary

Haraken

Ahmed Durak – Captain of the *Money Maker*

Alain de Long – Director of security, twin and crèche-mate to Alain, partner to Tatia Tachenko

Alex Racine – President of Haraken, partner to Renée de Guirnon, Star Hunter First (Swei Swee name)

Amelia – Close friend of Christie Racine

Angelina Monti – Assembly member, daughter of Tomas Monti

Asu Azasdau – Assembly member, captain

Avery Crosser – *Last Stand* deck commander

Benjamin Diaz – Pioneer, Minister of Mining, "Rainmaker," Little Ben

Bibi Haraken – Assembly member

Cedric Broussard – Z's New Terran avatar

Central Exchange – Haraken financial system

Christie Racine – Alex Racine's sister

Claude Dupuis – Engineering tech, program manager for SADE avatars

Cordelia – SADE, Julien's partner

Dane – SADE

Darius Gaumata – Fighter captain

Darrin Hesterly – New Terran TSF surgeon, who immigrated to Haraken, became CMO

Deirdre Canaan – Wing commander

Duggan Racine – Alex Racine's father

Edouard Manet – *Last Stand* captain, partner of Miko Tanaka

Elizabeth – SADE

Ellie Thompson – Wing commander

Eloise Haraken – Fiona Haraken's great-granddaughter

Eric Stroheim – Ambassador

Espero – Haraken city

Étienne de Long – Director of Security, twin and crèche-mate to Alain, partner to Ellie Thompson

First – Leader of the Swei Swee hives

Flits – Single person grav-drive flyers

Founding Day – Celebration of the founding of Haraken

Franz Cohen – Wing commander

Helmut – Z's avatar

Hive Singer – Mutter singing to the Swei Swee in their language

House Alexander– Military House Alex and Renée created to offer credibility to their actions in the Confederation

José Cordova – *Rêveur* captain

Julien – SADE, Cordelia's partner

Karl Schmidt – Captain, later manufactured flits with Hezekiah Cohen

Katie Racine – Alex Racine's mother, Haraken Assembly member

Libran-X – Warhead

Lucia Bellardo – Wing commander

Michael "Mickey" Brandon – Senior engineer, partner to Pia Sabine

Miko Tanaka – *No Retreat* captain, sister to Hatsuto Tanaka, partner to Edouard Manet

Miranda Leyton – Z's femme fatale avatar

Mutter – SADE, Hive Singer to the Swei Swee

Nua'll – Aliens who imprisoned the Swei Swee

Pia Sabine – Assembly member, partner to Michael, "Mickey" Brandon

People – Manner in which the Swei Swee refer to their collective

Renée de Guirnon – First lady of Haraken, partner to Alex Racine

Rainmaker – Name for Benjamin Diaz, also called Little Ben

Rosette – SADE

Robert Dorian – Assembly member, commander of military pilot training school

Sean McCrery – Fighter captain

Shadow – Z's spider, spying device

Sheila Reynard – Haraken fighter commodore

Star Hunter First – Swei Swee name for Alex Racine

Swei Swee – six-legged friendly alien

Svetlana Valenko – Wing commander

Tatia Tachenko – Admiral, ex-Terran Security Forces major, partner to Alain de Long

Teague – Six-year-old son of Alex and Renée
Terese Lechaux – Medical expert
Tomas Monti – Assembly speaker
Willem – SADE
Z – SADE

Méridien
Albert de Guirnon – Leader of House de Guirnon, brother of Renée
Assembly – Méridien government assembly of House Leaders
House – Organization of people headed by a Leader
Bartosz Rolek – House Leader, food production
Confederation – Collection of Méridien worlds
Confederation Hall – Government building housing the Council of Leaders
Council – Organization of Méridien Leaders
Con-Fed – Méridien language
Devon O'Shea – House Leader, terminals and planetside transportation
Didier – Le Jardin Orbital Platform SADE
Emilio Torres – House Leader, citizenry records
Esther – House Diamanté SADE
Gregorio – *Il Piacere* SADE
Gino Diamanté – House Leader, infrastructure and environmental services
Hector – House Ganesh SADE
Independents – Confederation outcasts, originally exiled to Libre, rescued by Alex Racine
Katarina Pasko – House Leader, implants
Le Jardin Orbital Platform – Platform above Méridien
Lemoyne – House Leader, Mahima Ganesh supporter
Lemuel Terminal – Shuttle terminal closest to Confederation Hall
Libre – Planet invaded, Alex Racine rescued people – Swei Swee now inhabit
Mahima Ganesh – Confederation Council Leader, House Leader, construction of commercial buildings
Oren Blumenthal – Le Jardin Orbital Platform director

Orso Quinlan – Lemuel Terminal manager

SADE – Self-aware digital entity, artificial intelligence being

Shannon Brixton – House Leader, SADEs

Teressi – House Leader, Mahima Ganesh supporter

Winston – Council SADE

New Terra

Clayton Downing – Former president of New Terra, convicted and imprisoned

Corona Mountains – New Terra

Darryl Jaya – Minister of Technology

Hailey Timmion – New Terran shuttle captain

Hatsuto Tanaka – Dagger pilot killed at New Terra, brother of Miko Tanaka

Hezekiah Cohen – Joaquin Station manager

Maria Gonzalez – New Terra president

Prima – New Terra capital city

Tara – voice on Alex Racine's *Outward Bound* ship

Terran Security Forces (TSF) – New Terran system police force

William Drake – Minister of Space Exploration

United Earth (UE) and Earthers

African Union (AU) – Earther political system

African Western Coastal Pac – Earther political system

Antonio García – *Reunion* mission commander, UE speaker

Boris – Wombo's friend, medical background

Dimitri Chofsky – *Hand of Justice* captain

Doultier – Fighter pilot, captain

Edward – Wombo's friend, lead physicist, mathematician

European-Indian Enclave – Organization of nations that sent a colony ship to GL-137

Final Wars – Earth's last series of conflicts in the 26th century

Francis Lumley – *Reunion* captain

Guide – Generic name for the controlling computer on United Earth ships

Hinnicky – Fighter pilot, captain

Jeffrey Hinsdale – *Reunion* master sergeant

Kyros Barbas – *Reunion* militia major

Laurent – *Reunion* comms officer, political appointee

Nema – Wombo's friend

North American Confederation – Organization of nations that sent the
   colony ship *New Terra* to Cepheus

Olawale Wombo – *Reunion* lead science administrator

Patricio Bunaldi – *Hand of Justice* mission commander, UE high judge

Resource Wars – Nations and states fighting about dwindling resources

Priita Ranta – Wombo's friend

Samara Theostin – *Hand of Justice* admiral

Shia Intifada –Fought with the African Union in the Third Union War

Storen – Wombo's friend, xenobiologist

Supreme Tribunal – Earth's highest political system

Third Union War – One of Earth's wars

Yoram Penzig – Wombo's friend, philosopher

Zhang Shin – Wombo's assistant administrator, *Reunion* science
administrator, political appointee

Planets, Colonies, Moons, and Stars

Arnos – System named for Libre star

Bevroren –Méridien outermost planet

Cepheus – Original star destination for the *New Terra*

Cetus – Last Confederation colony established, first colony attacked by the
   Nua'll

Delacroix – Méridien next-to-last planet outward

GL-137– Planet circling the star, Mane, where an Earth colony ship was
sent

Haraken – New name of Cetus colony in Hellébore system, home of the
   Harakens

Hellébore – Star of the planet Cetus, renamed Haraken

Libre – Independents' ex-colony in Arno system, now home to the
   remaining Swei Swee hives

Mane – Original name of the home of the Méridien Confederation

Méridien – Home world of Confederation

New Terra – Home world of New Terrans, fourth planet outward of Oistos

Niomedes – New Terra fifth planet outward

Oistos – Star of the planet New Terra, Alex Racine's home world

Seda – New Terra ninth and last planet outward, a gas giant with several moons

Sol – Star of solar system where Earth is located

Ships and Stations

Destiny – United Earth explorer ship, destroyed en route to target star

Freedom – Haraken city-ship

Hand of Justice – United Earth battleship

Il Piacere – Méridien House Diamanté premier liner

Joaquin Station – New Terra orbital station

Last Stand – Haraken carrier

Le Jardin Orbital Platform – Platform above Méridien

Lemuel Terminal – Shuttle terminal closest to Confederation Hall

Money Maker – Haraken freighter converted to carrier

New Terra – Ship that left Earth as a colony ship a millennium ago

No Retreat – Haraken carrier

Outward Bound – Explorer-tug owned by Alex Racine

Reunion – United Earth explorer ship

Rêveur – Haraken passenger liner

Travelers – Shuttles and fighters built by the Harakens based on the silver ships of the Swei Swee

Unsere Menschen – Haraken city-ship, translated as *Our People*

My Books

The Silver Ships series is available in e-book, softcover print, and audiobook versions. Please visit my website, http://scottjucha.com, for publication locations. You may also register at my website to receive email notification about the publish dates of my novels.

If you've been enjoying this series, please consider posting a review on Amazon, even a short one. Reviews attract other readers and help indie authors, such as myself.

Alex and friends will return in the upcoming novel *Sol, A Silver Ships Novel.*

The Silver Ships Series
The Silver Ships
Libre
Méridien
Haraken
Sol (forthcoming)

The Author

I have been enamored with fiction novels since the age of thirteen and long been a fan of great storytellers. I've lived in several countries overseas and in many of the US states, including Illinois, where I met my wonderful wife thirty-five years ago. My careers have spanned a variety of industries in the visual and scientific fields of photography, biology, film/video, software, and information technology (IT).

My first attempt at a novel, titled *The Lure,* was a crime drama centered on the modern-day surfacing of a 110-carat yellow diamond lost during the French Revolution. In 1980, in preparation for the book, I spent two wonderful weeks researching the Brazilian people, their language, and the religious customs of Candomblé. The day I returned from Rio de Janeiro, I had my first date with my wife-to-be, Peggy Giels.

During the past thirty-four years, I've outlined dozens of novels, but a busy career limited my efforts to complete any of them. Recently, I've chosen to make writing my primary focus. My first novel, *The Silver Ships,* was released in February 2015. This first installment in a sci-fi trilogy was quickly followed by books two and three, *Libre* and *Méridien. Haraken,* the fourth book in the series, has continued the exploits of Alex Racine and company, and begins a two-part story that will conclude in the following book, *Sol.*

I hope to continue to intrigue my readers with my stories as this is the most wonderful job I've ever had!

Made in the USA
Middletown, DE
15 December 2017